Tyrant
STALKER

USA TODAY BESTSELLING AUTHOR

ISABELLA STARLING

TYRANT STALKER
Copyright © Isabella Starling, 2021

This is a work of fiction. Names, characters, places, and incidents either are the product of the author's imagination or are used fictitiously. Any resemblance to actual persons, living or dead, events, or locales is entirely coincidental.

All rights reserved. No part of this book may be reproduced in any form or by any electronic or mechanical means, including information storage and retrieval systems, without permission in writing from the publisher, except by a reviewer who may quote brief passages in a review.

First ebook edition April 2021

Cover design: Isabella Starling
Editing: John Hudspith & The Plot Thickens
Formatting: Cat at TRC Designs

Tyrant Stalker

USA TODAY BESTSELLING AUTHOR

ISABELLA STARLING

"There's a dark side in all of us. Mine unveil on paper, with words…"

- Mary Laberge

Please refrain from spoiling this book for yourself or others.

A WORD OF WARNING

Tyrant Stalker is a DARK romance novel that has a lot of disturbing, cruel, and twisted scenes that may upset the more sensitive reader. Please heed this warning. For all questions or inquiries, you can email me directly at authorisabellastarling@gmail.com.

AUTHOR NOTE

Welcome to the dark and ominous world of the Millers. I hope you enjoy Dove and Nox's story. If you do, I would absolutely love it you post a review for it on Amazon. It helps me out so much!

You're also welcome to subscribe to my newsletter and receive some free books when you join!

I hope you're ready for the darkness that awaits you beyond this page…

ALSO BY ISABELLA STARLING

Don't Miss The Next Tyrant Dynasty Romance!

1: Tyrant Twin

(Kade and June)

2: *Tyrant Stalker*

(Dove and Nox)

Coming SOON

3: Tyrant Daddy

If you want to be the first to hear about my updates, make sure to join my Facebook group! Members of Good Girls Love Bad Boys are the first to hear about my news.

I am dedicating this book to the memory of Mary Laberge.

Mary, who understood the darkness, and was never afraid of it.

Mary, who would hold my hand as I wrote this and would have cried with me.

To you, Mary, for inspiring me not to be afraid of my dark side.

Your Isa.

PROLOGUE

NOX

Every love story has an expiration date.

I believed mine had already expired. When I tumbled into that abyss below the cliffs, I thought my life was over. But I had a guardian angel watching over me. Too bad I wasn't worthy of fucking saving.

When I woke up, they told me I'd been in a coma for six years. Six fucking years of my life, wasted while I was plugged into machines that helped me breathe.

I asked about them first. Kade and June.

They told me they were alive and well with three children. I fucking hated them even more when I found out about that. But after finding out about their happily ever after I stopped giving a damn. There was still one person though, one addiction from my past I couldn't bring myself to let go.

That addiction had a name – Dove Canterbury. I fixated on her like I had done on June before. I slowly recovered, my thoughts filled with the desire to own her again. It was in part what helped me recover, giving me the strength to overcome all the difficulties of my new life.

TYRANT STALKER

But I did it. I got through it all with one person on my mind – the little bird that was the only one to escape my gilded cage unscathed. Well, not completely unscathed.

I smirk as I put out my cigarette under my boot. I'm standing in an alley facing a small house on the outskirts of LA. It's busy here, busy and fucking hot. But I don't give a shit about that. All my attention is focused on the door of that house, glued to it as I wait for the only inhabitant of 1490 Westwood Boulevard to show her pretty face.

It's fucking gut-wrenching. This moment could change the rest of my life, and hers. I know where she lives now. There will be no running anymore. I've got her right in the palm of my hand.

As I wait, I notice a purple butterfly land on the handle of her front door. She's like a Disney fucking princess too, apparently, attracting critters and shit.

The door opens and out she comes. Long, flowing dark locks, glossy, hiding her beautiful face. She doesn't wear makeup anymore, but she hasn't stopped trying. She carries herself like a woman that knows her worth, even though you'd never think it from her outfit. Baggy black clothes hide her body, but from where her wrists peek out, I can tell she's thin. Painfully so.

She looks so different than she used to. Gone is her light blonde hair, replaced with a pitch-black color. I think it's her natural hair, and it looks beautiful.

My cock hardens in my pants as I watch her leave the house. She's carrying a small grocery bag in one hand. I'm curious as she heads into a side alley and I stay closely behind, breathing in the remnants of her scent as I follow her. I stay in the shadows, making sure she won't see me. I'm not going to expose myself so fast. No, I'm going to play Dove's mind like a goddamn instrument, pulling and playing with the strings until she's convinced she's going fucking insane. I can't fucking wait.

I watch her approach a homeless man in the alley and my fists tighten. I don't want her interacting with other men. But she doesn't seem afraid of the slumped figure on the ground. She offers him the grocery bag and they chat before she heads back home. My cock can't handle the sight of her. Six years of obsession, of dreaming about her for six goddamn years, are back to haunt me. And now she's here, the personification of all my desires, right here, at the touch of my fingertips.

I'm no longer Parker Miller. I stopped being the crazed, abused boy who was so angry at the world a long time ago. Now I'm Nox. I live in the night, in the shadows, and I'm never going to look for excuses for who I am anymore. My brother and his wife think I'm a monster. I think they're fucking right. And I'm done fighting what I should have admitted a long fucking time ago.

I watch Dove disappear back inside her house. I don't want to leave. The binds that tether me to her are pulling, taut and strong, reminding me she's the one who has the power here, because she holds my sick, twisted heart in the palm of her hand.

I fight the urge to palm my cock and turn my back to the house she lives in. I can't stay here for too long, can't risk her noticing. I have to stay in the shadows. I've been patient for so long, biding my time until I take her, steal her back, give her the home she deserves in a cage by my bed. I can keep waiting, as long as it fucking takes. Because I know she's going to end up as my goddamn property.

Walking down the street, I find the café where I'm supposed to meet him. Marissa's father, my benefactor, the poor fucking sod who's dumb enough not to blame me for the death of his only daughter.

Sometimes I wonder whether Thom Hodge secretly knows I'm the one who killed his kid. If he does, he's never mentioned it or shown any suspicion. His love for his only child is overshadowed by what he sees in me. Even in death, Marissa is worthless to him.

I don't think about her often, because the thought of her fills me with an emotion I'm not familiar with – guilt.

Hers was the first life I took. Not the first blood I spilled, but the first time I hurt deeply enough to watch her life essence drip out of her. She's gone now, so it's no use obsessing over the fact she's dead. Her father sure as fuck isn't.

I slide into the booth next to Hodge, avoiding his gaze. He looks hopeful, the poor fucking fool. He has so much hope, sees so much potential in me. But I'm not the genius artist he wants me to be. I'm just an abused kid who grew up into a monster and likes to unleash the full fury of his anger on a blank fucking canvas.

"Hello, Nox," he greets me politely. "I'm so glad to see you settling in."

I narrow my eyes at him. The poor fuck flew in from New York just to see me, trying to convince me to do a show, to go public with my work and stop just selling it to loaded collectors with a taste for the gruesome art world. I'm not going to do what he wants, though. I don't want my brother and his wife finding me, not now that I'm so close to claiming my little bird, caging her and crushing her fragile wings so she can never leave me again.

"Why did you come here?" I ask him.

Hodge places his intertwined fingers on the table and smiles at me. "I already ordered for us."

"I'm not eating or drinking."

"Are you taking care of yourself, Nox? You look strong enough."

"Answer my fucking question," I hiss in lieu of an answer.

Hodge smiles and moves back as a waitress places two plates of food before us. I am hungry, but I'm not going to eat in front of this man. Once the woman disappears, he begins talking, and it's the same old shit, just a different day. Some gallery opening, so many opportunities, if I would just come to one of them, speak to some of the owners, the collectors, the benefactors. Everyone wants to know the sick, fucked up mind behind the shit I create. But I'm not some goddamn zoo animal, inviting people to poke and prod at my brain. I keep my thoughts private because I don't trust a soul.

"You came here for nothing," I hiss at Hodge. "I'm not doing a show."

"Nox, I know you need the money."

"Just sell more of my shit then."

"You'll have to paint more so I can do that."

The bastard's right, though I'll never admit to my own wrongdoings. He has nothing to sell because it's been months since I've painted anything. Art doesn't come easily now. It feels like I'm squeezing water out of a fucking stone. When I was younger, I was filled with inspiration, with the desire to paint, to put my filthy thoughts on paper. But not now. Now, it's a chore to get anything out that doesn't feel pretentious as fuck. A part of me does miss it. The part that's hoping Dove will inspire me, if for nothing else than to create something for Hodge to sell before I blow all the money I have left.

I live a humble life, and it doesn't seem as if Dove needs money, but I've gotta be at least self-sufficient. I'll be fucking damned if I let someone else pay for me.

"I'll do my best," I mutter, pushing the plate of food away from me as I get up. "You can go back home now."

"Please, Nox."

"No." I brush down my leather jacket. "I told you over the fucking phone, I'm not interested in doing shows or anything where I have to be there in person."

"I hope someday I can change your mind. Until then, Nox." Hodge smiles his stupid fucking hopeful grin. "Keep creating."

I want to fucking punch the bastard. I don't even understand why I hate him so much after all he's done is help me.

Ignoring my instinct to pummel his jaw into dust, I walk out of the café and back into the hot street. I hate this fucking weather. It's too fucking hot for me. I thrive in the cold, in the darkness. I'm a New Yorker, not a basic fucking LA bitch. But LA has Dove, and New York doesn't, so I'll stay here for the foreseeable future.

I should head back home, but I can't resist the urge to drop by Dove's house one more time.

Her window is open and the sound of calming, sad music pours out into the street. I check to make sure there's no one around and slide into the shadows of her house. I look through her window. The place looks good, tidy and organized. I can hear the sound of her shower running. The door of her bathroom is open. I could walk right in there and take her. Right now. No regrets.

Fighting the urge seems like an impossible fucking task. All I want is to wrap my fingers around Dove's sweet little throat, squeeze until she has trouble breathing. But I can't. Not yet.

Patience was never a virtue of mine, so it takes everything in my beat-up body to pull away from the window. As I start my walk back to the nearby motel where I'm renting a shitty room, I think about Dove. How she did this to herself, because she's the only person in my sad fucking life that ever loved me.

I remember her as a teenager, barely legal, so fucking stunning. I couldn't see it back then, too crazed by my obsession for June. But I see it now. I see her beautiful, tortured soul beneath the dark exterior she's built up for herself. I know she still loves me. That kind of obsession never goes away. I should fucking know.

Smiling to myself, I find myself wondering how soon I can twist her mind, how soon I can hold her throat in my clenched fingers again.

It's a funny thing, love. And there's such a thin line between love and obsession. A line I love skirting over, dancing on the edge, pushing myself and the object of my affection, holding her over the precipice of madness.

Falling in love means allowing your mind, your body and your soul to be consumed by the other person.

Unfortunately for Dove Canterbury, falling in love with me also meant signing her own death sentence.

CHAPTER ONE

DOVE

I will never be as beautiful as I was before my face was ruined by a madman.

It's a hard truth, a bitter pill to swallow, but one that I've come to accept. My fingertips glide over the puckered scar. My reflection stares back, judging my appearance. I was pretty once. Years ago, before he cut me. I was pretty, careless, young, and stupid. I'm none of those things now.

"Dove, are you coming?"

"One second," I call out, untucking the dark strands of hair and allowing them to fall over my cheek, covering the scar. Like this, I look almost like I used to. I'm not the innocent nineteen-year-old I used to be. I'm twenty-seven now. I'm on a new path. I have a new life. A different kind of life. Sometimes I wonder if I would've been happier without the scar. But it's a dangerous path to go down. Better to focus on what I have than what could never be.

"Dove!"

"Coming!" I peel myself away from the mirror, sighing as I tuck my hair behind my ear again. There's no point in hiding the scar. They all know it's there. It's the reason I got this job, after all.

I leave the bathroom, my nude form wrapped in a black silk robe, exiting into the studio where the bright lights blind me. I groan inwardly. Why the hell did I agree to do this again? Because of Robin, I remind myself. Because I'd do anything for my brother. He's all I have.

"Where do you want me?" I ask, standing awkwardly in the middle of the brightly lit space.

Raphael glances up from his camera, shooing his assistant. His brows knit together when he sees me. "You messed with your hair."

"I'm sorry," I mutter, fighting the urge to play with it again. "It was too perfect."

He approaches me, critically examining my features as he toys with the strands of hair framing my face. He doesn't touch or mention the scar, and I'm grateful for it. I know how hard it is to ignore.

"It looks better this way, actually," he finally says, more to himself than me. "You'll have to take the robe off, though."

"Sure," I nod. "What am I wearing?"

Raphael returns to his setup, making sure his camera is connected to the computer screen. He doesn't look at me, fiddling with the cables as he says, "Nothing."

"Nothing?" Panic seizes my body in a deathly grip, my heart nearly jumping out of my chest at the thought. I do my best not to show it. I don't want to spoil this for myself. "What do you mean?"

Finally, Raphael glances up from the screen. "This is a nude shoot. Didn't I mention that?"

Wordlessly, I shake my head. The lump in my throat is getting bigger and bigger. What the hell did I get myself into? Damn Robin. He never mentioned this little detail. I wonder if he knew. My hands shake as I tug on the tie holding the black silk robe in place. I don't want to take it off, but what choice do I have? Raphael Santino is a world-renowned photographer. Booking this shoot was an honor. I can't let him down now.

"Sit on that chair," he says, staring through the lens of his camera as he points me underneath the bright lights. They all point at the chair, and I walk over there. It's hot under the lights, but not hot enough for me. I thrive in the heat. The cold always reaches my bones, making me feel more alone than ever. "Robe off, Dove."

I glance at everyone else in the room. There are two assistants, a lighting guy, as well as the makeup artist and hairstylist. I want to ask if they're all staying for the shoot, but I'm too embarrassed, not wanting to show just how inexperienced I am.

"*Pronto*, Dove," Raphael sighs, then follows my gaze to the rest of the people in the room. He seems to have picked up on my nervous energy. "Would you be more comfortable if we were alone?"

I contemplate his words. It would be easier to have just one judging pair of eyes on me instead of five. But out of all the people here, Raphael is the most intimidating by far. The Mexican photographer is gorgeous. Messy black hair, the most intense dark gaze and a body that looks like it's carved from stone. I've seen his Instagram feed. Even his selfies look like works of art, and he has beautiful models throwing themselves at him all day long. So what the hell does it matter? It's not like the guy's interested in me, anyway. He doesn't care what I look like. I'm not his girlfriend – I'm just his inspiration of the day.

"Yes," I finally manage.

He clicks his fingers and my watchers file out of the studio while casting curious glances at me. I can tell the hairstylist, Katya, is jealous. She was eating Raphael up with her eyes earlier. She must be hating this. The thought gives me a sick kind of satisfaction, yet I'm dreading what I'm about to do.

"When you're ready," Raphael says, returning his eye to behind the lens.

I get to my feet, the bright lights unforgiving, my hands trembling as I tug on the tie and the robe comes undone. I let it fall off my pale shoulders, gathering at my feet in a pool of silk. I can feel Raphael's gaze on me as he drinks in my body, and shame threatens to burn me up from the inside.

But the photographer doesn't mention any of my imperfections. Not the fact that

TYRANT STALKER

I'm painfully thin, emaciated. Not the tiny cuts covering my body, scars from years ago and some as fresh as a few days back. He doesn't talk about my visible rib cage, or the hip bones painfully protruding through my pale skin. Doesn't mention the scabbed scars on my thighs. And it's a welcome relief.

This is who I am. This is what I look like. If he doesn't like me, that's fine – I just hope he's quick and as painless as possible when he turns me down. But the words never come. Instead, I'm blinded by the flash of light as he snaps a photo.

"*Hermosa*," he mutters, admiring his own work on the screen. "Just fucking beautiful."

It's been a long time since I've been called beautiful.

For the next three hours, I work hard as Raphael's muse. He positions me in different ways, neither of us stopping for a second. I'm naked for the entire shoot, but it doesn't feel icky like I feared when Raphael first mentioned it. He doesn't look at me like a sex object. He looks at me almost impersonally, as though I'm a work of art he's been sent to capture. Like a true artist.

By the time he finally announces we've finished, I'm feeling exhausted.

"Do you want to see the photos?" he asks as he stares intently at the computer screen, scrutinizing our hard work. "I think they came out—"

"No, that's okay," I cut him off. I don't want to hear the ending of that sentence. "As long as we're done here, I'd like to head back home."

"Of course." He gives me a curious glance. This time, he doesn't look at me like I'm an object. He looks at me as a woman, and his gaze lingers on my puckered nipples, at the patch of hair on my neglected center. I flush, letting my hair fall over my face to hide the traitorous blush in my cheeks. Picking the black silk robe off the floor, I put it on as fast as I can. Once I'm covered by fabric again, I can finally breathe.

"Thank you for this opportunity," I say, my gaze meeting Raphael's. "I'm really grateful."

"Of course you are," he smirks. Cocky. But why wouldn't he be? "It was my pleasure, honestly, Dove. We have something amazing here. I'll be in touch in a few weeks with the final selection."

His eyes drink me in again as I head to the clothing rack where the clothes I came in are still hanging. I rummage through my purse first, seeing a couple of missed calls from my brother. He's probably anxious to know how everything went. I didn't expect for the shoot to take this long.

I smile to myself. Robin's way too protective, but I'm grateful for it. I can't trust my own judgement, never could. Robin makes sure I'm okay, and not getting into too much trouble.

"Unless..."

"What?" I turn back to face Raphael who is still staring at me intently. "Unless what?"

"Unless you'd like to see me before then." He smirks. The cockiness would be unbearable on any other man, but Raphael has a certain kind of charm that makes it impossible to hate him for being so forward. "I like you, Dove. You're... different."

Not special. Not beautiful. *Different.*

But it's a compliment, nonetheless. I stare back into the photographer's gaze, pondering his words. There's no way I can live up to the flock of picture-perfect, barely legal models that decorate his arms at public functions. I'm not as pretty, and I'm too broken. But maybe that's exactly why he likes me.

"Are you asking me out?" I wonder out loud, and he laughs.

"You're really straightforward, aren't you?" he asks, and I shrug in response.

"No point in pretending. I am what I am," I reply.

"I like that." He sets his camera down, grinning at me. "I *am* asking you out. Have dinner with me. Tonight."

"Tonight?" I shake my head. "No, I can't tonight."

"Got another hot date?"

I think of my plans. Dinner with Robin, then curling up in front of the TV, binging the same TV shows for the thousandth time. "You could say that."

"You're a popular girl, Dove Canterbury," Raphael smirks. "I'll settle for tomorrow then. And don't give me another excuse. I want to see you again, soon as I can."

I weigh the pros and cons. The negatives by far outweigh the positives, but despite that, I find myself nodding in response to Raphael's question. I grab a pen from his desk and scribble my address on a pink Post-It note, handing it to him.

"Pick me up here. Eight p.m. tomorrow."

"Do I get your number too?" He raises his brows, obviously amused. I hesitate, but then scribble that down, too. "And your social media? Instagram? Facebook? Do you have Twitter?"

"No," I reply firmly. "I'm not on social media."

I neglect to mention my Instagram account, but I don't want him to know about that. Not even Robin does.

"You're an enigma, Dove Canterbury," he reflects. I ignore his words and get dressed in the studio while his gaze swallows me up with curiosity. What's the point of hiding now? The guy's already seen me naked from every angle.

"Well, you got yourself a deal. I'll pick you up tomorrow. Say hi to your brother for me, alright?" Raphael says once I'm back in my baggy clothes that hide a multitude of sins.

"Sure." I smile awkwardly and grab my purse, hoisting it on my shoulder. "You have a good day."

I exit the studio into the office area. The hairstylist glares at me, but I ignore her, saying my goodbyes and heading out while ordering an Uber on my phone.

I wait. It's warmer here than it was in the air-conditioned studio, but still not enough to warm my cold bones. Nothing can stop the cold spreading from the inside.

As I wait for my driver, I scan the passersby for any sign of trouble. But no one pays me much attention. I'm invisible like this, in my all-black, baggy clothes, natural makeup, and my hair covering half my face – the ruined half.

But then a mother walks by, holding a little girl's hand, and my heart jumps. The girl is cute, wearing a pink tutu and light-up pink sneakers. She must be about four.

Really freaking cute. I smile at her, and she gives me a curious look while her mother impatiently tugs on her hand.

Tucking my hair behind my ear absentmindedly, I push my tongue out and make a face at her.

Her eyes widen as she notices the scar on my cheek. I almost forgot about it. Almost.

But as the little girl's smile changes into a grimace, I know I can never forget.

I'm ruined. A monster. And nothing will ever change the fact that Parker Miller destroyed my life eight years ago. I hate the bastard.

CHAPTER TWO

NOX

Little bird is not so little anymore.

I raise the cigarette to my lips, inhaling the smoke. It's hot out here. Outrageously fucking hot. I hate it. Hate being in this heat. It doesn't agree with my body, but Dove doesn't seem affected by it at all. My eyes follow her into the office building. I don't know what the fuck she's doing there, but once she disappears inside, I use the opportunity to scour the metal plates with business names on them.

Raphael Santino Photography.

Bright Idea Marketing.

Sweet Buns Bakery.

What the fuck is my little bird doing here? Not knowing is driving me fucking crazy. But I don't have a choice – there's no way for me to find out what's happening here, not unless I can get a hint somehow. All there's left for me to do is to wait for her to be done. And fuck me, it's taking forever.

I linger in an alleyway close to the building, keeping an eye on the revolving door. People come and go. Some carry sticky buns in brown paper wrapping, from that bakery I saw mentioned on the plaque. Others carry briefcases, wearing smart business outfits. Nothing like the misshapen, baggy clothes little bird wears to hide her true beauty.

For the life of me, I can't figure out what the fuck she's doing in there. The tension of not knowing bothers me, and my nails dig into the palms of my hands, forming red crescent moons of pain.

I wait. I loiter. No one notices me. I'm invisible in my all-black outfit, the hood of my sweatshirt pulled low over my face to hide it. It's not like anyone would recognize me here, anyway. LA is a long way from home. My past is in New York City. But Dove is my present and my future. She just doesn't know it yet.

Finally, what feels like hours later, Dove emerges from the building. She looks different than she did when she went in, and it pisses me off. Her hair's doing some weird curly shit. It looks as glossy as always though, and she's still wearing the same clothes. The light makeup on her face enhances her features but does nothing to hide the scar on her left cheek. I smirk at that. It pleases me.

I watch her interact with a little girl. I see the pain on little bird's face when she sees the kid's fear. I make a mental note of it. As she waits for her ride, I realize I'm being watched, too.

The girl's mother has left her outside, disappearing into the building Dove just came out of. What kind of fucking idiot leaves their kid on a busy street like this? My hands form fists. That woman needs to be punished.

I allow myself to sink into a dark place where I can take out my anger on the girl's mother. I imagine carving her, putting welts into her body as she screams. It doesn't matter what she looks like or if I'm attracted to her. All that matters is taking out my fucking rage on something.

A moment too late, I realize the girl is watching me. When I do, she's already coming toward me. I can't risk Dove noticing me, but I see her Uber's just pulled up, and she's getting into it right when the little girl comes to a stop before me.

"Hello," she says softly, and I groan as I watch Dove's ride drive down the street.

Fuck.

"Move it, kid," I hiss at the little girl.

"What's your name?" She stares up at me expectantly. The dumb little thing feared my little bird because of her scar, but she doesn't even flinch in my presence. She doesn't know a monster when it's staring her in the fucking face. "I like your jacket."

I decide to humor the kid. I kneel next to her, waving my hand in front of her and producing a red lollipop out of thin air. The girl gasps as I hand it to her.

"How did you do that?" she asks with wonder in her young voice.

"Magic. You like cherry flavor?"

She nods. "My favorite."

"Enjoy it, kid." I pull away from the shadows of the alley, ready to follow Dove. I'm guessing she went back home. She rarely leaves the apartment, so her little outing today is fucking inexplicable to me.

"Where are you going?"

I turn to face the little girl again, glancing at the building her mother disappeared into. "Where's your mom, kid?"

She smiles. "She's getting us some sticky buns. She says I have to wait here."

"Why wouldn't she take you with her?"

The kid shrugs, rubbing the hem of her pink tutu between her fingers and drawing lines on the asphalt with her toe. She's kind of cute, and I feel bad for leaving her alone on the street. The desire to keep following Dove is strong, but I do my best to fight it. My conscience may be nearly non-existent, but at least it's strong enough so I don't abandon this girl in the middle of the city, unlike her fuck-up mom.

"She likes a boy that works there," the girl mutters. "She says I'll spoil it for her if I come along."

My blood boils with rage. This poor kid. I have a soft spot for children with fucked up situations at home, obviously. And now I can't leave. I'll think about the kid all fucking day if I do.

TYRANT STALKER

With a groan, I lean against the wall. I'm fighting the urge to pull out another cig, but I don't want to be a bad influence on the girl. Talk about being a fucking hypocrite.

"I'll wait with you," I mutter carelessly. "But don't tell your mom about me. She'd probably be pissed, right?"

The girl nods with a conspiratorial smile. Knew I fucking liked her.

"Mommy says not to speak to strangers."

"Mommy's damn right," I grunt. "You don't know what's hiding in people's heads, kid. Humans are unpredictable. *Dangerous*."

"I like you."

I laugh out loud, fighting the urge to tell her off. She's not my goddamn kid and I sure as fuck won't be the one to discipline her. But then I see her mother exiting the building, holding a greasy paper bag. This is my last chance to give the kid some life tips. I kneel next to her once again.

"Don't trust a soul, kid," I tell her. "People suck."

"I know," she smiles widely.

"Good girl." I smirk and pick myself back up, leaning against the wall so I'm hidden by the shadows again. "Your mom's back, you better run along."

She nods and smiles up at me before walking back to the office building. She doesn't say goodbye, and I like that. Goodbyes are too fucking final. Maybe I'll see her again someday.

I watch her get scolded for wandering off by her mother, who doesn't even notice me. Stupid goddamn bitch. She should be thanking me, but she doesn't even know I exist, which is better for her, really. If I get too close to people, I end up hurting them. *Physically*.

As they pass the alleyway, her mother is oblivious to my presence, but the kid finds me in the shadows and waves. I wave back.

Hours later, I'm lingering in the street where Dove lives. I know she's home – the lights are on in her modest Spanish-style home. She's alone for now, but I figure her brother will be dropping by soon. He always does on Fridays.

I kind of like Robin, as jealous as I am of the guy. He's a year older than Dove and has an insufferable girlfriend called Elise. She's some kind of Instagram influencer, obsessed with perfection. I hate girls like her.

But Robin's a good fucking guy. He cares about Dove, really cares about her. He visits her almost every day, bringing food, because he knows she doesn't eat, and little, thoughtful gifts because he knows she needs a distraction from her shitty life.

Glancing at Dove's window, I make sure the lights are still on as I light another cigarette. I raise it to my lips, my eyes still on the house until I see a red car pulling up in front of it. Like I suspected, Robin is back again tonight.

The guy gets out of his Mustang with his hands full. He's got a bag of takeout that I know Dove won't touch, but he's as hopeful about his sister eating something as I am. In his other hand, he has a potted plant. It's not elegant like an orchid. It's barely even green anymore, all dried up and kind of rotten at the same time.

I watch him ring the doorbell, getting myself ready for the moment my little bird appears on the doorstep. A second later and there she is. She looks tired today. Her little venture into the outside world must've taken its toll on her. Still, Dove's face lights up as she sees her brother and invites him inside.

The door closes, pissing me off. I want to be privy to their conversation, but I can't fucking hear it from here. I need to figure out a better way of keeping an eye on Dove. Maybe I can bug her space. Then she really wouldn't have secrets from me.

I watch brother and sister unload things in the kitchen, Dove shaking her head when her brother offers her some Thai food – her once favorite. She keeps shaking her pretty head and Robin keeps telling her off, until he finally gives up. He should know better than that. My little bird doesn't eat in front of other people. In fact, she barely eats at all.

I watch them head into the living room next and settle in front of the TV. They put on some shitty sitcom I've seen them watch a thousand times and settle into a comfortable silence. The potted, half-dead plant is on the windowsill in the bathroom. I have no doubt it'll be thriving in no time. Dove has green fingers.

They spend hours together just like they always do. From my vantage point, I can see Robin glancing at his phone every few minutes. No doubt his vain wannabe model girlfriend is blowing it up with notifications. She's so fucking jealous of Dove. I can't stand her. And it amuses me that Dove hates the girl, too. Little bird doesn't hate a lot of people, but she can't stand Elise.

Finally, Robin makes an excuse to leave Dove for a moment. He heads outside to take a phone call in the street, and I smirk. He's so weak. That Elise woman needs putting in her place and some bruises to go along with it. I watch him argue on the phone with her before he heads back inside and feeds Dove some bullshit lie neither of them believes.

It's interesting how I can imagine their conversations going without ever hearing them. My resolve to bug Dove's house strengthens. I want more of her voice. I want more of *her*.

An hour later, a shiny, custom-color bubblegum pink Porsche pulls into the street, and I smirk to myself, halfway through my sixth cigarette since I got here. This'll be fucking good.

Elise gets out of the car, her yapping Yorkshire terrier barking from the safety of her Louis Vuitton handbag at *every-fucking-thing* they pass. Robin bought the dog for her a few weeks ago, and she complained because it wasn't a more expensive breed. Fucking bitch.

It's weird, knowing so much about people who don't even know I exist. Well, I suppose they do, they just think I'm long-fucking-gone.

Dove relishes in the belief that I died years ago. I bet she's shed some tears over my supposed death, though. After all, she was fucking obsessed with me back then, up until I carved her pretty face.

Sometimes I regret doing it. Not because of the scar, but because I frightened her off. It took me fucking years to realize Dove was it for me. Years after being blind-fucking-sided by my bastard twin brother and his slut bride. June Miller, née Wildfox, was never the one for me. But her former mini me is.

I watch Elise press the doorbell down for so long she nearly breaks one of her talons. I lean back against the wall of the alley and smirk. This ought to be fucking good.

CHAPTER THREE

DOVE

"**H**ey, kid."

"Robin!" I let him kiss my cheek and step aside so he can follow me into the apartment. "You're late. What happened?"

"Elise happened," he says. "I had to walk Pepper for her."

I groan. That freaking yappy little dog is the bane of my existence, but I choose not to mention it, focusing on something else instead of picking a fight the first few minutes my brother is here. I ignore the bag of takeout he brought and focus on the half-dead plant in his hand. "This for me?"

"If you can save it." Robin sets the food down on the counter and we inspect the plant together. "I don't know what I'm doing wrong. Every plant I get dies. And even worse, it's taking me less and less time to kill them."

"Good thing you have me," I grin, reaching for my watering can of tepid water and carefully pouring some into the plant's cute cat-shaped planter. "I'll have it back to life in no time. You gonna let me keep this one too?"

"Why not?" Robin laughs. "It's not like you need another plant, but at least it won't instantly die in my house."

He's right. My house is like a jungle. I can't resist a pretty plant, and I somehow always come back with something new, leafy and green when I leave home. Even if I don't, Robin supplies me with his castoffs more often than not. At this point, I'm pretty sure he's killing them on purpose so he can cheer me up with a new addition every week.

"So?" he asks, the excitement clear in his voice as we settle on the sofa in the living room. "How did the shoot go? You didn't say anything earlier."

"I wanted to tell you in person." I pick up the TV remote and click on play and one of our favorite shows starts to play out on the screen. We both know it by heart now. Half of the time we spend together is just quoting the freaking show to one another. "It went well, I think."

Robin reaches for the remote and pauses the show. He's always afraid he'll miss something if we talk while we watch it, even though we've both seen every episode a thousand times. "Well, tell me everything. I got a text from Katya. She said the photographer was really impressed with you."

I laugh out loud. Katya, one of my brother's ex-girlfriends, whom he stayed in touch with – much to Elise's dismay – was the hairstylist on set. She's the one who told Robin that Raphael was looking for unique models. And then Robin wouldn't leave me alone for weeks, begging me to go through with it. He thought it would be good for me, and as hesitant as I was about the whole thing, it ended up working out.

"Well, first of all," I start, narrowing my eyes at him. "You didn't tell me it was a nude shoot."

He laughs, nervously scratching the back of his dark-haired head. "I figured it would be. But you're cool with that, right?"

Robin knows I'm nowhere near cool with that. Not that nudity is the problem. No, it's being exposed – all my scars plainly visible for the viewer. But I find myself nodding now, as if it isn't a problem at all.

"It was actually kind of fun," I admit. "And really exhausting. I must've been there for five hours or even more. Two to do the makeup and hair, and then another three of shooting."

"So, what's Santino like?"

"He's..." I struggle to find the right words. "Intense. Interesting." Freaking hot as sin, I want to add, but I force myself not to. Although Robin knows me so well, I'm pretty sure he can tell what I was going to say next. "I'm glad I went, anyway. Thanks for making me go."

"You're welcome," Robin beams before wiggling his brows at me. "Heard the guy asked you out."

I groan. "Katya really can't keep her mouth shut, can she?"

"Nope." My brother's grinning from ear to ear. "So, how'd you turn down this one?"

Despite the scar, I've been asked out a fair number of times in the past years since I moved out to LA. But I almost always turn down the men who ask me. After a few disastrous experiences – including one where my date turned out to be a plastic surgeon and spent half of dinner explaining how he could fix my scar – I've pretty much sworn off dating altogether.

"I didn't," I finally say. "We're going out tomorrow."

"What?" Robin's mouth gapes open. "You agreed to go out with him?"

"Why not?" I shrug weakly. "I haven't been on a date in almost two years. Figured I might as well try again before I fully commit to being a green-fingered spinster."

"Cute." Robin stares me down. "So what are you doing on your date?"

"Dinner," I blurt out, my cheeks flushing a deep shade of red as I feel his penetrating smile on me.

"Dinner," he repeats. "Wow. You must really like this guy."

Robin knows as well as I do, I never do dinner dates, because I hate eating in front of other people. It's always awkward, and I don't want to deal with their prying questions about why I'm just picking at the food on my plate and not actually eating anything.

"What are you wearing?" my brother asks next and I shrug.

"I don't know. The usual?"

"Nuh uh, no way." I groan as I look into his determined eyes. "Why don't you borrow something from Elise? I'm sure she'd be happy to lend you something, and you're the same size, too."

We're only the same size because his tiny girlfriend starves herself on a daily basis to fit into a size zero. But then again, am I not doing the same thing? Even though it's for different reasons, I'm no better than Miss Instagram model/resident bitch Elise Howard.

"Fine," I finally groan. Elise will fucking love this. For some unknown reason, she's obsessed with me. She constantly offers to do my hair and makeup. To take me shopping, to get my nails done. I've fought it off successfully for the past year she's been with my brother, but I guess this is my freaking breaking point. She'll be thrilled.

"Perfect," Robin says. "I'll shoot her a quick text to let her know."

He pulls out his phone, narrowing his eyes at the screen.

"Trouble in paradise?"

"She's texted me twenty-seven times in the past ten minutes," Robin groans.

"God, how do you put up with it?" I shake my head. "She's *so* possessive. It's just as well she likes me. What the hell does she do when you're around other women you're not freaking related to?"

"You don't wanna know," Robin mutters, his fingers busy as he types a reply. For the next few minutes, he glares at his phone. "She's not replying."

"Maybe she's driving," I offer, which is a lame excuse, because we both know Elise texts while driving. "I'm sure she'll get back to you soon."

Just then, the sound of the doorbell rings out through the room. We exchange glances and get up from the sofa, both heading for the door. I open it, and of course, Elise stands on the doorstep in one of her bubblegum pink outfits to match her Barbie car, Pepper barking his head off at us from her designer purse – no doubt another one of my brother's gifts.

"Dove!" she exclaims, giving me air kisses on both cheeks as that insufferable dog barks and barks. "So good to see you, darling."

"What are you doing here, Elise?" Robin asks before I can reply, and his girlfriend gives him an innocent look. "We agreed to meet up tomorrow, not today."

"Well, you weren't answering my texts, honeybear," Elise pouts. God, that fucking nickname. It's so hard not to laugh at my brother when she uses it. "I thought something was wrong."

"I told you, I'm spending the evening with my sister," Robin insists. Why do his words make me feel so guilty? I feel like I'm taking away from Elise's time with him, and guilt threatens to swallow me up whole. "I don't have time to hang out today."

"Why can't we all hang out together?" Elise whines next. "I won't even complain about watching that stupid show again. Please? Let me come in. Please."

She's practically begging at this point, and I can tell my brother's resolve is weakening.

"Why don't you just go back to your place?" I suggest. "I can handle a night on my own, Robin."

"Absolutely not." Sigh. It was worth a try. If only Robin weren't so overprotective. "We'll all stay in tonight."

He steps aside to let Elise in. I groan inwardly. The last thing I want is to spend an evening with the woman, but it looks like I have no choice. The blonde walks inside with a triumphant smile and sets her purse on the floor. Pepper jumps out, stopping to growl at me before raising his leg at a plant I've barely managed to save from dying. Just fucking perfect.

Elise doesn't even scold him, and we all file into the living room. The silence would be awkward, but there isn't any. Elise is desperate to fill every second of the time we spend together with her ramblings. It's almost worse than the dog's constant yapping.

My brother tells her about the date I have the next day, and I cringe inwardly when she shrieks and tells me we must meet up the next day to do some maintenance. I don't have a clue what *maintenance* means, but by her critical gaze as she examines me up close, I'm guessing it'll take up most of my day. I'm already dreading it, but Robin's always so desperate for me to be close with Elise, I find myself agreeing to meet her in Rodeo Drive the next day.

I think of my mom then. I don't like to think about my parents very often, but I know she'd love that I'm going on a date. As annoying as she can be, I'm actually looking forward to our call this time. At least I'll have some good news to tell her.

Robin insists on staying until midnight's come and gone. I'm grateful Elise is here though, because I know Robin understands I won't want to eat in front of her. While they feast on the Thai takeout he brought, nobody forces me to eat, and I'm grateful for it. I watch Elise picking at her vegetables – she's pescatarian on Tuesdays and vegan for the rest of the week – and wonder where her issues with food came from. I know exactly why mine are present. It all stems from my mother's belief that I'm damaged goods.

When they finally get up to leave, I'm grateful for the peaceful night ahead. Robin shows me all the leftovers, including an untouched Pad Thai they left for me, and I promise him I'll have some, crossing my fingers behind my back. I walk them out and wave them off as they drive away in their separate cars and then I lock the front door.

My tummy is rumbling, but I pay it no mind. It's not worth the trouble to eat. I pile the leftovers and the untouched food into a brown paper bag and head outside again. The street is colder than earlier, but the night is pleasant. I walk down the street to the alleyway where Sam is already waiting.

"Robin come over again today?" he asks with a wide smile.

"You know it." I hand him the paper bag. "It's Thai today. I left the plastic cutlery in there. And I got you some sweet buns when I was in town earlier. Those are in there, too."

"Thanks, Dove." He gives me a bright smile. "Heading back already?"

"I have to," I say, winking at him. "Got a hot date tomorrow."

"A date?" Sam laughs out loud. "Who's the lucky guy?"

"That photographer I met today," I admit. "He was kind of cute, actually."

More like unbearably-fucking-hot, but I'm not about to admit that to Sam. He'd never stop making fun of me.

"I'll see you tomorrow?" he asks, the hope obvious in his voice, and I have to shrug apologetically.

"I brought you the buns because I'll be away for most of the day," I explain. "But I'll drop by the day after with some food. You need anything else?"

He shakes his head, even though we both know there are a lot of other things he needs.

"You want to come in the day after tomorrow? You could take a hot shower. I can brush your hair." I grin at him. His hair is a rat's nest, but he refuses to let me pay for a barber.

"No thanks, Dove," he replies firmly. He never wants to come into my house, no matter how many times I suggest it. I'm desperate to do more for him, but it was hard enough to get him to accept the food. Maybe with time, I can help him some more. "I'll see you the day after tomorrow, yeah?"

"Of course." I blow him a kiss and he laughs, retreating to his makeshift bed on the sidewalk.

I wrap my black cardigan tight around my body as a chill blows right through me. I've done everything on my to-do list now, but the night stretches ahead, promising hours of insomnia.

Maybe if I could finally catch a wink of sleep, things would be different. But as I lock the door behind me, I know it's not an option. Not with the shadow of my past hanging heavy above me with every step I take.

CHAPTER FOUR

NOX

After Dove gives her dinner to that homeless guy she's so intent on saving, and returns home, I decide to call it a night, too. As much as I want to watch her sleep, I have to fight the urge to break into her house. I need to bide my time.

Instead of keeping an eye on the little bird, I head back to Motel 97 where I'm renting a shitty room. I don't need much when it comes to sleeping arrangements, and I don't want to spend unnecessary money on a place to sleep. Although now that I've been following Dove for a few months, I'm starting to think I might need a more permanent place in LA, if only to avoid suspicion.

The bored-looking receptionist whose name I keep forgetting is popping bubblegum as I walk into the motel and grunt for her to hand me my keys. She perks up right away. I can tell she likes me. A few years ago, I would've taken advantage and had her in my bed the moment I first got to Motel 97. But not now.

Now, my attention is focused solely on Dove. She's the one I want, not some random redhead with a butterfly tramp stamp. So fucking generic it hurts. I smirk at the girl and swipe the key from her hand when she hands it over.

"Got plans for tonight, handsome?" she asks, and I fight the urge to roll my eyes. "Maybe you could treat me to dinner, and we could have some fun together..."

"I'm taken," I hiss instead.

"Oh yeah?" She pops her bubblegum again. "That don't matter to me, handsome."

"Well, it does to me." I turn my back on her and head to my room, but she slides around the counter and reappears in front of me. She's a goddamn pest. So fucking annoying.

"How come I ain't never seen this mystery woman, then?"

"She's shy," I grumble.

"Maybe that's cos she's imaginary," she laughs, popping her gum in my face. She glances down the hallway, then lifts up the cropped band tee she's wearing. I bet she can't name a single Nirvana song. "How 'bout these?"

I glance at her perky little tits and am left unimpressed. She doesn't compare to Dove, not even in the slightest. Plus, she's a redhead. Not even my goddamn type.

"Hard pass," I mutter, walking around her and feeling her pissed-off eyes on my back all the way to my room. She must hate me now. Not that I give a shit. As long as she stays out of my way so I can get what I fucking want.

I lock the door of my room when I'm inside, throwing my hoodie on the bed. With a groan, I pull my shirt over my head. A look in the mirror reveals not much has changed – my body is as toned as ever, given my rigorous exercise regime. But the scars are still there. Puckered. Ugly. Obvious.

I kick off my jeans and head into the shower. It's seen better times. There's black mold growing in it and the water runs brown for at least thirty seconds before it clears up. Finally, I step under the hot steam, allowing the water to beat down my back. I wash away the grime of the day, the cigarette smoke, the sweat. I wash myself until there's nothing left but burning skin and the scars that won't go away no matter how hard I scrub. Neither will the memories.

I wrap a towel around my waist and walk back into the shitty bedroom. Right there, on my bed, the redhead from earlier is sitting, legs spread and still incessantly popping that fucking gum. I groan.

"How the fuck did you get in?"

"We have security keys," she smirks. "Don't pretend like you're not glad I'm here."

I don't respond, and she picks herself up from my bed, sauntering up to me and grabbing the knot of my towel. She pulls me against her body and for some reason, I let her. But the rage inside me builds.

"Do you remember my name?" the redhead purrs, and I shake my head. She pouts at this but doesn't let it disturb her for too long. She tugs on the knot. My towel threatens to come undone, exposing my dick which is still throbbing from thinking about Dove in the shower. "It's Hanna."

"Hanna, is that right?" I say and she nods with what I'm sure she thinks is a seductive smile. I grab her wrist then. "Well, Hanna, you should get the fuck out of my room before I make you regret coming in here."

"How are you going to make me regret it?"

With a single move, I twist her arm behind her back, and she shrieks in pain. I know the human body well. One more twist, a few inches to the left, and I'll break her tiny wrist. The thought thrills me.

"I told you," I hiss at her as she looks up at me, her eyes terrified. Fucking finally. "I'm taken. Now get the hell out of my room before I break your arm. And then your neck."

I let her go, and she stumbles back, her expression wounded as she picks herself up, dusting off her denim cutoffs and that stupid fucking Nirvana shirt. "You don't want me?"

"No," I grunt. "For the thousandth time, I'm not interested. Now get lost."

She cradles the wrist I twisted in her other arm and leaves without saying another word. Once the door closes behind her, I breathe a sigh of relief. Fucking women. They just can't resist me.

TYRANT STALKER

The next morning, I follow Dove's Uber to Rodeo Drive. I'm surprised to see her there. Dove's not really the shopping type, and much less a designer kind of girl. But my doubts are quickly quashed when I see the Barbie car pull up.

Elise Howard, of fucking course. This should be interesting.

For the next few hours, I follow them around as they shop for ridiculous fucking outfits. That Elise bitch keeps trying to force my little bird into something pink, but luckily, the girl is smart enough to resist. Through the windows of one of the high-end boutiques, I watch her try on a black number. It's got long sleeves and a cowl neckline but reaches down to her knees. The dress is tight, and it pisses me off how hot Dove looks in it. Elise helps her pick a pair of simple black heels to go with the outfit, and little bird buys her a wallet for helping her.

I don't know what she's getting ready for, but if it involves a man, I'm going to fucking kill him.

After their shopping is done, the girls exchange air kisses and say their goodbyes. Elise leaves in her ridiculous car and little bird orders an Uber. I linger close by as she waits for her ride, holding the shopping bags in her hands. The temptation to approach her is fucking overwhelming. Maybe just a little bit closer... close enough to inhale her scent. I barely remember it. I haven't let myself get close to her for years, and I'm craving the unique perfume of her skin.

I do my best to remember it – the powdery mix of her own scent, the rosy smell of her perfume. But nothing is as good as the real thing.

I put out my cigarette under my boot and slip closer, hidden in the shadows. I stop five feet away from her. Dangerously fucking close, but little bird is oblivious. She needs to be more careful. But I'm close enough to smell her now. Close enough to fill my nostrils with her unique blend of soft, velvety rose petals and baby powder. Goddamn, she's amazing. My obsession deepens.

She's close enough that I could reach her, grab her by the throat and drag her into the shadows I emerged from. I have to fight every instinct to stop myself from doing it, and when her Uber arrives and she steps inside, my hands form fists. I want her. I won't be able to hold back much longer.

I hitch my own ride and follow her Uber back to her place. It's almost six p.m. and she still hasn't eaten. My own stomach is grumbling as much as hers must be, but she doesn't make anything to eat at home. Instead, she tries on her outfit and fusses with her hair and makeup in front of a mirror.

She's going on a fucking date. She has to be.

My lip twitches as I think about her with another man. If he touches her, I'm taking her tonight. I have to. I can't let anyone else have her. My blood is pumping, adrenaline rushing through my veins. The desire to finally take what's mine is fucking overwhelming.

The car that pulls up on her street is flashy. A driver exits, opening the door for a dark, messy-haired tall guy wearing an all-black suit. His slightly shabby hair is slicked back. He's handsome. But not good enough for my little bird.

If there was any doubt about him being my girl's date, it disappears when he rings Dove's doorbell. I hiss out loud I'm so pissed off. I don't know if I can watch this happen. Maybe I should just get it over with and slit his throat right now.

"I know what you're doing."

I snap my head around to the sound of the voice. It's a shabbily dressed man with wise eyes and a scraggly, auburn beard. His complexion is ruddy, but his teeth are straight as he grins at me.

It's little bird's charity project.

"What am I doing?" I ask, raising my brows at the man.

"Watching her." He motions to Dove's house. "You're not as invisible as you think. What's your name?"

I hesitate. I've had two names, but my first belongs to the past.

"Nox," I mutter.

"Interesting." The guy's hazel eyes drink me in, from my all-black outfit to the hoodie obscuring my face. "Does Dove know you've been watching her? What are you, a disgruntled ex-boyfriend?"

I smirk. "Something like that."

"What you're doing isn't right," the guy grumbles. "But I'm sure you know that already."

"Are you going to tell her what you saw?" I ask, hoping he doesn't. If he does, I'll have to kill him, and I don't want little bird to wonder what happened to him. A part of me expects him to ask for money in exchange for his silence, but he doesn't. Instead, he laughs out loud.

"Not yet. But I'll keep an eye on you."

I glance back at her house just in time to see the flashy car pull away. I curse out loud, kicking at the wall when I realize it's too late for me to follow them. I turn back to face Dove's friend.

"Do you know where they're going?"

"To dinner," he replies.

"But Dove doesn't eat in front of other people."

He smiles. "You seem to know a lot about her. Does she care about you as much as you care about her?"

"Not anymore," I answer truthfully. "But she did. A lot. Before I hurt her."

"That's the way it always is," he sighs, offering me a grimy hand. "The name's Sam."

I regard his dirt-stained palm, then reach forward and give him a firm handshake. I can tell he likes the fact that I haven't recoiled in disgust. We exchange inquisitive looks. I want him to trust me. I could use him on my side.

"Will you help me get her back?" I ask him.

"Maybe." The man's eyes sparkle. "If you prove to be worthy of her."

"I'm more than worthy," I hiss.

"No need to get so defensive." He laughs again. "I'm guessing you have to go make sure that smug-looking guy doesn't hurt her."

"That's right." I smirk at him, pleased that he seems to understand. "Can I trust you not to tell Dove about this?"

Whatever his answer is, something tells me it won't be a lie. Finally, he nods. "I won't tell her."

"Thank you." The two words slip from my lips with effort. I haven't said them in a long time, not to anyone. "I'll see you around, old man."

"See you around, Mr. Night," he says, making me look over my shoulder and smirk. He knows what the name I gave him means. It's Latin. He must be educated. I wonder how he ended up on the streets.

CHAPTER FIVE

DOVE

Raphael Santino is a gentleman.

He holds the car door open for me, pulls back my chair to help me sit down. He orders for me, but not before checking for my preferences. He even compliments my outfit, and I can tell he means it, because his eyes devour me. He wants me. A man hasn't wanted me in a long time.

Raphael orders our wine, an expensive red. I don't drink, but tonight, I need the extra courage, and I sip at the blood-red liquid throughout the evening.

"So," Raphael smiles after ordering our food. "Who is Dove Canterbury? Besides an enigma, of course."

"I'm just a regular girl," I mutter, sipping on the wine. The tart flavor is pleasing, and I try not to think about the calories in the glass. "Nothing fancy, really."

"I don't buy that for a single second," Raphael says, toasting me with his glass. "You're different. Definitely special. So, tell me everything about yourself."

"Everything?" I laugh, setting my glass down. "That's a tall order."

"I want to know." His dark eyes sparkle with amusement, boring into mine.

"Everything about you, Dove. So tell me."

I shrug, unsure of where to start. "I'm the younger of two siblings. My brother, Robin, is a year older than me. He lives in LA, too. We're very close. We spend at least three evenings of the week together."

"That's wonderful. And your parents?"

"My parents... They're back in New York, where I was born." My teeth dig into my bottom lip. It's always painful explaining this to people. "My dad worked as a CEO at a Fortune 500 company. He died a couple years ago. My mom was a socialite and married for money." I shrug. "She has other people now. Lovers, boyfriends. She's still beautiful."

"Are you close with her?" I don't know if he's doing this on purpose, but he's striking exactly where it hurts, and I'm trying not to let it show.

"Not at all." I clear my throat, glancing around the restaurant so Raphael won't notice I'm getting emotional. "Since this happened..." I point to my scarred cheek. "I haven't been interesting to her."

His brows knit together in worry. "What do you mean?"

"I was like her before the... accident. A socialite."

"How old were you when the accident happened?"

"Nineteen," I mutter. I don't tell anyone what happened when Parker Miller scarred me. That's my own shame, my own fault, and I have to bear the consequences of my actions. The only people that know are Parker, his brother Kade and his wife June, and Robin. And I've sworn them all to secrecy – except for Parker. Parker's dead.

I feel a shiver go down my spine.

Isn't he?

"So, your mother judged you for having the scar?" Raphael goes on.

"She said I'd never amount to anything with it," I admit. "No man would look at me, and my career as a socialite was pretty much over."

"So you moved out here?"

I nod. "A few years later, for my twenty-first birthday. I bought a house with the money Dad left me. I have enough to cover me for the rest of my life."

"But what about having a life? A career? Don't you have dreams of your own?"

I shrug again. "It's not like it's an option for me. The scar makes people judge me. Makes them afraid of me. Not a lot of people would risk hiring somebody like me."

"I think you're being too negative."

"Am I?" I smile, but there's a hint of sadness lingering on my face.

"Definitely." He grins. He is ridiculously handsome. Distractingly so. "What do you spend your days doing?"

"I volunteer a lot." I toy with the napkin in my lap. "I work at a soup kitchen downtown. I volunteer at an animal shelter. And I sometimes work at a plant nursery downtown too. They give me a symbolic payment. But it's fun. I don't have to interact with people a lot."

"You strike me as a very selfless person."

"I wasn't always. But this..." I point to the scar again. "This changed everything for me."

"I can imagine. You're living a very different life than you were in New York, aren't you?"

"Definitely."

"Do you miss it sometimes?"

I take a moment to think about his question. "I miss my best friend, June."

"You aren't in touch anymore?"

I shake my head. "It was... too painful. Difficult. She's married now, has kids. I'm happy for her. But I don't think there's room in her life for someone like me."

It's Raphael's turn to nod now, and just then, the waiter arrives with our appetizers. Raphael digs in with gusto while I pick at my food. He doesn't mention it, and it's a relief. Guys always wonder if I'm on some crazy diet that makes me unable to eat. But not him. He glances at me every so often, but he doesn't mention the fact that I've dissected the meal before him.

The waiter raises his brows at me when he picks up our plates. I'm not fooling him. Then again, this is LA. A lot of people pick at their food. He takes our plates away.

"What about you?" I finally ask Raphael. "I've been going on for ages. Why don't you tell me about yourself? How did you become a photographer?"

"My father was one," he explains. "I inherited all his equipment and started early. I always loved taking photos. I got the opportunity to work with the New York City Ballet for years. That got my work noticed. Then I started doing private exhibitions, getting hired to shoot for fashion magazines. I got to work with a lot of famous people. Word spread. *Et voilà*."

"That's the Cliff Notes version?" I grin at him.

"Pretty much." He smiles back.

"What about your family? Are you an only child?"

"Most likely not." He sighs. "My father was somewhat of a womanizer. He never married my mother, but I think he loved her, in his own way. They were happy together until he died, though my mother knew she wasn't his only one. We never knew about the others. Not the women, not the children I'm sure he had all over the globe."

"Was he a fashion photographer too?"

Raphael shakes his head. "He was... a different breed of creative. He worked for National Geographic for a number of years. His series on war crimes won several awards."

"That must've been difficult."

He smiles, but it's tinged with another emotion, a sadder one. "You wear your scar on your cheek, Dove Canterbury, but a lot of people wear theirs on their hearts."

His words strike me as true, and I take my time to ponder them while our mains arrive.

Raphael ordered some kind of pasta dish, which even I have to admit smells divine.

"What is this again?"

"Penne alla vodka," he says. "You like it?"

"It smells good," I admit reluctantly.

"Try it," he suggests, returning his eyes to his own dish. "I want to know if you like the taste."

His encouragement is soft, but kind, and it actually makes me want to eat. It's been a full day since I've had anything but water, and my stomach hurts. Tentatively, I spear a piece of the pasta with my fork and raise it to my lips.

I know people are watching, judging me. But as I glance at Raphael, I realize he isn't one of them. He seems fully engrossed in his own meal, not minding what I do one bit. I stick my tongue out and lick the smallest morsel of sauce off the pasta. It's good.

Raphael doesn't comment on the fact that I'm finally eating, but he does smile at me from across the table. I'm grateful he doesn't make a big deal out of it.

"It's good," I find myself saying. "I love the sauce."

"This place is great," the photographer nods. "Do you like Thai?"

"It used to be my favorite." Before... *Before*.

"I know a great Thai place too," he goes on. "Maybe we can go there next time."

The thought that he wants to see me again is exciting, and I find myself nodding along. I want to tell him I'm grateful for his kindness, but the words don't want to leave my lips. I keep eating though. I leave most of the pasta, but I scoop up the sauce with my fork, and by the time the waiter arrives to collect my dishes, I don't feel awkward telling him I enjoyed the meal.

"Did you have a nice time?" Raphael asks after we agree we're too full for dessert.

"I did," I nod, surprising myself. "Really nice."

"I'm not going to invite you back to my place tonight." He grins at my crestfallen expression. "I think it's too soon, and I want you to know I respect your limits. But I would love it if you came with me for a walk on the beach."

"I'd like that." I don't know how I'll handle the sand in my sky-high heels, but the idea is enticing and I don't want tonight to end just yet. He doesn't let me pay, covering the bill himself, and I don't fight him on it. When we walk out of the restaurant, I stumble on my heels, and Raphael grips me with a firm hand.

"Not used to heels?" he asks, looking amused. I'm embarrassed to admit it, but I'm really not. I must be so unlike the models he's used to dating. My confidence takes a huge dip then, and I shake my head wordlessly.

"I'm sorry, I'm such a mess."

"You're not a mess." He tips my chin back. When his fingers touch my skin, I feel an electric charge moving through my body, filling my veins with excitement. I haven't felt this way since...

I shake my head to get the thought out.

"Don't apologize," he goes on. "Take those shoes off. We're almost here anyway." He points ahead to where the sand is starting. I lean on his arm for support and undo the straps, then hold the shoes in one of my hands and run toward the sand. The gritty grains feel good. I curl my toes in it, grinning as I turn to face Raphael.

"Join me."

He does, and together, we make our way to the water's edge. There's no need for words, and for a few minutes, neither of us speaks. The silence is welcome and companionable.

While we're walking, Raphael's hand somehow slips into mine. This has happened on dates before, and I was always incredibly uncomfortable, but not this time. I let his fingers intertwine with mine, my heart skipping a beat as he pulls me to him to avoid the wave crashing on the shore where I stood moments later. I giggle.

There's a bonfire party on the beach and when we pass the crowd that's gathered, someone calls out Raphael's name. Instantly, I remember why I don't leave the house, why I never go anywhere, why I don't trust people.

A gorgeous brunette with a wide smile approaches us. She does a double take when she sees me, her eyes drinking in my scarred face. I can see her judging me silently, but before she has a chance to react, Raphael distracts her.

"Hey, Selma. I totally forgot you invited me to hang out tonight."

"I see," she purrs, toying with his shirt collar, letting her fingers linger on it. I find myself gritting my teeth together. I'm... jealous. What a weird feeling. "Found better company for tonight, did you? Where are you off to?"

"Just taking a walk."

"Moonlit night, a walk on the beach... Sounds romantic enough to me," the girl laughs, throwing me a look. "You're more than welcome to join us, if you'd like. We have marshmallows. And plenty of booze."

Raphael glances at me, but I can't quite meet his eyes. My shoulders sag with relief when he speaks up again. "Nah, I think we're good. I'll see you soon, Selma."

"Sure." She looks pissed as she glances at me. "You know where to find me. I'll be around... even when your latest conquest isn't."

I don't think Raphael notices, but when she leaves, she kicks sand right at me. I pretend not to notice either.

"I'm sorry about that," he mutters once we're out of earshot. "Here. Let's sit down."

He takes off his blazer and places it on the sand. I'm about to object – I'm sure it cost a lot of money – but I have a feeling he wouldn't listen. Instead, I sit next to him, and he puts his arm around my shoulders, cradling me against him. The moment is peaceful, serene. I'm relishing in the thought that he doesn't push me to kiss him, though the promise of it hangs in the air, sparkling and magical.

His fingers gently travel down my back. I want him to kiss me. I haven't wanted *anyone* to kiss me in years.

"Dove." I look up into Raphael's eyes. "I'm really glad we went out tonight. You made my week. My month. My year, even."

I laugh, shaking my head. "Don't exaggerate."

"I mean it."

Our eyes meet. There's something special in the air tonight. But then the spell breaks when Raphael is suddenly kicked aside. Sands flies everywhere and I feel someone snatching my purse away from me. I scream, but the attacker is already running off, blending into the night in his dark clothes.

What the *hell* just happened?

CHAPTER SIX

NOX

I take off sprinting, holding onto Dove's handbag. I can hear someone shouting, coming after me, but I'm faster. Until I trip on something in the sand and come crashing down. That smug bastard Dove was on a date with reaches me, grabbing me by the lapels of my leather jacket, but I'm too fast for him. Before he can see my face, I smash my fist into his, and he stumbles back, clutching his nose which is already bleeding profusely.

I disappear into the shadows, blending in with the night. I know they won't find me now. I watch them from under the nearby pier. Dove is consoling that photographer prick, and someone from that bonfire party runs over, calling the cops.

I need to get the fuck out of here before anyone gets the bright idea to check under the pier. I open Dove's bag and dig through her shit, smirking when I see her phone in there. Fucking *jackpot*.

While I walk back to the restaurant, I use Dove's phone to look up the photographer she was out with. I'd researched the companies in that office building she left days ago, and I instantly recognized the bastard when he picked her up for the date.

TYRANT STALKER

Now, I realize the idiot has used his home address for his company. I smirk. I know where I'll be spending the night.

Because I was tired of having to hitch a cab every time I needed to follow Dove, I decided to invest in a ride of my own. As I approach the rusty Harley Davidson I splurged on earlier, I grin to myself. At least I'm fucking traveling in style now.

I stash Dove's bag in the storage compartment and drive to the address I found. Raphael's not back yet, probably still giving a statement to the cops at the beach. But I'm fairly certain I ruined their little moment. Dove will be scared now. She won't let him kiss her anymore. I smirk to myself, pleased with my work.

I only have to try three times to find the right code to unlock her phone. It's her birthday. Not careful enough, little bird. I'll have to teach her better.

Her phone is filled with texts from her brother and a few from guys trying to get her attention and miserably failing. Some prick's been texting her every month for two years. *Give up already, you're embarrassing yourself,* I think to myself. Besides, she's fucking mine. I block the guy's number. He won't be bothering my little bird again.

Dove's camera roll reveals only a few selfies. The rest of her photos are ominous shots of LA, nothing like the vibrant, colorful atmosphere people associate with the city. There are no social media accounts except for Instagram. I click through to that, knitting my brows together when I see she actually does have an account. And one helluva lot of followers. Fifteen thousand of the fuckers.

I scroll through her page. It's private, none of the selfies are on there – but the dark, moody shots are. I'm impressed with her as I peruse the pics. She has a good eye.

It doesn't take long for me to install the software that will track every move she makes on her phone. I'll be one step ahead of her now, always, and the thought pleases me.

Just then, I see Raphael's driver pulling up to his building. I slip into the shadows, Dove's phone in my pocket, and watch the guy go inside while clutching his still bleeding nose. I got him good there.

I'm pleased to see he returned to his apartment alone. That means Dove will be home now, too. I'll drop by before I head to the motel, make sure she's okay.

Just as I'm about to leave, I notice a familiar ride pull into the parking lot before the building. My eyes narrow as the bubblegum pink car comes to a screeching halt. Two long legs emerge. The girl flicks her long blonde locks, clutching another designer purse holding her insufferable pest of a dog.

Interesting. What the fuck is Elise Howard doing here?

I watch her ring one of the doorbells and argue with someone over it. The doors don't open, and she paces the pavement in front of the building until a man emerges. It's Raphael.

I smirk at the sight. So there's another connection here. One that excites me, because it means I can fuck things up for the photographer even more. I watch from the shadows as Elise and Raphael argue, the dog yapping into the night. Looks like a lovers' spat to me. And my suspicions are only confirmed when Elise throws herself at the guy, kissing him with desperation.

Raphael has enough common sense to push her off, rubbing his temples. She starts begging then, the little drama queen, even adding some tears for show.

Finally, the guy seems to cave. He unlocks the door and they both head inside the building. Laughing out loud, I get back on my bike. I did the right thing by coming here tonight. I fucking *knew* that smug piece of shit was hiding something.

Twenty minutes later, I'm back in front of Dove's house. The lights are off everywhere except her bedroom, and I already know she'll be up for hours still. Little bird doesn't sleep much.

I think about my next move. I wonder whether that guy Sam is still around. Leaving my bike parked a couple streets over, I walk to the alleyway, and sure enough, there's Dove's little buddy. Except he looks much worse for wear today, what with the fucking needle sticking out of his arm.

"Sam," I mutter, kneeling next to him. "Hey, Sam."

He doesn't respond. I pull the needle out of his arm and toss it aside. I shake him then, and with a groan, he finally wakes up. It takes him several moments to come to, and the first thing he does is reach for the needle I already removed before meeting my eyes guiltily.

"Nasty little habit you got there," I smirk. "Dove know about it?"

"She's trying to get me to quit." His eyes are hungry as they meet mine. "Do you have any stuff?"

"No," I reply firmly. "I don't mess with that shit, man. And you shouldn't, either."

Since I've spent several years on the streets, I know firsthand how dangerous these addictions can be. I've seen them kill too many people to count. I don't want Sam to be one of them.

The thought is surprising, the fact that I somewhat care about the old bastard. I don't care about anyone but Dove. Well, at least I didn't until now.

"Don't tell me what to do," Sam mutters in response.

Oh boy. "I'm not," I hiss. "Just trying to fucking help. I don't want Dove all depressed when she finds you kicked the bucket someday."

"I'll be fine," he waves his hand dismissively. He groans, picking himself up. Whatever high he was on is gone now, and he groans, running his fingers through his messy hair. "You got something to eat?"

"Sorry," I mutter. "I'll bring you something next time. But here." I fish a twenty out of my pocket and offer it to him. He hesitates, but then pockets the cash anyway. "Get some food. Not anything else."

"Yeah," he mutters. A part of me already regrets giving him the money. Something tells me he won't take my advice.

"Dove got home okay?" I ask, and he nods, giving me a curious look.

"Where were you?"

"Keeping an eye on someone else," I mutter. "Did her date drive her home?"

"No, she came in a cab. I saw it pull up earlier."

"Good." I can tell he's itching to get away, probably spend the money I gave him on something he shouldn't buy. "You kept your promise, right? You didn't tell her about me?"

"Haven't spoken to Dove today, but your secret's safe with me."

"It better stay that way," I say.

"What?"

"I said it better fucking stay that way."

His brows shoot up. "Are you threatening me?"

"No," I say. *Not fucking yet, at least.* "I'll see you soon, Sam. You take care of yourself."

"I will," he mutters, already distracted. "See you, Nox."

Still, there's some kind of silent companionship in the air, and I appreciate that. It's nice to have a friend.

Tonight is the night I finally get to break into Dove's apartment.

I have some unfinished business and I can't resist any longer. I want to see her. I want to smell her. I want to fucking touch her. Little bird's a light sleeper though, so I need to be careful.

It doesn't take me long to pick her lock, and with a click, I'm in.

The door opens into her apartment and I walk in, closing it soundlessly behind me. The apartment smells like her. Everything in here has that powdery, rosy smell that's been driving me wild since I first caught a whiff of it.

I'm quiet walking through the rooms. Years of sneaking around has taught me how to stay hidden in the shadows. The thought that she's only a couple doors away is so fucking exciting my cock twitches in my pants.

Even though the desire to break down her door and claim her right the fuck now is overwhelming, I force myself to take a breather. Instead of going upstairs, I head to her kitchen.

Everything is tidy. There are no dirty dishes except for a coffee mug on the counter. I pick it up, inspecting it. There's still a trace of her lipstick on the rim. My cock jumps to attention.

TYRANT STALKER

I raise the mug to my mouth and lick the rim. By now, I'm sure my cock is fucking leaking with precum. I want her. I want her so fucking much.

I set the mug back down and rummage through her pantry next. There's barely any food, barely anything in there. She seems to be a coffee addict though. She has bags upon bags of coffee beans. The other thing I notice are the plants. Plants fucking everywhere. Her place is like a goddamn greenhouse.

It's getting harder and harder to ignore the fact that she's so close. My cock wants her. *I* want her.

Busying myself with the rest of the lower floor, I flick through her magazines and books. I go through her laundry in the bathroom and find the black lace thong she must've worn to her date tonight, because it was at the top of the pile. I hold the thong to my nose and breathe her in. A musk so sweet I can't help squeezing at my goddam aching cock. I pocket the thong and I want to take more, but I don't want to arouse her suspicious just yet. I only want to fuck with her head for now. Make her think she's imagining shit.

Finally, the urge overwhelms me. Quietly, I sneak upstairs. Her bedroom door is closed but I can hear her mumbling something in her sleep. I wait until she quietens down before closing my hand around the door handle.

The door opens with a creak, and I cringe inwardly, but she doesn't stir. I wait another few moments before entering the room. The window's open, and I'm grateful for the sounds of the street.

I pull out her purse from under my arm and place it on the green velvet armchair in the corner of the room. Her phone's inside, and she will be none the wiser about the tracking app I put on it. Finally, I turn to face her.

I haven't been this close to my little bird in a long time.

Wanting to touch her, I reach out, but change my mind at the last moment. I can't risk it.

Instead, I let my fingers linger just above her scar. It still looks so angry. She'll never be able to move on. I ruined her life.

I smile at the memory of putting the scar on her face. She wasn't as pretty then as she is now. I wish she knew that.

My time with little bird is coming to an end. The sunrise will be here soon, and I need to disappear into the shadows before it happens. I fist my hand before I have the chance to touch her. I just can't fucking risk it.

Eyes wandering over her pretty face, I commit every feature to memory. Her curved Cupid's bow, the way her nipples strain against the oversized shirt she's wearing. Her hand is fisting the sheets, and her lips are open, a soft O-shape taunting my cock to take her, claim her, push myself into her throat and just put an end to my misery already.

But I can't.

I shouldn't.

Not yet.

I force myself to pull back and I leave her room, closing the door softly behind me.

My fingers wrap around her panties in my pocket, and I smirk.

At least I have a memento of tonight to keep me busy until I see her next.

CHAPTER SEVEN

DOVE

I wake up with a start. I had one of those dreams where I was falling, and my body twitches as I come to, finding myself in the comfort of my own Egyptian cotton sheets. I breathe a sigh of relief when I realize I've slept through the night in God fucking knows how long.

I pull myself up, push my feet into my slippers and head for the window. I always leave it open, but the room's chilly now, and I need some warmth. I close the window and when I turn around, I stop in my tracks as I take in the sight before me.

My purse, the one that the thief stole from me last night, is resting on the armchair.

This can't be right. I rush toward the chair, grabbing the bag as if to make sure I'm not still dreaming. But it really is there. And when I open it, I find everything in there that I took with me last night. My lipstick. My keys. My phone. My wallet. Nothing is missing.

I don't understand how this is possible. My first instinct is to call Raphael. Make sure I didn't imagine that guy taking off with my purse last night just as my date and I were sharing a moment on that sandy beach. But I don't. I don't want to be the crazy girl that doesn't even remember everything that happened.

Did I drink that much last night? I wonder. I had two glasses of wine with dinner, and it's true I'm not used to alcohol... But I'd remember something like the robbery correctly. *Wouldn't I?*

Worrying my bottom lip between my teeth, I scroll through my messages. There are a few from Robin, asking how my date went last night, and nothing from Raphael. I send back a quick reply, not mentioning that I got mugged on the beach. I'm still not sure whether the whole thing is just a figment of my imagination.

I'm working at the plant nursery later, but before then, I owe someone a visit.

I change into one of my regular, baggy outfits and head outside. It's not a very warm day, and I wrap my free arm around my body, so I don't get cold. In the other, I'm clutching some snacks I had at home, making a mental note to pick up something more nutritious for Sam next time. He refuses to go to the soup kitchen where I volunteer, claiming other people need it more than he does. I admire him for his selflessness.

My opinion quickly changes as I make my way into the dark alleyway that's been Sam's home for the past two years. My friend is slumped on the ground, and next to him, there's a needle.

He promised me he wouldn't do this again. He promised he'd do his best to get clean this time. That he really wouldn't spend any more on drugs. Where the hell did he even get the money? I never give it to him anymore because we both know it ends up with his dealer.

"Sam," I say, shaking him on his makeshift bed of newspapers and cardboard boxes. "Sam, wake up."

His eyes fly open, and a huge weight falls off my chest. I've found him like this too many times to count, and the fear that one of these days, it'll be too late, is twisting my stomach into knots.

"Sam, what did you do?" I ask as he picks himself up, clearing his throat and dusting off his dirty jacket.

"I guess you saw it," he mutters croakily. "And we can't just pretend you didn't?"

"No, Sam." I groan, running my hand through my hair before handing him the paper bag. "Here. It isn't much, but I'll bring you something else for tonight."

"Thanks." He looks embarrassed as he takes the bag from me. An awkward silence follows. I know this is hard for him. He told me he never had friends – not even before he started living on the street. He also told me I'm the closest thing he has to a daughter. But none of that matters, apparently, because he still hasn't kicked his nasty drug habit despite me begging him to stop countless times.

And the worst part is, I know this is what drove Sam to part from his family.

He told me about his wife and daughter before. He got divorced early, but he still got to spend time with his daughter until his addiction took over his life. When it did, his kid cut off all contact. He has two grandchildren he's never met. I know how much it hurts him. I can see it in his eyes.

But today, I don't feel sorry for him. I feel too angry and betrayed for that.

I pick myself up and give him one last look. "I'll see you later."

His eyes meet mine, and the pain in them is almost unbearable. Before he can say another word, I walk away.

I spend the rest of the day working at the nursery, but my mind is swimming with too many thoughts to count. I try not to focus on Raphael. On my purse reappearing in my bedroom. On Sam.

My mind circles back to the events of one fateful night eight years ago. And once I go down that rabbit hole, I know there's no turning back.

I never could outrun Parker Miller.

8 YEARS AGO...

We're alone in the Miller-Wildfox house. The help is all asleep. June's still out, doing God knows what. Now it's just me and her stepbrother, Parker. The guy I've been crushing on for freaking months, begging and begging for my best friend to introduce me. Finally, she caved.

We went out to a nightclub called Pulse and I proceeded to get mind-blowingly drunk. But it worked out in my favor, because now I'm alone with Parker – just what I fucking wanted. And so what if I exaggerated how drunk I was? I got exactly what I wanted. Just like I always do.

Parker's lying next to me on the bed, swallowing me up with his hungry eyes. I'm wearing a short dress, my strappy heels still adorning my feet. I know I look good. I work hard for it. Hours in the gym, at the hairdressers, at the nail salon. Every inch of me is perfect. And Parker's approving look tells me he agrees.

"I want to see you naked," he murmurs. "Take that excuse for a dress off."

I stand up, never taking my eyes off his as I slip the straps of the dress down. My tits bounce free. They're not as big as June's, but they're perky and my nipples are rosy pink. Parker groans as I undress right down to my pink thong.

"You look good, little bird," he says. "Thong off, too."

I hook my fingers in the pink lace and tug them down, doing my best to seduce him. Parker doesn't know it, but my heart is beating a thousand times per minute. I don't know if he's figured it out yet. That this is my first time... But I wouldn't want anyone else to take my virginity.

I snap the elastic of the thong against my hips.

"I told you to take it off," Parker grits out. "Now."

Hesitantly, I push the thong over my ass. Just like the rest of me, my pussy is perfect. Waxed to perfection. His eyes drink me in, watching me with a look I can't quite describe.

"It's boring how perfect you are." I pout at the sound of his words. "You're missing something, little bird. You're just like all the others now."

"I don't think so," I smile in response, turning around seductively to give him a view of my pert ass. "I work so hard to look this good, Parker... Don't you like it?"

"I do," he smirks. "But I'd like it better if you didn't look like a copy of every *fucking Instagram model with a couple thousand followers."*

"I have more than a couple thousand," I brag.

"I don't give a shit."

"So what, then?" I put my hands on my hips. "You want me to look like June, is that it?"

He grits his teeth together, not answering me. Of-fucking-course that's it. It's painfully obvious my date is obsessed with his stepsister, just like I'm obsessed with him.

"Get on the fucking bed," he growls, and I do as I'm told, crawling on top of him. He lets me straddle him, and my heart pounds when I feel his thickness, hard and throbbing, under my pussy. I start grinding on him. "You're gonna leave a wet spot on my pants, little bird. Do you want everyone to know what a little slut you are?"

"Maybe." I grin wickedly. "Don't you want to fuck me?"

"You'll do for the night, yes." His words hurt, but I'm determined to change his mind. I'm not going to leave him alone after this. Parker and I are meant to be together. There's nobody else for me.

"Then fuck me," I whisper in the shell of his ear, grabbing his hands and putting them on my tits. But he's barely responding, as if his mind is preoccupied with something else. Someone else. Probably June. God, I don't want to hate her, but the jealousy I feel is overwhelming.

"You a virgin, little bird?"

I stop moving, my teeth digging into my bottom lip. "Is that a problem?"

"It might be." Parker props himself up on his elbows. "You like it rough?"

"I don't know," I manage. "Do you?"

"Of course I fucking do, Dove. Don't be stupid."

"Well, then I do, too." I smirk at him mischievously. "I like whatever you like. I'll be whoever you want me to be. Do whatever you want. Anything."

"Anything?" His gray eyes sparkle darkly. "Any-fucking-thing?"

"Of course," I chirp, hoping I sound more certain than I feel.

The next moment, Parker grabs me by the wrists, flipping me over so my body is caged underneath his on the bed. I whimper as he slams my arms down and my breaths are coming hard.

"Anything you want," I tell him, "Any way you want it. I really do like you, Parker."

"You won't after tonight," he growls at me, and my heart jumps with excitement. "I'm going to make you regret this. Regret liking me. Regret making a move."

I struggle beneath him, but he won't let go. It excites me, and I whisper, "Are you going to pop my cherry?"

He shakes his head, grinning. "I'm going to pop all your fucking cherries, Dove Canterbury."

His words send a shiver of excitement down my spine, and I stare up at him intently as he lowers his lips against mine. His kiss isn't sensual or sweet. It's a punishment. He nips at my mouth, biting, sucking me. I mewl against his lips and he deepens our kiss, claiming me as his property once and for all.

"You know you're signing your death sentence when you kiss me like that?" Parker mutters against my lips. "I'm sick. I'm going to get obsessed with you, and I'll never fucking let you go."

"Fine by me," I grin against his lips. He grabs me by the hair, pulling my head back and exposing my neck to his mouth. He doesn't kiss it, he fucking bites, and I love it so much.

"Let me have that mouth first." His words are laced with a dark promise, and I watch him unbutton his jeans, my heart pounding as his hard cock springs free. "I've been dying to fuck that little mouth of yours, little bird..."

I don't get a chance to answer. He climbs on top of me, my body caged beneath his as he forces his cockhead into my mouth. I've never done this before, and I'm afraid I'll be clumsy and bad at it, but when his tip slides into me, a fervent desire fills me and instinct takes over.

I lick him and he groans. I kiss his cock like I want to kiss him, and Parker's *fingers tighten in my hair.*

"Not hard enough, Dove," he growls. "Suck it. Work for it. Show me how good you can be for me."

I take his words to heart. I'm desperate, eager to impress him. I want him to keep coming back to me, to keep taking me, to mark me as his forever. So, I do my best to satisfy him, eagerly eating up his cock and sucking hard.

"Fuck," *he mutters. His fingers are twisting, pulling on my hair painfully.* "Keep doing that, little bird. Take it. Fucking take it!"

Encouraged by his words, I allow my throat to accept him deeper. But then something switches inside Parker. I see the darkness take over him and pull him under. He grips my hair so tight it makes me squeal and when he starts to fuck my throat with angry thrusts of his hips I choke and gag and splutter.

He's loving it.

And it hurts.

But I fucking love it.

CHAPTER EIGHT

NOX
8 YEARS AGO...

It's hard to fight my brewing obsession with Dove Canterbury. The need to mark her as mine is overwhelming. I keep thinking about ways to claim her. To let the world know that I was her first, and I'll be her last, too.

She sucks my cock clumsily, but I love it nonetheless. Her little mouth wraps around the tip of my dick, trusting eyes finding mine as she sucks and licks at me. I want more, so I grab her by the hair and push myself deeper into her mouth. I'll always want more than she'll want to give me. But if Dove doesn't want to get hurt, she'll let me have it.

"Where do you want it next?" I grunt as her eyes bulge, taking me deeper and deeper until she gags. I pull my cock free and she splutters up so much saliva, the sight is almost enough to make me come. "Tell me, little bird. Tell me where you fucking want it."

"In my pussy," she breathes. "Please, I don't want to be a virgin anymore, Parker."

"Show me!" The words are nothing but a hiss as I move down her body. She *opens her legs for me, nice and wide, and I position myself at the tip of her untouched entrance. I want her. I'm going to fucking have her. And I'm going to kill any man who dares to claim her after me.*

Her fearful eyes find mine as I rub my cockhead over her sweet pussy lips. I know she's scared, but I don't offer any reassurance, no words of encouragement. She can deal with the guilt and the shame on her fucking own. I'm not here for that – I'm here for three reasons, and two of them are yet to be taken advantage of, between her legs.

"You ready for me, little bird?" She nods, teeth digging into her bottom lip as her eyes beg me to take even more than I already have. "Tell me your pussy is mine. Forever."

"It's yours," she manages hoarsely. "It's yours, forever, Parker..."

"You better not be fucking lying," I hiss as I toy with her, wiping the precum off my cock with her cunt, grinning at her as she whimpers. "Because I'll hunt you down... I know who you are, where you live. You'll never escape me now, little bird."

"I don't want to." Her words excite me. She's such a willing victim. I fucking love it. "Take it, please, Parker, I don't want to keep it, I don't want to have it anymore, please... Take my virginity... I want it to be yours."

With a groan, I push myself into her dripping wetness. She tenses as her snatch stretches around me, her walls desperately trying to accommodate my girth, but it ain't fucking happening. I'm too big for her. I'm going to tear her the fuck up.

"You ready for this?" I growl. "It's going to hurt..." I have no interest in making this easier for her. I get off on this. On the scent of her fear, on the taste of her sweat, blood, and tears. "Tell me you want me to hurt you."

"Hurt me," she breathes in desperation. "Please, Parker, fucking hurt me..."

I give her what she wants. With a single thrust of my hips, I bury my length inside her. She screams, but I don't give a shit. I'm too far gone in my obsession to care about what my victim wants. All that matters is pleasing my cock, feeding my addiction. I have an appetite, and I'm going to use my little bird to sate it.

"It hurts," she cries out. "Please, Parker! It hurts!"

"I don't care," I growl, driving myself in and out of her again and again. It's hard to give a shit now, when I'm so fucking close, when her desperation tastes so damn sweet. The walls of her pussy are closing in, holding me prisoner in her cunt. There's no goddamn way I'm pulling out now. "Just take it. Tell me how good it feels."

She cries out but doesn't try to stop me. Instead, her little fingers wind through the strands of my hair, gripping me, holding on for dear life as I fuck her harder, rougher, meaner. Every thrust of my hips marks her. Every time I push my cock deeper, she cries out in pain. With each second that passes, my obsession grows.

Until I finally pull out. She cries at the loss of my cock, accusing eyes meeting mine. "Don't stop, Parker..."

"You have one hole left," I grunt. "I'm taking that next."

"No, p-please." Now she's stuttering, growing paler by the second. "You already took so much from me... Please don't take any more."

"I'll take whatever the hell I want," I hiss. "You're mine. Repeat it to me."

"I'm..." She bites her bottom lip. I can see her getting worried when she looks at me. She's scared. "Please, I..."

"Say it!" I demand.

"I'm yours."

"Forever?"

"For..." She swallows. "Forever, Parker..."

I grab her, throwing her over to her belly and propping a pillow under her. I spit on her ass, watching it dribble between her cheeks, her skin so pale and beautiful, completely unmarred. I wish I could leave more marks, and the desire to carve my name into her grows.

I'm sick. I shouldn't be thinking this shit. And I'm already obsessed with someone else – my stepsister. Dove is just a fucking kid. She doesn't deserve this. Doesn't deserve to be hurt by me.

None of that helps, though. I still want her, and before I can change my mind, I thumb my spit over her tiny asshole, making it wet before massaging her puckered hole with the tip of my finger.

"You were innocent before," I mutter. "But no more. Not again. Not after I'm done with you."

"P-Please," she begs as I grab her by the throat, twisting her head so she's forced to look at me. "Please, Parker, don't hurt me."

"You were begging for the opposite moments ago," I remind her cruelly. "Which is it, little bird? Pain or no pain?" I ask her as I push a finger into her.

She doesn't answer, merely mewls in response, but I'm too far gone to give a damn. Instead of waiting for Dove to make up her mind, I line my cock up and force it into her, growing harder and needier as I push deep. I break that cherry, too. She screams as I fill her up, and my cock grows, throbbing in tune with her desperation.

I can tell she's hurting. She seems to be drifting in and out of consciousness now, her body limp beneath mine. But still it isn't enough to stop me. I fuck her like it's my last time. I don't have mercy for this girl. I can't let myself have mercy, because it would mean I care, and I don't care about anyone.

I keep going until her moans and cries grow softer and softer. And when I finally come in her tight little hole, she doesn't even respond. She's gone somewhere in her head, a dark place where everything is okay and the monster from her nightmares isn't holding her captive on this bed.

Filling her ass, I finally force myself to pull out. I look at her then, really look at her, her body bruised and broken by the sheer force I fucked her with. Her puckered hole dribbling with my cum. Without even speaking to her, I know she's ruined. She'll spend the rest of her life looking for this. Searching for the same things I gave her tonight, for the looming darkness that will hang just outside her reach as long as she's alive. But she'll never find it again. Not without me.

I force myself to pull back as she opens her eyes with a groan. She must be in so much pain. I want to hate myself, but I don't. Not when it felt so fucking good to rip Dove's innocence away from her.

Now it's time for me to leave. I can't stay here, not after what I've done. I can't *risk giving her false hope. She's already infatuated with me – what I just did will only make matters worse. I don't want to destroy her. I just wanted to take something beautiful and ruin it.*

As Dove's broken gaze finds mine, I know I've succeeded.

I remember fucking her like it was yesterday. The day I took Dove's virginity, I didn't know how deep my obsession ran already. I would fight it for months to come. Months without knowing who the real woman I wanted was. But not anymore. Now, I was certain. Dove Canterbury is the one for me.

I wake up from the memory with a groan, my hand fisted around my cock. It's the next day – has to be. I managed to make it back to the motel and fell asleep in my clothes on top of the bedspread. My head is pounding and I'm exhausted.

Today isn't a Dove day, it's a workday, and I'm fucking dreading it. I have to talk to that old bastard Hodge, who will buy any bullshit I feed him. He still doesn't know I'm the reason his daughter is dead.

I don't regret many things, but I regret killing Marissa Hodge. She didn't deserve to die, but she fell victim to my own rage. I couldn't see straight back then. All that mattered was the red mist that descended every time I thought of my twin. Marissa was collateral damage. But Hodge still won't admit it to himself that I'm the reason his only daughter is dead.

Sometimes I think about telling him. The dark, vicious side of me wants to do it. Wants to punish this man who's only done good things for me. I'm sick like that. I take something beautiful and I twist it and work it until it's no longer pretty. I did it to Marissa. I tried to do it to June. And now I'm doing it to Dove – the only obsession I could never truly escape.

Picking up my phone, I see a number of missed calls from Hodge. I call him back, preparing myself for his cheeriness. It's such a sharp contrast to the black hole that replaces my heart, I need to mentally prepare myself for it.

"Nox, hello!" I was right. He sounds delighted to hear from me. That stupid fucker. If only he could admit to himself what I did. "Have you given any more thought to the exhibition?"

I groan, rubbing my temples. Of course, he would bring that up again. He's been incessant in his efforts to get me to have another show, right here in LA. But after all these years, I don't want to risk my twin finding me. He would kill me if he did. I'm sure of that.

"I don't want to do a fucking show," I grunt in response. "How many times do I have to tell you?"

"Nox, I –"

"No," I hiss. "Tell me some good news instead. Did any more paintings sell?"

Since everything went down, my work has still been selling, and I've been creating darker and darker things as time goes by. My art completes many macabre collections of loaded, private billionaires who keep their sadistic streaks hidden, unlike me. But my most dedicated benefactor died a few months back, and we've been having trouble moving canvases since then.

"Not yet," Hodge admits. "But they will, when we do the show. People want to know you, Nox. They want to see the man behind all these incredible works of art."

"Too fucking bad, because I'm not interested."

"It would really help," he reminds me. "I know you need the money."

I think about his words. I don't need the money, he's wrong. I've got enough saved up to last me at least another year or two, even without moving any more art.

"You don't want to sink," Hodge persists. "Now is the time to show yourself. Nobody will connect you to your old life, Nox. Nobody in LA knows who you are."

"Kade could find me," I remind him.

"Your brother's too preoccupied," Hodge says and jealousy twists my stomach into knots. Why did Kade get his happily ever after and I didn't? It's fucking unfair. "He has three children now, and he's still running the company. He never suspected anything. Far as he knows, you're dead."

"And I'd like to keep it that way," I mutter. "He can't find out about this. Not now, not ever."

"What if I could promise you that he wouldn't?"

"You can't."

"I can." Hodge sounds so confident I almost believe him. "Trust me, Nox. Just agree to this gallery showing. One exhibition. That's all I'm asking for."

I've had enough, and I don't know how to make myself any clearer than I already have, so I cut the call short. I turn off my phone and pull on a jacket before heading outside. The receptionist isn't there, and I'm grateful for it. The last thing I need to deal with is a horny little teenager. Although the thought is tempting, I only have eyes for one woman.

I head to the nearby newsagent to pick up some smokes. Barking my order at the woman behind the counter, I wait for her to get them for me, scanning the magazine covers as I wait. I almost miss it, but it's unmistakably her. My little bird is on the cover of the most famous fashion magazine of the city.

I grab a copy off the counter. I'm so pissed off already, I crumple the paper, ignoring the saleswoman as she hisses I'll have to pay for that. I throw some money on the counter, grab my smokes and the magazine, and head off, eyes still trained on Dove's beautiful, scarred face staring back at me with trusting eyes that have seen so much pain already.

That bastard put my woman on the cover of a goddamn magazine. *Naked*.

My hands tighten around the magazine. I raise it again to see the image in its full glory, and that's when I see it. The scar I put on Dove's face is not the only one she has. Her body is full of them – little cuts, small but deep enough to scar. Some of them look newer than the others. She's hurting herself.

I wanted to kill the photographer, Raphael whatever-the-fuck-his-name-is, but now, a need to protect little bird is twisting my stomach into knots. I have to save her. Not from me, but from herself.

CHAPTER NINE

DOVE

My own face is staring back at me from the cover of a magazine. It's been a long time since I've seen myself in print, and now I understand why.

The image is beautiful, but I'm not. The scar marring my face is too prominent. I thought maybe Raphael would edit it out. I signed an agreement that said the photos were his property, but I didn't expect him to exploit me like this. My blood boils, anxiety taking over as I pay for my copy of the glossy magazine. The vendor's eyes drink me in curiously. He's recognized me. I need to get the hell out of here.

I rush across the street. Raphael sent me a text this morning telling me to pick up a copy of the magazine, Void. He probably thought I'd be thrilled to see myself on the cover of it, but I'm far from thrilled.

There's no denying the photograph is beautiful. It's intimate. It shows me in a vulnerable light. In a way I very rarely show other people. I allowed Raphael in, showed him myself at my most vulnerable, and he exploited it. I shoot him a text, asking him why he did it. I hope he can tell I'm pissed about this. Despite our date going well, I'm not going to hide how I really feel about what he did.

TYRANT STALKER

The worst thing about the photo isn't the scar on my face, but all the others on my body.

Because I'm naked on the portrait, and Raphael has barely edited the photo, every little cut is obvious. I look awful. Crazy. Broken. I hate him for doing this to me.

I arrive back home in time for Raphael's reply. He's asking me out again, mentioning that Thai place he told me about on our last date. Furiously, I type back a reply.

You really think I'm going to forgive you for doing this? I can't believe your audacity.

Do you like the photo? he texts back, making me roll my eyes.

Doesn't matter. How'd you get in Void anyway? I thought those spreads book months in advance.

They saw the portrait and loved it. You should, too. So. Dinner?

If you think you can make me forget about this with one meal, you've got another thing coming.

We'll see after you try it, he replies. *Best pad Thai in town, hands down. I'll pick you up. Seven p.m. No need to dress up, it's a casual place.*

Frustrated, I pocket my phone again. I can't believe he's acting like this, and at the same time, I'm glad he is. He's making light of the situation. But all I can think of is my mother picking up Void and seeing the face she told me was ruined staring back at her from the cover. She would hate this. Hate my imperfections being exposed like this. After the accident happened, she thought I should move, go in hiding. She didn't want anyone to see her precious daughter ruined. Neither did I, and for a while, I took her advice. I locked myself in, didn't leave the house. I saw surgeon after surgeon, discussing my options. But there was nothing anyone could do – not even the insanely expensive, experimental, painful procedures would hide the damage done to my face.

That's when I started hating Parker Miller. I spent years wishing him dead, but when I got the news that he was gone, it didn't help matters much. I felt sad for losing someone I once cared about. The scar might've closed up, but the emotional wounds

Parker left behind didn't. They rotted and festered instead.

Despite being upset with Raphael, I feel a frisson of excitement as I get ready for our date. I pick out a casual outfit – black faux leather pants and a pair of heeled black ankle boots. I decide on a black silky camisole with lace I would never usually wear, wondering whether I'm doing this because I know it accentuates my cleavage. Do I want Raphael to make a move?

I shake my head to get the thought out. I don't need a romance right now. I need to tell Raphael just how angry I am about the photo, in person.

I pair my outfit with a long, fluffy white cardigan to break up the all-black. But looking at myself, I decide I look too cheery. I keep trying things on and the pile of clothes on my bed grows as I discard items. Finally, I settle on a light gray cardigan over the camisole. I brush my hair, so it falls in rich dark waves down my back, and put on a slick of red gloss and some mascara. There. Done.

By the time Raphael arrives to pick me up, I've almost managed to forget about the mugging thing. But then I remember my bag reappearing in my bedroom. I still can't explain it, but I'm too afraid to bring it up with my date. I don't want him to think I'm crazy... There has to be a rational explanation for everything, and I'm determined to believe that. If I don't... I'll go mental.

Raphael opens the car door for me. This time, he's driving himself. The drive to the Thai place is quiet and tense. I refuse to look at him, and when he realizes I don't want to make small talk, he turns on the car radio. A ballad blares out on the speakers, and I stare through the window as we pull up in front of the restaurant.

He's booked us a table, and the waiter is already waiting with two steaming hot plates of food. My stomach rumbles and I groan inwardly. In my anger, I forgot about having to eat tonight. And this place is packed – every table is taken.

I watch Raphael eat with gusto, while I pick at my food. Even though it's my favorite, I can't bring myself to take a bite. Not with all these people here.

"So, you're mad at me." The photographer grins at me. "I promise I wasn't trying to piss you off or exploit you."

"Then why'd you do it?" I cross my arms defiantly. "Why did you put that shot on the cover?"

"Because it's beautiful," he answers simply. "It's art. Sometimes, art has to transcend your own feelings on the matter. Do you know that's the least edited image that's ever been on the cover of Void?"

I shake my head.

"Well, it is. They loved it just the way it was. They want to book you for another shoot with an in-house photographer."

"Pass," I mutter.

"Would you let me finish, woman?" He laughs, shaking his head. "Anyone ever tell you how stubborn you are?"

I shake my head again. "Of course not."

"No, no, of course." Raphael grins, glancing at my untouched food and motioning for the waiter. "Can we get the leftovers to go, please?"

"But you haven't finished your meal," I argue. He doesn't listen, paying for the meal again and taking the doggy bags in one hand, and my palm in the other.

I'm tempted to mention the mugging as we make our way to his car, but I'm too worried what he'll think of me. I'm also a little disappointed he's cut our date so short, but I guess I only have myself to blame. I've acted cold toward him all night.

Raphael pulls me past his car, sitting on a bench and pulling out the containers of food.

"What are you doing?"

"Finishing my dinner," he shrugs. "You will too, right?"

I glance around us. The boardwalk is deserted. The only one who would see me eat here is Raphael, and he doesn't seem to care, tucking into his own food as he pats the bench for me to join him. Reluctantly, I do. I take out my chopsticks and eat, slowly, bite by bite. Raphael was right. This is the best Thai dish I've ever had.

We finish our food in comfortable silence. I don't eat everything, but at least half of it, and it feels good. I put the rest back in the bag for Sam later.

"You've got a little..." Raphael points to my face.

"Here?" I wipe, and he laughs, leaning in close.

"Let me." His thumb wipes the corner of my lip. He raises it to his lips and sucks it clean. For some reason it makes me need him. I want him to kiss me. I want him to touch me.

I look away, unable to handle the weight of his gaze, but he keeps his eyes trained on me.

"Dove," he mutters. "Look at me."

Wordlessly, I shake my head. But he takes my chin in his fingers, gently tipping my head back. My eyes meet his. They're burning with a cool, quiet desire. I realize I want him to kiss me, and the next second, he does.

His lips meet mine, hesitant at first, as if he thinks I'll push him away. But I don't. I can't. I'm so starved for some kind of connection, I lean into him, kissing him back.

Encouraged by my response, Raphael deepens our kiss. I push the leftovers aside and he hoists me up on his lap. Suddenly I'm straddling him, and we're kissing like our lives depend on it.

Fuck. I never realized how much I wanted this. How much I missed human contact... Kissing, fucking, making love. It all hits me like a ton of bricks. I'm so tempted to ask him for more. Whimper and beg for more. I've only done that with one other man. And he ruined my life. I can't let Raphael do that.

I pull back, forcing my heartbeat to slow down. Raphael traces his fingertips over my lips, as if to remember their shape. I don't regret kissing him, but we've moved fast – from an innocent peck to a full-on makeout session on a bench, like we're two horny freaking teenagers.

"I'm sorry," I whisper. "It's... it's so fast."

"Don't be sorry," he replies. "I'll give you all the time you need. But I do want to kiss you again..."

I look up at him and nod. I don't want to, but I need more comforting.

His lips meet mine again. This time he's patient, slow, kind. Somehow, still passionate. I melt into his embrace, my body molding into his as he holds me close.

"Do you want to come back to my place?" he mutters in my ear. "Or yours... Whatever you want, Dove, I just want to be with you. Fuck, I know it's too fast, I know I shouldn't say all this, but I can't help myself."

I battle with my decision, but deep down, I know I'm not ready yet. And if he truly cares about me, he'll be willing to wait. I pull back and shake my head, "It's too soon. Can you take me home? I have something else I need to do."

"Of course." Such a gentleman. He takes my hand and we walk back to his car, hand in hand. The whole drive home, his right hand rests on my knee, and I don't mind it one bit.

He parks in front of my house and gets out to walk me to the door.

"I actually have another errand," I mutter apologetically. "I really would invite you in, I just..."

"No need to explain." He squeezes my hand. "I'll wait, Dove."

"Thank you," I manage. He leans in and kisses me again. Soft, beautiful, special. The kiss is fleeting, and when he pulls back, I feel lost. "Will we go out again?"

"Of course," he smirks. "I'm not taking no for an answer. And about Void... Can I give your number to the photographer they work with?"

"I'm sorry, but no." I shake my head. "It was a one-time thing for me."

"Understood." He smiles. "In a way, I'm relieved. It makes the portraits I took of you so much more special."

I smile back and we say our goodbyes. I wave as he drives off before heading into the alleyway where Sam should be. It's late – I spent more time with Raphael than I thought I would. I expect to see my friend asleep on his makeshift bed, but when I get there, the newspapers, cardboard and my blanket are abandoned.

"Sam?" I call out, but there's no answer. Just silence. Worry instantly pierces my heart. Sam is always here. Always. Something must've happened.

I leave my bag of leftovers on his makeshift bed, and head back to my house.

Whatever happened, I just hope he's alright. He has to be.

Besides my brother, he's the only friend I have.

CHAPTER TEN

NOX

"You have to stop doing this, Sam."

"I know." He groans, picking himself up in the hospital bed. Several tubes are leading out of his veins and his nose, pumping him full of more drugs to help lessen the effect of what he did last night. "Don't tell Dove."

"I won't," I say firmly. Sam doesn't know I haven't spoken to Dove in eight years, and I'd prefer to keep it that way. "But only because it would hurt her to find out what you've been doing to yourself. You have to get a grip, man."

"I know," he repeats weakly, just as a blonde nurse strides into the hospital room he's sharing with four others.

"Mr. Benedetto, your insurance isn't valid," she tells him bluntly. "How are you planning on paying for your treatments?"

"I'll handle it," I mutter, taking the papers from her and signing my name on the dotted line.

"You can't do that, Nox," Sam groans. "It'll be expensive… a nightmare."

"How else are they going to help you?" I hand the papers back to the nurse and she scurries out of the room. "Just let me do this for you, and promise you'll get better."

"I don't know if I can." Sam looks so small and frail in that hospital bed, it even tugs on the strings of my own black heart. "I think it's too late for me. I don't think I'll ever get better."

"You have to try," I insist. "For Dove. For me."

"Why do you care?"

"You're my friend, aren't you?" He nods hesitantly. "There you go. You have two friends now, who both care about you and want to help you get better. Here." I reach inside my coat pocket and pull out the prepaid phone I bought in the gift shop earlier. "I got you a phone. And this power bank. I have one too, we'll exchange them when I come visit you. My number's in there, and Dove's is, too."

"Why are you doing this for me?" Sam stares at me with something akin to anger, which I don't understand. "I told you, it's too fucking late for me. There's no way I can get better. I'm doomed."

"I don't believe that." I truly don't, and I take him by the shoulder as he raises his eyes to mine. "You're a man, Sam. A strong man. You can turn things around, and I believe you will. Just stay strong."

I will never forget walking into that alleyway Sam calls home hours earlier, seeing him crumpled and convulsing on the hard pavement. He'd had a seizure, an after-effect of all the drugs he'd done that day. It was devastating – the only reprieve being that I found him, and not little bird.

A part of me was desperate to protect Dove from the ugly side of her friendship with Sam. In my years on the streets, I'd seen the ugly side of addiction too many times to count, and I'd be damned if I was going to lose another friend to the needle.

"If you want, I can get you a room at the motel where I'm staying," I say.

"No," he shakes his head vehemently. "No, I don't want that."

"You could even stay with me," I offer next. "There's a couch in mine and –"

"No." He stares at me hard. "I don't want your pity."

"Then stop this," I hiss. "Stop ruining your life, because you're also ruining Dove's in the process. You're like a father to her. Do you understand that? It would kill her to lose you."

He nods, staring at his dirty palms as I pace the hospital room. Neither of us says another word until Miss Blondie, the nurse, reappears, and tells us Sam is free to go.

I pay the hospital bill in silence. It's gonna eat away at my savings, but that doesn't matter. Next, I load Sam up on my bike and hand him my helmet. I only have the one.

In silence, I speed off to the alleyway. When we arrive, we find a crumpled note on his messy blanket and the makeshift bed he's made out of newspapers and cardboard.

Where were you, Sam? – Dove

My chest tightens at the sight of her loopy handwriting. She must've come looking for him in the night. I can't imagine how worried she was, seeing him gone from his usual spot.

"Don't tell her," Sam begs me again.

"I won't this time." I put the helmet on my head. "But if this happens again, I'll be forced to."

He nods and silently waves me off as I pull out onto the road. I go to the motel and take a quick shower to wash the hospital smell of antiseptic and sickness off me. As I exit the bathroom with a towel wrapped around my waist, I scroll through my phone. I need to check up on Dove. The fact that I haven't seen her in so long is eating away at me.

I open the app I use to track her phone, scrolling through her messages. Robin, Robin, Robin. Someone from the plant nursery. And Raphael. Over and over again, his name pops up. Fucking Raphael!

I snarl at the screen as I start reading through their messages.

I had a great time last night :)

Me too. I want to see you again soon, Dove.

TYRANT STALKER

You can. Are you going to kiss me like that again?

I feel like I'm about to fucking explode. That slimy fucking bastard kissed her. He put his lips on my woman, my property, *my* little bird. And now he has to die.

A snarl rips itself from my lips as I inspect more of their texts. There are so many. They've been texting all day today. She even told him about Sam.

I toss the phone to my shitty motel bed. I can't accept this. She trusts him. She spends time with him. He's her friend, and he'll soon turn into something more if I don't intervene. But I have another ace up my sleeve – I know about Raphael and Elise. And I'm more than fucking willing to expose their sordid affair. I'll do any-fucking-thing to get my little bird back in my arms... even if it means breaking her sweet little heart.

I parked my bike a couple of streets over, and now I'm standing in the shadows on the street where Raphael lives. My teeth are gritted together as I wait. I know she'll come. I'd bet anything that the girl showed up here every single night since Raphael started seeing Dove.

And as if on cue, the ridiculous bubblegum pink car pulls up, and Elise exits. Her dog is stuffed into another one of those ridiculous overpriced purses, and she rings the doorbell incessantly. I watch her argue with him over the intercom until she finally smiles and he comes downstairs to deal with her.

Fuck.

He didn't invite her up. Why didn't he invite her up? Doesn't he want her anymore? Despite her many shortcomings, Elise is fucking hot. There can only be one reason as to why Raphael doesn't want her in his apartment.

He's starting to like Dove more than this designer Barbie doll.

My nails dig into the palms of my hands as I watch Elise burst into tears on Raphael's doorstep. He's telling her off, explaining she can't stay, and ordering her to go back home. As his whiny mistress cries, the stupid dog starts yapping again. My head hurts. I can't fucking stay here.

I wait until Elise leaves with her shoulders slumped before getting on my bike again. I follow her, knowing full well who she's going to see next. And I'm right. She pulls up in front of a terracotta apartment building downtown. Robin, Dove's brother, opens the door for her, concerned when he sees the traces of tears ruining her perfectly painted face. She dismisses his worries, waving her hand as if it's nothing. Little fucking liar.

So, Elise is a fucking mess, but what else is new? Now I just need to wait until the perfect moment to hurt all four players involved in this sick little game. The perfect moment to drive a wedge between Dove and Raphael and make sure they don't end up together.

Another short bike ride later and I'm back in front of Dove's house. The lights are off, except the one she keeps on in her bedroom. The desire to go back inside her house is fucking overwhelming. I want to be close to her. I want to watch her sleep, to caress her cheek, to inhale her scent. I want another pair of her panties.

I fist my hands in my pockets, making sure the street is empty. I shouldn't, but I have to be near her. I need to see what she's doing, what her life has been like today. I can't bear the thought of waiting for her outside all night. I need her.

I use the spare key hidden beneath a flowerpot. I saw her use it when I stole her bag. I let myself in, allowing the forbidden shivers to go down my spine as I enter her private space. Quickly, I check if everything is in place on the ground floor. I snatch another pair of panties – dark red, lace – from her hamper, holding them to my nose and filling myself with her sweet scent. But that's not enough, not this time, so I lick them, taste her sugar on my tongue. She tastes so fucking good. Even sweeter than I remember.

I stash the panties in my pocket and head upstairs. The door to her bedroom has been left ajar, and I'm worried as fuck she's going to wake up, since she's such a light sleeper. But I brought reinforcements this time because I want to stay longer tonight. I want to play with my toy, and nothing is going to fucking stop me.

I take the small wrap from my pocket, unfold the end, and let the white powder fall into the glass of water she keeps by her bed before finally turning to face her. She's sleeping naked – it's a warm night. The sheets cover up everything apart from one nipple, the bud hardened by the breeze coming from the open window. And just like that, I'm hard. Fuck, she's mesmerizing. I can barely take my eyes off her.

The temptation to touch her is so damn great, but I force myself to keep my distance. The drink on her nightstand fizzes as I move quietly through the room. Her phone's next to her, probably filled with more fucking texts from that smug Mexican bastard. Her dark hair is fanned over the pillow and she looks as breathtaking as ever. I want her. I want her so fucking much my balls ache.

I'm back in front of her bed soon enough, barely resisting the urge to touch my fingertips to her porcelain skin. The scar is a permanent reminder of what I've done to her already. Raised and puckered, it would feel so fucking good against my fingers.

Before I can stop myself, I reach out and touch it. She doesn't move, and my cock swells as I trace my fingertip over the length of the scar that mars her beautiful face. I see the other scars too. The ones I saw on that magazine cover. There are so many of them, small, big, some deep, some shallow. And some wounds are recent. She's been hurting herself. She's been hurting herself for a very long fucking time.

Just as I pull my hand back, she stirs, as if disturbed by the loss of the comforting touch on her cheek. Fuck. She's going to wake up, and yet I don't want to move away. Every cell in my body is screaming for more. I want to part her legs and see that pretty little snatch. I want to grab her by the hair and feel the weight of her dark mane in my hands. But she's going to wake up any second. The longer I stay here, the more dangerous this is. She's almost awake... so very close to busting me.

Her pretty mouth opens and she mutters something, and then her eyes fly open, and I know I'm fucked... but maybe that's exactly what I've wanted all along.

CHAPTER ELEVEN

DOVE

I could swear Parker was just in my room.

I rub my eyes, glancing to the window, but I know I'm the one who left it open. There's no one there anymore, nothing but the soft breeze blowing in and ruffling the white silk curtains. With a groan, I pull myself up. I guess I was expecting too much by hoping for another night of uninterrupted sleep.

Picking myself up from the bed, I shut the window. It's chilly in the room, and I'm parched. I reach for the glass of water on my nightstand and down it in one go. It tastes bitter, and I make a face, wondering if I'd kept the glass on there for too long.

I'm certain I won't be able to fall asleep again, but a few moments after finishing my drink, I realize just how bone tired I am. I get back in the bed and pull the sheets up, burrowing in the comfort of my duvet, my eyes feeling heavier and heavier as I start drifting off. I must've imagined Parker right there, in my bedroom.

There's no other explanation.

Parker is here again, but so is Raphael. The rational side of me knows it's a dream, but there's nothing I can do to stop the two mirages from having their way with me – not now that they've tied me down. The silk ropes feel amazing against my skin, holding me captive as the two men circle me, their cruel intentions making their eyes sparkle with darkness.

I know they're going to fuck me, I just don't know which one of them is going to go first.

Raphael approaches and I notice he's holding a knife. I begin to thrash against my restraints, but it's no use. He's going to hurt me, and my eyes go to Parker's, desperately pleading for help. But help doesn't come.

Raphael raises the knife and I close my eyes so I don't have to see the blood. But he doesn't cut me. No, instead he starts sawing against the ropes in an effort to get me free.

That's when Parker loses it. He roars to life, knocking Raphael out and kicking the knife out of both our reaches.

"You're never leaving," Parker snarls at me as Raphael groans weakly on the ground. "You're mine, Dove, you're fucking mine, and I'll never let go."

I descend into a cacophony of pleas, pleading with him to let me go, but I know it's no use. Parker will never leave. Parker will never let go. Parker and I are tethered together, our sick, dark connection meaning we'll never be apart. I feel the invisible strings pulling me to him. There's no fighting it.

"You want me to fuck you in front of him?" Parker hisses in my ear. "Want your boy toy to watch how a real man fucks you, little bird?"

I shake my head, opening my mouth to scream, but no sound comes out. Parker fondles me, my hair, my tits, the embarrassingly wet spot between my legs. He touches me gently. Caresses me like he cares, like he's not trying to hurt me at all. But I know him. I know the monster hiding behind his handsome face. He gets off on it – the darkness, the pain. And now, he's more determined than ever to hurt me.

His fingers plunge into my wetness and he fucks me hard while more soundless screams escape my lips. I hate him as my body vibrates from his roughness. I hate him as he spits and snarls with every thrust, but it feels so fucking good. And when I moan, the sound finally comes while Raphael watches helplessly from the ground.

"I'm sorry," I mouth at him. "I'm sorry, but I want him... I want Parker, I don't want you. I'm so sorry..."

"Keep apologizing," Parker mutters in my ear. "Keep telling him it's me you want... It's me you choose... I'm the one you're going to end up with, little bird... We all fucking know it. You're mine. My property. My little bird."

"No!" I cry out.

"Yes!" he snarls back. "My property... my girl... my. Fucking. Girl."

I start crying but he pays it no mind, continuing his vicious assault on my barely resisting body, stretching me, hurting me.

I hate him.

I want him.

I love him...

I wake up with a start. Fuck.

My head is heavy. My mind feels thick like a fog has descended upon every thought, and my mouth is dry as hell. I rub my eyes, thanking my lucky stars the mirage and everything that followed was all just a dream. But there's something else... something that hurts.

Getting up from the bed, I wince when I feel a strange weight between my legs. My hand shoots between my thighs. My pussy is soaked, and I flush in embarrassment as I realize just how much my dirty dream turned me on. But there's something else. Something cold and hard. And it's not in my pussy. It's wedged tightly in my ass.

I keep feeling around, running to the mirror on the wall and bending over. And there it is – a silver metal thing, with a pink crystal heart. It's a plug, and it's lodged deep inside me.

My hand flies up to cover my mouth that has opened in shock. What the fuck? I don't own a butt plug, so what the hell is that thing doing inside me?

I tug on it to get it out and a sensation I've never felt before makes my knees weak. Fuck. How am I going to get this thing out? And, more importantly... am I going to come pulling it out of my body?

I worry my bottom lip between my teeth as I lie back on the bed, raising one leg up to my chest. My fingers wrap around the base of the plug and I start tugging on it in an effort to get it out.

It feels good. So fucking good, my teeth draw blood from my lip as I keep going. Except now I'm not pulling it out. No, I'm playing with it, twisting it, pushing it in and out as I bring myself closer and closer to an unwilling orgasm. I can't explain the toy stuck inside me, and worry twists my insides into a thousand knots. Finally, I pull the plug out with a soft scream as it pops out of me. I can feel how much it stretched me. Another few minutes and I would've come from it.

I toss it aside, unable to even look at the stupid thing as I rush to the bathroom.

My cheeks are burning up as I begin scrubbing myself. It feels as if I'm washing years of dirty secrets down the drain, and I scrub until my body is burning and red.

Wrapping myself up in a thick towel, I go back to the bedroom, my eyes instantly going to the corner where I tossed that metal plug.

It's not there.

My towel falls to the ground as I raise my hands to my mouth. How can it not be there? Didn't I just toss it aside? Didn't I just have it in me?

With a start, I remember the handbag, the thief. Now the plug. Am I going crazy? What's happening to me? Why can't I remember the simplest of things?

I push all the worries to the back of my mind. I can't think about any of it right now. Instead, I focus on one person who always manages to calm my racing mind.

Sam.

I was so worried when I didn't find him in his usual spot last night, and I cross my fingers as I load up some food for him in a brown paper bag and head to his alley.

My heart soars when I see him there, crumpled in a heap on his makeshift bed.

"Sam!" I rush toward him, kneeling in front of him on the dirty pavement. He won't look at me. "I came looking for you last night. Where were you? I was so worried."

"I had something I needed to do," he mutters, motioning to the brown bag. "That for me?"

"Yes." I pass him the bag and he digs into some cookies. "I brought something yesterday, but you weren't here. What happened, Sam? Where did you go?"

"I told you, I had something to do." Am I imagining it, or is his reply strained and unwelcoming? Either way, he's making it clear he doesn't want any further questions. But I can't help myself.

"Oh, Sam, it's not the drugs again, is it?" He keeps eating, refusing to look at me. "Please tell me it's not the drugs. I was worried sick, Sam."

"Don't worry about me, Dove," he says finally. "You have better things to do than worry about an old man everyone else was wise enough to forget."

"I could never forget you, Sam," I tell him firmly. "You're important to me. Much too important to forget."

He doesn't respond, just eats his cookies in silence. I guess he just doesn't want to talk to me today, so I pick myself up.

"Well, I better go," I finally mutter. "I'm working at the soup kitchen today. Do you want to come over? It's chowder night."

He shakes his head without looking at me. "Thanks for the food, kid."

"You're welcome." I kick at a pebble, unsure what to do next. But Sam won't even meet my eyes, so I decide to write today off as a bad day for him. I quietly mutter a goodbye, but he doesn't respond as I head back to my place with slumped shoulders.

I spend the rest of the day at the soup kitchen, working hard to fill more hungry mouths than we can handle. At the end of the day, I sign another check for a sizable donation to the soup kitchen, and the head, Velma, thanks me profusely. I just smile tensely in return. The feeling that I'm still not doing enough is still there, convincing me I'll never be good enough.

As I come back to my place, my face lights up when I see Robin sitting on my doorstep.

"What are you doing here?" I ask jovially as we hug.

"Thought you could use the company," he grins, holding up a bag. "I brought Mexican food today."

My smile falters because I don't want to eat after everything that's happened today. Still, I'm thrilled to see Robin, and I invite him in. We settle on the couch in front of the TV and quickly catch up while he digs into the quesadillas he brought with him. I know he's going to pressure me about food tonight – I can tell from his tense demeanor. So I'm grateful when his phone starts going off.

"Elise?" I ask. He nods, groaning and running his fingers through his hair. "Maybe you should ask her to come over."

"Elise?" Robin looks shocked, laughing. "What, you didn't get enough of her when you went shopping the other day?"

"I just thought it might be fun to watch a movie. All three of us." I smile innocently. If Robin can tell I'm only doing this because I want to distract him, he doesn't show it, but he does look suspicious.

"Maybe," he finally mutters, his eyes lighting up with an idea. "I'll do it, under one condition."

"What's that?"

"You invite your new crush over, too." Robin's grin is mischievous. "You know, the Raphael guy."

"You want to meet him?" Despite my stressful day, I find myself grinning as my brother nods. "That's actually not a bad idea. But do I look alright? Am I a mess? I've been working all day."

"You look great," my brother insists. "Now call him. I want to meet this mystery guy you're so head over heels for."

"Oh, shut up," I mutter, but for some reason, I can't keep the smile off my face.

"Okay, I'll call him. Elise won't mind?"

"Why would she?"

"I don't know."

"Just call him already," Robin laughs. "Let's see if he's worth you getting all flustered over."

CHAPTER TWELVE

NOX

The white powder I put in Dove's drink works like a charm. She's out in moments, leaving me free to do whatever the hell I want with her body. She doesn't even wake up when I pull the duvet off her. For such a light sleeper, she is deeply slumbering now – there's no way she'll wake up. I've dosed the powder carefully, making sure not to harm her, but also ensuring she'll be fast asleep for the duration of the time I play with her.

After I pull the duvet off her, I take some time just to admire her stunning naked body. The scars are marring her, but they don't take away from her beauty. She is beautiful in an inoffensive way that strikes me to my very core. Her perky pink nipples stand erect, just begging for me to take them in my mouth. Her pussy is waxed bare save for a strip of dark hair running down to her sweet center. She is painfully thin, though, her bones nearly protruding from her pearlescent skin.

Dove is ruining herself. Day by day, she gets weaker, thinner and succumbs more to the disorders plaguing her mind and body. I vow to make things better for her. To make sure she'll be okay, that she'll eat right, that she won't starve herself any longer.

TYRANT STALKER

But I'm running out of patience. I need to touch her. Need to feel her silky skin beneath my fingertips. I reach out, laying a hand on her stomach. I expected it to be cold, but she's warm, hot-blooded under the pearliness. I groan.

With my free hand, I reach in my pocket and pull out the toy I bought especially for her. I saw it in a shop a couple weeks back and bought it with Dove in mind, already fantasizing about putting it in her tight little asshole. I still remember taking her virginities, every single one of them, while she writhed in pleasure and pain. Tonight's going to be even better, because tonight, Dove can't fight back.

My fingers roam over her body, exploring every forbidden inch. I slide them under her breasts, feeling the weight of them in my palm. Finally touching her feels fucking surreal. I dig my teeth into my bottom lip, breathlessly whispering her name. I almost want her to wake up. To see me. To realize I'm the one who's been fucking with her all this time. But I fight the urge and stroke her instead, allowing my fingertips to familiarize themselves with the layout of her body again.

God, she's beautiful. Her porcelain skin marred only by the scar I gave her and the ones she gave herself, shimmers in the moonlight. My cock is so hard it's straining against the fabric of my jeans, and I can't stand another moment of not having my fist wrapped around it. I pull it out, stroking my impressive length over Dove's naked thigh. My pre-cum smears from my tip, marking her as my property as I stroke myself harder to draw out the seed from my balls.

I can't resist reaching between her legs. With two fingers, I part her silky folds, allowing my spit to drip from my lips to her hot little center. I rub it in, groaning when she stirs in her sleep, so very eager for more. I want to fucking devour her.

Turning around the plug I brought with me in my hands, I put it up to my mouth and make it wet with my spit. I play with her then, running the toy over her pearlescent body, touching it to every bit of her, stroking the tip of it over her puckered nipples, sliding it down over her stomach and between her pussy lips with ease. She's wet. Always so fucking ready for me, begging me to do more to her sweet, unconscious little body. God, I want to fuck her so badly. Desire is twisting up my insides, demanding I give in to the darkness that is eager to wreak havoc on Dove. But I can't. I must resist a while longer.

I start fingering her. One finger first, then two, then three, stretching her tight little snatch as much as I can. My cock is fucking dripping with pre-cum. I want to be inside her, but I need to keep fighting those urges. Instead, I finger her hard, toying with her asshole with the plug I brought. It'll slip in soon, filling her up, allowing her ass to stretch the way it will have to when she inevitably takes my dick in it. I push the plug in by a good inch, stretching her sweet asshole around it. I toy with her with one hand, the other massaging my throbbing cock. Finally, I push the plug fully inside. As her asshole swallows it up, a gasp escapes Dove's lips and her eyes flutter open. I pause. I'm convinced she's woken up, but those pretty eyes flutter closed again, saving me from getting busted. She moans in her sleep, restlessly shaking as her body accepts my gift.

I'm so fucking desperate to come. I want to fill her. To mark her as mine. But I need to fight those instincts. I need to hold back before it's too late. I'll fuck her soon enough.

Still, I can't resist the urge to swipe my cockhead against her lips, leaving a trail of wetness in my wake. Dove's pink tongue darts out, licking at the remains of my pre-cum, and she smiles in her sleep. She's such a good girl. I want to reward her, so I toy with her some more. Fingers disappear in her soaked pussy while my other hand twists the plug in her tight little hole. I could spend hours doing this. Toying with her, showing her what pleasure is all about. But I'm going to get busted if I stay here for much longer. The effects of the powder will wear off soon, and I already risked getting caught when her eyes flew open the first time. God-fucking-damn-it, it'll be hard to leave her, though. With her mouth parted and my pre-cum still glistening on her lips, it takes everything in me not to fuck her there and then.

I tear myself away from Dove's bed. But it's getting late – or rather, early.

She'll be groggy and confused when she wakes up. I wish I could be here to make everything better, but I shouldn't. I need to get the fuck out of Dove's house.

I consider taking the plug out, but on second thought, I decide to leave it to fuck with Dove's head more. Smirking at her restless figure, I snap a quick photo with my phone before leaving the room.

I let myself out and remember the bag of sweet buns I got for Sam. I grab it from my bike's storage and head into the alley he calls home.

My new friend is leaning against the brick wall of the building behind him and seems excited when he sees me.

"Brought me something good?"

"They're a little stale, but they should still be fine." I pass him the bag and sit cross-legged opposite of him. "Hope you're hungry."

He nods to acknowledge me and digs into the food. He doesn't need to express his gratitude – his warm eyes speak volumes by themselves.

We sit together in amicable silence as he makes his way through the food. I like Sam, I realize. He's the first person I've met who I want to be around, who I want to be my friend. He doesn't pressure me, doesn't call me out. He just accepts me with all my flaws.

"See you soon?" I ask as I pick myself up, and Sam's eyes meet mine. I wonder whether he knows how I feel. How much this simple moment means to me.

"Very soon," he grins in return. "Thanks for the grub."

I raise my hand in a silent greeting and leave him there. My heart doesn't feel as cold tonight.

The next morning, I wake up early and decide to resist my relentless desire to follow Dove around. Instead, I decide to check up on the slimy photographer, Raphael. I need to know more about him. I need to know if he's serious about Dove, or if he's fucking around with a bunch of other bitches behind her back.

I follow him from his apartment to the office building where he works. I go up to the bakery, buying food I won't eat so I can keep an eye on the guy. I watch him interacting with a group of gorgeous models through the glass walls that enclose his office. The guy may look sleazy, but he's the perfect gentleman. He doesn't touch one of them inappropriately, doesn't flirt, doesn't let the girls' looks distract him from doing his job. He's a class act.

I grit my teeth together, waiting for him to finish in a side alley. He meets up with a woman later on, but it seems like a business meeting – they greet each other with a firm handshake. I'm starting to realize this guy is serious about Dove. He wants her. He's not going to do anything to fuck up his chances, and that pisses me off, because I want my little bird for myself.

Later on, I park in the side alley close to Dove's place. I watch Robin, her brother, come over, and decide to use the app I planted on Dove's phone to listen in to their conversation. I hear her brother's stupid fucking idea of inviting Elise over, then the follow-up of Raphael coming over, too. By then I'm grinning wide. This'll be fucking perfect. It's time for the secrets to come out.

Raphael arrives first, and the brother-sister duo greet him with excitement. Elise pulls up fashionably late, and I'm intently listening to the conversation on my phone as they all meet in Dove's house.

"This is Elise," Robin introduces his girlfriend. "Elise, this is Raphael, a friend of Dove's."

"You look familiar," Elise purrs suggestively. God, to be a fucking fly on the wall in that room. I'd love to see the smug bastard's expression right about now.

"Yes, I believe we did a shoot together a couple months back," Raphael replies. Why does he sound so fucking calm? He shouldn't be calm. He should be shaking in his fucking boots. "I remember you. Elise Howard, is it?"

"Yes," the bitch replies. "I remember you too."

I bet you fucking do, I think to myself. You've been trying to get into his pants for fucking months. Too bad he only has eyes for my girl. There's no way he's giving you what you fucking want.

I listen to their awkward conversation as the evening goes on, mindlessly scrolling through Dove's Instagram as I do so. Finally, I can't resist anymore. My account is a throwaway anyway – there's no way Dove will figure out it's me.

I comment something generic on one of the moody photos of the city, and listen to her phone going off on the audio transmission.

"Oh, Miss Popular," Robin teases her. "Who's that?"

"Just a notification," Dove giggles. "I'll check it later."

This pisses me off. I want her to look at it now, so I leave another comment.

"Looks like one of those fans is pretty insistent," Raphael laughs. "You should reply, Dove."

"Oh, alright." I imagine her picking up her phone. The surprised expression on her face when she sees my comment. I imagine her fingers moving lightning fast across the screen to type back the reply.

I stare at my own comment as I wait.

Nice image. Is that you on the cover of this month's Void?

Her reply comes a moment later.

How did you know that? There are no photos of me on my profile.

I grin to myself, quickly typing another reply.

Let's just say I'm your secret admirer. I know lots of things.

Okay... Well, I'm glad my work has a fan.

I'm not a fan of your work, I reply. *I'm a fan of you.*

"Almost done?" Raphael cuts in, and I realize the three others have been sitting there in awkward silence waiting for Dove to finish up, which makes me grin even wider.

"Of course," Dove says hurriedly. I picture her pocketing the phone. "I'm sorry about that. Let's get back to our evening."

Yes, let's, I think to myself, smirking as I wait for the cat to leap out of the bag. This is getting fucking better by the goddamn second.

CHAPTER THIRTEEN

DOVE

I want to touch myself.

The desire to do that has been missing from my life for a long time. Being raised fairly traditionally, I could never get past the guilt that surrounded pleasuring my own body. And yet as I lie in bed this morning, I find myself yearning for pleasure only I can give myself.

Tentatively, my fingers find their way between my thighs, brushing against my overheated center. My teeth dig into my bottom lip. It's been a long time since I've had an orgasm, and the urge to bring myself closer and closer is overwhelming. Closing my eyes tightly so I can pretend it's someone else doing this to me, I start massaging my clit and getting myself to the edge.

But just like every other time I've done this, the same thing happens. Parker appears in my mind, his darkly handsome face twisted into a painful grimace. I can't help it. My obsession with the fucker is unrelenting, even eight years after he carved my face. I wish I wasn't so obsessed with the man who ruined my life. But the fact that his body was never found makes me think he's still around somewhere. Watching me. I can't get rid of the feeling, and it only makes me more excited as I breathe out a moan, my fingers trembling over my exposed wetness.

I'm getting closer, my fingers working more frantically as I try to get the image of that bastard out of my head. But nothing is helping. Parker Miller is firmly lodged in my brain, refusing to leave.

I'm so close now I can taste the orgasm on the tip of my tongue. With a moan, I plunge two fingers inside myself, working my dripping pussy to an orgasm that escapes me if I don't think about him. I try to trick myself, force the image of Raphael into my mind, but it doesn't work.

My body doesn't want Raphael, it wants Parker.

My lips part as I feel the orgasm ripping itself from my body. But it doesn't bring any relief. No, instead it fills me with guilt, reminding me just how broken I am. That I'll never be able to feel better, not until Parker's body is found.

Frustrated, I get up from my bed. It's early morning, but I'm exhausted by the thoughts in my head. I take a scalding hot shower to wash away the remnants of my sins. The beating water colors my skin in shades of red, and I groan, avoiding the area between my legs. I'm afraid any more stimulation will bring me close to an orgasm again.

The intense need to punish myself for what I've just done is fucking overwhelming. My eyes find the razor in the shower, the one I use to keep my pussy bare. It would only take a moment to take it apart. To hold the gleaming silver razorblade in my hands. To sink it into my skin again, slicing, cutting, relieving the pressure underneath my complexion.

With trembling hands, I reach for the razor. The voices ring in my ears. Robin. My mother. My father. My therapist. Sam. Dear, darling Sam. They would judge me for what I'm about to do. They'd be so disappointed that I'm back to my old habits, the ones I've spent years running away from. But I can't help myself. The guilt is too much.

The blade slices into my skin. I cut deep this time, because nothing but the most overwhelming pain, the darkest blood, will soothe my nerves.

My scarlet blood mixes with the water. The pain is blinding, and the razorblade drops from my shaky hand. I'm bleeding profusely but the pain doesn't help this time, it only makes matters worse. I regret doing it, and yet I don't. My sick brain has convinced itself this is what I need, what I deserve. I'm forever punishing myself for the thoughts in my head that only I know about.

I know what my mother would say. She'd sign a check to my psychiatrist, and he'd pump me full of pills again. The pills never helped. They just made me drowsy and numb. I still hurt myself on them, just so I could feel fucking something.

I get out of the shower and bandage up my arm. I get dressed. The cut leaves dark droplets of red blood on my clothes. The blood sinks into the black fabric, disappearing. If only my problems could do the same.

I want to go see Sam, so I load up some food into a paper bag in the kitchen, throw on a black leather jacket, and lock up the house when I leave. Sam is an early riser just like me, and when I approach the alleyway, I see him sitting up against the wall. A tentative smile lights up his face when he sees me.

"Got something good for me?" he asks with a grin. He looks worn-out and tired as hell, and for the umpteenth time, I find myself wishing he'd take me up on the offer to treat him to a motel room, at least. But I know he won't – he's too proud to accept help like that.

"Always." I hand him the bag, my eyes discreetly scanning the surroundings for signs of needles. But there's nothing. It seems Sam is clean tonight.

I sit next to him on the ground, not caring if I get my clothes dirty. I'm here for Sam, not to worry about my appearance.

He's digging into the food without saying much, and my heart beats with uncertainty, eager for the reprieve of some calming words from my friend.

"Is everything okay?" I find myself asking. Sam nods, but doesn't look at me. "You seem so far away..."

"I'm right here, Dove." He puts the paper bag down and reaches for my hand. My eyes fill with tears for some inexplicable reason, and I wipe them away with my free hand. "What's wrong, kid?"

"I'm just..." I shake my head, laughing to make light of the situation. "I feel alone."

"You're not alone, you have me."

"But..."

"No buts." Sam smiles wide. "I'm always here for you, Dove. You know why?"

"Why?" I whisper.

"Because I care about you," he goes on. "I care about you like you were my own daughter. I love you like I love my child. And I want you to know, even if you lose me, or anyone in your life, that love remains. In your heart, in your memories, in your mind. Do you understand?"

It's the most he's opened up to me, and the tears are burning my eyes again. "Thank you, Sam. I do."

"Good." He picks up the bag and starts eating again, looking at me with a warm smile. "Remember what I told you."

"It feels like you're saying goodbye," I mutter. "Are you going somewhere?"

"No way," Sam grins with his mouth full. "You're stuck with me, kid."

"Good." I laugh again as I pick myself up. "I'll see you soon, then."

"Very soon," he smiles in return.

I lean over to grab the wrapping off the food and when I do, my sleeve rides up, exposing my bandaged arm. I see Sam's eyes dart to it, and I quickly pull my sleeve back down.

"Dove." I ignore him, balling up the paper, distracting myself with the crinkling sounds. "Dove, look at me."

Except I can't. Because if I do, I'll cry and want to tell him the truth. That I'm a wreck. That I can't help hurting myself. That I still believe I deserve this.

"Dove, you didn't."

"I'm sorry," I breathe, but the tears don't fall.

"You can't keep doing this, kid. You can't keep hurting yourself."

"I know."

"Then why do it?"

"Because I deserve it."

"Now, that's some real bullshit." Sam grabs me by my unharmed arm and forces me closer. "Dove, I'm worried about you."

"Don't be."

"Do you have someone you can talk to?"

"I have Robin."

"But you won't tell him, will you?" Wordlessly, I shake my head. Sam knows me better than I know myself. There's no way I'm going to my brother with these problems. I don't want to worry him. "Dove, you need to talk to someone about this. You need to stop it with the guilt."

I nod, but we both know I'm pretending. Sam doesn't know about Parker. He never asked how I got the scar on my face, and I never told him. If I do, it will only make things more real.

"I have to go," I mutter, pulling away from him. I try to hide my disappointment when he allows my hand to slip out of his. "I'm sorry, Sam. I'll try to get better, I promise."

"You better," he mutters. "Because I need you here, kid. Who else is going to lecture me without you around?"

I manage a weak chuckle.

We wave each other off, and I leave him with a bright smile on my face despite the tears.

I'll always have Sam. Of that, I'm sure.

Raphael has been texting me all day, and I've been sending back half-assed replies. I can't bring myself to commit to liking him. It's too much. Too much to handle when my mind is still reeling from the first man I fell in love with.

But my self-preservation instincts are kicking in, and I send a text to Robin, asking him if he wants to come over. He's quick to respond, as if sensing something's wrong. He offers to bring over some food, and I agree. I need to make him think I'm at least partially okay. Besides, I don't even remember the last time I ate, and my stomach hurts. I'll have to put something in myself if I want to survive. *But do I?*

I shake myself to get the thought out. I never let myself go to the darkest of places. It's too hard to get back out of them.

Robin arrives with a lasagna dish thirty minutes later. I let him in. I can tell he knows something's off from the moment he appears on my doorstep. I heat up the lasagna in the oven and we settle in front of the TV. We eat straight out of the dish, for which I'm grateful, because at least he won't see the leftovers on my plate.

"Did you hurt yourself again, Dove?" My eyes snap to my brother's. I would deny it any other day, but something's making me unable to shake my head.

"Why do you ask?"

"Just a feeling." He knows me so well.

"I... I had to," I mutter.

"Dove." I refuse to look at him, picking at the burnt cheese on the dish. "Dove, I thought you weren't doing that anymore."

I hadn't, not for months. I thought I was getting better, but I reached my breaking point today. I couldn't help it. I had to hurt myself. I deserved it. But all of this is too much to put into words for my brother, so instead I just chew on my bottom lip, hoping he'll drop the subject.

"I'm just trying to help you."

"I know," I whisper. There are so many other things I want to say. Like that he won't be able to save me – no one will. That I'm not worthy of his help. That he should spend his precious time on someone who he can actually make better. That there's no hope for me. Instead of saying any of that, my mouth remains firmly closed, my eyes locked on the TV screen but not seeing anything.

"I want you to get better. Don't you want to get better?"

"I don't think I can," I manage.

"Of course you can." He squeezes my hand gently and I try not to wince, because it's the arm I hurt today. "I believe in you, Dove."

"I don't," I manage to chuckle. "You're the only one who has such blind faith in me."

"Because I know you can do it." I shake my head. "Please, Dove. You have to try. For me. For that friend of yours, Sam. For Raphael."

My eyes snap to his. "What about Raphael?"

"Don't you like him?" I nod. "Well, how do you think he'd feel if he knew about this? The self-harm?"

"He knows," I mutter. "He saw the scars." *He thought they were beautiful.*

"You need to get better for every one of us who needs you here," Robin tells me. "Because we do need you. You're the brightest part of my day, Dove, and I know you can get better."

"Thanks." I wipe my eyes even though the tears never fell, then busy myself by clearing the coffee table. I stop, picking over my words. "Robin, if it's not too much trouble... Could you spend the night?"

"Of course," he replies.

"You're not seeing Elise tonight?"

"You're my priority, Dove."

"Thanks," I smile weakly.

I don't want to be an obligation for my brother. Hate the thought of him giving up things so he can spend time with me. And yet I find myself grateful for his sacrifice.

If he wouldn't stay with me tonight, I know I would hurt myself again.

CHAPTER FOURTEEN

NOX

Getting into Dove's apartment is getting almost too easy. It makes me worried about someone else breaking in, taking advantage while she sleeps soundly. She isn't being careful enough. I make a mental note to tell Sam about it, convince him to bring it up with my little bird, since I can't.

Finding her key under the same flowerpot where it always is, I sneak in easily again, having arrived at her house in the middle of the night. I've finally caught up on some much-needed rest after weeks of following her night-and-day, but I am still pissed with myself for not getting there earlier. I should be keeping a closer eye on her. Who the fuck needs sleep? All I need is her, my little bird.

The house is quiet as always, all the lights off except the night light in Dove's bedroom. I make my way to the bathroom first, digging through her laundry like I always do. My fingers wrap around her worn panties, a cheeky pair of hipsters this time, simple black lace. I inhale her scent. Roses. God, I want her. It's getting increasingly harder to stay away from her, to convince myself I shouldn't just barge into her bedroom and alert her to my presence. So what if she resists? I can easily overpower her, and she doesn't need this life. Doesn't need the patronizing Robin or his stupid, fake girlfriend. She would miss Sam, that's for sure, because I would, too. But everyone else is disposable. Including that photographer prick who's been trying relentlessly to force his way into Dove's life. I'll deal with him soon enough.

While I'm going through her stuff, a noise rattles me. But when I turn around, there's nothing. The house is still in the night with no movement at all. I must've imagined it.

I keep going through her things, making a mental note of every little change she's made in the apartment since the last time I've been here. But there isn't much. Dove doesn't really shop for food, not unless she's getting something for Sam. It makes me worry about how much she's eating. I remember her skeletal body when I played with her the other night. She was painfully thin, emaciated. I'd take better care of her than she does. If only she'd see that.

"What the fuck do you think you're doing?"

I spin around. Dove's brother, Robin, is standing in the doorframe as my heart beats into overdrive. He's wearing pajamas. I realize he must've come over to spend the night with Dove. Fuck. Fuck. *Fuck.*

I should've known I wasn't careful enough tonight. I didn't even check the driveway for his car, I was so fucking eager to get into Dove's house and see her again. But he's here, in the fucking flesh. And as his eyes take me in, realization dawns on him like someone's hit him with a ton of bricks. He knows who I am. He knows what I've done. And now he's going to cut my Dove fantasy short. But I can't let that happen.

"Holy shit," he mutters. "It's you."

I approach him but he holds up his phone as a warning. I speak in slow, hushed tones, because I don't want to wake up Dove. "It's okay. I'm a friend of Dove's, I'm just checking up on her because –"

"Do you think I'm an idiot?" Robin hisses at me. His look is one of pure disgust, and he's snarling the words at me, obviously having recognized me. I remember the bruise he gave Kade, having mixed us up years ago. Does he know I'm not my brother? Has he realized I'm not dead at all? "I've already called the cops. The game is up. Get the fuck away from my sister's stuff."

My heart threatens to beat straight out of my chest. For the first time in my life, I'm fucking terrified. Not because I know I'm going to jail, but because I know I'm going to lose Dove if I do.

And I can't let that happen. I can't lose Dove. Even if it means...

"Fuck," I mutter.

"Yeah, fuck is right," Robin snarls in disgust. "What the hell were you thinking? You thought you wouldn't get caught? I'd kill you myself for what you did to her, you sick fuck. Get away from her stuff. I'm not telling you again."

I move away from the laundry basket. One of my hands goes behind my back while I raise the other one in surrender. My heart is beating a million miles a minute and I know this won't end well. Getting busted never does.

The possibilities run through my head. I could run. But then Robin would reveal what he knows to Dove, and she'd spend a lifetime looking over her shoulder. I would never be able to get her.

The other option is to dispose of the man who just caught me. I've killed before. I could kill again. But as I stare at the man in front of me, I remember how much he means to Dove. That he's one of the rare bright lights in her life. I can't take Robin away from her. *But what fucking choice do I have?*

I lunge at him, clutching the chloroform-soaked rag I pulled from my waistband. His eyes widen, but I'm too fast, and he can't fucking stop me. I press the rag against his mouth, holding my breath while he struggles. The fumes are making me dizzy too, and my rapidly beating heart isn't helping. But I can't stop now. I have to go through with this. I have to get rid of Robin.

Dove's brother's body goes limp in my arms. The fucker's heavy, and I lay him down gently on the ground, mouthing curse word after curse word as I contemplate what to do next.

TYRANT STALKER

But either way I turn it, there's no happy ending for Robin. Not if I want to keep Dove in my life. He'd never let us be together. No, he'd keep an even closer eye on me. I have to dispose of him.

I kick at the laundry basket, cursing out loud this time. I pray Dove won't wake up as I drag Robin through the living room. His unconscious body is heavy and I'm thanking my lucky stars when I realize there's nobody on the street outside. I'm risking a lot for Dove. I have to, because we belong together.

I bring my bike closer and position Robin in front of me. I ride out carefully. The last thing I need is to get stopped by cops, even though a twisted part of me is almost hoping it will happen. I don't want to kill Robin. I want him to disappear. Let me have my own happy ending. *But that's not going to happen, is it?*

I drive close-by to the motel where there's a trash site. Robin's starting to stir by the time I get there and my own guilty conscience weighs heavily on me as I leave his unmoving body on the ground. Fuck. I can't do this. I can't kill him. I don't want to hurt Dove. I want to make her happy, not miserable with worry. But I have no choice.

I pull out the gun I bought from a guy a couple alleys down from Sam, just in case. I guess that just in case moment is happening right now. Pointing the barrel at Robin, I groan out loud, running my hand through my hair. Just then, Dove's brother stirs awake, and I'm momentarily stunned, watching him pick himself up, disoriented and scared. Then, he stares down the barrel of my gun.

"No," he mutters. "You're not going to kill me. I'm not letting you get away with this. You can never have her."

"I have to," I mutter.

"You don't." The hint of desperation in Robin's voice makes me sad. "We can talk about this. You don't have to do this. I won't tell anyone."

He's lying, and we both know it. If I let him go now, he'll go running straight to the cops, and I can't let that happen. I can't lose Dove, not now, not ever.

"I'm a human being," Robin rasps. "Don't kill me... I deserve to live... I deserve to –"

The shot rings out into the dark. The gun falls from my hands. For the first time in decades, I feel tears stinging my eyes. He didn't give me a choice.

Hours later, it's closer to morning than night. I've downed half a bottle of whiskey and I'm a goddamn mess as I show up on Sam's street. The old man's curled up on his makeshift bed. There's a spoon nearby, and a needle sticking out of his arm. This time I don't mention it. I can't, my mind too preoccupied with what I've just done.

"Up early?" Sam asks me, taking the needle out. His pupils are insanely dilated, but he seems mostly out of his daze. He disposes of the evidence of his night. *Just like I did with mine.*

"Couldn't sleep," I mutter, half-collapsing on the ground next to him.

"Jesus, kid, you fucking reek," Sam mutters. "Did you visit a distillery?"

"Something like that," I mutter. I don't elaborate, and Sam doesn't ask me to. I feel sick to my stomach, like I'm going to throw up any second. I want to die. For the first time in my life, I feel disgusted enough with myself to take my own life. How could I do this to her? How could I ruin Dove's life like this?

She can never find out what I did. It'll be my best kept secret. Because the moment Dove finds out I killed her brother, it's officially fucking over for us.

"You sure you're okay, kid?" Sam asks next, and I look up into his kind eyes. The closest relationship in my life right now is this – my friend is a homeless man who cares more about me than my own family. And yet I can't tell him the truth. Can't risk Sam hating me, too.

So I tell myself I'm allowed this – a single moment of weakness. Tears sting my eyes but they never fall. I shake my head, unable to answer Sam's question. Sobs begin to wrack my body, but no tears fall. Even I'm disgusted with myself.

Sam pats me on the back as I howl into the night, not giving a shit who hears or sees me. I don't know how long I'm there, but Sam consoles me through it. He doesn't take his hand off my back until I calm down, and when I can finally breathe again, I pull away from him, my face stoic as I tuck my hands into the pockets of my jeans.

"I'm sorry for taking up your night," I tell Sam harshly. "I... I got overwhelmed."

"This got something to do with Dove?"

I hesitate, but finally nod. "Doesn't it always?"

"I think you should show yourself to her," he tells me resolutely. "I think she'd be grateful to have you. You seem like a good man. I trust you."

You shouldn't.

I don't say anything, merely nodding with the ghost of a smile on my lips. There's nothing left to say anymore, nothing I can do to make this better for either of us. I raise my hand in silent goodbye and Sam does the same. With my hands in my pockets, I make my way back to my bike, kicking at the gravel.

I've committed the most heinous crime. Now I have to make sure Dove never finds out about it. One person will never forgive me – and it's myself. But if Dove found out, she would hate me forever. And I can't have that. Because I need her. I can't live without her. And I'll just have to live with my own guilty conscience for the rest of my life.

I can do that.

If it means I eventually get my little bird in my arms, I can do fucking anything.

CHAPTER FIFTEEN

DOVE

When I wake up the next morning, Robin's gone already. I'm sad he left without saying goodbye and can't help but feel guilty about it, so I call his cell, but the operator tells me his number isn't available.

Groaning, I end the call.

I try to go about my day, heading to the plant nursery where I stay in the back, moving stock, sweeping floors and cleaning shelves, anything I can do so I don't have to deal with customers. I don't have it in me today to deal with people.

I call Robin three times that day and every single time, I get the dreaded not available message. His phone must be switched off... But Robin never switches off his phone. He always tells me I can call him anytime. Finally, I decide to bite the bullet and call Elise. Maybe she knows what's up.

"What's up?" she answers on the fourth ring.

"Hey, Elise." Fuck, I already sound panicked. "I was wondering if you heard from Robin."

"I thought he was with you?" My heart pangs when she says that. "He was supposed to call me this morning, and he never did."

"Are you sure?"

"Of course I'm sure," she mutters. "Do you think something's wrong?"

I hesitate, not knowing what to tell her. "Can we meet at his apartment in an hour?"

"Sure," Elise says, sounding more bothered than I would have liked. I wanted her to make me feel better, to console me, but the call has done exactly the opposite of that.

Thirty minutes later, I leave the plant nursery and head to Robin's apartment downtown. Elise is already waiting, and I'm relieved to see her yappy dog isn't with her. We use Elise's keys to get in. The apartment is empty. He's nowhere to be seen.

"This is weird," I say. "It is, isn't it?"

"I... I think so," Elise manages, wiping her eyes. She's already crying. So much for not panicking.

"We have to go to the cops," I tell her.

"But they won't do anything. All the TV shows say you have to wait twenty-four hours before you report someone missing, don't they?"

"I don't care. Are you coming with me or not?" She nods wordlessly. We get in her car and ride to the nearest police station in a silence that's charged with worry. I feel sick to my stomach. Instinctively, I know something's wrong. Robin would never disappear without telling me where he was going. Something bad has happened.

We both give our reports at the police station. Elise was right – until the twenty-four hours are up, we can't do anything. And it's been only seventeen since I last saw him going to sleep in my living room. Anxiously, I wait for the time to pass, grabbing coffee with Elise in a hipster cafe nearby. It's flavored with something ridiculous like orange blossom, but I barely even notice the flavor. I scald my tongue on the hot beverage, downing it in quick gulps that do nothing to soothe me.

"I'll have to go soon," Elise mutters apologetically. "Pepper's alone at home... I need to walk him."

"Okay."

"Are you going to be okay?"

"I have to be," I mutter. "I'm going back to the station soon, in another few hours. They have to start the search then."

She picks up her purse and putting down some money for our drinks. "Dove, I know it's none of my business, but... Please eat something."

My eyes snap up and we stare at one another.

"You look so thin," she says softly. "Painfully thin. Please eat. That's what Robin would want."

I nod. I don't trust myself to say anything right now.

When Elise leaves, I order a slice of pecan pie. It arrives, prettily arranged on a patterned plate, and I stare at it, picking at the crust with my dessert fork while my stomach rumbles loudly.

I'm hungry. Starving. So why is the thought of eating only managing to make me feel sicker?

My phone dings. It's a message from the account that commented on my Instagram the other day. He or she has sent through a photo, an abandoned cup of coffee with lipstick on the rim. No words. The image is black and white save from the hot pink of the lipstick. I manage a shaky smile.

I reply, if only to distract myself from the inescapable truth of my reality – that Robin is gone. My gut says so, and my gut is never wrong.

Good eye.

Thanks, little bird.

You have a nickname for me now?

Don't you like it?

This is dangerously close to flirting, and I find myself thinking of Raphael guiltily. I haven't returned his text and call from this morning, but I have time to chat to this stranger.

Instead of replying, I force myself to get up, the abandoned plate reminding me just how weak I am and how disappointed Robin would be. I leave Elise's money on the table and head to the precinct.

I'm introduced to Detective Goldin, who's going to lead the investigation. He tells me nonsense I don't believe, like that Robin probably went on a bender, or wanted to escape for a few days. I don't buy any of it, and I head back home with the sinking feeling that he's gone. For good.

Somehow, two weeks pass. I've been dodging Raphael's calls apart from telling him Robin's gone missing. But I just don't have the energy to show my fear to someone else. Because deep down, I already accepted he isn't coming back. A sister just knows.

Elise is getting on my last nerve, too. She's unwilling to accept that Robin's missing and keeps pressing me for details, like I'll magically remember something I've skimmed over. Of course I won't remember anything. I remember that night well – I've replayed it in my mind a thousand times.

I visit Sam that night with a box of cookies and a paper cup of warm soup. He knows all about Robin's disappearance and has been my lone shining star in the time since my brother has been missing.

"Any news?" he calls out when he sees me approaching.

"Nothing," I mutter, handing him the cup. He starts sipping on the chicken noodle soup while I sigh, crumpling on the blanket next to him. "I just wish they'd find... something."

"You've accepted that he's gone."

"I don't want to," I mutter. "I just feel it. I know he's dead."

He shakes his head. "I'm sorry, Dove. Have you called your mother?"

"Yesterday." The call was fucking painful. Mom was awkward and cold like always, although at least she got a little emotional when it came to the subject of Robin. She always liked him better than me. But she was as clueless as we all were as to Robin's whereabouts.

"No news there?" Sam wonders, and I shake my head. He pats my hand, and I'm grateful he hasn't tried to give me some bullshit reason why Robin's gone. He accepts my grief, doesn't question the fact that I *know* he's gone, like Elise does.

I stay with Sam until he finishes his soup, leaving him the cookies for later. He tells me to come by again, and I promise I will, heading back home to find a familiar face at my doorstep.

"Raphael?"

"Hey." He smiles, offering me a bouquet of yellow roses. "I thought they might cheer you up."

I smile weakly, accepting the bouquet with a soft thank you as I let us into my apartment. I don't tell him I don't like cut flowers. I don't explain they remind me of the inevitable end.

We sit down in the living room, making small talk and avoiding the topic of Robin. I'm grateful as well as resentful that he doesn't ask about my brother, and my own confusing feelings twist my stomach into a thousand knots.

"I'm sorry I just barged in here," he finally says. "I've been really worried about you. Are you eating?"

I shrug noncommittally. Robin was the only person besides Sam in my life who cared about that.

"Do you want me to order something?"

The truth is, I can't remember the last time I ate. Can't remember eating at all. My eyes fill with tears for the first time in days. I'm hungry. I nod gratefully at Raphael's idea, and he quickly places an order at a taqueria downtown.

"Dove."

I can't bring myself to look at him. If I do, he's going to see the sadness and despair in my eyes, and I don't want him to acknowledge it right now.

"Dove, I think we should get drunk."

"What?" My eyes snap up because I'm so shocked by his statement. "How's that going to help?"

"You'll forget," he says. "At least for a little while."

Somehow, forgetting seems like a good option right now.

We discover some long-abandoned margarita mix in my pantry, probably left over from one of Robin's visits. Raphael blends ice into the mix and adds tequila, serving us ice-cold drinks in tall mason jars.

Our food arrives soon after. We sit at the coffee table, flicking through Netflix as we eat our fill of the food and drink ourselves silly on the margaritas. I'm glad he came over.

I'm feeling pleasantly tipsy as time moves on, and I keep glancing at my phone.

I've been messaging back and forth with the man – I know he's a man now – who commented on my Instagram profile. We don't talk about my real life, and it's a welcome change not having to discuss Robin or the loneliness, the eating disorder, the obvious depression. But there are no messages from mystery man, and Raphael has surely noticed by now I keep staring at my phone, so I put it away.

I even manage to laugh during our dinner, even though it's barely a chuckle. In a matter of two hours, we're both drunk as fuck.

"You can't drive back tonight," I say.

"I can get an Uber."

"Don't." I surprise myself as much as I do Raphael. "Spend the night. You can... You can sleep on the couch."

"You sure?"

"Yeah." I nod. I am sure. I don't want Raphael in my bed, but I'll be comforted knowing someone's in the house with me. Since that incident with the butt plug – and the thief who stole my bag – I've been feeling unsafe in my own place.

I set up the couch for Raphael and we down the rest of our margaritas. I'm exhausted by the time everything's ready, and relieved to be going to my own bedroom. At the same time, I'm grateful Raphael hasn't made a move on me. I don't think I could reciprocate tonight.

"Oh, I almost forgot." I turn in the direction of Raphael's voice. "I know it's not really your cup of tea... But I thought it could help you get your mind off... you know."

"What is it?"

"I'm hosting an art party in a club downtown. It's called Pulse. They just opened their LA division."

I nearly faint at the name of that club. I still remember my wild nights at Pulse in New York, when I wasn't even legally allowed to be out and drinking. The night I met Parker in Pulse is still so fresh in my mind, even though it was over eight years ago. But there are some nights you just don't forget.

"Okay," I find myself saying. "I'd love to be there."

"Really?" Raphael seems almost as surprised as I am. "You sure? I'd really love for you to be there as my date, but if it's too much..."

"It's not," I manage. "I want to support you."

And I need to start getting over Robin's disappearance.

And I also need to stop calling it a disappearance, because deep down, where it matters most, I know the truth – that my brother is dead.

CHAPTER SIXTEEN

NOX

It's so easy to become a part of Elise's life. Call it morbid fascination, or obsession if you want. But when I run into her at a grocery store downtown, I can't help but approach her. My need to remain close to Dove, to stay in her life, is fucking sickening.

Elise is easy. I compliment her dog and the little shit yaps at me, not shutting up for a second while I hit on its owner. Ten minutes later, and I have a date I don't want. How easy it is for her to move on from Robin. It fucking disgusts me.

Of course, I have an ulterior motive. I know about Raphael's little club event, and thanks to the listening device I planted on Dove's phone, I know she's going there with him. They may not have kissed at her apartment last night, but they sure as fuck will at the club. Dove's looking for something, *someone*, to drown her pitiful sorrows in, but I'll be fucking damned if it'll be Raphael.

It's time for me to make an appearance in Dove's life again.

I'll act like I didn't know she was there, of course. How could I? It's not like I've been stalking her for years. She has no fucking clue about my sickness. No idea she's still the object of my obsession.

But tonight's going to be special. Dove will be back in my life and I'll be back in hers. I'll be her shoulder to cry on. I'll be her savior, the man who saves her from herself, even if I can't save her from myself.

"Do I look good?" Elise fusses with her hair in the rearview mirror. She didn't want to take the bike, so I've been forced to arrive at Pulse in her fucking bubblegum princess ride. I give her a quick glance and mutter something positive in response, forgetting about it the moment I close my mouth. She does look good, but I don't give a shit about her appearance. She could look like a million bucks and I'd still only have eyes for Dove.

"Aren't you going to help me out of the car?" Elise pouts as she looks at me, and I look her dead in the eyes, finally seeing her for what she really is. A fucking idiot, who's already moved on from Robin. Tonight isn't about us, it's about Elise following around that schmuck photographer and throwing herself at him when Dove isn't looking, which suits me just fine. At least she'll keep Raphael busy while I make Dove mine again.

"Help yourself," I growl at her, opening the door and getting out of the princess wagon. Elise huffs and puffs behind me, following me into the club. We face our first issue – the bouncer holding up a guest list. But I slip him a couple hundreds, and just like that, we're in. The blocky, huge guy raises the red velvet rope, and into Pulse we walk.

My eyes drink in the inside of the place. Swanky. Pretentious as shit. Art is displayed on the club walls and lo-fi, chilled music plays through the speakers. People are drinking ridiculously colored cocktails and mingling in small groups. Elise stands out like a sore thumb, but then again, so do I.

My date is wearing a tight bandage pink dress that clings to her sexy body, and sky-high heels with the tiniest handbag known to humankind. At least Pepper's not with her, because I'd lose my damn mind if I had to listen to that thing bark all fucking night long.

I stand out just as much in my beaten old leather aviator jacket, accompanied by ripped black jeans and a white V-neck. Elise tried to convince me to wear a shirt, but I wasn't having any of her shit.

Scanning the crowd, I realize Dove isn't here yet, and neither is photographer prick. Fucking good. It gives me some time to get my bearings, even though it makes me fucking paranoid about them making out when I'm not looking.

I buy Elise a ridiculous overpriced cocktail and myself a twenty-dollar bottle of beer. I fight the urge to throw an insult at the guy manning the bar who gives me a smug grin as I grab the drinks from him. Elise wraps her glossy pink pout around the straw in her drink, and I guzzle the beer, my heart pounding in tune with the music.

The moment Dove enters the room, the entire atmosphere of the place changes in an instant. I can feel her, smell her. I don't even see her yet but her electrifying presence has made the hairs on my neck stand on end.

"Oh God," Elise mutters next to me.

"What's up?" I take another swig of the beer, feigning casualness. As if I didn't fucking know this would happen. I planted the idea of coming here in Elise's head. It barely took any coercing.

"My ex is here," she groans, but she sounds fucking delighted to me. As depressing as it is how fast she's moved on from Robin, I find relief in the way her eyes devour Raphael who enters the room in an all-black outfit that costs more than my bike, probably. "Fuck. And he's with…"

She doesn't get to finish her sentence. Raphael's gaze finds us, darkening. I half expect him to march over, readying myself for the inevitable face-off. Instead, he puts a proprietorial arm around the woman standing next to him, shifting his body so she can't see us.

But I'd recognize Dove anywhere, from any fucking angle. I've been stalking her for long enough that every feature of hers is engrained in my mind, for-fucking-ever. Her hair is a glossy dark sheet of silk, straightened to perfection. She's wearing a long-sleeved black dress with a scooped back. She doesn't have any scars there. It doesn't escape me how she keeps correcting her hair, though, making sure some of it is always falling over her face to cover up what I did to her.

I wish she wouldn't do that. I wish she'd be fucking proud of my gift, show it off to everyone around her. They should know she's mine. They should know I'm crazy enough to kill for her. I don't have limits anymore. I'll do any-fucking-thing to keep Dove tethered to me.

I wait not-so-patiently for her to notice me. I keep Elise entertained, making her down one cocktail after another. I keep it to one beer – I need to keep my wits about me if I want to impress Dove. The more Elise drinks though, the more of a mess she is, which works fine for me. She's going to embarrass herself, and I'll leave Raphael to deal with it while I leave with Dove on the back of my bike, which I parked up here a few hours ago. There's no fucking way I'm leaving with Elise tonight.

No, I'm leaving with my little bird.

I make a mental note not to call her that. I need to keep up pretenses with the game of messages we've been sending to one another through Instagram. I don't want her to know it's me yet, and a part of me wonders why I'm keeping that a secret. Maybe it's because I feel safer knowing I have one last card up my sleeve.

Elise is getting impatient. She's fidgety, eager to see Raphael, to speak to him, and we both know she won't last much longer. When she finally comes up with some bullshit excuse to go see her 'old friend' and asks me to come with, I nod along. She hooks a proprietorial arm through mine and totters over to where Raphael and Dove are standing.

I've been close enough to her to sate my immediate need to have her nearby, but this is on another level. I get to speak to her. I get to see the look of pure shock in her face when she realizes it's really me. And I can't fucking wait to wreck her all over again.

"Raphael?" Elise speaks up in her squeaky voice, and the slimy asshole turns around to face her. But I miss his reaction, because my eyes are zeroed in on Dove, a sly smirk playing on my lips as she also turns around.

She looks at me, really fucking looks at me, and the sight of those eyes on mine makes me hard as fuck. Her pupils dilate. Her breath catches in her throat. She looks fucking terrified, unable to look away.

"P-Parker?" she whispers.

"Hey, Dove," Elise jumps in, practically purring with excitement as she wraps her friend in a hug. "This is Nox, um, er..." She looks at me, desperately begging for help. The bitch doesn't even know my fucking last name. But I refuse to help her out, just staring with a smirk. "Well, this is Nox. Nox, this is Dove. And Raphael. He's a photographer."

"Hello," I answer easily, focusing on the guy and shaking his hand. He has a strong handshake, confident. I lazily turn my attention to Dove next, giving her a crooked smile. "Hey."

"His name isn't Nox," Dove hisses, surreptitiously touching the scar on her face. Good, it feels fucking good to scare her like this. "It's Parker, Parker Miller."

"Huh?" I raise my brows, staring her down. "You must be confusing me with someone."

"You know I'm not." Her words are coming out in a snarl, and Raphael looks at her with concern.

"You okay, Dove?"

"No, I'm not okay," she mutters.

"So, Raphael," Elise cuts in, running her fingers over his arm. "I haven't seen you in a while. How've you been?"

For a moment, Raphael takes his eyes off Dove, but a moment is all I need. Dove pushes through the crowd and I follow, hot on her trail. I reach for her arm, and she pulls it away from me, turning around to snarl.

"Stay the fuck away from me."

"I can't," I mutter, quiet enough so she can't hear it. I keep following her like I always do. She pushes through the back exit into the alleyway behind the club and I'm still hot on her trail.

"Dove, wait."

"No," she shakes her head vehemently. "Just leave me alone, Parker."

"It's Nox these days."

"No, it's not." She looks pissed off. Her face is red, blotchy, apart from the scar that mars it, which is strikingly pale. She's never looked more beautiful, but then again, I come to that conclusion every single time I see her. "It's not Nox, it's Parker. Stop fucking lying to everyone."

"I'm not lying." I make another grab for her, thirsty for the feeling of her skin against mine, but she dodges me. If she wants to play this cat and mouse game, I'll play it with her. But only because I know she'll be mine in the end. The cat always fucking wins. "Dove, please. Would you just listen to me and let me explain?"

"Explain what? That you're somehow back from the dead? Back in my life? That you're fucking sick? I already know all of that, Parker." She comes closer. My heart threatens to beat right out of my chest as she grabs the front of my shirt and pulls me in closer. "You're sick. I don't know how you found me. I don't know what you want. I just want you to leave me alone."

I contemplate her words. She thinks she hates me, but she's fucking wrong. I release a long breath before snaking my hand up around her neck. I grab tightly. She gasps and I feel her throat opening for a breath I won't give her beneath my fingers.

"You don't tell me what to do, Dove," I say. "You never could. Remember? I remember everything. How you followed me around like a lost little lamb. How desperate you were for me. How much you fucking wanted me. And now I'm back. And you can't keep running."

"I'm going to report you," she grinds out through gritted teeth. "I'm going to call the cops on you."

My heart beats into overdrive. I remember the night at the junkyard. Robin's body. Getting rid of him as if he meant nothing. He meant everything to her. That's over. There's no room for anyone else in Dove's life. Just. *Me.*

"You are?" I ask with a smirk. "You're going to report me, Dove? Why don't you do that right now?"

I pull out a phone from my pocket and dial 911. I hold the phone up to her, my smile unrelenting as I wait for the operator to click on.

"911, what's your emergency?"

"Say it," I mutter at Dove. "Tell them. Tell them and this ends here and now."

CHAPTER SEVENTEEN

DOVE

It's like a mirage. A figment of imagination. There's no way this is the madman who ruined my life eight years ago. But my eyes don't lie. Parker – Nox – stands before me in the flesh. Somehow, he survived that fall in Hawaii, and now he's back to haunt me. And something's telling me he won't give up this time.

I swallow thickly. The operator is asking if I'm okay. Nox is staring at me with his twisted smile and his cruel eyes and his unfairly handsome face. I want to claw that face. I want to ruin it like he ruined mine. But I'm not brave enough.

"Sorry, accident," I mutter into the phone. Without saying anything, Nox ends the call and pockets his phone. He doesn't address what just happened, and I stare down at the floor, feeling tears gathering in my eyes. But they don't fall. I don't let them.

"So, this is how it's going to be from now on, Dove," he says, gently taking my chin in his hands and tipping my head back so I'm forced to look at him. But I don't want to. I can't look at him. I can't meet his dark eyes. So, I close mine, refusing to give him any more of my attention. "You're going to be a good girl for me like you were all those years ago. Right now, you're going to head inside and tell that prick you came with you have to go home. If you want to tell him it's over right now, be my fucking guest. Otherwise you'll do it tomorrow."

"You don't own me," I hiss at him. "You don't tell me what to do."

"Think again." His grip moves to my throat. Hard, unrelenting, clenching down on my neck. Suddenly I can't resist. I need this. The darkness I've been trying to avoid my entire life is overwhelming. I've been running from him my whole life. That ends now. "I'm back, and you're done fucking fighting this. Got that?"

Fingers tightening. Menacing words escaping his lips. He's dark, ominous and so fucking exciting. It's the first flash of temptation I've had in years. And I should've known it would come from him... my damnation.

"Let me go," I whisper, but it's more for show than anything else, and of course, he does nothing of the sort. Instead, he laughs in my face, letting his fingers wander up my neck, over my lips, parting them.

"Suck my thumb," he mutters, and when I don't, he raises his hand like he's going to slap me. I flinch but the slap never comes. I open my needy mouth then, and close my lips around his thumb as he pushes it inside. I start sucking. Slowly, hesitantly, but sucking nonetheless. "That's right, you little fucking slut. You got better at that, didn't you? Had lots of practice?"

My eyes find his, silently begging for a reprieve I know he'll never give me. He grins while his finger continues to travel. Now, it slips over to my scar. He taunts me by touching it, pressing his fingers into it, smirking at me when he sees the pain in my eyes.

"I did this to you," he says. "It's beautiful. Maybe I'll add more."

"Don't, you sick –"

"Shut up." The hand is back, a silent warning hanging in the air, forever reminding me I'm at his mercy now. "You don't talk back to me. You try that again, you get fucking punished. Stand up against the wall. Back to the bricks, right the fuck now."

I obey him because I can't help myself. I flatten my back against the brick, eyes silently begging him to stop, even though we both know he won't. I don't know if this is real. It has to be a nightmare. There's just no fucking way Parker is actually here.

But he ends that little fantasy as he tells me to spread my legs. The hand rises again, and I obey, too afraid of what will happen if I don't. I know full well what he's capable of. I still bear the scars of his anger.

"That's right," he mutters as he slaps my thighs apart further. "I bet you're fucking wet already, aren't you?"

"No." I glare at him, closing my eyes tightly when he pushes his hand between my legs. Fuck. Fuck. God. This can't be happening. This. Can't. Be. *Real*.

"Let's see how big of a liar you are." With one easy motion, he snaps my panties away from my body. I'm exposed to him now. He hitches up my dress, prolonging the moment he'll feel for my arousal. But then he does. Finally. I'm almost relieved when I hear his dark chuckle in my ear. "You lied, Dove. So many lies. You're gonna have to get out of that habit. Or maybe I'll break it for you."

"Fuck you."

"You will," he replies easily. "Soon enough, you will. Now let's see..."

His fingers probe between my legs, smearing my wetness all over my thighs.

"Please stop," I whisper weakly, even though we both know it won't do any good. I can't resist this man. I never fucking could. "Please. We can end this right now. Nobody has to know. I won't tell anyone. Please."

"You better beg for something better," he tells me, pulling his fingers away from my exposed pussy and bringing them to his lips. He sucks them clean, the sound obscene, making my cheeks flush hot. "Beg for something I'll actually give you, little slut. Something we both want."

"Please." I can't help begging. A part of me still hopes this is just a sick, awful nightmare I'll wake up from soon. "I won't tell anyone. Just let me go."

"Never." His voice is fierce and sends a shiver of excitement through my body.

"This is a dream," I whisper, barely loud enough for him to hear. "This isn't real. You can't hurt me."

"Wake the fuck up, Dove." He pinches my arm, hard, and I wince. "This isn't a dream. This is real fucking life. Your nightmare's happening, here and now. I'm fucking back."

"Dove?"

Our eyes snap to the doorway. Up until now, we were alone in the back alley. But now the door is open, and Raphael is standing there, his troubled expression telling me he's worried about me.

"Everything okay?"

"Everything's fine," Parker calls out. "Dove and I go way back. We were just reminiscing."

"Dove?" Elise appears behind him, wearing a sugary sweet smile. "We were wondering where you went. Come inside for a drink!"

Parker leans against me, painfully squeezing my thigh as he mutters in my ear, "Remember what I told you to do. We're getting the fuck out of here, right now."

I swallow, giving him a barely perceptible nod before turning my fake brave face to the other two.

"I think I'm actually g-going to head home," I manage to get out. "I don't feel so good."

"I'm happy to give you a ride," Parker says.

"I'll handle that," Raphael cuts in. "She came with me."

"But Raphael," Elise pouts. "It's your special night. Do you really want to leave early?"

"I don't mind," he says, his eyes firmly locked with mine. "Come on, Dove. Let me take you home."

Parker peels his back from the wall, coming to stand in front of my date for the night. He gives a lazy smile to the man I came here with. "I said I'd handle it, man. I'm taking her home."

"Thanks, but that won't be necessary," Raphael says firmly.

I can see a fight brewing, so I step forward, awkwardly repositioning my dress and hoping neither Raphael nor Elise have noticed how high up on my thighs it is.

"It's fine. I'll go with Nox tonight, Raphael."

"That's right. We got some catching up to do," he grins at my date. "You and Elise just hang out."

"No, I don't think so," Raphael shakes his head.

Ignoring his words, Parker turns to face me with that wicked smirk of his. "Ready?"

I nod, following him through the alley.

"Dove." Raphael grabs me by the forearm. His fingers dig into my skin, painfully hard. I yelp as I turn to face him. "Wait."

"Get your motherfucking hands off her." Parker is standing between us in a flash, his eyes burning with a fire so intense it puzzles Raphael. "Are you deaf, you fucking jackass? Hands. Off. Her. Now."

"Jesus, okay." Raphael raises his hands in the air, glaring at me as Parker leads me away. I feel his and Elise's eyes on us as we make our way around the corner.

"That guy's a piece of shit," Parker mutters under his breath. "You dating him?"

"I don't know," I manage.

"Well, it's over now. You won't have time for him anymore, so unless he catches on fast, you'll need to tell him it's over."

"Why do you think you suddenly control me?" My cheeks are burning up and I'm feeling pissed off with how proprietorial he's being, even though it turns me on at the same time. Not that I'd ever admit that, of course. "You think you own me or something? I'll never do what you want. I'm only humoring you because –"

"Shut up, Dove," he stops me in my tracks. "You're embarrassing yourself. Keep that pretty mouth shut and keep walking."

I don't know what compels me to obey, but I do. I follow in his footsteps until we reach a bike and he pulls out a helmet, holding it out for me.

"Put this on."

I obey, and he snaps it closed under my chin. The intimacy between us is thick and heavy with anticipation. My heart has never beaten faster. I've never been this excited. Not since the last time Parker appeared in my life.

"Don't you have one?" I wonder out loud as he gets on the bike in front of me.

"Don't need one."

"Oh, you're suddenly invincible?"

"I survived Hawaii, didn't I?" He grins at me, revving the engine. I hold on to his waist, pressing my body close to his as he pulls away. He asks for my address and I whisper-yell it in his ear. We keep moving to my house, and when he parks twenty minutes later, I regret having to leave the warmth of his body. I nervously chew my bottom lip as we get off the bike.

"What now?" I ask.

"Now we go inside," he shrugs. "You offer to make me a coffee and I fuck you on the countertop."

"You aren't going to fuck me."

"Says who?" His brows shoot up in amusement.

"Me. Don't I have a choice?"

"No." He laughs at me, pulling me across the street. "Come on. Which one's yours?"

I guide him to my house, unlocking the door despite my best judgement and letting him inside. Everything I've done tonight feels utterly surreal. I can't believe this is real. That Parker Miller is now Nox and he's somehow back in my life. My mind knows I won't outrun him this time, and it's not because he won't give up – it's because I want this. I crave it.

I *want* him hurting me.

I long for him to do more, to mark me again, to prove that I'm the one he's been obsessed with all these years.

As I make the coffee, I guiltily remember I haven't thought about Robin since Parker walked back into my life. I cling to the memory of my brother, but the moment I walk back into the living room and see Parker standing there with one of my picture frames in his hand, my thoughts go out the window again.

"Put that down."

"Who's this?" He points to the man in the photo, holding me close.

"My brother," I manage without breaking down. "His name was Robin."

"Was?" He raises his brows again, contemplating my words.

"Yes, was," I reply firmly, setting the mugs down with such force brown liquid sloshes over the edge. "Now are you going to tell me what the fuck you want from me?"

CHAPTER EIGHTEEN

NOX

I put down the frame that upset her. Approaching her, I notice with a smirk that she still flinches when I'm near her. I resist the urge to touch her, to taunt her by running my fingertips over the puckered scar. Instead of doing just that, I sit down on her couch, making myself comfortable. It's fucking weird being in here after watching her in the house for so long. Finally, I'm a part of her inner circle. Now it's time for me to sink my teeth into my delicious victim.

"So, what are you doing here, Parker?" Dove demands. "And what's with the weird new name?"

"Do you know what Nox means?" She shakes her head no. "It's Latin for night."

"So ominous." She actually smiles when she says that, and it's beyond fucking adorable. The urge to make her mine is uncontrollable. I'm going to go fucking insane if I don't sink my dick into her. Right now. But instead of showing her how much I want her, I return the mug to her coffee table, leaning back on the sofa. "You still haven't answered my other question, *Nox*."

"I like the sound of my weird new name on your pretty lips," I tell her.

"My question? Answer it," my little bird demands.

I sigh dramatically. "Who are you talking to?"

She sighs right back. "Nox, answer my question."

"That's better. I'm here for you," I shrug. "Isn't that obvious?"

"But I have a life of my own now," she goes on. "You can't just waltz in and not expect me to be scared... I know what you did. I know what you did to June and Kade."

"Don't fucking say their names," I hiss, losing control for a split second. I clear my throat and run my fingers through my hair. I abandoned my brother's undercut years ago. Now I wear my hair the way I like – a little messy, dark as ever, and permanently in need of a fucking haircut. "I don't want their names on your lips, Dove. We don't talk about them. Not now, not fucking ever."

"Fine," she hisses, obviously upset by how defensive I've gotten. "But you still can't be here. If Kade and – if *they* knew, they'd drag you away from here. Away from me."

I know she's right, but I'm not going to acknowledge it. There was no way my prick brother was getting between us. He'd already ruined my life once, I wasn't going to let him get the best thing that ever happened to me – Dove Canterbury.

"Don't worry about them," I mutter. "They don't matter at fucking all. I'm here for you, Dove. Because we belong together."

"You're fucking delusional." She runs her hand through her hair, obviously frustrated with me. "God, you're really making me crazy."

I don't tell her how crazy I've been for her all these years. That I've spent months, years, tailing her, taking the same streets, following her around the city until I had all her movements down pat. I know everything about her and have for years. And yet Dove is just now coming to terms with the fact that I'm back in her life.

"I'm not leaving," I tell her. "You can't get rid of me now. You had your chance to call the cops, tell them I'm here, and you didn't take it. So now you'll just have to deal with me being around."

"I could still do it." Her eyes bore into mine with defiance. "The moment you leave, I'll call them to tell them about you."

"Sure you will," I smirk at her, stepping closer and grabbing her by the wrist. "We both know you're a terrible fucking liar, Dove. So why don't you just shut the fuck up and do as you're told. It'll make matters a lot easier for both of us."

She's putty in my hands and we both know it. For whatever reason, her body hasn't forgotten its obsession with me. Her bones, her marrow, her skin, still recalls my phantom touch, and she's now shivering in anticipation of more abuse, teetering on the edge and hoping I'll push her right the fuck over.

"You still want me to leave?" I grind out. "You want me out of your life? You never want to see me again? Say it. I fucking dare you."

"Fuck you, Parker," she spits out. My free hand moves to her throat, lighting fast. I hold her in place, roughly enough to tell her this is her place.

"It's Nox. You make that mistake again, I'll make you fucking pay for it. Got that?" I squeeze my fingers in warning. "Answer me."

"Y-Yes," she manages. "God, I got it! I'm sorry!"

"Damn right you are." I let go of her. She heaves a deep breath, glaring at me as I easily take a step back. "Aren't you gonna give me a tour of your place?"

"No," she says. "Because I want you out of here. Now."

"Oh, you're not getting rid of me. Why don't you tell me about your little boyfriend, then. What was it, Raphaello or something ridiculous? Like the candy?"

"Raphael," she hisses. "You've got no business asking about him, Nox."

"I'll make it my fucking business. You two serious?" She gives a non-committal shrug, making me approach her. Dove shrinks away as if she's scared I'll hurt her again. "I asked you if you're serious. Unless you want more pretty scars added to your face, I suggest you answer properly. A shrug isn't an answer, Dove."

"We just started seeing each other."

"Oh, how precious." I smirk at her. "Young love. How is he in bed? You fooling yourself into thinking anyone will be as good as me?"

"Fuck you."

"You keep saying that. I guess you really fucking want it."

She groans. "Look, it's getting late. Can you please just leave me alone? I'm tired and I want you to leave."

"I'm staying here tonight."

Her eyes widen. "Excuse me? You can't just –"

"What are you going to do?" My grin is wide as I face her. "Call your boyfriend?"

"He's not my boyfriend."

"Ah." I smirk. "Not putting a label on it just yet, I see. That means that spot is mine."

"You're not my boyfriend, you sicko."

"But the position is open," I wink at her.

"Not for you." She walks over to the front door, opens it wide and motions for me to leave. "Get out. I don't want you in my house or in my life. I don't want you anywhere near me. So just fucking leave. Now."

"Oh, Dove. I'm not going any-fucking-where. Don't you get it? I came here for you."

"Well, you can't have me," she hisses, but realizes fighting me is pointless so she slams the door shut. "If you aren't leaving, I am."

"And where are you going to go?" I smirk. "Your brother's?"

A painful expression takes over her pretty face. The words hurt, stinging hard even for me.

"Elise's," she finally replies.

"I'm sure she'll be delighted to see you," I mock her. "Especially since she was all over your non-boyfriend tonight. You really still think she didn't leave with Raphael?"

She hesitates, which fills me with a sick sense of success. I put the seed of doubt in her mind, now I just have to water it and make sure it flourishes.

"You can't stay here," she says again, shaking her head. "Don't you have some other place to go?"

"No," I lie. "If you don't let me stay, I'll have to sleep on a park bench or some shit."

"Great." She groans in frustration, pacing the room while my eyes follow her, appreciating her beauty. The need to have her, to make her mine again, is fucking overwhelming. I can barely concentrate on anything that isn't her. It's impossible to keep a clear head around Dove. So, when she passes me, I grab her again, flattening her back against the wall. A gasp escapes her lips and her wide, trusting eyes meet mine. "Don't hurt me anymore."

"Why not?" I ask, genuinely curious. "I thought you liked it."

Her teeth dig into her bottom lip. "I don't like being abused. You made me a victim. I hate being a victim."

"Then don't be one," I tell her. "You always have a choice, Dove. And I know you want this. I know you crave me just as much as I crave you... Even now... after all this time. Isn't that right?"

She doesn't answer, averting her gaze. I've still got her pressed up against the wall, and I can't resist the urge to lean in, inhaling her sweet scent, filling my nostrils with the concoction that is so uniquely Dove it makes my mind spin.

"Get off me." She tries to push me off, but I don't budge. She's forced to stay there, pressed between me and the wall with no chance of escaping. "You're such a fucking freak."

"Call me whatever the fuck you want, Dove, you're not getting rid of me." I tower over her and I fucking love it because I know it makes her feel so very vulnerable. My eyes land on her lips, drinking in the seductive shape of her Cupid's bow, the tremble in her bottom lip, the way her mouth parts as if she expects me to kiss her already. "You want me to kiss you, don't you?"

"I'd rather die than endure that," she grits out, lying through her teeth.

"Prove it."

"I..." Her eyes flash with anger. "Just fuck off already, Nox. I don't want you here."

"And yet we both know you're lying." I smirk at her. "Do I need to prove that to you yet again? Should I reach between your legs and show you just how much I fucking turn you on?"

"Don't touch me."

"You say that, but you seem so very desperate for it. Tell me more. Tell me how much you hate me. How you'll never let me have you again."

"Damn right I won't..."

My eyes travel down her body, her dress tight over her tits. I can practically see her nipples hardening under the weight of my gaze. She wants this. She wants my abuse. She fucking lives for it.

"Keep denying it then. Keep telling me no. It only turns me on more."

"You can never have me," she insists. "We both know how wrong this is. That you don't deserve me. Haven't you hurt me enough? Isn't one scar enough?"

"Never," I hiss in the shell of her ear. "It will never be enough."

I trace my lips along her jawline, making her gasp out loud. She's so fucking weak when I'm around. It's like prey playing dead when the predator arrives. It only makes my job fucking easier. Luckily for Dove, I don't need the thrill of the chase to get my dick hard, because I know we're meant to end up together. And even if we weren't... there's no way she can outrun me.

"You're so desperate for it," I mutter against her skin. "Body shaking, lips parted... You just want me to take what's mine."

"N-No."

"Still lying? I'll force the truth out of you, Dove. Don't you fucking worry."

At the last moment, before my will breaks, I pull away from her. I can see the disappointment in her eyes because it mirrors my own. But this is how I get the girl. I make her crave something, then yank it away before her palm can wrap around the prize.

"Let's go to bed, Dove."

"Where the fuck do you think you're sleeping?"

"Next to you," I smirk. "Maybe on top of you. Maybe you on top of me. Depends on my mood."

"Dream on." She hesitates before motioning to the couch. "You can sleep there, but tomorrow you have to find a new place to spend the night. I'm not playing hostess for some sicko from my past."

"Sure you aren't." She hesitates again. "Waiting for something?"

A goodnight kiss, perhaps?

"No," she finally mutters. "I have something else I need to do."

"Want me to come with you?"

"No," she replies sharply. "Go to sleep. And be gone when I wake up tomorrow."

I smirk, not replying, because there's no goddamn way I'm leaving. Not now, when I've got her eating out of the palm of my hand.

CHAPTER NINTEEN

DOVE

There's only one person who can make me feel better after the night I've had.

I load up a paper bag with some food and juice boxes and leave through the backdoor. My head is pounding. Every thought I have revolves around Parker, or Nox, or whatever. But I force myself to push it all aside. He can't be the only person on my mind. I need to remember the people who really matter. Like Robin. Like Sam.

But there's a weird, sinking feeling in the pit of my stomach as I keep walking, turning the corner near the alleyway leading to Sam's spot. Like I'm about to walk into something terrible. And my heart sinks the moment I round the corner and see him.

Sam's leaning against the brick wall behind him like always. He's covered up with my old blanket, and still has the paper bag I last gave him next to him. But his eyes are open. Open in a way they shouldn't be, staring ahead blankly, unseeing.

"S-Sam?" My voice is already breaking, as if my body instinctively knows what's happened before my mind accepts it. My paper bag falls to the ground. I run toward him, stepping on a juice box as I do. The cold juice soaks my shoes, but I don't notice it. I don't notice anything.

TYRANT STALKER

I'm kneeling before him. His eyes, his kind, wise eyes, stare into mine, but he can't see anymore. I want to fucking scream, but when I open my mouth, no sound comes out. I know I'm breaking. My mind is in pieces, my heart in tatters at my feet. With shaky hands, I reach for my phone. I call 911 and rattle off my address, but when the operator asks me what's wrong, I can't bring myself to say it. Can't reduce my friend Sam to what he is now – just a body.

"Just c-come," I manage, and the phone drops from my hand as the full weight of what's just happened dawns on me. I can't move. I'm frozen to the fucking spot, eyes glued to Sam's unmoving gaze. Slowly, I lower my gaze to his arm. There's a needle sticking out of it. I swallow the scream fighting its way from inside me.

"You promised," I whisper. "You promised you wouldn't do that anymore. You promised, Sam. You promised!"

I start hammering my fists against his chest as the tears finally fall. In two months, I've lost the only two people who've ever mattered to me, and I don't know if I can live without them. I don't even know if I want to try.

"Don't leave me, you can't leave me, you can't do this to me. I'm not ready, Sam. I'm not ready!"

"Dove, Dove, Dove." The voice is calming and kind, but I know its owner is anything but. Gently, he pries away my hands from Sam's body. He holds me tight on the ground, sitting behind me and embracing me, rocking me back and forth as I scream my frustration at the world. I am breaking, but the sicko who ruined my life is here to hold the pieces together for a while longer.

He must've followed me after I left the house, which should only make me angrier, but for some fucked up reason, I'm grateful Nox is here.

Nox, a hero in the *night*. What the hell is his game?

By the time the ambulance pulls up with its sirens blaring, I feel numb. There's so much pain I don't feel anything anymore. My mind has retreated to a place where nothing can hurt it. Not even the man gently whispering in my ear, telling me everything's going to be okay.

The paramedics rush out, but the moment they see Sam, they stop in their tracks. We all know it's over. There's nothing they can do to help him.

The truth of what's just happened is too heavy, and a sob rips from my lips as I watch them load up Sam's body onto a stretcher. A blonde woman gently closes his eyelids, which makes me irrationally angry. I want to scream at her, fucking attack her. I want to tell her he doesn't trust cars, they'll have to figure out a different way to get him to the hospital. But it doesn't matter. None of it does. Because Sam.... Sam's gone now. Forever.

One of the paramedics starts asking me questions but I don't even hear them. I hear Nox though, arguing with the guy and telling him to fuck off and leave me alone. The guy leaves with his hands raised in defeat. Nox insists we're going to the hospital with them.

I don't even remember the ride there. He takes me there on his bike and tells me to hold on tight, so I do, even though I just want to slip off the fucking bike and to my certain death on the road.

We wait in the hospital for what feels like hours. Nox offers me sandwiches, drinks, but I can't even reply. I just stare blankly ahead, just like Sam did when I found him.

Finally, Nox sits next to me. His reassuring palm comes to rest on my knee, but I don't feel its warmth. I don't know if I'll ever feel warm again.

Nox buries his face in his hands then. I mourn the loss of his palm on my knee, but I don't mention it. But when he stands up and screams, punching the wall, even I'm surprised.

He sits down next to me with his knuckles bleeding while two security guards rush toward us.

"Sir, you can't do that in here," one of them tells Nox, already reaching for his taser. "We're going to have to ask you to leave."

"I can't leave," Nox hisses. "I need to help my... my Dove."

"You just punched a wall," the other man says. "You're scaring people. You need to get out of here, now."

Nox nurses his twisted, bloodied fingers in his hand, standing up and getting up close to the guard. "I said I'm not fucking leaving."

The guy backs off. Nox's intimidating presence scares anyone who comes near us, and the guards reluctantly leave me alone with him.

"Why are you so angry?" I ask softly as he sits back down next to me.

"I..." He shakes his head. "I don't like seeing you upset."

There's more to it than that, and we both know it. But I'm tired. Bone tired. Too exhausted to demand more details. We sit there together, and I lean my head against his shoulder because I need some kind of comfort.

The doctor appears what feels like hours later. He's apologetic, kind, but his tone does nothing to help with the message he's come to deliver.

"There was nothing we could do," he says gently. "It must've happened right after he took that lethal dose of heroin. I'm sorry. Are you his next of kin? There's the matter of the bills..."

"I'll cover it," Nox cuts in, signing his name on a stack of papers the doctor hands him. "We'll call you with further arrangements for the..." He swallows thickly. "Funeral."

That word makes me feel sick. I curl up into a ball on one of the shitty plastic chairs. The doc prattles on about helplines and support they offer grieving family members. I just want him to shut up so I can close my eyes and sleep forever and a day.

"Come on, Dove. Please, come with me." I'm vaguely aware of Nox helping me stand up, but my legs won't hold me. I can't be here anymore. This can't be real. I didn't just lose him, the last bright light in my life. Sam isn't gone. He can't be. Without him, without Robin... what do I have left?

When he realizes I can't stand up, Nox simply raises me into his arms. I don't fight it. I just wrap my arms around his neck and allow him to carry me out of there. The cold, fresh air outside hits me hard, and I gasp for breaths that aren't coming, just like they'll never come again for Sam.

Nox sets me down on the seat of his bike, carefully putting the helmet on me.

He buckles the strap under my chin while my eyes stare emptily ahead. Nox doesn't speak, and I'm grateful he doesn't interrupt my mind that's already going a mile a minute. He simply tells me to hold on tight and drives me back home without saying another word.

He walks me up to the house, lingering on the welcome mat as I unlock the door and let myself in. I stand there with my hand on the doorknob, wondering what the fuck I'm supposed to do next.

I know I shouldn't invite Nox in, but I don't want to be alone tonight. In fact, I don't want to be with anyone but him. So, I cock my head to the side, managing a weak, trembling smile, as I say, "Aren't you going to come in?"

He nods, accepting my invitation and walking into the room. He shuts the front door behind him.

"I'm going to take a shower," I mutter. "I'll see you later."

I almost wish he'd argue, but he doesn't. I walk to the bathroom feeling like a shell of myself. There's nothing left of Dove Canterbury but this shell I'm forced to live in. And yet it's more than Sam has right now.

Swallowing back a sob, I strip my clothes off in the bathroom. I set the temperature to scalding hot in the hope that it will warm my tired, exhausted body. As the hot water beats against my body though, I find no comfort in its warmth. I still feel numb. There's nothing anyone can do to make it better. But I can do something.

My eyes go to the razor in the shower I shave my legs with. It took me years to be able to have it in the open like that, and now I know why. It's dangerous, too easy. I could just take it apart and hurt myself, right here and right now. Nox would be none the wiser. Nobody would have to know.

With trembling fingers, I pick up the razor and take it apart. I take out the razorblade and leave the plastic. I feel sick as I touch the blade to my skin, not cutting, but just holding it there, reminding myself I'm the one who holds the power. I'm in pain, but that pain can go away, *will* go away when I cut into my skin and make it bleed. I can make it all go away. What Nox doesn't know won't hurt him.

I press the edge of the blade into my skin. It parts easily and the blissful pain takes over, so overwhelming I'm able to tune out the pain of losing Sam, of losing Robin. I cut deeper. The razor slides into my skin with such ease it's almost a relief. With a sigh, I watch the bloody drips swirling down the drain.

"What the fuck are you doing, Dove?"

I want to look at him, but I can't. I'm too tired. The razorblade slips from my fingers and the water beats down on my new cut, a new scar to remember Sam by. I forgot I'm naked. Nox will see me like this, vulnerable and exposed. None of it matters anymore, because the razor did its job. I don't feel the pain of the loss anymore. I focus on the physical pain, on the broken skin, the bleeding cut. And I tell myself it's all going to be okay, knowing full well I'm lying to myself.

But what else am I supposed to do?

CHAPTER TWENTY

NOX

"Stop fidgeting." I grab her hand and inspect it up close. "Christ, Dove. Why did you do this? Where's your first-aid kit?"

She mumbles something in response as I sit her down on the stool and I realize she's retreated to a part of her that won't be able to give me the answers I need. I rifle through her cabinets until I find the kit. She doesn't even wince as I disinfect the cut. I apply some antiseptic cream and wrap it up, and the whole time, Dove just sits there, her eyes so far away.

Dove is still naked, but now's not the moment to admire her body. I ask her if she can walk and she doesn't respond. Finally, I gather her in my arms like I did at the hospital. I carry her upstairs and into her bedroom and she doesn't fight me. Putting her in her bed, I cover her with a blanket, unsure of what to do next. There's an armchair in the room where I could sleep, but when I move to walk away, her fingers tangle in my shirt and she pulls me back.

"Don't go, Nox."

Simple words, but so powerful. The fact she used my new name is enough to make my dick swell and my balls tighten. Oh how I want to fuck her right now. I climb on the bed next to her, fighting every instinct inside my body that's telling me to just do it. Take advantage, take what's mine, and pay no mind to whether she wants this or not. But I can't bring myself to do it. In Dove's weakest moment, my humanity has reared its ugly head. And I just can't hurt her more than she has already been hurt.

I lie down, my head on her pillow, and she cuddles me, lying practically on top of me, which is fucking torture for my already hard dick. But the moment I put my head down, the truth of what's happened hits me like a punch in the gut.

Sam is gone. My only friend in the world is dead. And I didn't even do it. This one wasn't my fault. Was it?

Maybe I should have told Dove how much he was struggling. Maybe I should have gotten him more help. Maybe, maybe, maybe... I can't change anything now. He's gone. I'm all Dove has left. Just like I fucking wanted.

I groan, the sound barely audible in the room, and pray Dove won't notice. A part of me wonders whether I'm really at fault for this, because I wanted her to myself. Well, I got my motherfucking wish. But at what cost? Losing the only damn friend I'd ever had.

I haven't cried in a fucking long time, but tonight I feel like I could. I feel the loss of Sam deep in my soul, where it hurts most. I force myself to push it to the back of my mind, where it can't cut me anymore. I'm not the priority right now. Dove is.

Soon after, her breaths get deeper and I realize she's asleep. She must be fucking exhausted after the night she's had, but there's no way I can sleep. So I gently extricate myself from her arms, and she fitfully turns to her side. I cover her up with the blanket again, tucking her in. Her expression is troubled, but she's certainly asleep.

I head down to the kitchen and pour myself a glass of water. The knock comes just as I down the cool liquid, and I wonder who the fuck it could be as I head for the front door. If that piece of shit photographer has the nerve to show up here tonight, I might up my body count before tomorrow morning.

My instincts weren't wrong. I open the door to find the prick on Dove's doorstep.

"Can I help you?" My voice comes out gruff and I do nothing to better the impression. The guy's brows furrow when he sees me standing there, and he glances behind me, searching for her.

"Where's Dove?"

"She's asleep." Not that it's any of your goddamn business. "What do you want?"

"To talk to her."

I realize then the guy is fucking hammered, smirking to myself. Oh, if only Dove could see him now. That illusion of the perfect billionaire playboy would be shattered in seconds. But I'm not going to wake her up just so she can see what a mess her almost-boyfriend is.

"She's asleep," I tell him again. "It's the middle of the night. I suggest you get an Uber and go home."

"I need to tell her something."

"Now's not the time. She just had some terrible news."

"About Robin?"

"No," I grunt. "About a friend of hers, Sam."

"Who?"

This piece of shit knows nothing about Dove, and I'll be damned if I let him disturb her.

"You need to get the fuck home."

"You don't tell me what to do." He almost lunges at me but loses his balance at the last second. The prick would look a lot fucking scarier if he wasn't standing on wobbling feet, close to passing the fuck out. "Who the fuck are you anyway?"

"I'm Dove's boyfriend," I lie easily.

"Bull-fucking-shit," the shit laughs. "She'd tell me if that was the case."

I shrug with a grin. "Guess you aren't important enough for her to fill you in."

His eyes flash with anger and for a moment, I'm convinced he really will try to knock me out. But I can take a pussy like him, easy. I hope for his sake he doesn't try, because he'll end up dead if he does.

"If you aren't letting me in right now, I'm calling the cops."

I laugh at the idiot. "And tell them what, exactly? That some girl you want to fuck is with someone else now and you're fucking butthurt? Nah, I don't think so, man. She's been through enough today. Go fuck yourself."

Something takes over him then, and a look of madness flashes across his face. He steps forward, all up in my face. He looks like he's about to throw a punch, but at the last second, he changes his mind. Without saying another word, he turns on his heel and staggers away. With the greatest pleasure, I slam the front door after him.

"Who was that?"

I turn around at the sound of Dove's voice. The sight of her makes my mouth water. She has an almost see-through silky wrap around her. And she's put on fresh black panties.

"It was your date," I say. "Checking up on you."

"What'd you tell him?"

"That you needed space. What are you doing up?"

"I'm a light sleeper," she mutters. "The talking woke me up."

"You need to get some rest."

"Don't tell me what to do." She walks past me into the kitchen and pours herself a glass of ice-cold water. I follow behind, leaning against her and placing my hands on the sink, caging her in front of me.

"But I like telling you what to do."

"I don't have the energy for this right now."

"I told you, you need to rest."

"How the fuck am I supposed to do that with you in my house?" Her shoulders slump as she breathes a sigh. "I'm scared of you."

"Why?"

"*Why?*" She turns around and I move in closer, pressing her body against the sink. "Because you're dangerous. Because bad things happen every time you show up in my life. Because I'm fucking afraid of what you're capable of."

"I'd never hurt you," I tell her, raising my hand to cup her cheek. But she flinches when I do.

"You already have. Too many times to count."

I don't argue with her. Instead, I wrap my fingers in her hair and tug on it. "I want you, Dove."

"Well, I don't want you."

"Then tell me to leave," I grunt. "Tell me to pack my shit and go. To never come see you again."

"I..." She struggles with the words, amusing me. "I n-never w-want to..."

"Yes?" I taunt her. "You going to finish that sentence?"

She doesn't. Instead, her eyes lock with mine and she stares me down stubbornly. But she doesn't say another word.

"When are you going to let me back where I belong?" I ask her next, running a finger down her bony chest, over her perky nipples and down between her legs. "In here... in your mouth... in your tight little ass. When are you going to admit you belong with me?"

"Never."

"I'm going to enjoy making you change your mind. You should've turned me in when you had the chance, Dove. Because now I'm *never* going to stop."

She pushes her fingers against my chest and I allow her to push me back. I laugh out loud at her, stumbling back as she advances on me. It would be so fucking easy for me to overpower her. To show her who's the real boss around here. But I'm saving it. I can't use my force on her just yet. I want her fucking willing for what's to come next.

"After tomorrow, I want you gone," she tells me. "I never want to see you again."

"Sure, liar," I smirk. My expression changes when I look into her eyes, though. She looks like she's in pain. Her eyes betray her. They show just how deeply Sam's death has hurt her. "Do you want to talk about what happened today?"

"Fuck off!" Her reply leaves no room for arguments.

"Do you want me to make it better for you?"

TYRANT STALKER

Her eyes narrow at me. "And just how the hell do you think *you* can make anything better?"

I kneel before her then, and her eyes grow wider and wider. I hook my fingers in her panties and gently slide them down her legs. Even I'm fucking shocked she doesn't fight me. But Dove stands perfectly still, eyes firmly closed as I slide her panties to the floor. I lift the silky wrap then, coming face to face with her exposed pussy.

"Don't," she whispers, the word barely audible. "Don't hurt me."

"Never." I kiss her. Kiss her hipbones, her exposed pussy, moving lower, between her legs. The feeling of her skin on my lips is intoxicating, overwhelming. I can't get enough, and from the soft mewl that escapes Dove's lips, I know she feels the same way.

"Why do you have to do this?" I look up at her, her eyes now open, tears welling in them. "Why can't you just leave me alone? This isn't love, Nox."

Once again, I'm smiling at my name on her lips. "No," I mutter. "This isn't love. It's obsession."

My mouth returns to her soft pussy lips and I part them with my tongue. This time she doesn't fight me, but she seems to be playing a game with herself, one where she can't make a single sound while I run my tongue up her sensitive flesh.

I want to remember the way she tastes in this moment forever. I want the taste, the feel of her, ingrained in my memory. Part of my fucking system. I can't stop now. I need more of her.

"I fucking worship you, Dove," I mutter against her skin, flicking my tongue at her clit. "You're all I want... all I think about... My obsession. My possession."

"I'm not property," she manages, but her voice is uncertain, weak. I see my window and I fucking take it, prolonging my licks, making her shake and tremble on the spot. "Ask me to fuck you, Dove."

"No."

"Beg me to take your holes again. How many men have been inside them since me? How many of them came in *my* fucking holes?"

She bites her lower lip, closing her eyes again without giving me an answer. But now I need to know because I'm a fucking glutton for punishment. I pinch her clit with my fingers, making her yelp in pain.

"How many, Dove?"

"Stop it," she hisses.

"Never. Tell me."

"N-No."

"Embarrassed? Just how much of a whore have you turned into, Dove? Tell me how many. Right the fuck now."

"None," she whispers. "Okay? Fucking none. I haven't slept with anyone. I have barely kissed anyone. I didn't let anyone fuck me. Not my mouth. Not my pussy. Not my ass."

I'm fucking shocked but delighted at the same time. "None? But it's been years..."

This time, the tears do fall. She pushes me away and storms off, and I struggle to wipe the self-righteous smile off my face.

None.

She's still fucking mine.

CHAPTER TWENTY-ONE

DOVE

"What are you still doing here?" I tap my foot against the floor, glaring at Nox as he leisurely pours a glass of water at the kitchen sink. "I told you, I wanted you gone in the morning."

"I can't just leave," he mutters, taking gulps of his drink. "I don't trust you by yourself."

"Fortunately for you, that's my problem, not yours."

"I'm not leaving, Dove." He sets the glass down and approaches me with a darkened expression. "You hurt yourself last night. I need to check your cut."

He reaches for my arm, but I snatch it away. I've reached the anger stage in my process and I hate him right now. I just want him fucking gone. From my house, from my life. I want him to leave.

"There's no need for that. Just go."

And yet, a part of me still hopes he won't leave. That he'll refuse to go away. That he'll insist on staying. And when he does, my heart soars for reasons I'd rather not damn well explore.

"Come here." He motions to the window, and reluctantly, I do as I'm told. He's careful as he unwraps the bandage covering my cut, but I still wince when he pulls it off. "It looks better than it did last night."

He disinfects it again and adds some antiseptic cream before covering it with a fresh bandage. It's strange seeing him like this. Strange to know he actually cares about me. He's so careful with me, like I was a porcelain doll. Every motion he makes, every stroke of his fingers is gentle. It's the opposite of what I know him to be – unforgiving, rough, and cruel.

"What are you going to do all day?" I ask him. "Do you have a job or something?"

He doesn't answer me, carefully arranging the bandage on my arm. "What are *you* going to do all day, Dove?"

"I'm supposed to go to the plant nursery, but I don't feel good," I mutter.

"The hospital called," he tells me. "They have... they have Sam's ashes. They asked if I wanted to arrange the funeral."

"I want to scatter them," I mutter. "Uphill somewhere."

"We can do that."

"I didn't include you on purpose, Nox," I hiss. "You're not part of this, so stop forcing yourself into the situation."

I can tell I've hurt him, and for a split second, I regret my harsh words. But I don't say sorry.

"I am part of it whether I want to be or not," he mutters. "We'll go on a hike tonight, then. I'll find a more secluded location where we won't be bothered by anyone."

I glare at him, wanting to fight him. And yet the temptation of having company for the final part of Sam's journey is tempting. I want him to come with me. I don't think I'm strong enough to handle this on my own.

"Get ready and we'll go to the hospital," he mutters, sitting down on my sofa and scrolling through hike locations. I take a few seconds to just look at him. I can't believe Parker Miller – Nox – is sitting on my couch. Fuck. I spent years trying to run from him, but here he is now, in the fucking flesh. And something tells me he's not giving up on me, especially after my confession last night.

But I hadn't lied. I wanted to, but I couldn't bring myself to do it. I really hadn't been with anyone since him. It was ridiculous. So many years had passed. I'd went on dates, I'd let men kiss me. But I never, ever felt what I felt with Nox. Not until Raphael.

Guiltily, I remember abandoning my date the previous night at the club. I feel so fucking terrible. I'll need to call Raphael and apologize, but I'm dreading the thought of speaking to him again. I don't know how the fuck I'm supposed to explain what's happening with my life right now.

As I get ready, I stare at my reflection in the mirror. I can't believe I'm letting the monster who did this to me closer and closer. I should be running away and calling for help, not inviting him deeper into my life. I hate myself. I hate the fact that I'm unable to fight my attraction to Nox.

I pick out an all-black outfit from my closet and furrow my brows when I think of all the weird stuff that's been happening lately. The stolen handbag on my date with Raphael. The butt plug I found inside me. Is it possible that...

I shake my head to get the thought out. No, I can't get paranoid now. Of course Nox didn't have anything to do with it. How could he?

And yet the seed of doubt has been planted, and as I walk back to the living room where he's waiting for me, I can barely look him in the eyes.

Outside, he puts the helmet on my head again and we silently drive to the hospital. There, we receive a standard urn filled with Sam's ashes. I can't even bring myself to look at it, let alone hold it, but Nox handles everything for me. He tells me he found the perfect location to scatter my friend's ashes, and we get back on the bike. He holds the urn with one hand until we arrive and park on the street.

"You're going to be hot as fuck in those black clothes," he tells me. "It's going to be a warm way."

TYRANT STALKER

"Whatever," I mutter, dismissing his words, even though I'm already burning up. I'm wearing black leggings and an oversized black sweatshirt with a huge pair of black sunglasses to cover the scar. I thought if it got really warm, I could strip down to my sports bra, but now I'm mortified by the thought and being so exposed in front of Nox.

What happened in the kitchen last night can never happen again. I'm not risking letting this maniac back into my life. Not after everything he's done to me.

I quickly come to regret my all-black outfit decision as we begin our ascent. It only takes me twenty minutes to give up on the sweatshirt, and I reluctantly pull it over my head and tie it around my waist. Nox merely smirks at me, not commenting on my bra or my exposed skin, covered in scars. We keep walking in charged silence. But I appreciate the quiet this time. It gives me time to think about Sam. This hike is about him, after all.

My thoughts fill with every memory I have of the man who's made living in LA so much better. He made me less lonely. He made me feel like I belonged. He was my best friend, even though our connection was strange and unexpected. There are so many things I wish I'd gotten to say to him, but now it's too late.

I wipe a traitorous tear from my eyes and keep walking. Nox is carrying the urn, but once our hike is halfway done, I ask him to carry it the rest of the way.

It's heartbreaking. All that's left of his life is in a simple black object. Sam was larger than life and now he's been reduced to this.

I worry my bottom lip between my teeth and keep walking. We reach the top of the hill after an hour, and I'm exhausted and out of breath, but the view from here more than makes up for it. It's gorgeous up here. You can see the city in all its glory. And we're alone, just like I'd wanted.

"Think this place will do?" Nox asks me, and I nod. "Whenever you're ready."

I sit cross-legged on the dusty earth overlooking the side of the hill, and Nox joins me. "I'd like to say a few things first."

"Go ahead."

But now that it's come down to it, I have no idea what to say. How am I supposed to put a life as impactful as Sam's into just a few words? I can try, at least.

"Sam, you meant everything to me, even though I never learned your last name," I begin softly. "You were my best friend. My confidant. I trusted you and I believed in you. You motivated me to be a better person even when you believed you couldn't be that for me. And perhaps this is how our story ends. With me carrying on your legacy. With me telling your story."

Nox and I get up and he helps me open the urn. I don't dare look inside, I'm already too emotional. Together, we scatter Sam's ashes into the wind and watch them disperse above the city that he loved so much. The city that gave him life and killed him.

Nox comes to stand behind me, gently wrapping an arm around my waist. "He would be proud of you."

"How can you say that?" I mutter. "You never even knew him."

He doesn't answer. We stand there for a long time, until I finally come to peace with the idea that Sam is gone for good now. Finally, I sniffle and pull back, softly asking Nox if we can leave.

Our descent is quiet again, and we run into two women on the way. Both of them eye Nox appreciatively, and I feel jealousy brewing in the pit of my stomach. He smirks at both of them, making me go fucking crazy. I hate that he looks at other women. I hate that other women look at him. He's fucking mine.

The ferocity of my own mind takes me by surprise, and I keep my lips tightly pressed together as they continue climbing the hill and we keep descending.

Halfway down, my phone starts to ring, and I blanch when I see the caller ID.

"Lover boy?" Nox teases me.

"Shut up." Reluctantly, I answer the call. I have to get it over with sometime. "Hey, Raphael."

"Dove." His dark voice is worried and relieved at the same time. "I'm so glad you're okay. Where have you been? I've been trying to call you all day."

"Sorry, I wasn't checking my phone. Something... happened last night."

"What, Dove? Can you tell me?"

I ponder the question. I could tell him, but I realize I don't want to. My relationship with Sam was too special, too unique to be cheapened into a simple sentence about him. "Maybe some other time."

"When can I see you, Dove?"

"I don't know," I mutter. "I'm... taking some time off."

"Time off from me?" I don't answer. "Dove? Please talk to me. I came by your house last night."

"I know."

"But I –" I stare at my phone that starts crackling with static.

"Connection's really bad here," Nox chimes in innocently, and I roll my eyes, cutting the call and pocketing my phone. He doesn't even try to wipe that self-righteous look off his face as we make our way back to the parking lot. This time, I see him checking out my ass as we walk, but I don't call him out on it. It's sick because I want him to look. I feel like I won over the two girls we ran into on the hike, and victory has never tasted sweeter.

"You're going to have to get a helmet for yourself, too," I tell him back in the parking lot as he straps the thing to my head, just as carefully as always.

"Is that so?" he chuckles darkly. "You planning on becoming a regular plus one on all my trips?"

"No, I..." I blush fiercely. "If you ever drive anyone else, I mean."

"There's no one else, Dove," he says firmly. "There was only ever you."

I swallow thickly at the sound of his words. I wish I was brave enough to tell him he was the only one for me, too. Instead, my lips remain firmly pressed together for our ride home, and I don't say another word until we're back in my house.

CHAPTER TWENTY-TWO

NOX

We return to Dove's apartment. She doesn't ask me if I'm coming in, but when we're finally in her apartment, she turns to face me with her arms crossed.

"You need to find another place to live."

"Why? I can keep an eye on you here. You'll feel safer with a man around."

She laughs at me. "As if, Nox. If anything, I'm more scared having you around."

"Stop lying to yourself," I mutter. "Come on, Dove. You need me."

"I don't fucking need you. I never did."

"Now that's a lie if ever I heard one."

"Whatever," she groans just as her belly rumbles. "Fuck."

"Are you hungry?" I narrow my eyes at her. "When was the last time you ate?"

"Doesn't matter," she shakes her head dismissively. That's when I finally look at her, really look at her. The girl is painfully thin. She looks on the brink of starvation.

"I'm ordering some takeout," I announce. "What are you in the mood for?"

"Nothing."

"So damn stubborn." I place an order on a delivery app while she disappears into the bathroom to take a shower. I want to suggest we do it together, but I have a feeling that won't go down very well, so I keep my mouth shut.

She emerges sometime later, giving me a dirty look, even though I didn't even do anything.

"Mind if I use your shower?"

"If you have to," she grunts. "But after we eat, you're out of here, Nox."

I just smirk at her, heading for the bathroom. The whole room reeks of roses and I groan out loud. That scent of hers is going to drive me fucking crazy. I get into her shower and stand under the hot spray of water. I'm fucking grateful for the fact there's no guy stuff in here, but it seems like I'm gonna smell like a fucking bouquet by the time I wash my hair. Everything's so fucking girly. I need to bring some of my own stuff in here, level it out.

Even though Dove seems to be determined that I won't be staying with her for much longer, there's no fucking way I'm leaving. I know the moment I walk away, that piece of shit Raphael's going to come in guns blazing trying to take my place. And that's just not fucking happening, not on my watch.

I hear voices outside and hurry up towel-drying my hair. I put my boxers and jeans on and walk to the front door where Dove's talking to some guy that's way too old to be delivering food.

She's laughing.

He's saying something and she throws her head back, laughing easily at what he's saying.

Jealousy bubbles under the surface. I want to fucking kill the guy, but I force myself to stand back and observe them. When they keep chatting, he asks for her phone number. My nails dig into my palms as I fist my hands. Like fuck am I letting this happen.

Dove stiffens as I walk up behind her, wrapping a proprietorial arm around her waist. "Thanks for the pizzas. You can get lost now."

"Nox," she hisses. "I haven't even paid him yet."

I pull my wallet from my jeans and hand the shell-shocked guy a fifty. "Thanks. Bye."

"So, about that phone number..."

"Are you fucking serious?" I hiss at him. "Can't you take a goddamn hint?"

"Whoa, chill out," the guy mutters. "What are you, her keeper?"

"Exactly," I hiss, taking a step forward. The prick must be feeling extra fucking brave, which is too fucking bad for him, because I'm in the right mood to kick out some of his teeth. "You were leaving, I believe."

"I was actually waiting for your friend to answer my question," the guy says.

"I'm answering for her," I growl. "Get. Fucking. Lost."

The guy sighs, laughing lightly as he puts down a pizza box. "You want a fucking fight, man?"

"Maybe I do."

"Please, can you not?" Dove hisses at me. "This is freaking embarrassing, Nox!"

"Go eat the pizza before it gets cold," I tell her, never taking my eyes off the prick in front of me. "Go on, Dove."

She reluctantly takes a step behind while I face off with the guy.

"Last chance," he tells me with a smirk. "I take tae-kwon–"

He doesn't get to finish his sentence, because I've already slammed my fist into his face. He falls to the ground while Dove shrieks behind me. I'm pretty sure I've broken his nose, because the prick's blood spurts out moments later. He groans on the ground, covering his face with his hands while I keep hitting and hitting.

It's been a long time since the red mist descended like this. When I killed Robin, I did it out of necessity. There was no joy in hurting him – he was innocent. But not this piece of shit. Mr. Pizza Delivery Guy had it fucking coming for so much as *looking* at my goddamn property.

"Stop it! Nox, fucking stop it! Stop! Stop! Parker, *stop!*"

Finally, when she uses my real name, the word comes through and I stop with my fist mid-air. Dove is sobbing behind me. The delivery guy is barely conscious, groaning on the ground. He never did get the chance to show me his tae-kwon-do skills.

"You're fucking insane," Dove tells me as she pulls me off him. My knuckles are bloody and my heart's going a thousand miles a minute. I blink, trying to get back in the moment as the guy picks himself up and limps to his car, driving off with the screech of tires on concrete. "How could you do that? Are you fucking crazy? You could've killed him!"

"That's what he deserved," I snarl, ripping my hand away when she reaches for it. "He had no right, Dove. No goddamn right."

"No right to do his job?" she hisses. "You're fucking crazy. Off the rails. You're just like you used to be, and I'll never, ever trust you!"

In tune with her words, she starts shoving me backwards and I stumble into her street. I'm still shirtless, only wearing jeans and boxers. Now we've caught the attention of passers-by and Dove's nosy fucking neighbors who are staring at us from their windows. I want to kill all of them.

"Dove, calm down," I tell her, raising my hands to stop her and quickly realizing that would only piss her off more since they're still stained with blood. "Look, I'm fucking sorry, okay? I... I overreacted."

"No fucking shit!" She slaps me. It's so loud and shocks me so much I actually laugh out loud, but that only makes her angrier. "You're insane. You need to get the fuck away from here. I want you out of my house and out of my life."

"I'm not leaving," I shake my head. "I can't leave."

"If you don't, I'm getting a restraining order."

"You don't mean that." I furrow my brows and shake my head. She wouldn't do that to me.

"You just beat up some guy I've never seen before for no fucking reason! I'm afraid you're going to..." She glances around us, hissing the rest of the sentence at me in softer tones. "Kill someone!"

I groan. "Let me get my shoes and my shirt at least."

"No," she grunts. "You'll just worm your way back into my life and my heart. And I don't want you in either."

Her words hurt, but I try not to let it show. I run my fingers through my hair, fighting the urge to scream at the people watching us and tell them to fuck off and mind their own business.

"Dove, you don't mean it."

"Of fucking course I mean it. I've been trying to get rid of you since you showed up here."

"You're lying."

"I'm not!" she screams in frustration, pulling at her hair. "Can't you see my life's gone to hell since you reappeared? I've lost everything. Everything. Sam. Raphael. And Robin... Robin..."

She swallows and I watch something click inside her like a switch. Her legs can't hold her up anymore and she collapses on the ground, staring at her open palms as if they hold the answer to everything that's happened. Everything I've done.

Because obviously, Dove's fucking right. I'm the one who's been making her life a living hell, and I have no goddamn regrets. I wouldn't take anything I did back. Not even Robin. Because it all meant I got her here, broken, with no one to help her but me.

And I'm the one who picks her up in the end.

I'm the one who guides her back in the house where the pizza boxes lie forgotten on the counter.

I'm the one who sits her down on the sofa and cleans her scrapes from collapsing on the pavement while she stares ahead, eyes unseeing.

I'm the one who force-feeds her some shitty vegetarian pizza concoction that turns my stomach.

I'm the only one who can make it better, and we both fucking know it.

"I'll leave now, if you want," I finally mutter once she's eaten two slices. "I just wanted to make sure you were okay."

TYRANT STALKER

She doesn't answer, and I pull back, coming to terms with the fact that I need to give her some space. But when I attempt to walk away, her hand shoots up and she wraps her fingers around my wrist, ever so gently pulling me back. She doesn't speak, but when her eyes meet mine, they speak the only word that matters.

Stay.

Except I know I can't. I can't stay here, because the mere fact that she reached out for me has already made my dick hard. So I pull my hand out of her grasp. Her face breaks into a painfully desperate expression.

"Don't go."

Now she's said it out loud. And yet I still can't stay. Not without revealing all the awful, humiliating things I want to do to her still innocent body. Not without breaking her.

"I have to leave. You need time to rest."

"I can't be alone tonight. I can't, Nox. I don't want to be alone."

I groan, running my fingers through my hair in frustration. "I can keep an eye on you. From the street."

"No," she whines. "Stay with me. Hold me. Take care of me."

The words falling from her lips fucking break me. I want nothing more than to stay, and yet I know I can't. Not without breaking the promise I made to myself – that I wouldn't hurt her unless she begged for it.

But Dove is still so pure. She doesn't know how ugly and awful the world is. How black my heart is. She has no idea of all the awful things I want to do to her.

My heart battles my mind as she awaits my answer. Finally, I shake my head.

"I can't."

She jumps up at this, a look of pure rage crossing her face. "You *can't*? You were so obsessed with owning me, you knocked out some stranger, and now you can't fucking stay?"

I shake my head. Whatever I say now will mean nothing, but I try anyway. "I'm sorry."

"Sorry? Sorry's not fucking enough," she snarls at me. "Why can't you stay? Why can't you do the right thing for once in your sorry fucking life? Why can't you? Why, Nox? Why?"

"Why?" I hiss.

"Yes, why!" she screams, hammering her fists against my chest. We're going to wake up all of her neighbors again, not that I particularly give a damn. "Why, Nox? Why won't you stay, why, why, why?"

I grab her hands. She goes still. I move her right palm over the bulge forming in my pants, hissing my answer at her.

"This is why, Dove. Because just being near you makes me hard as a rock. Because seeing you naked has been giving me blue balls all day. Because I want to fuck you. And I'm going to fucking hurt you if you make me stay. Do you fucking understand?" I pull her against me, glaring into her wide eyes. "Do you, Dove?"

CHAPTER TWENTY-THREE

DOVE

My hand rests between his legs. I'm too afraid to move, to do much as let out a breath. My eyes are glued to his and the air between us is thick, the tension sparking with electricity.

"You can't handle it," he mutters. "You never fucking could."

He takes a step back and my hand falls from his crotch. My mind is screaming for me to cling to him, to beg him not to leave me, to take me with him, to never let me go. And yet I stay glued to the spot, unable to move a single inch. He shakes his head. He's put on his shirt, but now he puts on his shoes too, and the whole time, I don't say a word, even though my head is swimming with things I want to scream at him to convince him to stay.

He laces up his boots and gives me one last look. "I'll be around."

With those words, he leaves me standing there, walking away from me as if I never meant anything to him at all. I feel like I'm going to be sick, and yet it takes me several minutes after the door shuts behind him to move to the sofa like I've been severely injured, collapsing on the plush pillows.

TYRANT STALKER

My life is a fucking mess. The sofa smells like Robin. Robin, who's gone. And Sam. And now Nox. I have nobody left.

My thoughts fill with people I could call.

Raphael. No. I don't want to explain what's been happening with me, and I don't want him to know I don't see a romantic future for us.

Elise. But what would I say? Even though it's been only weeks since Robin went missing, I know she's already moving on. The way I'll never be able to.

My mother. The thought makes me laugh out loud. As if she'd even want to talk to me.

I lie on the couch for what feels like hours. Nox doesn't come back. Evening turns into night, and the fear starts creeping in, heavy, dark and crippling. At some point, I force myself to drag myself upstairs and into my bed.

I'm convinced I won't be able to fall asleep for hours, but the adrenaline rush has tired me out, and my eyelids grow heavier and heavier by the second. Thankfully, I don't get a chance to dwell on what happened with Nox. My mind saves me, mercifully plunging me into a world of numb darkness, where I don't have to feel a thing.

I wake up because I can't breathe. My eyes fly open, my chest reverberating with the beat of my own heart. The room is dark, and there's someone in here with me. Instantly, I'm terrified. That is, until my eyes find his.

I'd recognize his gaze anywhere. Grey, dark, promising a world of pain and trouble. And yet for some reason, his presence calms me, and my heart beats a little steadier despite the fact that Nox has his palm pressed against my mouth.

"Don't make a fucking sound," he tells me. "Just nod and shake your head. Understood?"

I struggle beneath him, but his free hand instantly finds its way to my throat, and he squeezes. Hard. I understand the game we're playing now. If I don't do what he says, he's going to hurt me. My heart soars with excitement, and I hate myself for it.

Finally, I settle and give him a simple nod. This seems to please him. He smiles at me, almost gently, lulling me into a false sense of security.

"Good girl." God, those two little words make me feel all the things I shouldn't. "Are you happy I came back?"

I nod, eyes fluttering open and closed fast.

"Do you know why I came back?"

I shake my head no. My chest burns. Every spot he's touching burns. I want him to take me. I want him to have me. I'll deal with the mess I made here tomorrow. Tonight, I just want to belong to him once more.

I was obsessed with Parker Miller once. And the thing about obsession is... it's un-fucking-curable. As I stare into his eyes, I know I'll never be able to quash the feelings I have for him. I'm doomed in this state, forever hoping he'll take advantage of me again, even though I've experienced his wrath too many times to count.

"I came back to fuck you, Dove," he mutters in the shell of my ear, sending shivers down my spine. "I came back to fucking take what's mine. Do you want that?"

He raises his face above mine. His lips linger inches away from my own, torturing me, taunting me with a kiss he won't give me. Not unless I tell him the truth.

My eyes close. I don't want to give him this power over me, to admit what I'm truly feeling, what I don't want him to know. Yet I know if I don't, he'll leave me wanting again. So, I nod. With my eyes closed, I nod, telling myself this doesn't change anything.

I'm still the brave girl who gets through whatever life throws at her.

I'm still the victim who pushed through the self-hatred and blame and became a better person.

Nox does not define me. Parker Miller does not define me. *What he did to me does not define me.*

"Beg me," he whispers in my ear. "Beg me to fuck your untouched cunt... And don't you dare fucking scream."

His palm leaves my mouth and I rasp, trying to get some fresh air into my lungs. But his impatient gaze tells me he won't wait for those words forever, his hand still lingering on the pillow, ready to cut off my air supply again at any moment.

"I-I-I..." I struggle to speak, tripping over the simple word, swallowing, blinking fast. "I... I want you to..."

"You want me to what, Dove?" He taunts me, mesmerizingly close to me, his lips a breath away from mine. I pray he'll kiss me. Everything else is forgotten, all those bridges burned. Nothing matters but Nox's lips on mine. Taking what's been his all along. "Speak up, be a good girl for me. Don't fucking disappoint me."

"I want you to –" I choke on the words, struggling to catch my breath. "I want you to fuck me, Nox..."

With a growl, he climbs onto the bed and positions himself between my legs. My heart is still pounding, my mind unwilling to accept this isn't just a dream. I pinch myself, and it fucking hurts. This is real. Nox is real. *We are real. This is happening.*

He slides my panties down my legs. I notice he's only wearing boxers, and he slides them off with lightning speed. My eyes widen at the sight of his cock. I want him. I remember him. How could I ever forget my first cock... my only cock...

He grabs hold of my knees and lifts my legs apart, smirking at what he sees. I can feel how wet I am, and when he leans in close and spits on me, all I can do is gasp for him. He pushes my legs back, positions his cock at my entrance. My heart pounds. Our eyes meet. He laughs at me as he presses his cockhead in the wetness pooling at my center. Laughs as he rubs his spit into me. "You really want it, Dove? Really?"

"Really," I whisper. "Really, really, really, really..."

"I don't believe you," he mutters. "Keep fucking begging."

But he doesn't make it easy on me. He keeps on rubbing the tip of his cock into my pussy, grinding me so much it's almost fucking painful, the denial he's putting me through. I find myself babbling, eager to get more, eager for him, for the love only he can give me.

"Please, Nox, please, fucking please, fuck me, all I want is you, all I ever wanted is you... Take it, it's your pussy, they're your holes. I spent all this time waiting for you. I wanted you... I always wanted you... Don't take this away from me, Nox, please, I'm begging you, please, fucking please, I need you..."

"So, you remember how to beg after all," he smirks. "Good to fucking know... I'm not going to fuck you tonight."

A gasp rips itself from my lips and my bottom lip wobbles in frustration.

"Make your peace with that now, little Dove. But I'm going to make it fucking unbearable for you. I'll make *my* pussy so damn desperate it'll be weeping, leaking at the sight of me. And you'll beg for everything I want to do to you. Every. Single. Fucking. Thing. Got that?"

"Yes," I manage.

"Yes, what?"

"Yes..."

"Focus," he smirks at me. "Be respectful. If you're not, I'm going to hurt you. What do you call me when we play?"

I remember everything I know about him, thinking hard about the answer he wants. I mewl in frustration, afraid of his reaction because I don't know the answer. But he doesn't seem angry. His palm finds my cheek and he gently runs his fingers over my scar. I close my eyes, anticipating a slap that never comes.

"You call me Sir, Dove. When we play, you call me Sir. Now say it. Say yes, Sir."

"Yes... S-Sir," I whisper.

"Say it again. I fucking like it."

"Please, S-Sir," I croak. "Please. Please. My pussy needs you. Fuck me. Fuck me, please, Sir."

"What did I tell you, Dove? You're not getting fucked tonight. Beg for other things. Things you might actually get."

"Cum." My voice is shaky as fuck and it's embarrassing. "I want your cum, Sir."

He smirks at me from between my still-raised legs, my pussy pouting at him. "You don't want to come yourself?" He presses his hard cock against my clit and it's enough to make me shudder and squirm.

"I don't care," I whisper. "You decide, j-just let m-me have yours... Please... Please, Sir."

"Good girl." He groans, rubbing his cock over my pussy. I feel him leaking, the precum sticking to my pussy, running between my legs. I'm so turned on I could scream, but I force my lips to stay pressed together. "Keep begging, Dove..."

"Give me more, Sir." I'm hungry now. No, ravenous. I want more of him. I want him to give me everything. "Give me your cum. Cum on my pussy. Cum on my clit, Sir. Please, just fucking please, let me have your cum, Sir."

"What a thirsty little slut." He smiles menacingly, wiping his dripping cock on my eager snatch. "And it's so fucking tempting. If I didn't have plans for you, I'd be tempted to give you your little wish."

"P-Plans?" I whisper. "What p-plans?"

"You'll find out," he replies easily. "But tonight, I just wanted to tease you. To get you to admit how happy you are that I came back for you."

I flush fiercely, part of me hating this and another loving the side of me only Nox can bring out.

"Are you happy I came back?" he asks, and I find myself nodding. "Do you want me to sleep on the sofa tonight?"

At this, I shake my head, desperately reaching out and gripping his wrists in my arms. "Please, here..."

"Here with you? In your bed? So close you can feel my fucking cock pressing against your tight little ass while you sleep?"

I swallow thickly, nodding without saying another word.

"Okay, Dove." He smirks. "I'll give you what you want."

He lets go of my legs, throws my panties at me, tells me to put them on, that it'll be too distracting to sleep next to me naked. I do as he says, so grateful for his presence as he lies down beside me. He pulls me against him, wrapping me up in his arms and inhaling the scent of my hair.

"Sleep," he mutters in my ear. "Sleep, Dove."

"I can't," I whisper.

"Why not? Because of me?"

I shake my head. Suddenly the reality of everything that's happened hits me fucking hard. The moment Nox stops distracting me with our bodies, I'm hit with memories. Thoughts. Words he said to me. Things he told me. How he took care of me. How much he loved me. More than anyone else. He was the only one who took the time to make sure I ate. But he's gone. I feel it in my bones.

"I miss him."

"Sam?"

I shake my head, feeling guilty as fuck.

"Robin?"

I narrow my eyes, looking up at Nox. "How do you know about Robin?"

CHAPTER TWENTY-FOUR

NOX

Fuck. Fuck. *Fuck*.

    I have to be careful now, or I'm going to get caught in this fucking lie. And it's too soon. I don't want her to find out what I did to her brother. Not now, not ever. I fucking slipped, and if I'm not careful, it's all going to come crashing down on me like a ton of shit.

    "I..." I struggle to find the words, my mind screaming at me to hurry the fuck up and think of something before little bird suspects something's seriously off here.

    "How, Nox?" She sits up in bed, and when I reach for her, she slaps my hand away. "Answer me."

    Fuck. I'll have to confess at least part of what I've done. I can't lie to her, but I can't tell her the whole truth either. I swallow thickly, hoping she can't see my guilty fucking expression in the darkened room.

    "The truth is, Dove..."

    I killed him.

    I killed your brother. I killed him in cold fucking blood. I did this, it's my fucking fault you're alone... I did I did it I did I did it I killed him killed killed killed I'm a killer I'm a killer a murderer it's my fucking FAULT!

"I've been keeping tabs on you."

"What the fuck's that supposed to mean?" She narrows her eyes at me.

I laugh, trying to make a joke out of the situation. Trying to distract her. Trying to do any-fucking-thing to get her to stop thinking about Robin and what happened to him. "Ever since that shit went down in Hawaii... I've been keeping an eye on you."

"Explain," she barks at me. "I don't understand what you're saying, but if it's what I think it is..."

"It means I've been... watching you." I know this won't end well, but it's the most I can give her. "Making sure everything was okay."

I reach out for her, but she shrinks away from me, a look of disgust in her pretty eyes illuminated by the moonlight. "You've been *stalking* me?"

"If you want to call it that."

"Yes, I do," she replies. "Because that's what it is. How long has this been going on for, Parker?"

"It's Nox," I remind her.

"No." She pushes the duvet off, getting up and crossing her arms in front of her body. "It's Parker. Stop fucking lying to me and yourself. Just tell the truth for once in your sorry fucking life."

"Why are you getting so upset?" I grunt. "I didn't touch you..." Well, that's technically a lie, but Dove doesn't need to know that, at least not right now.

"God, I was so fucking stupid," she whispers to herself. "I thought I was going crazy. You said you didn't touch me. But you did, didn't you?"

Fuck. I just stare at her, hoping she won't come to the right conclusion.

But Dove's smarter than I give her credit for.

"The butt plug," she mutters. "The handbag. That was you, wasn't it?"

I need to accept I've lost this one and admit it. It's better than her realizing I'm the one who killed Robin.

"Yes," I tell her, keeping my eyes trained on her.

"Fuck," she whispers. "Fuck. Fuck. Fuck."

My thoughts exactly, little bird.

"You had me thinking I was going crazy." Her eyes find mine again, angry, hurt. "I thought I was imagining stuff... seeing things! You had me thinking I was crazy, that I'd have to see a doctor, get pills, get treatment! How could you do that to me?"

I can't say anything, because the only thing I can think about is the other thing I did, the one I now pray she won't ever find out about.

I can tell she's spiraling now, getting angrier and angrier as she spews curse words at me, pacing the room as she yells her frustrations. I understand, I really fucking do. But this doesn't change anything. It just means my plan will be set into motion sooner than I thought. Luckily, I got everything ready when I left for a couple hours earlier. My little bird's cage is waiting. It was only a matter of time, anyway. I never could fight the darkness that well.

"You have to leave," she realizes out loud. "I want you out of my house. I want you out of my life. Stop following me. Stop fucking stalking me. Stay away from me."

"Sure," I say, moving closer to her. She doesn't step away to avoid colliding with me, and it's the biggest mistake she's made all night. "Just do me one favor first, and then I'll leave you alone."

"What the fuck could you possibly want after everything you've done to me?" she hisses.

I reach into the pocket of my jacket that's hanging over a chair.

"What are you doing?"

I give her a reassuring smile as I reveal the chloroform-soaked rag. "Smell this."

I press it firmly against her mouth. She doesn't fight me for long. Her body is helpless to the odor, and I hold my breath until she goes limp in my arms, then toss the soaked fabric away. I gather her in my arms, holding her close. I inhale her scent, filling my nostrils with it.

She'll hate me for a while after I do this, but needs must. Soon enough, Dove will realize this was for the best. That I'm only doing all this so we can finally be together, the way we're supposed to.

The way it was fucking meant to be.

"Good morning, Dove," I say gently as she wakes up with a groan. "Slept well?"

"Where the fuck am I?" Her voice is croaky, heavy with sleep. "What the fuck did you do?"

"I did what I had to," I tell her with a smile. "You were fighting this. You won't do that for long. I'll train you to accept me. To love me. To want me."

She turns her red-rimmed eyes to mine, not saying a word. Instead, she raises her hands to the metal collar around her neck, the one that's connected to an O-ring on the wall with a heavy, long chain.

"What did you fucking do?" she whispers. "Where am I, Parker?"

"It's Nox," I remind her gently. I don't like this new little habit of hers where she defies me by calling me a name I've long since forsaken. "Or preferably, Sir. Remember when you called me Sir? Remember what a good slut you were for me? That was only last night, Dove."

She takes a look around, only then realizing what I've done. "What is this place? Why are there mirrors everywhere?"

"So you can see yourself," I smile. "Look at your own reflection all day long."

"N-No," she whispers, clawing at the collar around her neck. "No, I don't want that."

"Unfortunately for you, Dove, it's not up for discussion." I stand up, approaching her from the shadows. "You're going to stay here until we fix a few nasty little habits of yours. Like that self-harming thing. It was cute for a while, but you're done doing that. If you hurt yourself, I'm making your stay in here a week longer. Each time I find a cut, a scab, anything I think you've done to yourself, I'm extending your time in the cell."

"N-No." Her eyes are horrified. "Don't do this, you can't, please don't do this to me."

"Of course I can," I reply easily. "I can do anything I fucking want to you. Nobody knows where you are. And before you start screaming... no one will hear you. So, I'd save my voice if I were you. You don't want your throat sore. I'll take care of that myself."

"Don't do this." Her voice is desperate. I have a feeling the worst part about this are the mirrors, because she's still stubbornly refusing to look at her own reflection, even though I've covered every surface in here with it. "Don't do this, it's not too late, we can still go back. No one has to know..."

"Of course not," I smile. "Which is why you won't tell anyone. And by the time I'm done with you, Dove, you won't even *want* to leave."

She doesn't answer me. Instead she panics, looking around the room for an exit that doesn't exist. There's a door, and she lunges for it, but her chain will only allow her to go so far. I laugh at her meager efforts.

"It's not even locked," I tell her. "Maybe I'll leave it open sometime, just to taunt you more."

"You're a-a monster," she whispers. "You can't do this to me. I'll kill myself."

"No, you won't," I smirk. "Here's the thing about hurting yourself, Dove. You only want to do it until you have to start fighting for your life. But I don't expect you to understand that now. Soon enough, though, you'll learn your lesson."

"Stay away from me," she hisses when I come closer. "I'm going to hurt you!"

"Sure you will," I smirk. "Sit on the floor in front of the mirror like a good girl."

She crouches, glaring at me as I close the distance between us. "I'll never obey you again."

"So naive," I tell her. "You'll change your mind soon enough. Now sit."

"Or?" Her eyes are full of defiance, and it's kind of adorable. "You're going to hurt me?"

"Not you," I smile. "Maybe Elise. Maybe Raphael. Someone in your life, anyway."

"You can't be serious."

"I'm *dead* fucking serious, Dove. Now sit the fuck down."

Her eyes sparkle with anger, but in the end, she does as she's told. She's such a good little girl deep down. So deeply obedient. I'll have fun bringing that side of her out to play.

"Good girl."

"Don't fucking call me that."

"Shut up, Dove." I kneel behind her. "Look at your reflection."

"No."

"You really want them to get hurt?" Gently, I move the hair off her collarbone so it falls in a silky waterfall down her back. "I'd be more than happy to oblige..."

She lets out a sound I can't quite define and finally, reluctantly, meets my eyes in the mirror.

"Good girl." I kiss the top of her head. "See how good it feels to obey?"

"Fuck you."

"One thing at a time, Dove," I smirk. "Now spread your fucking legs."

She doesn't fight me this time, but I can tell how much she wants to. Still, she spreads her legs wide, knees falling open to reveal her naked pussy. She's shocked by the sight of it, glaring at me.

"Show me your cunt," I order her. "Spread those pretty lips. Show me how beautiful that achy snatch is for me."

Hesitantly, she reaches between her legs, slowly opening herself up for me. She may say she hates me, but her pussy doesn't lie. And I see how glistening wet it is for me, eager for me to plunge myself inside her.

"So beautiful," I mutter. "So fucking tempting. You want me to play with it?"

She shakes her head no vehemently.

"You sure about that, Dove?"

She just glares, but I take it as an invitation. Reaching between her legs, I elicit a gasp from her lips the second my fingertips connect with her sweet little cunt. She attempts to close her eyes, but I warn her with a stern flick of my fingers against her clit. She yelps, her eyes fly open, and she's staring at us in the mirror again while I smirk at her.

"Doesn't it feel good? Doesn't it make you love yourself a little more, knowing how good your body can make you feel?"

"No," she hisses, fighting the moan I know is fighting to escape her lips.

"You can lie to me all you want," I smirk. "But the truth is written all over your face, Dove."

I start massaging her tender clit and she struggles against me to no avail. I know exactly what I'm doing – bringing her closer and closer to an orgasm she doesn't want. I can't fucking wait to hear her moan for me. It's going to make my cock so goddamn hard.

"Look me in the eyes," I whisper in her ear. "In the mirror."

She does. I know it's a welcome reprieve for her, the fact that she doesn't have to look at herself.

"Tell me you love me," I grunt.

"No," she hisses instantly. "No fucking way."

"No?" I repeat innocently. "You want another task? You have to do that one, or someone gets fucking hurt. Let's say I'm feeling merciful."

"Anything else," she grunts.

"Look at yourself then," I laugh. "Right into your own eyes. Tell the girl in the mirror you love *her*, Dove. I'm going to keep toying with your sweet little cunt until you do."

CHAPTER TWENTY-FIVE

DOVE

I want to fucking kill him. But I'm helpless here. He rules me in this room and we both know it. So, I close my eyes and pray for it all to go away. Pray that this is just a bad dream and I'll wake up back in my room, with Robin close by, with Sam still around. But I know it won't happen. This is my reality now. I'm Nox's captive.

A gasp rips itself from me as he continues his assault on my pussy. He's gentle, painfully gentle, bringing me so close to an orgasm I have to fight my own instincts so I don't moan his name. But every time I get just close enough, a finger's brush away from an orgasm, he takes the pleasure away.

I know what he wants me to do but I won't give it to him. Yet with every stroke of his fingers, I get closer to conceding, to admitting he's won one battle, if not the war.

I open my eyes, staring at the girl in the mirror. Maybe if I pretend it isn't me, I can say the words he wants to hear. My bottom lip trembles as I struggle to get those traitorous words out. I tell myself I don't have to mean them. I just have to say them for his benefit, so he'll leave me the fuck alone.

"Go on, Dove," he mutters in my ear. "Be a good little slut for me... Show me how good you can be, and I'll reward you."

"I..." I bite my lower lip. How can it be this hard? They're just words... They don't have to mean anything. "I love..."

"Say it," he taunts me, fingers brushing against my clit and bringing me a step closer to madness. "I love myself. Go on, Dove. Just fucking say it. Be a good girl for me."

Everything in my body resists this, but I know he won't stop if I don't say it. And yet a part of me doesn't want it. A part of me is desperate for him to continue his assault on me. I want to blame him for everything bad that's happened to me these past few months... And at the same time, I never want him to fucking stop.

"I love... m-myself." I shift my gaze in the mirror, glaring at him as he pulls back with a smirk on his face. "Aren't you... aren't you going to..."

"What?" he laughs in my face. "Make you come? Dream on, Dove. You'll have to beg a lot harder for that."

I stare at him incredulously as he walks toward the door. "Wait."

"Oh?" He grins at me. "Ready to beg already?"

"Where's the bathroom? Where's the water? What am I going to eat?"

"Behind that mirror is a small bathroom." He motions carelessly to the right. "You can use the toilet and wash up in there. Water's there too along with a glass. Don't even think about hurting yourself or trying to hurt me, because I'll punish you so much, you'll never make the same mistake again."

I purse my lips, staring at him with annoyance. "People will look for me, you know."

"Oh, will they now. Maybe I'll just make you write a note to let them know you're okay."

"You're sick." My lip curls at him in disgust. "You're a monster."

"I've been called worse, Dove."

With those words, he leaves me alone in the room of mirrors. I close my eyes and lean back, wishing this wasn't real. Wishing he would have let me come. Wishing for him to never take me away from here... Because it means being with him. And my sick heart yearns for nothing more than to be his unwilling toy.

I'm going to die in this room, alone.

A shiver travels down my spine, chilling me to the bone. I don't know how long I've been alone in here for, but it feels like hours. I've tried to keep count of the minutes ticking by, but I have no real idea of time here, with these mirrors on every wall instead of windows. I found the bathroom which was small as Nox described. I washed up. I drank water. I wished I were brave enough to end my own life.

But Nox was right. There's nothing like one's life being put in danger to put things into perspective. And I'd never been more eager to survive.

He reappears what feels like hours later. The entire time, I'd lain on the mattress in the corner of the room, eyes firmly closed so I didn't have to stare at my own reflection on the ceiling.

"Having fun?" Nox asks as he enters the room again.

"Fuck off." I refuse to open my eyes. I don't want to look at him, don't want to see him. All I care about is time passing, because it brings me one step closer to someone suspecting something's wrong. Someone coming to rescue me. I will never trust a man again after this, of that, I'm sure. I grit my teeth together refusing to look at Nox even as he kneels next to me, gently brushing his fingertips over my face.

"I have to lock you in the bathroom for a while," he tells me. "I'm not going to hurt you. But I have something special planned for you, to make you feel less alone in here. Come with me."

He pulls me to my feet and guides me to the bathroom. There's a hole drilled in the door through which he feeds the chain before reattaching it back to the wall on the other side. I wait listlessly in the room while he gets everything ready in the mirrored space. I hate him.

I eye the glass I drunk out of earlier. I could break it. But am I really capable of killing Nox?

My heart and mind both say no, and I know as desperate as I am to get the hell out of here, I won't be able to hurt him. Not like that, not permanently. A big part of me still has feelings for him. Wants him to love me, like I once loved him. But I'm not letting that part win. Not now that he's kidnapped me.

I weigh the glass in my hand, contemplating slitting my own wrists. But for once, I don't feel the pull of that temptation. I've spent a lifetime hurting myself, but this is the first time I don't long for the cuts on my skin. I want to get the fuck out of here so I can have my revenge on Nox. I want to punish him not just for everything he's done to me, but for everything he's threatened to do to the people I love, too.

"Almost ready," he calls out from the other side of the door. "I think you'll like this, Dove. I thought of it especially for you. Just give me a couple more minutes."

My teeth grit together in anger. I don't answer. I have nothing else to say to him, the monster from my nightmares. He finishes up in the mirror room and again unclips my chain. Finally, I decide to go through with it. Right before he enters, I smash the glass against the sink, holding a shard in my shaky hand as he enters the bathroom.

"What are you doing with that, Dove?" he asks with a grin when he sees me. "You really think it'll take some glass to bring me down? I survived Hawaii, I can sure as fuck survive you, too."

"Get away from me," I hiss, waving the shard at him as he attempts to come closer. He raises his arms, chuckling, the chain still in one of his hands. "I'm going to hurt you if you ever touch me again, you sick bastard."

"Don't threaten me, Dove," he mutters. "I don't fucking like it. Don't you want to see the surprise I'm giving you? Don't you want to see how much I *care* about you?"

"No," I get out through gritted teeth. "I don't want anything to do with you. Just leave me the fuck alone."

"I can't," he admits. "Now put that glass down before you hurt yourself, and come with me."

"No." My hand tightens around the shard, the glass digging sharply into my palm. I know I'm bleeding, but I almost don't notice it. I'm too focused on hurting Nox. I need to get rid of him. Maybe not kill him, but hurt him badly enough so he won't touch me ever again. "Don't come any closer or I'll fucking kill you."

"While I'd love to see you try, I've had enough of these childish games," he grunts at me. "Now, put the glass down. You've already cut yourself, silly girl."

My hand tightens even more around the glass. "No."

"Why are you being so fucking stubborn, Dove? Put it down!"

"No!" I grip it tighter, making him groan out loud as he approaches me. What pisses me off no end is the fact that he isn't even worried about his own well-being. Like he's convinced I'll never fucking hurt him. And the sad part is, he's fucking right. I can't bring myself to slash his veins with the shard. I can only hurt myself. But that'll work out just fine, since I seem to be the only person he cares about anymore. "One step closer and I'm cutting myself."

I touch the glass to my wrist, hands shaking as I wait for Nox's reaction. And I get one alright. His gaze darkens and he snatches my wrist with his fingers. I yelp, fingers flying open and the shard landing on the ground, blood oozing from my fresh cut.

"Crazy fucking girl," Nox mutters against the shell of my ear. "Don't you dare do that again."

I try to punch him, but he twists my good arm behind my back, making me cry out.

"Relax," he hisses. "I won't fucking break it. Just stop resisting for one fucking second so I can help you."

With those words, it's as if every last bit of the fight I had left in me leaks right out. I crumple to the ground and he kneels in front of me, checking my cut while I listlessly stare ahead.

"It's deep," he mutters. "It might need stitches."

I shake my head. "Don't make me go."

"What?" He knits his brows together. His features dance before my eyes as I try to focus and fail miserably. "Dove, I'm worried."

"I don't want to go," I whisper. "They'll take you away from me."

We're both quiet for a moment after that, allowing what I've said to sink in. He doesn't say another word, and allows me to sit on the floor while he gets a first-aid kit. I don't try to run. I think if I did, he wouldn't try to stop me. Not this time.

Nox cleans my cut with antiseptic and covers it up with a bandage. Once he's done, he gently wraps a blindfold on, leads me outside and leaves me waiting, still unchained, in the other room.

I know there's a carpet here because I feel it under my toes. There must be windows too, I feel the air coming in and the light warming my skin. I turn my face toward the sunlight, savoring it.

When Nox pulls the blindfold off my eyes, I don't expect him to have come true on his promise. Knowing him, something nice might have been a new toy to torture me with. But no. He's brought me into a beautiful, hotel-like room with an attached bathroom, with a real tub. And the room is filled with flowers. They're wilted. Nearly gone. I look at him with an unreadable expression on my face.

"What's this?"

"Your reward." He points to my ankle. "No more chain, either."

"Because I hurt myself?"

"Because you showed me and yourself what a good girl you are," he growls. "And I heard you like flowers. So, here's the deal."

"The deal?"

"Of course," Nox smirks. "You didn't think there wouldn't be a deal, right?"

I glare at him and he laughs at me before continuing.

"When the first plant sprouts a new leaf, I'll touch you again. Until then, you water them. You take care of yourself. Pamper yourself. Anything you want that I can bring here, I'll give to you. Food, drinks, treats. Anything, Dove."

"Why are you doing this?" I ask.

"Spoiling you?"

"Torturing me," I hiss.

"Because you fucking love it, and need it. Now listen carefully. I'm going to limit my time with you, because you need to learn how to take care of yourself. You'll have toys. You can play with yourself."

"As if," I scoff.

"But you should know there are cameras in this room," Nox goes on. "And I fully intend on watching the little show you're going to put on for me."

"Dream on."

"We'll see." He smirks. "As long as you know, anything you do in here, I'm sure as fuck going to watch. Every night, put a list of what you want under the door. Don't do anything stupid. And enjoy it."

"Enjoy it?" I glare at him with pure, undiluted hatred. "How can I enjoy myself being a fucking captive?"

"You'd be surprised. Right, little bird, I'll leave you to it." He makes a move to leave but I tug on his sleeve, pulling him back. "What is it?"

"I'm going to go crazy by myself in here," I say. "Can't I see you at least?"

"No," he grunts. "I'll be too tempted, and I can't touch you for a while. Show me the plants every day. There's a phone in here, nothing works on it but the camera feed which transports to me so I can watch it. Show me how they're recovering. Show me yourself. Make me proud, little bird."

"Stay with me," I whisper, my heart pumping into overdrive as I realize how desperate I am. "You fix me."

He takes my shoulders in his hands and looks deep into my eyes. "I can't. This time, Dove, it's on you. I'm doing what I can to help. Now, I have to go. This is already too fucking hard and I hate goodbyes."

"Fine." I push him away, glaring at him. "Leave then. Like everyone else."

"It's not about me leaving," Nox hisses. "It's about you learning that you can survive my absence. Goodbye, Dove."

I run to the door but I'm too late. He's already slammed it shut.

Turning to face the half-dead plants in the room, I notice several cameras dotted throughout the beautiful suite. I flip them all off.

CHAPTER TWENTY-SIX

DOVE

I do have to admit, the new room is much nicer than the dump he put me in before. The first chance I get, I take a long, hot bath, filling the tub with stuff he left in the bathroom for me. The bath salts smell like roses, my favorite. I don't even want to know whether that's a coincidence.

After finishing up in the bath, I lather myself with lotion and leave my hair to dry in natural waves. I lie on the soft bed and appreciate every inch of my skin touching the pillows dressed in pure silk.

A piece of paper slides under my door, and I remember the list I'm supposed to write. There are so many things that come to mind I'm shocked – usually I'm not one for little treats like this.

I add a chocolate bar, a matcha latte, and one of my favorite books, Rebecca, to the list. After thinking about it for a moment, I add a toy too. If I'm going to be stuck in here by myself, I might as well make Nox's life a living hell.

I pass the note back and crawl back into the bed. It doesn't take me long to fall asleep. The silky sheets work their magic and for the first time in years, I sleep like a baby.

I have no idea what the time is when I wake up. My head is still full of the dream that took over my sleep, with Nox fucking me, torturing me until I was begging for an orgasm. With a groan, I roll over onto my belly. That's when I see it. There's a small wicker basket by the door.

Heart pounding with excitement, I pick myself up and rush to it. The basket has everything I asked for – an old, beaten up copy of Rebecca, a glass tumbler with a green concoction, and a chocolate bar. And right there, in the middle, there's a long, velvet bag.

I tear into the chocolate bar and dig my teeth in. Halfway through it, I realize this must be the first time in years I'm enjoying a snack without feeling guilty. But I can't even think about my eating habits right now – my attention is focused solely on the velvet bag in the basket.

Crumpling the wrapper, I toss it aside and lift the velvet bag out of the basket. Inside, there's a toy. It's a massage wand, with a thick, rounded top, and no wire. I turn it on and it rumbles to life, making me flush.

I take it with me to the bed. The phone Nox mentioned is waiting on the bedside table and my heart pounds as I pick it up. Just like he said, nothing works but the cameras, which are already recording.

I shouldn't give in to his demands, but a part of me wants to make this as difficult for Nox as it is for me.

Before I go on, I strip my clothes off until I'm bare. I climb on the bed and get myself into position. My mouth is watering at the thought of Nox watching this, knowing what I'm doing for his pleasure alone. I position the wand to my center. The rounded tip fits perfectly between my pussy lips, and the pressure on my swollen clit is already almost too much.

I offer the nearest camera full view of my drenched pussy. I turn the toy on, and it vibrates to life with low, rumbly sounds.

I close my eyes, trying to ignore the alarm bells going off in my head. The silence and being alone combined are doing things to me. I want him to watch me. I want him to *fuck* me.

Need uncurls in my belly, deep, dark and alarmingly fast. I rub myself with the toy, eliciting shaky moans. I want to say his name, beg him to fuck me, but I don't. Instead, I just get myself off with the toy, imagining him watching the feed wherever he is right now. The orgasms come fast, my legs and eyes fluttering as I allow the relief to wash over me.

"Fuck," I breathe, pushing the toy, bringing myself so impossibly close my eyes roll back from the effort not to come. I flick my clit with my free hand and moan again. Is he watching? Why isn't he here yet? Doesn't he want to fuck me?

I close my eyes and I come again, then again. I didn't even know I could push myself this hard, but my body is pent up, needy for a release. I could keep going for ever. In my mind, I make a stubborn promise to myself – to keep fucking myself until Nox loses his patience, barges in here and gives me what I'm so very fucking desperate for.

I keep going, never letting myself stop. One orgasm melts into another as I rub myself with the wand, teasing my cunt by pushing the vibrating tip inside myself every so often. I'm getting so fucking close I know it's going to happen eventually; I'm going to fucking soak this bed. I'm going to come so hard my pussy will squirt out all the frustration my stalker makes me feel.

And then it happens, almost without warning. I scream his name and then I'm gushing. A stream of it covers the silky sheets, and then I'm sitting in a puddle, crying, laughing, whispering his name like a mantra meant just for me.

I'm so far gone I barely notice the sounds of approaching footsteps until the door is unlocked. It flies open the next moment, slamming into the wall and bringing down some plaster. My eyes widen in shock as they connect with Nox's at the door.

"What the fuck do you think you're doing?" he snarls at me.

He doesn't approach me. Doesn't make a move to stop or help me. It only pisses me off more. "What does it fucking look like? Giving myself the orgasms you've been keeping from me."

"Put the toy down."

"No," I hiss in response, pushing it against my center again and groaning in frustration.

"Fucking obey, little bird."

I don't. He takes several steps to reach me and rips the wand away from me, throwing it at the wall. It hits the surface with a thud, crashes to the floor and blinks a few times before dying.

"You can't take it away from me!" I howl.

"I can do anything I fucking want, Dove," he replies, getting up close and snarling in my face. "You're at my mercy now, and you're playing my goddamn game."

"Then make me come," I hiss. "Give me orgasms, fuck me, give me what I need!"

"No."

"Why not?"

"Because you're not fucking ready."

"You don't know me," I accuse him. "You don't know when I'm ready. You don't know shit."

His hand wraps around my throat so fast I don't even get a chance to fight back. He grips me so hard there's no way for any air to get in, and I let out a gargled moan as he lifts me off the bed. He slams my back against the wall and I struggle pointlessly, feet kicking into air. Terror and fear wash over me. He's killed before. He could kill me right now.

"Don't... hurt... me..." I manage to get out.

"Why shouldn't I?" he growls. "You disobey orders. You try to get me to lose my patience. You fuck with my head. You fuck with my dick without ever wrapping your mouth or cunt or tight little ass around it."

"Then..." I sputter. "Fuck me. Please."

"No," he grunts before letting go of me. I crumple to the floor, choking, coughing for my next breath of air. "I'm not going to fuck you. I don't fuck brats."

I glare at him, heart hammering in my chest as I crawl to him. "I know you want to. Do you think I'm fucking blind, Nox? Don't you think I know how desperate you are to plunge your big fat cock inside my dripping pussy? Don't you think I know how much you want to cover me in your seed? You're so fucking obvious... Everyone knows you love me."

He flinches at that and my heart soars.

"You do, don't you?" I purr. "You love me..."

"Don't say that word," he grunts.

"Why?" I smirk, tugging on his leather belt. The way the buckle rattles excites me. "Because it's fucking true?"

"I don't love you."

"Liar," I hiss, opening his belt buckle. He doesn't stop me. I undo his zipper next. My hands have started to shake, and I feel my bottom lip wobbling as I pull down his jeans. He's wearing a pair of silky black boxers and his dick is hard underneath the fabric, painfully straining against it. "I'll suck it... Just tell me."

"I'm not telling you anything."

"Really?" I smile, pulling his boxers down. I don't look at his cock right away, even though it nearly slaps my face when it comes out, it's so fucking big. "You don't want me to suck your huge fucking cock? You don't want that, Nox? My pretty mouth wrapped around your tip, sucking out everything you have to give me?"

"Fuck," he curses, running his hands through his hair and taking his eyes off me. "Stop, little bird."

I don't.

In fact, I disobey his order. I take a look at his cock and lick my lips at the sight. He's so fucking big, throbbing, the veins making his dick look angry, enraged. I want it on my tongue, in my mouth. I want him to come so deep down my throat I don't even get to swallow.

"Stop," he grunts, but I don't.

Instead, I wrap my mouth around his tip and start to suck like the greediest little whore. I play with him with the tip of my tongue, bringing us both closer. When his hips involuntarily thrust forward, I scoot closer, taking more of him in my mouth, licking him eagerly, with desperate need fueling me to keep going.

"Stop," he repeats.

"Never," I manage with his cock in my mouth. I can fucking feel him throbbing. My tongue slides along the longest vein on his dick, feeling the blood running into his cock. A sick desire to bite, to make him bleed, overtakes me. It fills my head. Punishing Nox. Hurting him like he hurt me.

But I can't.

I should, I want to, and yet I can't.

All I want is to keep going, keep sucking, keep stealing his orgasms until they all belong to me.

"Please," I whisper, my eyes going to his. "Feed me."

"Fucking hell," he grunts, closes his eyes, and then grips me by the hair. His eyes remain closed as he forces my mouth down on his dick, deeper, closer, until he's filled me completely. He keeps me that way, unable to breathe, smelling his scent, becoming his toy. "Right there, little bird, don't you dare fucking stop."

I choke on his length and sputter but he doesn't stop. Long ropes of saliva drip down my chest and I turn my eyes up to his to show him how much I love this. We're caught in this moment now, with no one to witness what we're doing, with no one to judge us. And I can finally be myself, give him everything, like I've always longed to do.

A silent tear drips down my face as he pushes his cock deeper, deeper still until he hits the back of my throat.

It's sick, fucked up and twisted.

ISABELLA STARLING

And yet I can't help the orgasm racking through my body as I feel him get closer. His cock jerks in my mouth, ready to spill, ready to give me everything I've ever dreamt of.

But at the last moment, Nox pulls back.

He groans and I cry out at the loss of him, watching him walk backwards until his back hits the wall. He curses and grabs his cock just as it explodes, spraying the air and the floor with his seed.

We watch each other, our breaths labored as he pulls up his boxers and jeans and zips them back up.

"That was the first and last time you disobey me," he growls at me. "I have to punish you now."

"You're the one that came in here," I hiss. "You're the one who couldn't fucking resist me."

"I'm locking you in, Dove. You won't see me again."

"You said that the first time," I remind him sweetly.

It takes him three steps to reach me again and slap my face, hard. I'm so stunned I can barely react, just stare up at him with accusing eyes.

"This journey is about you, not me," Nox hisses. "I want to heal you. Make you better. Not empty my balls down your throat. Now you either fucking obey, or I'll make you stay in here even longer. Without me. Without anyone."

"N-No," I stutter.

"Then be a good little bird and don't tease me like that," he grunts. "I'm taking the toy. I'm taking it all until you learn some goddamn manners."

"No!" I cling to his legs. "Don't leave me, don't go!"

"How do you expect me to stay?" he growls. "How do you expect me to fix you?"

"I don't want to be fixed."

The gentleness with which he takes my chin in his hands shocks me, and I turn my eyes to his. "Please, Dove. Do it for me."

His fingers leave my skin before I can react. He doesn't even look at me again before slamming the door and locking it. I sit on the floor, naked, shivering and on the verge of tears.

My eyes roam to the puddle of his cum on the floor and I crawl to it on all fours. Shakily, I lower myself to the ground and dip my tongue into the clear liquid. Shivers go through my body. I lick it and close my eyes to pretend this isn't happening. That I'm not desperate enough to fucking lick my stalker's seed off the floor.

But deep down, I already know Nox has won already.

CHAPTER TWENTY-SEVEN

NOX

I knew watching her in that room would be hell, but I never realized just how bad it would be.

She's been in there for three days and she's had her hand between her legs the whole time, even when she's fucking sleeping. I haven't taken my hand off my dick either. Jerking off while she sleeps in her luxurious cell, or while she makes herself come to annoy me.

But she's getting better, I can tell. Every evening, she gives me a list of items she wants, and it includes food and drinks most of the time. I'm proud of her. But I also know I won't be able to last much longer with her only a couple of doors down from me.

On the third day, she finally gives in. She starts watering the plants, reviving them slowly. From then on, there's no other option but to take care of the greenery I've filled her room with. She takes care of them like a good girl, and in turn, starts taking care of herself too.

I can see the battle behind Dove's eyes. I can see the part of her that's convinced herself she doesn't deserve to revive her own body. And I keep working away at it, hoping it'll get better. On the next day, I leave her some plant food as a reward. Her eyes light up as she shows me herself on the camera feed, wordlessly feeding the plants. She doesn't say a word that day. She remains quiet, thoughtfully pondering her innermost desires.

During the day, Dove is a good girl. But when her body naturally transitions into nighttime, the horny little slut inside her comes out to play. She's such a good fucktoy for me, abusing her sweet holes and showing me every second of her self-inflicted torture. After the trouble she gave me before, I vow not to let my dick decide for me. And as much as I want to kick down the door to her room, I don't. Because she needs this time to heal.

The dry leaves fall off some of the plants. I can tell some are beyond salvaging, but even those, Dove treats with love. She is consumed by her need to help another living thing, but because there's nothing else to do, she doesn't forget to take care of herself. I leave her three meals a day, along with the snacks she wants, and she eats them all. When she fucks herself, I still see her bones, but her skin isn't as painfully tight over them, and that fills me with an unwelcome emotion I'm not familiar with.

Hope.

It's a strange fucking thing.

The days pass painfully slowly, but it's worth it watching Dove bloom. On the eleventh day since I've last seen her, she starts the camera feed with a bright smile.

"Look," she whispers, holding up an aloe vera plant. "Right here. Do you see it?"

She points to the smallest green leaf unfurling slowly in the middle of the plant, and my dick fucking tightens.

She's done it. She's healed the plant. But is she ready for me to rip her out of this false sense of security? Am I going to undo all this progress if I move forward with the next part of my plan?

Even if she isn't ready... I can't hold back anymore.

I make her room unbearably warm that day, toying with the thermostat. By the time two hours are up, she's screaming at me on the camera feed. She knows I'm fucking with her, but she soon realizes it's helping the plants too. She waters them dutifully. Three hours in, she goes for an ice-cold shower, and I strip naked before silently entering her room.

She doesn't hear me and doesn't sense me. The sight of her in the flesh after an almost two-week long deprivation is almost too much for my cock to handle. I'm instantly hard, precum dripping off my cock as I enter the walk-in shower and press my body against her. She tries to yelp but she doesn't get the chance, because I've already put my palm over her mouth and caged her arms behind her back. Dove's eyes roll up to look at me and she mumbles my name, lashes fluttering when our gazes meet.

"Listen to me," I mutter. "Do you want to get fucked? Nod if you do."

Her pupils dilate and she nods eagerly.

"Then you don't make a sound," I go on. "I don't want to hear a word or a moan out of that slut mouth. You got that?"

She nods again and I smirk, adjusting the temperature of the shower.

"Good girl."

She yelps when the water runs hot and I slap her ass.

"Quiet. Not a fucking word."

She closes her eyes as I run my hand down her naked tits and between her legs.

"You just fucking listen today, Dove. I want to tell you some things and I don't want you fucking interrupting me. So be a good fucktoy and just. *Listen.*"

She nods again and I push two fingers inside her. She struggles against me but doesn't make a sound. Lowering my lips against her ear, I start to whisper.

"You've been teasing me for eleven days. So now I'm going to punish you for all the shit you pulled. By the end of tonight, you're going to swear to me you're mine."

She tenses in my arms, but I pay it no mind, pushing her into the warm water. She resists but doesn't make a peep.

"You proved to yourself you can beat your own demons," I mutter in her ear.

"Now you're going to beat mine. You know what my demons want, little bird? They want your tight little holes. They want to fucking abuse you."

Dove whimpers and I bring my hand down hard on her ass. I can't tell if she's crying with the water running down her face, but my dick decides she is, tightening even more. I position my fingers against Dove's asshole, not pressing in, just letting her know what's about to happen.

She looks at me, petrified as I turn off the shower with my hand still between her legs.

"Put your hands on the tile."

Dove obeys and I slap her thighs apart. She's shivering, dripping with water, and yet her cunt is hot as fuck, ripe for the taking. I position my cock over her puckered hole and twist her wet hair in my fist.

"Look at me. Bend your head back."

Doing what she's told, she whimpers again.

"What did I fucking say about making noises?" I growl into her ear.

"I can't help it," she mewls, and it's as if a dam has opened. "Please, Nox, please, I can't take it, I can't take it, help me, you have to help me."

"Help you?" I laugh against her goose-bumped skin. "I'm only going to make it worse, little bird."

I choose to ignore that she's lost our little game. Her words are turning me on.

I test her asshole with my thumb first, and she gasps when I slide it in. I fuck her like that until her knees shake, then push in another finger. She's moaning my name, shivering uncontrollably. She wants an orgasm, but she won't get one from me, not now. I love to see her suffering too much.

When I pull out of her, Dove whimpers. But my fingers are soon replaced by my cock, and the way it fills her up makes her roll her eyes back. She's so fucking tight. She feels so goddamn good. I never want to leave this tight spot, off limits to anyone else but me. She's my whore. She's always been mine. I just have to convince her of that. Make her submit.

"Beg me then," I whisper in her ear. "Beg me to fuck your filthy slut hole."

"N-Nox," she manages, trembling in my arms. "Fuck me."

"I didn't hear a single please," I hiss, burying my cock deeper to the sound of her moans. "Beg me, little bird. Beg for my fucking cock."

"Please, I... I'll do anything," she admits brokenly, lashes still aflutter. "I'll do anything for your cock, Nox."

"You'll take care of yourself?" I grunt in her ear. "You fucking swear you'll take care of yourself for me?"

"I'll do everything for you," she breathes. "Anything, everything you want."

"You admit it?" I push myself all the way inside her. "You're my whore? You're my property?"

She tenses again, refusing to give me an answer. Her body fights her, her ass clenching around my cock, but the words never come, and she doesn't nod either.

"We'll see," I hiss. "I'll make you say it, my pretty little whore."

"You... you fucked June like this?" she stutters.

I'm so shocked by her words, I stop pushing inside her for a second. "What the fuck?"

"I said, did you fuck June like this?" Her words are filled with venom yet dripping with pain, and she turns her accusing eyes to mine. "I bet you did. I bet you're doing all this to get back at her. You still want her, don't you? You're still in love with her, you still want her, you're still as obsessed with her as you were when we first met! Just fucking admit it, *Parker*!"

"Shut your damn mouth," I grunt, pulling my cock out. "Don't say her name. This is about us. You!"

"Liar," she yells, struggling against me. The claws come out then and she attacks me, digging her long talons into my skin. "You're a fucking liar!"

I grab her by the wrists, making sure to hold her firmly enough so she can't hurt either of us and yet with enough gentleness that I don't leave marks.

"Breathe, little bird," I mutter as the next batch of hot tears slide down her pale cheeks. "Breathe for me, in and out."

"No," she manages, shaking in my arms. I hold her wrists with one hand and open the shower with the other. The moment is over, she doesn't need my cock anymore. She needs me to make her feel whole again.

Gently, I guide her out of the shower. She seems numb now, shaking with her eyes misty. I wrap her in a thick white towel and lead her to the bed. She climbs in without fighting me, pretty eyes focused on anything in the room but me. She can't even look at me. I should've known this would happen.

"Do you want me to go?" I grunt as I tuck her in. "I'll leave you alone, let you breathe."

"No," she whispers, still without looking at me. A silence follows and she toys with the edge of the duvet before finally looking at me. "I'm sorry."

"Why'd you do that?"

"Because..." She shrugs with a shaky smile. "I guess my shrink would say, because I wanted the validation. Seeing you stay after I tried so hard to push you away."

"You really worried about June?" She shrugs again. "I don't give a shit about her, Dove."

"You did back then."

"That was years ago. But you're right," I growl. "I should've realized then that she wasn't the one for me."

"And I am?"

Refusing to answer her question, I pick myself up from her bed.

"Don't go," she calls out after me.

"I got you a present," I mutter. "I'll get it and you wait here. But you need to calm down, so I'll be back in an hour. Don't touch yourself."

"Don't go."

Her eyes fill with tears and she desperately clings to my hand, pulling me back as she sits up in the bed. Everything inside me is screaming at me to leave. Not to let her in, not to let her see my vulnerability. I don't want Dove to know she's my fucking weak spot. I don't want anyone to know that, because they'd sure as fuck use it against me. Especially my little bird.

"Please," she mewls. "Just stay with me. We don't have to talk. Sit by me. Hold my hand."

I want to resist but I can't. Not when I see Dove's hopeful eyes.

I don't fucking love her, I tell myself in my head. It's obsession, not love.

There's a fucking difference.

CHAPTER TWENTY-EIGHT

DOVE

I don't know how long we stay like that on the bed, but Nox holds me close the whole time. I feel the beat of my heart slowly growing steadier, less erratic. Once it returns to a normal pace, I finally start to breathe again, and I'm grateful for every atom of oxygen that fills my tired lungs.

He starts caressing my hair, his palm sliding over my locks to my cheek. I cuddle up against him, my head unable to believe what's happening. But for the time being, I simply accept it, let him in and let myself feel every emotion he's brought out of me in these eleven days of solitude.

"Do you feel better?" Nox asks roughly. I can tell this is hard for him. That giving a shit, showing me he cares, is so difficult for him. I shouldn't be grateful, I should hate him, but my heart melts for the man, nevertheless.

"Yeah," I whisper.

"Good," he grunts. "Then we can move on."

He leaves the bed, leaving a cold spot behind between the sheets. He collects something from a paper bag he brought with him earlier and presents it to me. It's a simple silver chain that's attached to a black leather collar. My heart pounds at the sight.

"What's this for?"

"For you," he smirks. "if you're a good girl."

"What do I have to do for it?"

"Obey me."

It sounds so simple yet my whole body wants to resist him. I don't want to give in to his demands. I don't want to admit he owns me, as true as we both know it is.

Without saying another word, Nox tightens the collar around my throat. The weight of it feels so good around my neck, I fight the urge to moan, turning my face to the side so my captor won't see me blushing.

"Are you going to be a good girl and do as I say?" He tips my chin back, making me look at him. "Maybe then I'll finally let you have my fucking cock..."

"Please," I manage.

"Answer me."

"I've been good."

"Not good enough," he hisses, tugging on my collar. "Give me more."

I shake my head wordlessly. A part of me is hoping I'll elicit a reaction from him, and I get what I want.

"You remember how obsessed you used to be with me?" Nox whispers in my ear, taunting me. "How much you craved my attention, my affection? You would've done anything for me. You practically begged me for that pretty memento you wear on your cheek..."

I swallow, unable to reply. The part of me that truly believes all this is falling for his cruel, malicious words. I'm succumbing to his old charm just like I always fucking do. I want him. I need this. I want him to use me.

"You wanted to be perfect," he keeps going. "So obsessed with looking like my stepsister... Blonde, pretty, a perfect Barbie doll. You know how much more beautiful you are now?"

His fingers tighten around my throat as I whimper and shake my head.

"Every man that sees you on the street wants a piece of that tight little ass. They all fantasize about you, little bird. Burrowing their thick cocks in your holes... but they're all mine, aren't they? You're not going to let anyone else have them, are you, Dove?"

I manage a wordless moan and he smirks at me, his finger gliding over my cheek, over the scar he gave me. I fucking hate the man and yet I can't resist his sweet abuse.

"You were so empty back then, little bird," he goes on. "So full of nothing. You're different now. You're not whole anymore. I broke you. You're not just an empty doll from a magazine cover. You're my beautiful, broken toy."

I shiver beneath his touch. My body longs for him to claim me, even though my mind is still fighting the truth. But he's done so much for me. He's fixed me. I'm confident I can make it now, even if he disappears again. It would break my heart, but it wouldn't destroy me. Nothing can destroy me now.

"Do you want a choice?" Nox whispers in my ear. "Is that what you want, little bird? For me to let you have your wings?"

"Please," I whisper needily as he lets go of the chain leash. I don't know what I'm asking for and I'm not sure Nox does either. But he lets the chain fall and takes a few steps back. I miss him already, my chest tightening as I watch him leave. He walks to the door and unlocks it, leaving it wide open.

"You can go if you like," he nods toward the hallway. My heart speeds up, wondering if he'll let me go or take my choice away at the very last minute again. "You're free, little bird. I won't keep you caged any longer. If you want to walk away from me, this is your chance."

My mind wants me to fight this. To beg him to keep me. But my body has different plans. I pull myself up from the bed, toying with the loose leash around my throat. I sink to my knees and keep my gaze trained on the floor, too ashamed to look at him. Wordlessly, I hand him the leash, my hands trembling as I wait for him to take it.

He doesn't.

"Say it."

"What?" I demand, looking up at him with a fiery expression.

"Say you're mine."

"I'm..." I struggle to say what he wants.

"Say it, or I'm making you leave."

"I'm yours." My eyes burn with hatred as they meet his. "Please."

"Not enough." My expression is mirrored in his dark gaze. "Tell me you're property. My fucking property."

"I'm..." I swallow thickly, closing my eyes so I don't have to look at him and face the humiliation of our conversation. "I'm your property, Nox."

"Look at me."

I shake my head wordlessly, eyes still closed. But he kneels on the floor next to me, gripping my face in his hands. "Look at me, little bird, I want you to fucking mean it."

My eyes fly open despite my instincts screaming at me not to do it. "I hate you."

"No, you don't. Now say it. Make me fucking believe it."

"I'm yours."

"Not fucking buying it," he growls. "Fucking convince me, Dove. Or I'm making you leave."

"P-Please." His words send a jolt of fear down my spine. "Don't make me go. I'll be good."

"Then *say it*." His fingers glide over my scar. "Last chance, little bird. You want me to let you go?"

I shake my head, fighting back tears.

"Tell me then."

"Don't let me go," I blurt. "Don't make me leave."

"Why not, Dove?"

"Because I'm yours, I belong with you."

"You're mine?"

I nod brokenly. "I'm your toy."

"What's mine?" he grunts, fingers traveling over my chest and pinching my already hard nipples. "Are these pretty tits mine?"

"Yes," I whisper.

"And what about this?" he traces his fingers over my lips. "Mine?"

"Yours."

His hand wanders down over my navel, barely brushing over my pussy, driving me crazy. "And this?"

"Yours, it's all yours."

"Beg me."

"What?" I turn my fiery eyes to his.

"Beg me to keep you. Degrade yourself."

"Why?"

"Because it gets me hard as fuck," he hisses. "And I'm done asking, Dove. Show me what a good girl you can be."

"P-Please. Keep me."

"More."

"Keep me as your prisoner," I whisper brokenly. "Don't ever let me go. I want to be yours. I don't want anyone else. Keep me, Nox. I want to be your... property."

"You already are." He grabs the chain and tugs on it. "You know what you just did, don't you, Dove?"

"I..." I avoid his gaze, unable to handle its weight. "Please. I want to be yours."

"I know you do, but now that you said it, I'm never letting you forget it." He tugs on the chain, smirking at my crestfallen expression. "Starting to realize what you did, aren't you, Dove? You know I'm never going to let you go again? You belong to me now. Forget about your little boyfriend. Forget about ever looking at another man that way again. You're my property now, and I don't let my property lust after anyone but me."

He tugs on the chain until I get up. He walks me over to the plants and my heartbeat speeds up yet again as I face the plant with the unfurling leaf.

"You're going to grow for me, just like that," Nox whispers in my ear. "You're going to be a good girl for me and heal, so I can abuse you all over again. Say it."

"I'll be a good girl for you," I whisper, the words barely registering though I believe them fully. "I'll do anything you want, Nox. I'll be so good for you, I won't disappoint you ever again, please..."

"What are you begging for, little bird?" He spins me around so I'm looking at him. That's when it really hits me, all of it.

How long I've been alone in here.

How much I crave the touch I've denied myself for a full decade.

How desperate I am for Nox to fuck me.

"Your cock," I find myself saying. Nox smirks at me.

"You want me to fuck you, Dove?"

"Y-Yes."

"It's been so long, hasn't it?"

"S-So long," I manage. "Please, please let me have it."

"Are you desperate enough for me?"

"I've never been more needy," I admit, my voice breaking.

"Get on the fucking bed," Nox growls. "Spread your legs as wide as you fucking can."

I scramble onto the bed, the chain links making clanking noises as I do what he tells me. I spread my legs, guiltily remembering the teasing I put him through these eleven days, fucking myself when he couldn't, showing off everything he couldn't have. Something tells me I'm about to get punished for disobeying him, that he's going to put me in my place. My hopes soar in excitement.

"Show me your cunt."

Nox's order should make me feel shy, but it doesn't. Feeling wanton and daring, I spread my pussy lips, watching him closely for a reaction. He doesn't disappoint, a grin pulling at his lips as I uncover my innermost center for him.

"Such a pretty fucking pussy. Touch it. Fuck it for me."

My fingers slide inside my wet little hole and a moan escapes my lips as I start to bring myself closer to an inevitable release. I could come already. Skirting this close to the edge makes me scared and yet I can't fucking stop myself, I have to keep going.

"That's right, such a good whore. Keep fucking that pretty cunt. Show me what's mine. Show me what I'm going to take tonight."

My teeth dig into my bottom lip as I bring myself closer and closer. My orgasm is imminent, waiting for me at the tip of my fingers yet so very far away, because I already know he won't make it that easy.

"Take your fingers out."

I do. The wetness makes an embarrassing sound and I flinch, flushing fiercely as I realize just how exposed I am for him.

Nox approaches me, eyes darkened with desire as they meet mine. "You want to come, little bird? You want my cock inside you, bringing you that orgasm you've dreamed of for years?"

"Y-Yes," I manage.

"Beg."

"Please fuck me."

"Beg more."

"Please, Nox, I can't take it," I struggle to get out. "Just fuck me, make me come, make me your whore, I'll be so good for you, I'll do it all for you, I'll never let you down again."

"That's right," he mutters. He looks almost crazed now and I've never been more attracted to him. "You're my property now, Dove. And I'm not done claiming you yet."

CHAPTER TWENTY-NINE

NOX

She's never looked more beautiful than right now, overwhelmed with need and desire.

"You want me to fuck you?" I ask her, and she nods eagerly. "Tell me I own you."

Dove swallows thickly, but the words seem to roll off her tongue with ease now that she's admitted it to herself. "You own me, Nox."

"Good girl." I allow my fingertips to glide over the scar marring her face. "There's one last thing we need to do before I fuck you. Are you ready?"

She nods blindly, not even caring enough to ask me what her final task is. I smirk as I pull the pocketknife out. I hand it to her, careful not to cut her with the blade, and Dove turns her quizzical gaze to mine.

"What's this?"

"You want to be mine, Dove?" I grunt. "I want you to get back at me for what I did to you."

"What do you mean?"

I trace my fingertips over my cheek, mirroring the puckered scar on her face. "Right here. You're going to cut me."

Her hand holding the knife shakes, but she doesn't let go. "I'm not going to hurt you."

"Why not?" I smirk. "How many times have you thought about it, little bird? Getting back at me. Doing the same thing I did to you. Hurting me. Now's your fucking chance. I won't give you another one."

She seems lost in thought. I knew this would go one of two ways – either she'd be eager and willing from the get-go, or she'd need a while to come around to the idea. But I decided I wanted this when I first saw how my scar had changed her life. It'll be the perfect way to show people she's my property. And I want to pay for what I did to her. Of course, it's not the main reason I'm doing all this. I'm doing it so Dove can grow as a person.

"You don't want to?" I ask and she shakes her head, staring at the knife in her hands while her bottom lip trembles. "But think about how good it would feel, little bird. Getting that revenge... hurting me like I hurt you. Don't you want to ruin my life, Dove?"

"I..." Her words are shaky as they come out. "I don't want to hurt anyone."

"You hurt yourself," I hiss. "You hurt yourself all the time. But you won't, not anymore. Now every time you want to cut into your skin, you're going to cut me instead. We'll see how quickly we break that nasty little habit of yours."

"P-Please," she manages, her voice breaking. "I don't want to do this."

"Are you sure?" I taunt her. "Are you absolutely fucking sure you don't want this, Dove? I thought you'd be eager to punish me. After all, you hate me so fucking much, don't you?"

"I..." She's getting confused. I can practically see the cogs turning in her brain as she tries to come to terms with her own thoughts. "I do hate you."

"Then fucking cut me." I kneel down next to her, grab her hand holding the knife by the wrist and gently press it against my cheek. "It would be so easy, Dove. You can take it all out on me, I won't punish you for it. I'll reward you. Now fucking cut me."

"N-No," she shakes her head vehemently, but I force her hand to dig the knife's tip into my skin. "No, Nox!"

"Yes." I grin at her through the pain. "Do it. Think of what I did to you. Think of how I ruined your life. All the things you missed out on, because of me. What I did. How I wrecked you. Ruined you. Took everything from you. You didn't want it, did you, Dove? Now is your fucking chance. Get back at me, little bird."

She lets out a yelp and pulls her hand back. The knife clatters to the floor and a droplet of blood runs down my cheek.

"Pathetic," I tell her. "You can't even bring yourself to hurt the man that took everything away from you, can you, Dove?"

"Yes, I can," she hisses. "I can. I will. I can."

"Promises, promises," I smirk. "So full of it, Dove. But I'm not buying your bullshit. You're gonna have to try fucking harder."

"I hate you."

"I know you do. So, take the knife."

Her eyes go to the bloodied blade on the floor. With shaky fingers she picks it back up and glares at me.

"I'm just trying to help you, Dove," I say, with a gentler tone. "I'm trying to help you heal and get better for me, so you can continue being an excellent slut."

"P-Please."

"Don't be weak right now," I demand. "Come here."

She comes closer, holding the knife in her shaky fingers. "I don't want to hurt you."

"You have to," I tell her, gentler than I thought I was capable of being. "It'll help you deal with everything that's happened. Place the blade on my cheek."

She raises a trembling hand and rests the cool blade against my cheek.

"Good girl. See how well you obey? I need you to listen to me, Dove. I need you to hurt me. I need you to cut me. I want us to wear matching scars for the rest of our lives. I want everyone to know we did this to each other."

"You're sick," she whispers, but I don't reply. And when her eyes find mine, I know everything I can't put into words is staring back at her. I can only hope she's strong enough to go through with what she must do to find some closure from the fucked up shit I've done to her.

"Please, Dove." I never fucking beg, and the words feel alien on my tongue. "Cut me. I want to be like you."

She lets out the smallest whimper. Her fingers go to her own scar, touching the surface, as if trying to memorize the exact way I cut her. I'm about to speak again, encourage her to do it, but she doesn't need it. The blade sinks into my skin, tearing at it.

"Good girl," I hiss through the pain. She looks strong right now, not like the fearful little girl I've got her pegged as. "Keep going. Make me look like you."

She doesn't say a word. I can tell she's concentrating now, focusing solely on her fucked up little task. The knife hurts as it carves me, but I'm too turned on to pay it any mind. She doesn't stop. When it's over, the bloody knife clatters to the ground once more and she covers her mouth with her palm, unable to believe what she's just done.

"That felt good, didn't it?" I hiss, ignoring the searing pain in my cheek. "You got back at me now, Dove. We don't owe each other anymore. Now I can use you as hard as I fucking want without any repercussions, isn't that right, little bird?"

"I can't b-believe I-I did that," she stutters, closing her eyes firmly.

"Look at me," I demand. "Look at what you did. I deserve this, Dove. You had to get back at me. I know how good it feels, I've been there too, little bird. Let it fill you. Let it overtake you."

"No, please," she whispers, my weak little bird once more.

I take hold of her shoulders and push her up against the wall, caging her body with mine. I can feel blood running over my face and down my neck, but I don't give a shit.

"I'm going to fuck you now," I tell her. "I'm going to hurt that pussy until you never have a doubt about who it belongs to ever again."

"Please." She sounds so fucking broken. I can't wait to make it worse.

"Tell me how much you loved it," I taunt her. "I know I did. Cutting into your face made me so goddamn hard. Not because it hurt you. Because I knew you'd think of me every single time you saw your reflection. You can never escape me, Dove. Never. I'll always be here..."

I tap my fingers against her temples and she looks up at me, no longer the timid, intimidated Dove Canterbury she was when I first brought her in here.

"I loved it," she whispers. "I fucking love seeing you bleed."

I crush my lips against hers the moment those words leave her mouth. I kiss her hard, my blood smearing her face, punishing her for every second we were separated. My cock hardens between us, throbbing, pressing against her with a silent demand to be noticed, to be touched. She doesn't ignore it. Her trembling fingers find their way to my zipper and belt, pulling, freeing my cock. She gasps when she wraps her palm around it, jerking me hard and fast until I'm groaning her name, ready to fucking burst.

"Not yet," I tell her roughly. "I'm going to fuck you first. You want that cock inside you, don't you?"

"Yes," she nods eagerly, burning desire in her eyes. "I want you to fuck me, I want you to give me everything, I want it all, Nox."

"Fuck, little bird." I grab her by the waist and she shrieks as I carry her back to the bed. I lay her down gently and kneel between her legs. She's still fucking naked and I've never been more tempted in my life. I'll fuck her soon, but not before I taste the sweet sugar of her cunt.

I start licking her, filling my mouth with her taste as it mixes with the metallic taste of my own blood. She's a moaning, whimpering mess in seconds. I know how to eat a girl out, and my favorite toy is about to realize she's never had it better.

Burrowing my face between her creamy thighs, I get my fill of her essence until she's gasping for breath as much as I am.

"Please," she begs. "Please, fuck me! I can't take this, it's torture."

With a grunt, I pull myself to my knees. I place my cock on her belly, just to show her how deep inside I'm going to go. "See that, little bird? My cock's too fucking big for you. Are you going to cry for me?"

A couple of drops of blood fall on her perfect skin and she shivers. "Yes. I'll cry. I'll do anything you fucking want."

"You better mean it, little bird."

I take hold of her legs and lift them, parting them wide, my cock throbbing at the sight of her blood-stained pussy. With one long push, I sink my cock balls deep inside her drippy little cunt. She gasps when I do, but it soon turns into a moan as I start rocking my hips inside her, making her wetter and wetter with each thrust of my powerful hips. God, I could spend an eternity doing this, torturing her. She feels so damn good on my cock. Dove is so beautiful when she's falling apart.

"I can't," she whispers brokenly. "I need to come."

"No fucking coming," I hiss. "Not yet. Not until you're ripe for it."

She whimpers as my hand finds her throat. Clenching my fist around her swan-like neck feels so fucking good I almost burst on the goddamn spot. I could fill her right now. Pump her full of my seed, not giving a shit that she's not on protection. Just fuck my cum so deep inside her we'll both know she's pregnant by the time I'm done.

I want to.

But I want her to beg for it first.

"You want it like this?" I ask her. "Raw, without anything between us? Is that what you want, Dove?"

"Yes," she begs. "Please, that's what I want, keep going, keep fucking me."

"Sick little bitch," I grunt. "You loved hurting me, didn't you?"

"You deserved it," she admits.

"Fuck yes." I pump inside her harder, losing all inhibition as I get closer and closer, but pull back before it's too late.

No way am I letting myself come yet.

I'm going to keep torturing my little bird.

That's what she was made for, after all.

CHAPTER THIRTY

DOVE

He's fucking me like this is his mission on the planet – to make me submit using his hands, his voice and his cock, and nothing fucking else. I'm a mess in seconds, still reeling from what he made me do to him. The wound on his face is dripping with blood and I know it needs stitches, but neither of us is stopping to get him to a hospital.

I'm almost feverish with desire. Overtaken with all those feelings I fought to keep out for fucking years. Nothing matters right now, everything other than Nox forgotten and pushed to the side. I don't think about Sam. I don't think about Robin's disappearance. All I can focus on is the cock punishing me for every minute we spent apart, driving into me with a punishing force that threatens to rip me up from the inside.

"Please, Nox," I whisper. "Please don't stop."

"Wouldn't dream of it, little bird. Keep taking it like a good fucking slut. Spread your legs wider for me."

I do as I'm told, ignoring the pain from having my thighs spread so wide my muscles hurt. Nothing matters but being his good little whore, submitting to him in every way he wants and giving him everything he desires. I want to be nothing more than a fuckdoll. An object he uses to fuel his desire, a fleshlight for him to fuck, a blow-up doll he can use and abuse any time and any way he fucking wants to.

His cock is impossibly hard inside me, tightening while I clench. I can feel the veins throbbing, making him harder than I thought possible. It's been so long since I felt Parker Miller inside me. But this isn't him. This is Nox. And Nox doesn't love June. Nox only sees me.

Getting lost in the carnage of the situation, I allow my eyes to roll back and my body to submit to his every wicked desire. I want so much more but I force myself to grit my teeth and stop fucking begging. I accept his rewards and his punishments together, my body letting him in, even when my mind refuses to do so.

He's stretching me so bad it hurts. I've never had a cock like his, this big, this fucking demanding. He's going to tear me apart and there's absolutely nothing I can do to stop him.

And I don't even want him to stop...

Crazed thoughts enter my mind and I dig my nails into his back, scratching, hissing his name as he continues to fuck me mercilessly.

"I missed your cock so much," I whisper, unable to help myself. "I missed it inside me, missed it fucking me..."

"It missed you too," Nox grunts. "I'm not letting anyone else have this pussy. You got that, little bird? All your holes are mine. If I see someone else ogle you, I'm going to fucking kill them."

"You're crazy," I breathe. "You're so fucking sick and twisted..."

"If you think that's going to stop me, you're fucking wrong," he roars, plunging his cock deep inside me and making me cry out in pain. "That's right, I want it to fucking hurt you, little bird. I want your cunt sore and desperate for my cum to soothe it. That's what you want, isn't it?"

"Y-Yes," I admit readily as blood from his face drips onto my tits. My head is too fucked to start wondering how fucked up all this is. I want him. I want to come on his cock. I want to be filled with his seed. I want to be dripping with his cum. I want to dip my fingers in and lick every drop he pumps inside me. "Give it to me, Nox. I want it, I'll do anything."

"Keep begging," he grunts. "I want to hear your sweet voice..."

"Please, Nox." My voice keeps fucking breaking and I flush deeply, realizing how embarrassing it is. Yet still, I continue, "Please, keep fucking me, fill me, give me everything, I want it all."

He growls and pulls me closer, sliding my body down until my legs wrap around his hips. He grabs my ass and continues to pound me while I close my eyes and shiver under the pressure of what we've done.

I'm fucking the psycho stalker who's been abusing me since I was eighteen years old. I've let him have it all, my orgasms, my life, my fucking dignity. And the worst part is, I never want him to give it back. I'm his property now – fully his. For ever.

"Fill me please," I beg desperately. "Give it to me, I don't want to wait any longer."

"Not done," he replies with a grunt. "You sound so pretty when you beg, but you need to shut the fuck up."

"Please, Nox, I –" I don't get to finish my words because he covers my mouth with his hand, pressing down hard.

"Don't talk. Shut up. Let me fuck you. I want to watch you struggle."

Every sentence that leaves his lips is like a nail in my coffin. I feel like I'm going to fall apart. But I still don't want him to stop. Even though my body knows this is bad, I don't want it to ever end. It's too addicting, getting lost in his abuse. Bending to his will. I don't want this to ever, ever end.

He grabs my legs by the ankles and holds them up. He pulls out, watching my pussy drip on the sheets before plunging his cock inside me yet again. I can feel him hitting my cervix with every thrust, hurting me so much I nearly pass out from the pain.

And yet I still don't want him to stop.

"Beg for my load," he hisses. "Beg for me to breed you, little bird."

His words take my breath away. I gasp for air but there's none there. My legs fall down uselessly when he lets go and whips me around into a doggy position. He forces my head back until I'm looking up at him, grabbing my hair with one hand and smacking my ass with the other.

"Beg for it, little bird!"

"P-Please," I manage, shocked by the impact of his hand as he smacks me again. "Please! Fill me!"

"Keep going, not good enough."

I groan in frustration. I want to rip my hair out. I want to fucking hurt him.

The blood from his cut drips down on my face. I push my tongue out and lick it. It tastes metallic, like iron. I feel so fucked up, so needy, I'm going to fucking come soon.

He fists my hair tight and pummels me hard and fast and my body is rocked by an orgasm I can't fight. I yell his name and he smacks my ass while I'm coming, over and over again and in the same spot, making sure I'm going to fucking bruise. He doesn't stop fucking me either. My pussy clenches, impossibly tight around his swollen dick and ready to milk every last drop of his seed.

"You want it?" he growls in my ear. "You want your slutty cunt filled with my cum? You want me to come right into your fucking cervix? You wanna be pregnant, little bird?"

All I can do is whimper and cry.

"Fucking answer me!"

"Please, yes," I whisper. "I want your baby. I want you. I want everything. Don't let me go."

"Never," he growls, grasping my throat and looking deep into my eyes as he pushes in one final time. "Take it."

I could cry from the pain of him being inside me fully. It feels like he's stretching me impossibly, making my pussy take so much more than it could possibly handle. I feel his cock throb. I feel the first spurt of cum inside me and I whimper his name as more and more follow. He's not moving, just letting my cunt clench and milk his cock. His eyes roll back and he smirks, my name a dying whisper on his lips.

I don't know how long it takes for him to stop coming. It feels like he's painting my cunt from the inside with his warm cum, and somehow, despite the pain, I feel happy, taken care of... and relieved.

Once he's done, I collapse on the bed and he pulls out. My shaky hand goes between my legs, cupping the seed that runs out. Deliriously, I bring my hand to my face and suck my fingers until there's not a trace left.

"You're such a good girl," Nox mutters, pulling me into his embrace. "I fucking love hurting you."

He holds me close, lips nuzzling my neck and hair as I start to sob. Once it begins, there's no way I can stop, and sobs rack my body, making me shake with the intensity of the orgasm he just gave me.

Nox doesn't offer comforting words and doesn't try to make it better. But his lips find mine, and he kisses me, proving to me yet again how very weak I am for him. His fingers absentmindedly find their way between my legs, toying with my clit, pushing his cum deeper inside me.

We stay like that for a long time, until I finally stop crying. Once he pulls back, I feel the loss of him and it fucking hurts.

"You need to get dressed," he tells me. "We're leaving."

"What?" I sit up in the bed. "Where are we going?"

"We need to go to my motel room and decide what's going to happen next. Where we'll live. Shit like that."

"You think we're going to live together?" I scoff.

"Won't we?"

I ponder his words and press my lips together, unwilling to give Nox an answer. To be honest, after this, I don't see my life without him. I don't think I can survive without Nox. I don't *want* to survive without Nox.

"Okay," I whisper.

He hands me his shirt and a pair of shorts. They're both too big on me, and the scars on my legs and arms are painfully visible. But I'm past the point of caring. My heart beats with trepidation and excitement, eager for our next chapter to begin.

We arrive at the motel a while later. The receptionist gives me a nasty look when Nox guides me to his room.

"What the fuck happened to your face?" she asks Nox as we pass, but he doesn't bother with an answer, just pulls me along, down the hallway and away from prying eyes. She calls out after us, but we both ignore her. "You need stitches or that's going to leave a nasty scar!"

The moment the door is closed, he rips my clothes off my body and admires me with a smirk on his handsome face.

"You need to clean your face," I whisper, and he nods.

"There's a first-aid kit in the bathroom. Get it, you'll clean me up."

I nearly trip over myself on the way to the bathroom. My heart is fucking pounding. I'm still trying to come to terms with everything that's happened. I can't believe I'm right back where I started. I tried so hard to run away from him, but I should've known I'd never be able to escape Nox.

I dig in the medicine cabinet in the bathroom but don't find anything. I check the storage closet next, but there's nothing there either. I exit the room to find Nox gone. I sit on the bed with an exasperated sigh.

There's something behind the pillows.

I lift one of them and furrow my brows when I see the offending piece of fabric. It's a gray hoodie, and it's stained with blood. The Columbia college logo is on it.

I've seen this hoodie.

I know this hoodie.

Dread settles in my stomach just as I hear Nox's keys turning in the lock.

"Got one from the reception," he grunts. "Realized we didn't have one here, and..."

His eyes find mine and he sees what I'm holding. The moment stretches into for ever. I can't believe this is happening. With a sickening crunch, I've landed back in reality.

And life will never be the same again.

CHAPTER THIRTY-ONE

NOX

"**W**hat the fuck is this?"

My mind is fucking racing. My eyes are glued to what she's holding. I'm doing damage control in my mind already, but my mouth won't open and say the words. I just need to explain. I can explain. I can get out of this.

"Is this my brother's?" Dove tosses the blood-stained hoodie at me. "Answer me! Is this Robin's?"

"Dove, I..." I raise my hands in the air defensively. How the fuck do I start? What the fuck do I say? I'm a terrible fucking liar. The truth is written all over my goddamn face. "I can explain."

"Explain, then," she hisses, glaring at me. If looks could kill, hers would've incinerated me. "Explain what you're doing with the hoodie my brother was last seen in, and explain why it's bloody!"

I can't answer her. I try to force myself, but the truth won't come out. I just stand there as she comes at me with her fists. She hammers them into my chest, punching, hissing my name, telling me I'm a monster.

"Explain!" she screams. "Explain it, right the fuck now! There has to be an explanation, right Nox? There must be a reason. You didn't do it. You didn't!"

"I'm sorry, Dove," I mutter.

"Sorry for what?" she growls. "Sorry for what, you fucking monster? Are you such a fucked up killer that you kept this... as some sick memento? Or as a reminder of what you are?"

I don't know why I kept it, so I don't answer her. She takes a step back and looks at me as if this is the first time she's seeing me. Seeing the monster my father saw when he beat me, when he put the scars on my back. Dove shakes her head, runs her fingers through that dark mane of hair, whispering, muttering something I don't quite understand.

"He's gone," she says. "He's gone. Robin's gone. You killed him. You took him away from me. You did this. You did this. You. Fucking. Did. This!"

I can't answer her. We both know it's true now. The hoodie is in my hands and she snatches it away from me, holding it up to her nose, inhaling the scent. When she pulls her hand back, her face is smeared with blood.

"You don't deserve it. You don't deserve a memory of him. You don't deserve to say his fucking name."

"Dove, I'm fucking sorry," I get out. "I thought I had to do it, I –"

"Don't give me your bullshit fucking reasons!" She's a banshee, one moment crying into the hoodie, the next discarding it to claw at me. I don't stop her. I feel like I have no right. "I don't want to know! I don't want you to tell me it's my fucking fault, my fault he's gone, because of you! Your sick, twisted fucking obsession with me made you do this! It's my fault! My fault he's gone, my fault, my fucking fault..."

She slumps to the floor. She's a mess, her makeup smudged, her hair ruffled, her eyes wild. My little bird is so fucking beautiful.

"You're a monster," she whispers. "I made you do this. He's gone. Robin's gone because of me."

I don't tell her it's not true, because technically, it fucking is.

I'm a cold man. Dove Canterbury is the only person I feel for. But I can't console her now. I did what I had to do. I did it so we could be together. I did it so she'd finally fucking realize she loved me. And it motherfucking worked.

"Whatever I tell you now, you're going to hate me more," I say calmly. "Let's talk about this when you feel better."

"Are you fucking kidding me?" She gets up and looks at me the way my father did. With pure disgust. "I'm leaving. I can't even look at you. You make me fucking sick."

She tries to walk past me to get to the door, but I take her by the forearm. She thrashes wildly so I let go, but block her way. "Let me make it better."

"Better?" she spits out. "You can't make a murder better. Are you turning yourself in?"

"What?" I shake my head. "No, of course not. I need to be with you. Take care of you."

"Then I want nothing to do with you." She walks past me and opens the door.

"Don't, little bird."

"Don't you dare fucking call me that," she hisses over her shoulder.

"You wanna make this hard on me?" I advance on her and slam the door closed. She glares and screams in frustration when I grab her, throwing her over my shoulder. "I'll make you fucking stay. I'll make you never leave me again."

I let her down on the bed. I hold her down with one hand and grab some rope from the nightstand with the other. My heart is fucking pounding in disbelief. But I have to do this, I don't have a choice. I can't let her get away from me. I can't lose Dove again.

I tie up her ankles and her wrists. She doesn't say a word, just stares at the ceiling. Once I'm done, I take a step back to admire her. No matter what, she's so fucking beautiful. One day she'll understand. I'll make her.

"I'll keep you like this as long as I fucking have to," I tell her. "Until you agree with me."

"I don't care," she whispers. "I don't fucking care anymore. You've broken me. I'm... I'm nothing anymore."

"Don't say that, little bird." I gently touch her cheek. It takes a lot of effort for me not to hurt her, because my body wants to abuse something beautiful, and she's the one I want to hurt most.

"Don't touch me," she whispers, tears gliding down her cheeks. "Don't touch me, please."

I pull my hand back. Usually, I wouldn't give a shit, but her pain is so fucking intense I can feel it, searing my bones. I feel bad for her, but not for what I did. It needed to be done. Means to an end. Anything so we can be together at the end of this.

"Dove, you'll get over this," I mutter. "You have to."

She doesn't say another word. A silent tear rolls down her cheek as she stares at the ceiling. I don't know what to do with myself, so I just fucking stare at her. I still think she's beautiful. Stunning. Perfect. I know I can make her think I'm perfect, too. She just needs to come to terms with that.

"You love me," I mutter. "You told me you love me. Remember, Dove?"

She shakes her head, "You didn't even say it back."

"You know I don't believe in that bullshit," I smirk.

"It's not. It's what normal people do, Nox," she whispers. "It's what I need. What I want. What you aren't capable of."

"You know how much I fucking want you," I hiss.

"It's not the same." Her voice breaks, and she keeps repeating it over and over again like a mantra. "It's not the same. It's not the same. It's not the same."

"Dove, do you want me to fuck you?" I sit next to her on the bed, my hands roaming her skin. "I'll make it better. Let me show you how much I need you. Let me own that body."

She laughs, cries, laughs some more. I don't stop touching her. But it's different now. Her skin's cold.

"I need to pee," she whispers.

"Swear to me you won't run."

"I won't."

I untie her and stand in the bathroom while she pees. She doesn't object, doesn't say a word. She just stares ahead while she does it, eyes blank, staring into nothing. After, she walks back to the room. She stares out of the window. It's raining.

"I want to go home," she manages.

"I can't let you go home."

"Then you'll have to kill me, too."

"Don't fucking say shit like that," I growl, standing behind her. I can smell her. Sweet roses and soapy skin. "I need you, Dove. I'm not spending another day of my life without you."

I lay a hand on her shoulder and she shivers.

"Every time you touch me," she begins. "I'll remember him. Every time I look at you, I'll know he's the last thing you saw. Every time I say your name, I'll remember you killed him because of me. You took something precious. You didn't just kill Robin. You killed me too."

"Dove..."

"No." She turns around to face me. "Every time you try to kiss me, I'll resist you. Every time you lay your fingers on me, I'll make myself sick after. And every time you put your cock near me, I'm going to hurt myself. Can you live with that, Nox?"

"I won't fucking let you."

"If you really want to stop me, you'll have to kill me, too."

"Dove, don't be fucking ridiculous," I grunt. "I'm going to take care of you, little bird."

She doesn't say another word. Her gaze wanders off into nothing and she just stares ahead. I touch her. I talk to her. She lets me walk her to the bed. She cries while I kiss her. I can't do this. I fucking can't.

"You don't want me anymore?" I whisper in her ear. She doesn't respond. She just keeps crying.

It's getting light outside and we haven't slept. She looks pale as a ghost and somehow sickly green at the same time.

"Let me fix it," I say. "Let me make it better. Let me make it right."

She doesn't say a word.

"Fuck." I get up. I have to use the bathroom, but I'm nervous about her leaving if I do. I leave the door open and take a piss but she doesn't try to run. She just paces the room.

When I come back though, Dove's holding a pair of scissors like a fucking weapon.

"Don't, Dove," I mutter. "You don't want to hurt yourself again, do you?"

"This is the last time you're going to see me."

"What the fuck?" I growl.

"If I ever see you again, Nox, I'm going to the cops and telling them what you did to Robin."

"Dove, don't." I rush to her. She waves the scissors but I don't let her intimidate me. I don't give a shit if she cuts me. I just want to convince her to stay. "I'll make it right. I'll do everything. Anything."

She just keeps shaking her head, her hand trembling. The scissors clatter to the floor. I don't try to move closer.

"I need to leave," she whispers. "I mean it, Nox. I can't forgive you. I'll never forgive you. If I see you again, you will pay."

"Dove, let me change your mind."

"No!" she roars this time. "No, you've taken fucking enough from me. I'm done letting you steal my life. My people. I'm done with you. Done."

"But Dove, I..." I bite my lower lip. Fuck. Can I even fucking say it? Will it make a difference now? I've known it for a long time. "Dove, I love you."

"It doesn't matter," she admits brokenly. "I don't love you. Stay away, or else."

She backs away. There's so much fucking fire in those beautiful eyes. Dark, resilient, angry fire. She's going to be okay. She's going to get through this. But she'll do it without me.

As for me, I'm not sure how I'll survive the hurricane that just came in and ruined my goddamn life.

The last memory I have of Dove Canterbury is her slamming the motel room door closed on me and leaving me the shell of a man I used to be. She even takes the hoodie. She has evidence against me now. She really could turn me in.

And yet my first thought isn't how to get over the woman whose life I've ruined. No, it isn't – because I'm sick, and I can't help myself, and I'm already fucking plotting how to stalk her until she gets over this. Until she changes her mind.

She has to.

CHAPTER THIRTY-TWO

DOVE

I don't know how I find my way home after everything at the motel. I'm in a delirious trance, bumping into people as tears stream down my face. My heart is pounding, my head heavy with disbelief and the shocking discovery I made today. Nox is a monster. A cruel, vicious monster.

I know he thinks he did this to help me. But he's destroyed my very soul. I already know I can never forgive him for what happened. I'll never forget what he took away from me.

Getting home, I slam the front door closed and fall to my knees. Now that I'm finally separated from him, I can see things clearly. I can see Nox for the monster he truly is. The deviant who's killed and hurt people to get to me. The stalker who kidnapped me and held me captive to fulfill his sick, twisted fantasy. And I almost fell for it.

Almost.

In a trance, I walk over to where my handbag lies discarded on the coffee table. I dig out my phone and plug it in to recharge the battery. Once the screen lights up, the pings never stop.

Text messages, calls, video calls. The soup kitchen, the plant nursery, and one number that stands out from the rest. I thought I had nobody left, but Raphael is here to prove me wrong. He's texted, called. The last text was only thirty minutes ago. He hasn't forgotten about me. He's worried about me. Unlike Nox, he wants to take care of me.

With shaky fingers, I hold my phone and stare at the last message he sent. He said he's coming over to the house again to check up on me. Fear squeezes my chest tight. That was thirty minutes ago. He'll be here any second. But am I brave enough to see him? I can never tell him what happened, I already know that. I'm not going to start a witch hunt against Nox, as much as what he did has destroyed me.

His punishment will mean nothing to me unless Nox himself is the one to seek it out.

He needs to realize he must repent for what he's done.

Until then, I'm done with the sick bastard.

The doorbell rings and I pick myself up from the couch robotically, stumbling over to the front door. I take a deep breath and open the door.

"Dove!" Raphael makes a move to embrace me but I take a step back, avoiding his inquisitive gaze. "Where were you, Dove?"

"Doesn't matter," I say, my voice devoid of emotion. "I'm back now. Not going anywhere again."

"I was so worried. Why won't you look at me?"

I close my eyes firmly, counting to five. Then, I open them and look at Raphael, the man who's only ever tried to help me since the very first day I met him. And yet I betrayed him. I chose the monster lurking in the shadows instead of Raphael. And now I'm paying for that awful mistake.

"Thank you," Raphael mutters. His dark eyes spark with worry and desire. There are so many things I wish I could tell him, but I'm uselessly tongue-tied, unable to broach the subject of my disappearance. "Can I come in?"

"Yeah," I nod, stepping aside to let him in. I've opened some windows but the air in here is still stale. My flowers and plants are desperately in need of water.

I put the coffee pot on and busy myself by watering the plants. I don't say anything and neither does Raphael. He just follows me as I move through the house, as if watching over me to make sure nothing bad happens to me again.

Fifteen minutes later, we settle on my couch, warming our palms on cups of warm coffee. Fresh air flows through the open window. My heart and head both hurt and I'm not ready for the conversation I know Raphael wants to have. I'm already dreading it. There's nothing I can tell him, anyway.

"Where were you, Dove?"

"I had to leave," I mutter. "It doesn't matter."

"You're pale as a ghost. What happened?"

"Nothing." I shake my head vehemently. Perhaps if I deny it out loud enough times, I'll start to believe it myself. "I'm back now. Everything will go back to normal."

"I missed you."

I risk a look at his handsome face. He's wearing a look of sincerity and I'm desperate to believe him. I want to know there's at least one person out there who has my best interests at heart, who doesn't want to hurt me, destroy me. I want to believe Raphael is here purely for me – to make me feel better.

"I missed you, too," I lie. The truth is, I haven't even thought about him. Not until I saw all the missed calls and texts.

"Are you going to be okay here on your own?" he asks. "You can come stay at my place for a while."

"No," I shake my head. I need to be alone, though I won't say that aloud, so I don't hurt his feelings. "I have my plants to take care of, and I'll have to head to work tomorrow, see if they'll take me back."

"I understand," he nods. An awkward silence falls between us, but Raphael breaks it soon enough. "Do you want me to leave you alone, Dove?"

"No," I say, surprising myself as much as I'm surprising Raphael. "I need a friend."

"I can be your friend. But, Dove..." He reaches for my hand and I fight every instinct in my body screaming at me to pull away from his touch. "I still like you... Want you."

"Okay," I nod. It's the most I can muster the courage for. I can't give him false hopes, promise anything other than to be his friend.

"Have you eaten?"

"Not for a while," I realize out loud. "Do you want to order some takeout?"

"Sure." If Raphael is surprised by the fact I've offered he doesn't show it. I scroll through my phone and we order together. Things feel surprisingly normal as I click on the TV and we settle in front of it, waiting for our food. This time, the silence is pleasant, companionable.

The food shows up soon. I load up our plates and eat hungrily. My stomach was rumbling. I needed this.

At least there's one thing I can be grateful for to Nox. He taught me how to take care of myself again. All those years I denied myself – for him, for my mother – feel inconsequential now. There's nobody in this world who I'll starve myself for, hurt myself for, again. I'm my priority now. I'm the only one who can take care of myself. And I fully intend on doing that.

"It's good to see you eating," Raphael tells me with a smile.

"This used to be my favorite," I mutter, picking up more noodles with my chopsticks. "Pad Thai. I ate it all the time back in New York."

"Seems like your life was quite different back then."

I swallow thickly. "Very. But I like it better here. And I'm done sulking and feeling sorry for myself."

Robin wouldn't want that.

At the mere thought of my brother, my stomach clenches with guilt and sadness. My appetite is gone in an instant. I put my plate on the coffee table and curl up on the couch, pulling my legs against my body. I want to cry, but I don't want Raphael to know what's wrong.

"Is there anything I can do?" he asks when I don't speak for a while.

I'm rarely this honest, but the truth flows from my lips easily this time. "Don't leave me. I need you."

"I won't leave." Raphael sets his plate down too, and brings over a blanket, draping it over my curled-up body. I look up at him, thanking him with a weak smile. "I'll clean up here. You get some rest, Dove, okay? I won't go anywhere, I promise you that."

"Thank you," I whisper. And then sleep is already pulling me under, promising a world of darkness where all my worries are gone, and I can float endlessly in the shadows where nothing can hurt me at all.

I don't know how long I'm asleep for. When my eyes fly open, my first instinct is to panic. But then I realize I'm not with Nox anymore. The truth of what happened hits me like a ton of bricks and I groan, burying my face in a pillow.

"Good morning, Sleeping Beauty."

I look up, remembering Raphael. Pulling myself into a sitting position, I rub the sleep out of my eyes and manage the weakest smile. "I thought you would've left by now. What's the time?"

"It's seven a.m.," he says. "I promised to stay, didn't I?"

"You didn't have to do that."

"I know I didn't, but I like to keep my promises," he grins. "I cleaned up a bit, changed the sheets on your bed, did the dishes. The house is nice and aired out now."

"Thank you." Somehow, the thought of Raphael going through my things doesn't annoy me as much as I thought it would. He's only trying to help after all.

"When will I see you again, Dove?" he asks.

"I don't know."

"Don't pull away from me." He makes a move to touch me but changes his mind at the last second. "Please. I don't want to lose you. I want to help you. Make you feel better."

"I don't think anyone can do that," I tell him with a sigh.

"Has there been any word from your brother?"

His innocent question threatens to destroy me the moment it leaves his lips. I force myself to remain calm. Not to think about the bloodied hoodie in Nox's motel room.

"No," I manage.

"I could hire a PI," he offers. "Help you figure out what happened."

"No," I repeat. "Don't."

"Dove, I just want to help," he goes on. "I was worried sick for you."

"I can take care of myself." For the first time, I'm not lying by saying that. I don't need anyone now, not anymore. I'm independent. Perhaps Nox did teach me that. And yet I can never not hate him. Not after what he's done.

"Just promise me you won't disappear again," Raphael says. "I want to stay in touch."

"Yes," I nod. "I'd like that too."

As independent as I want to be, I will still need a friend. I just hope Raphael can accept I'm not ready for anything romantic. Not with anyone. Not after Nox.

"I have to head to work soon," he mutters, checking his phone. "Can I take you out to dinner tonight?"

I ponder his question. Perhaps I should say no, pretend like I don't want his company. But the truth is, I'm eager for someone to be around. Someone who doesn't see me as an object, a sex toy. I want Raphael to be that person. I only hope he can accept I'm not going to be in a relationship with him.

"Yes," I finally say. "But, Raphael..."

"Dove, you don't have to say it." He picks himself up and grins at me. "I'm a big guy, I can see what's happening. I've seen heartache too many times to count. I know what it feels like. Just let me make it better for you. No strings attached."

"Thank you," I manage weakly. Somehow, without me having to put it into words, he realized exactly what I needed.

"I'll see you tonight."

"Yes."

We say goodbye at the door and I lock up after he leaves, but not before checking the street to make sure nobody's there.

No sign of Nox.

Fucking good, I tell myself. If he showed up here again, I'd be forced to call the cops. He better keep his fucking distance, or else.

CHAPTER THIRTY-THREE

NOX
3 MONTHS LATER

Some things never change.

I was always a monster. Despite my father's best efforts, he couldn't beat the evil streak out of me. And now, I've finally accepted it. I'm done running from who I am. I'm done denying myself the pleasure of watching Dove, my little bird, live her life even when she doesn't want me in it.

I'm a stalker.

And I'm never going to change.

I'm following her again today. I've been doing it since she left my motel room after losing her shit with me, but she hasn't noticed so far. I've been sticking to the shadows, hiding in plain sight, and it's worked well. I have no doubt Dove would keep her promise of turning me in if she spotted me tailing her. But I have no intention of being noticed. After all, I'm most at home in the shadows.

The pain from her rejection cuts deep, but what's worse is the feeling that she's in the wrong.

I desperately want to convince Dove I'm the right man for her, but I also understand she won't want to listen to me until something changes. And I'm not turning myself in.

She's been talking to Raphael. I saw him come to her house that first day when we parted ways. Jealousy squeezed my heart in its long fingers, threatening to make me lose my mind again. But since my argument with Dove, I've realized I can't hurt anyone else she's close to. She won't understand. She'll only hold it against me.

I never was a patient man, but I'm starting to realize I'll have to change if I want Dove back beside me.

She's working at the plant nursery today, settling back into her normal life and her regular routine. Under her green thumb, plants flourish and life thrives. Even her own, personal issues are getting resolved. My little bird is taking better care of herself, eating right, not hurting her pretty body. She's healing. And I'm the reason why. Yet I can't reap the rewards, not without coming back into her life and stealing back what's always been mine.

I know she's going to see that prick again today, and it pisses me off to no end. I don't want her around Raphael. Hate the thought of him touching her, consoling her. It should be my job to do that. Soon enough, Dove will come around and I'll take that bastard's place. Soon enough.

I saw her having dinner with him only last night. The guy's obviously in love with her. You can see it from the way he looks at her, obsessing about her actions, wondering whether it's too soon to make a move again. When I see those wheels turning in his head, I want to fucking scream at the guy, tell him he'll never have her, not like I once did. It's all surface level between them, but not between us. Our scars run deep. So very deep.

At least she's eating. It's a small consolation to know I've helped Dove heal, but it fucking hurts to watch her explore this new version of herself with somebody else. Somebody who should be me.

Somehow, I'll force my way back into her life. I just need to figure out how and play my cards right. But I have no doubt that Dove will be back in my arms. That's where she truly belongs, after all.

Today, they're going out again, probably for dinner. It's almost a daily occurrence now. Dove will meet Raphael in front of his office and he'll take her to a new restaurant every night. They're growing closer, getting attached to one another, and it fucking kills me to watch. I want to destroy the prick who's taking what's mine. I want to steal her back. But Dove doesn't want me – she's made that clear enough.

Before I got here, I touched my cock thinking about her. Thick, long ropes of cum decorated my shower tile as I brought myself off, thinking about my little bird. Whatever she does, she can never escape me. I'll always keep an eye on her. Watch her, make sure nothing bad happens. She's mine. *Mine.*

I know eventually, Dove and Raphael will fuck. I also know that's one thing I won't be able to stand by and watch. I'll burst on the scene and physically separate them if I have to. I can't fucking bear the thought of his dick, his fingers, inside her. Those holes are mine and I will do every-fucking-thing in my power to keep it that way. And yet I need to remain unnoticed, hiding in the shadows and hoping neither of them notices me.

I don't know how much Dove has told Raphael, but I'm betting it's not the whole truth. He seems like a self-righteous prick, the kind that would report me, track me down and make me serve time for everything I've done. But Dove wouldn't. Dove loves me too much to condemn me to such a fate. Now I just have to twist her pretty little mind into submission, convince her that obeying me is what she's wanted all along.

I wait for them to meet in front of his office building. It's only been a few months since they met for the first time. Surely, she doesn't feel as much for him as he feels for her. My little bird doesn't fall so fast, and I know for a fact she's still hung up on me. I know, because I listen to her fucking herself while she whispers my name, coming to the fantasy of me that she can never have in real life. Not because I don't want her to. Because she decided it has to be this way. And one day I'll change her mind.

My gaze is focused on the entrance to the building. But instead of seeing Raphael exit or Dove arrive, I see a young woman pulling a little girl along.

The woman is short but pretty, with an innocent looking face that tells me she's younger than me. She's wearing an angry expression though, pulling along the kid wearing mismatched clothes. My curiosity is piqued, and I watch them approach the building, the kid tearing her arm out of her mother's grasp.

The girl stomps and shakes her head, crossing her arms in front of her little body. Her pretty face is streaked with tears. She's refusing to go inside with her mother.

It takes me a moment to recognize the little girl, but when I do, my expression turns thunderous.

I've seen her before. The little girl was here when Dove had her photoshoot, but she never told me her name.

The woman only tries to convince the kid for a few minutes before she shrugs and disappears inside the building, abandoning her child. The little girl bravely wipes her eyes, and that's when she sees me. Slowly, a tentative smile pulls at the corners of her lips and she raises her hand, waving timidly.

I shouldn't engage, shouldn't talk to her. But as she starts coming over to where I'm hiding, I realize just how eager I am for some human contact. How desperately I want to talk to somebody else, even if it is just a silly little kid. I've been stuck dealing with the receptionist, my only human contact, somebody I can't stand. Somehow, I'm starved of conversation, and the kid seems like a better bet of having a good talk with than most adults.

"Hello," she greets me shyly, and I smirk at her.

"Hey, kid. Long time no see."

"I was hoping I would see you again."

I nod in acknowledgement of her words, then nod toward the building. "Your mom still hitting on the guy that works in there?"

"Yeah." She sighs. So grown up for such a little thing. "My stepdad would be so angry if he knew."

I watch her closely, wondering how hard life must be for her. Whether she has anyone on her side, anyone to help her. Before I can come to a conclusion, the kid points to my face.

"You have a new scar."

I touch my fingertips to the mark Dove left on me. Sometimes I almost manage to forget it's there now that it's all healed up. "Yeah. Makes me look like a villain, doesn't it?"

She shrugs. "Sometimes heroes have scars, too."

Her words are so profound I find myself clearing my throat in an effort not to show my emotions. I need to change the topic, and fast.

"So, you said your mom's married?"

She nods. "I don't like the guy."

"Why not?"

Wordlessly, she reaches for the sleeve of her lilac shirt printed with dalmatians and pulls it up. There are traces of fingers being dug into skin there, deep and bruised, an angry dark purple.

"He did that to you?"

She nods, avoiding my gaze. "I don't think he likes me."

My blood boils at the fucking sight. Who hurts an innocent child? I remember my own father then and what he did to me. How he abused me. How he twisted things around to make it seem like I deserved it, like it was part of a lesson I needed to be taught.

"What's your name?" My heart speeds up. I shouldn't ask. I shouldn't get involved. But because of my own trauma, when I see a kid in trouble, I can't help but try and get them out of their shitty situation.

"Willa," she whispers.

"Cute name," I grin, and she smiles back. "Where do you live?"

"Not far from here," she says, glancing at the exit of the building. "Oh, my mom is back. I'll..."

She turns away but I've already blended right back into the shadows. Her eyebrows crease, but she seems to understand the nature of our forbidden friendship. She waves to the empty alley and skips over to where her mother is waiting. At least she seems less miserable now than she was when she first got here.

Breathing a heavy sigh, I already know my plan for the day is fucked. I need to follow the girl, Willa, now, not Dove. Dove has other people taking care of her now, but Willa doesn't. And she deserves help just as much. She's innocent. An innocent little kid that needs my help.

My fists tighten, my nails digging into the skin of my palm. Not waiting for Dove to appear, I slink into the shadows and begin trailing the little girl and her mother. I don't know when I fucking turned into a protector of the city, but I don't have a choice. My conscience which has sat undisturbed for decades is back at it, reminding me it's my responsibility to help the kid. After all, she doesn't have anybody else.

The woman is impatient, constantly tugging on the little girl's hand and dragging her along. I can tell Willa isn't excited about going back home. The sick side of me is almost excited at the prospect of meeting her stepdaddy. I can't wait to beat the shit out of the guy. Maybe even slit his fucking throat. That's what the bastard deserves for fucking up an innocent child.

Finally, the two of them arrive at a small, shitty house that's falling apart. The mom goes in first, leaving Willa on the doorstep.

What the actual fuck? She needs a lesson in bringing up a child.

Willa sits on the pavement, hugging her knees close to her chest, and my stomach tightens.

I watch until the door opens again. A stocky, once handsome guy, appears on the doorstep, glaring at my new friend. He mutters something I can't hear and she follows him inside with her shoulders slumped, and the door slams shut behind them.

I lean against the brick wall behind me, lighting up a smoke.

I have a new mission now, something to distract me from Dove. I can only hope it will be enough to take my mind off little bird, the way she wanted.

CHAPTER THIRTY-FOUR

DOVE

It's another Saturday night just like the ones before it. I'm out to dinner with Raphael again, mindlessly stabbing the vegetables on my plate with my fork.

"You're somewhere else today, aren't you?" At the sound of Raphael's voice, my head snaps toward him and I offer an apologetic smile.

"I'm sorry. Just really tired."

"Dove, you know I'm here for you, right?" His palm covers mine on the table, but I'm still averting his gaze, unable to bear the weight of his watchful eyes. "I'll do anything to make you feel better."

"It's okay," I reply jovially, even though it's the last thing I feel right now. Because, like clockwork, the nighttime rolls around and my mind goes back to the man I can never have – Nox.

After all, the monsters come out to play only when the sun is gone... And Nox did always feel most at home in the shadows.

I've forced him from my mind most days, but when night falls, he's back with a vengeance. His voice is burned into my brain, endlessly demanding attention.

TYRANT STALKER

Attention I refuse to give him or his memory that lives within me, because the prick doesn't deserve it.

He's a killer. A murderer. And he should pay for what he's done. Because of him, I'll never see my brother again. And now Sam is gone too, and the only person I really have left is sitting in front of me, and here I am, still thinking about Robin's murderer. I deserve a punishment, so I dig my nails into my palms underneath the table.

Raphael seems to sense my discomfort, seeing how my teeth dig into my bottom lip painfully. He reaches for my hand under the table. My palm opens up, allowing his fingers to gently trace the crescent-shaped wounds I've given myself.

"Please don't hurt yourself," he says. His tone is soft but his intention is clear. He wants me to stop what I'm doing. But I can't. Not for him.

I think of Nox, then. Imagine his handsome face, the scar I put on it. He'll carry me around for ever now. He can't run from me either.

And my fingers relax. I stop hurting myself, stop digging my nails into my palm. I close my eyes shut and exhale, telling myself I'm doing this for Raphael, even though my mind and body both know it's a lie, a betrayal. I'm doing this for Nox. To make him proud. And as sick as it is, the smallest sliver of me hopes he's watching, and that he's proud.

"Sorry," I say quickly, mostly to get rid of the thoughts invading my mind.

Raphael rewards me with a smile and we get back to our food. I'm feeling marginally better and he seems pleased by that, though I don't dare tell him it's because of Nox.

Strangely enough, Raphael hasn't asked me about him, despite their somewhat strange meeting. Perhaps he knows it's better not to ask.

After dinner, we leave the restaurant and decide to go for a walk on the beach again. Raphael's hand finds its way into mine. I carry my sandals in the other hand, the pleasantly cool sand slipping through my toes. The atmosphere is peaceful, the breeze gentle against my skin.

"Dove..."

I raise my eyes to Raphael's, swallowing thickly. I know what's coming and I'm scared.

"Will you ever let me kiss you again?"

I feel the lump in my throat growing bigger and bigger. What am I supposed to tell him? LIE! my subconscious screams at me. Lie to him!

And yet I can't. Somehow the words don't leave my lips and I merely stare at Raphael, hoping he understands.

"You don't want that?" he asks.

"I don't know," I whisper. "I want to want it."

He groans. His hands cup my face and I look down, unable to handle the weight of his gaze. But it doesn't stop him. Slowly, passionately, Raphael touches his lips to mine. The kiss is perfect – anything and everything a girl could dream of. He's a gentleman, so much different than Nox, so much less demanding, so much more giving. And yet I feel nothing.

"I'm sorry," I whisper against his lips as he pulls back.

He watches me closely. A tear slips down my cheek. I don't want to be weak in front of him. I don't want him to see how broken I really am, because a part of me still wants to impress him.

"Don't apologize," he mutters. "You never have to apologize to me, Dove."

I nod, even though his words don't strike home. I feel like I owe him for everything he's done for me. He's never implied it, and yet I can't help the feelings of not being good enough for anyone.

"But Dove, I have to ask," Raphael speaks up again. "Do you want me to wait for you? Because I will. I'll wait months, years. Because I already know you're the only one I want."

His words make my heart tighten in my chest, as if someone's squeezing it with an iron grip. What the fuck am I supposed to tell him?

"I don't know," I whisper brokenly. "I can't say. I can't ask you to do that."

"Just know I'm willing to wait as long as it takes." He smiles at me. He's so confident. Handsome. He could have any woman in the world. And he picked me. "You're worth it, Dove."

"Thank you," I manage.

"I know we've been hanging out a lot," Raphael goes on. "But how would you feel if we start dating? Absolutely no pressure, of course."

"I..."

"We don't have to do anything," he rushes to say. "I just figured it was the next step... We're already spending a lot of time together."

I shake my head. "I can't."

"You don't want to?"

"No," I cut him off sharply before he can continue, my eyes blazing with silent fire. "I *can't*."

Of course I want to. Deep down, I know it's the best choice for me. Raphael is safe. Nox isn't. And yet I can't force myself to accept his proposal. Not when there's a stalker out there that I feel so much more for. A stalker I never want to see again.

Not until he pays for his crimes.

"Okay," Raphael says. We don't speak of it again. We take a nice, long walk without saying much. The silence is pleasant, companionable – something you'd expect from a lifelong partner. Raphael is so many women's dream match. But he's not mine.

Once we reach the far end of the beach, he calls us an Uber. We sit close by, his hand softly touching mine, full of hopes and dreams and promises of a future I can never give him. And yet I'm the selfish bitch that won't let him go. I need Raphael. He's the only person that keeps me sane, the only one I have left after Sam, after my brother.

We pull up in front of my house first. Our eyes meet and he nods at me. "Go ahead."

I'm grateful he doesn't offer to walk me in, because I don't want to say no. I smile and kiss his cheek on an impulse, then get out of the car. I watch the Uber pull away and let myself in, my heart still pounding from the weight of my conversation with Raphael. My conscience is out for vengeance, reminding me how stupid I am. Obsessed with the man who hurt me instead of the one who would do anything for me. I deserve this. I deserve to be alone.

And yet there's a small voice deep within me. A voice that was born in that room with all the plants, the one Nox locked me in. The voice feels like it doesn't belong to me. It belongs to a woman who's much stronger and more capable. But maybe one day I can grow up enough to *be* her.

I lock the door behind me. Out of habit, I check every room. They're all empty. I'm alone.

Fighting back the feeling of disappointment, I peel off my dress and take off my bra with a sigh. I get between the sheets in nothing but my black lace thong, fingers wrapped around a vibrator I bought last week.

I'm a woman and I have needs, and I'm going to embrace them. Fuck what anyone else says.

I turn the toy on and it rumbles to life. Shutting my eyes, I push the fabric of my thong to the side and toy with my clit, pressing down the vibrator. In an instant, relief and pleasure wash over me. It's sick, the fact that this is the only thing that makes me feel complete anymore.

Sex.

Fucking.

I've become a toy. But this toy only plays by itself.

It feels somehow powerful to be in charge of my own body. To extract moan after moan from my own lips. I hold the power now. Too bad I can't control where my thoughts are going.

Once again, I find my mind circling around Nox. What I did to him, what he did to me. How we fucked each other up beyond repair. Most of me wants to hate him, but there are parts, and those parts are determined as hell, that want him, need him back. I dream of him. At night, he's back in my head, controlling me, pulling the strings that make my body obey him without question.

I'm a woman obsessed. And I know there's no way out of this – it's a hell of my own making, one I can never escape.

But it's a small consolation, nevertheless, to know I'm not letting him near me again. He can't hurt me if he isn't around. He can't keep stealing people, memories, he can't wreck my future if he isn't here.

My eyes fly open, the toy incessantly buzzing between my legs. I want the release I'm keeping from myself, and yet it feels like a waste because my stalker isn't watching.

"Fuck you, Nox," I mutter, the words barely above a whisper. "You don't own me."

Knowing I'm lying to myself, I bring myself closer to an orgasm. I'm a finger slip away from coming, from giving myself the pleasure I don't deserve. It will be a small consolation for what I've done to myself. For cutting Nox out of my life.

The climax begins and I pull my toy away, denying myself. My thoughts are swimming with images of him. Nox. Fucking me up even when I've forced him to stay away. Stubbornly, I push the toy back and force myself to think of Raphael.

How unbelievably handsome he is, with his dark hair, clear brown eyes, his perfect complexion. How he towers above me, his shoulders broad, his mere presence protective. His deep voice, his calming words. He could be the one.

But he isn't.

Still, I grit my teeth and force myself to keep him on my mind. I think of Raphael as gasps escape my lips, as the inescapable orgasm threatens to rip me apart.

"Please," I whisper to nobody but myself. "Please, make me come."

I grit my teeth, knowing how very close I am. I'm almost done. And when I come without thinking of what shouldn't be on my mind, I'll be free. Free of Nox's control over me.

Except the moment I think of his name, he's back.

He laughs at me. He mocks me for thinking of someone else, when we both know he's the only one for me. His invisible fingers take the toy and bring me closer, toying with my conscience. I want it. I want this. I want him.

I fight back tears as the orgasm rips through my body. My teeth dig into my bottom lip and I silence my own scream of pleasure and frustration. My orgasm, this time, is silent.

But Nox has still won.

CHAPTER THIRTY-FIVE

NOX

I'm developing a new obsession. You could almost call it wholesome.

The little kid, Willa, has a tough life. She reminds me of myself, of what I went through at that age. How I found a darkness deep within me, and how I was forced to quash it down years later when my father found out. But the thing about darkness is, if you shut it out, it festers and rots. That's what happened to me, and I can't let that happen to Willa.

I've kept my distance from her for now. I'll get in touch again soon, but first, I need to learn more about the kid and the way her life and the people around her work.

There's one thing I'm already sure about – her so-called parents are pieces of shit. I've seen her stepfather strike her, and it took everything I had in me not to storm into their house and rip her out of his abusive claws. Her mother's a drug addict, but not in the quiet, ashamed way Sam was. Willa's mom doesn't give a shit. She'll snort coke in front of her daughter. She'll do anything she can get her hands on just so she can be in a perpetual state of numbness. Her forgotten daughter is left to fend for herself.

She must be six or seven years old. She walks to school alone, with me trailing

TYRANT STALKER

behind her in the shadows to make sure she's okay. She's brave. She doesn't let anyone put her down. At school, she's alone. Sometimes, she eats her lunch in the bathroom. Sometimes, she sits by herself in the enclosed sitting area by the school.

That's where I choose to make contact again.

I wait until the school day is over. I wait until she's walking home, and peel my back from the shadows. She notices me right away, grinning wide as her eyes meet mine.

"Hey, Willa."

"Hello," she replies, still a little cautious. "Your scar is healing."

I nod, even though it's fucking painful, because it reminds me of how much time has passed since I've spoken to Dove.

"I got you something."

Her eyes light up as I pull out a crumpled brown paper bag. I've noticed she only eats at school. Her mother doesn't even check if she's hungry, and there's rarely something for her to eat at their house.

First, Willa pulls out some nutritional bars. She makes a face, making me chuckle darkly.

"They're not that bad," I promise her. "You can keep them hidden in your room. For when you're really hungry."

Her eyes light up. "How did you know?"

"Don't ask," I grin. "Check the bag, there's something else."

She keeps digging underneath the stacks of bars. "Oh!"

Her little hand pulls out the plushie. It's a grizzly bear, with feather-soft fur and eyes that almost look intelligent.

"He'll keep you safe," I tell her. "And we'll make a little deal."

"What kind of deal?" She holds the teddy close, unwilling to let go, as if I'm going to take him away already.

"Sometimes I walk by your house," I go on easily. "So, if you put the bear in your bedroom window, I'll know you're okay. And if you don't, I'll know something's wrong and you need my help."

"Okay," she nods thoughtfully. "I can do that."

"Great. You should go back home now, your mother is probably waiting."

She hesitates, drawing circles in the sand with her foot. "You promise you'll help me?"

"Yeah."

"I won't tell my mom about you."

I laugh out loud. "Yeah, you shouldn't, kid."

"I'll see you soon?" She turns her hopeful eyes to mine.

"I hope not," I grin. "Unless something's wrong."

She smiles, tucking the bear back inside the bag. When she looks up, I'm already gone, but she doesn't seem surprised. She starts taking small steps toward her home, dragging the bag with her. She looks so small. SO vulnerable. And I sure as fuck don't need another helpless creature to take care of, to be my responsibility. But I can't help myself.

I return to the hotel room with a heavy mind, my shoulders slumped. At least the front desk girl has ignored me since the scar, since she saw Dove.

After a hot shower in the shitty bathroom, I dig out my phone and find another slew of missed calls. Hodge has been calling. What the fuck does he want now?

Reluctantly, I call him back. He answers on the second ring, as if he's been waiting by the phone.

"Nox. I've been waiting for your call."

I swallow my frustration, silently wondering why I'm such a piece of shit to this man who's done nothing to deserve it. "What's up?"

"I was hoping we could talk about the exhibition again."

I groan. I should've seen this coming. He's constantly pressuring me about the same shit. "I don't want to do an exhibition."

"I know, but it would help your recognition so much. We could sell more. Have you been painting?"

I glance around the crappy motel room. I haven't touched a paintbrush in months. I have a sketchbook that I'll draw in with charcoal, but that's it. "No."

"You should come back to New York, Nox. It's your home after all."

He's quietly insistent, never pushing too hard. The man is a goddamn saint, but it only makes me hate him more. And I'm starting to realize why. He reminds me of my father. And for some reason, hurting him makes me feel better.

"I can't leave LA."

"Why not?"

I hesitate, unsure of my own answer. What the fuck am I supposed to tell him? Definitely not the truth.

"I can't. Not yet. I got people here counting on me," I finally mutter. Dove and Willa's images fill my mind. I can't walk away from them. I can't break these obsessions. I have to keep going.

"Alright, Nox," Hodge says, ever the patient saint. "You sure you don't want to come?"

"No," I repeat.

"Alright." For a moment, I'm convinced our conversation is over, but then he speaks up again, his tone changing, his voice darker, crueler. "I know what you did to my daughter, Parker."

"What?" I hiss.

"You killed her."

I haven't heard him speak the truth out loud. For years, I was convinced he was shutting his own eyes. Somehow replacing his daughter with me, as if her murderer could somehow make Hodge's pain better.

"Hodge, I..." I don't know whether to defend myself or deny it. It's rare that I'm lost for words.

"Spare me the bullshit." Suddenly, his voice drips with venom. "You killed her.

Don't worry, *Nox*, I'll never make you pay the way you should – behind fucking bars. But there's something else for you to do. Obey me. Give me what I fucking want."

"What's that?" I ask through gritted teeth.

"Come to New York. Do the exhibition."

"But my brother –"

"You don't even have to see him."

"He'll know I'm there."

"We'll keep him away from you," Hodge insists.

"Why are you so obsessed with this?" I hiss. "Why can't you let fucking go?"

"Because you took everything I had away from me," he growls. "So now I'm making you pay."

The truth hurts. I remember what happened just hours ago, how I promised Willa I'd be there for her. But what choice do I have?

"And if I don't?" I ask, anticipating Hodge's answer.

"I'm turning you in," the older man says. "You're going to jail for a very, very long time."

I want to tell him to go fuck himself, but I tighten my jaw, refusing to let my emotions out. My mind reminds me of the darkness within. Rotting, festering. I'm only making things worse.

"Are you blackmailing me?"

"Call it whatever you want," he says, and I can practically feel him smirking. "I'll send you a ticket over email. I'm expecting you in New York in two days."

"What about my life here?" I demand.

"What life?" Hodge seems to revel in hurting me. "You're a monster, Nox. You have nothing, no one. Whoever is in your life will be better off once you leave. They don't deserve to get hurt, do they?"

They.

I think of them.

Willa. Innocent, young. Hurt, abused. On her own without me.

TYRANT STALKER

Dove. Broken by me so many times neither of us knows if she can be put back together again.

Maybe Hodge is right. Maybe I'd be doing them a favor by blending into the shadows once and for all, disappearing, unburdening their lives.

Maybe I should do what he says. Seems like I don't have a damn choice, anyway.

I end the call, unable to handle the conversation. A moment later, an email rolls in, telling me I have a flight the next day at noon. It barely gives me any time to say my goodbyes. I have to pack up my meager belongings and get out of here in a few hours.

With a groan, I towel-dry my hair and tell myself the few hours I have left in LA are enough.

I get dressed again, heading to Willa's house first.

The bear is in her bedroom window, silently watching the street. I get closer, dangerously close, telling myself I'll risk it this time, because I know it's the last time.

I peek inside her bedroom, or what passes for it. It's trashed. Her mattress is on the floor and there's a thin blanket covering Willa's sleeping body. I think of calling out to her but think better of it. She needs her rest. But now I've fucked up – just one more thing to add to my endless list of mistakes. I've given the kid false hope. I've made her a promise that I'm breaking the very same day.

I walk away from the house with my hands in my pockets. My conscience is heavy tonight.

There's one more stop I have to make – Dove's house. And if it's hard leaving Willa, leaving Dove will be like ripping my heart out of my body, and trying to fucking survive.

She's alone tonight, no Raphael in sight. There're a few lights on, which means I should keep my distance, because little bird is still awake. And yet I can't help myself.

I stand close by, catching a glimpse of her here and there. I'm grateful she's not in full view. It would only make what I have to do worse. I don't think I'd be able to leave if I saw Dove properly tonight. Something pulls me back to her every time, reminding me my blackened heart belongs here, with her.

"Hey, creep. Got a problem?"

The words take me by surprise and my heart beats into overdrive as I spin around. And there he is, Raphael Santino in all his tall, dark and handsome glory.

"What are you doing here?" he demands as realization dawns on him. "Hey, I know you."

"No, you don't," I mutter, bumping my shoulder into his, hard, as I make my way away from Dove.

"You need to stay away from her."

"You need to shut your mouth before it gets you in trouble," I hiss.

He grabs me by the shoulder. He may be bigger and broader but I'm fast, and I've been defending myself my whole life. I slam Raphael against the wall of Dove's house, not giving a shit.

"Don't fucking touch me," I snarl at him. "And... take care of little bird."

The guy knits his brows together. "We finally getting rid of you?"

I don't answer him, just slam him against the wall again and snarl at him like a wild dog.

"Don't come back here again," Raphael calls out after me. "If you know what's good for you."

I smirk as I put more and more distance between myself and my woman.

I never was very good at following orders. But I'll give Dove the space she needs to heal.

For now.

CHAPTER THIRTY-SIX

DOVE

"How does that make you feel?"

I fidget with the hem of my dress. I'm not wearing leggings or tights underneath it today, and the dress hits the top of my thighs, exposing minimal scarring. I feel confident, though. When a woman stared me down on the street, I stared right back. I'm not letting anyone intimidate me anymore. I've been through enough to know I'm strong enough to fight back.

She looked away, and I kept walking with my head held high until I reached the offices of Dr. Christensen. This is my third visit, and Dr. Christensen says I've already made progress on my journey. That's what he calls this path of healing – a journey.

I shrug. "I don't know. She seemed to be judging me and that hurt. I felt like... I felt like my mother was watching me."

"Does your mother judge you?"

I laugh bitterly. "Always and forever."

"Is that why you've cut off contact with her for the most part?"

Dr. Blake Christensen must be my age, or a little older. He must be fresh out of medical school. His diplomas line the walls in his office. He's handsome – someone my mother would adore. She'd love it if I brought a guy like him home. Educated, probably loaded. But I have no interest in him, and he's been nothing but professional, focused on getting me to a better place.

"Yes," I finally nod. "She was always a negative influence in my life. Toxic. She's a narcissist for sure."

The doctor chuckles, writing something down in his pad. "I see we've reached the same conclusion, Dove."

I manage a weak smile as he leans forward, watching me closely. "Our time is almost up, but I'd love to know more about your relationship with your brother."

Instantly, I look away. I fumble to find my purse and my jacket, not meeting the doctor's gaze. "I should go. I'm meeting Raphael after this."

"Alright," Dr. Christensen says softly. "But one day, we'll have to talk about Robin, Dove."

"Not today," I cut him off sharply, then take a breath of air, filling my lungs. "Not today, please."

Christensen nods and walks me to the door, offering an encouraging smile. "I'll see you next week, Dove."

"You will," I reply, managing a smile as I leave his office.

Raphael is already waiting outside, his wide grin making me feel guilty as fuck. "How'd it go?"

"Okay," I mutter. "As usual."

He doesn't pry. "Want to get some food?"

I nod eagerly. Since Nox's cruel and vicious *therapy*, my appetite is back with a vengeance. Of course I'm still watching what I eat, but at least I'm not being as paranoid about it as I used to be.

We get an Uber downtown to grab sushi at one of our favorite places. While we wait for a table at the bar, I catch Raphael looking at me and laugh nervously, tucking my hair behind my ear.

"What? Do I have something on my face?"

"No," he grins. "You just look... different than when I first met you."

I cock my head to the side. "Happier?"

"I'm not sure," Raphael admits. "But definitely more confident. Like you're ready to take on the world."

"Thanks." I manage a smile before the hostess shows us to our table. Raphael puts in our order, remembering what I like perfectly, but once again, my smile is weakened by my heavy heart.

"It's good to see you eating," he interjects our small talk later, while we eat. "So good. I'm so proud of you, Dove."

I nod. "You've helped a lot."

He disregards my lie and digs in his pocket, handing me a key. "I want you to have this."

"What is it?"

"A key to my apartment." He opens my palm and places the key inside it. "I want you to move in with me, Dove."

The moments those words leave his lips I feel all the air leave my body as if I've been sucker-punched. It instantly feels like a betrayal. All I can do is imagine how pissed Nox would be about this. I can't do it.

But Raphael's been nothing but patient with me. He hasn't even kissed me. He's remained the perfect gentleman throughout, ever since Nox appeared. He deserves this. And yet I don't want to give it to him.

"I can't leave my house," I whisper. "I... I love it too much..."

"Ok." He smiles to reassure me. "Then let me move in with you, Dove. I want to be with you. Always."

"I..." I bite my lower lip, bad habits coming back to haunt me. "I can't do it. I'm sorry."

I can feel Raphael's gaze on me, but I can't look up. I hate myself for doing this to him. But any other man would've given up sooner. Would have walked away. Not

Raphael, though.

"Then answer me this, Dove," Raphael speaks up again. Am I imagining it, or is there a hint of cruelty, an edge of darkness to his voice? I lift my eyes to meet his, and his expression softens. No, I was wrong. He's too warmhearted for me, too kind, too giving. Nox has made me crave the opposite.

"What do you want to know?" I ask.

"Do you want me to keep waiting?"

I don't know the answer to his question. A part of me believes that even if I told him to stop, he wouldn't be able to walk away from me. So, I decide to torture us both, prolonging the inevitable break-up of our friendship. Because that's all it will ever be – at least for me.

He merely nods and we eat the rest of our dinner in silence. But instead of feeling upset about it, I allow my emotions to mellow by listening to the calm, melodic music playing in the restaurant. I remember the doctor's words, how he told me to distract my mind and find strength from the simple things. By the time Raphael and I are finished with our meal, I'm feeling more confident and ready to take on the world again.

We're walking back home when we run into her.

I should've spotted Elise from a mile away with those tottering heels and Pepper barking his head off in her designer purse. She's all but disappeared from my life lately. Partly because her reasons shifted. Partly because I haven't been able to answer any of her messages since I found out the truth about Robin.

"Raphael!" she squeals first, before her eyes fall to me.

Oh.

I forgot about that little detail.

"Dove?" She takes a step closer and her dog growls at me as she kisses each of my cheeks. "How have you been? You two still see each other?"

"Yes," Raphael answers for me, relieving me of the burden. "And we've had a very long day. So, if you don't mind..."

"Oh, sure." Elise's expression falls and she smiles, but it's shaky. "Dove, will you give me a call sometime? I haven't... I haven't forgotten."

My nails try to dig into my hands again but Raphael's strong palm replaces them and he gives me a meaningful look.

"You're okay," he says softly, and I find myself nodding.

That's the thing about Raphael. He's good for me. Unlike Nox, he tries to help me and has me in mind every step of the way. He wants the best for me. He would never hurt somebody I love under the pretense of doing it for our relationship.

As I remember my brother, my stomach tightens into an impossible-to-untangle knot. It hurts. Merely hearing Robin's name is fucking me up. Someday, I'll have to deal with my emotions. But not today. Today, I can keep fucking running.

"I'm sorry," I say to Elise, feeling my voice betray me. "I'll call you when I can. When I feel a little better."

She nods, but the way she looks at us tells me she isn't pleased one bit. I can tell there's something between her and Raphael. If it were Nox, I'd already be losing my mind from the jealousy. But not this time. I'm finding it hard to even care.

Raphael takes my hand and gently tugs me along. "Come on, Dove, we better get going."

I fall into step behind him, leaving Elise standing there. I risk a look over my shoulder, and my eyes connect with the blonde's. She's staring me down, hopeful in a way and annoyed in another. I can tell she doesn't like the friendship I've got with Raphael.

That's too fucking bad, because I'm not going to stop.

"Can you turn your shoulder slightly to the left?"

I oblige Raphael's request and he snaps another shot. He grins at me and I offer up a nervous smile. I don't know why I agreed to let him take more photos. But something about the way he does this makes me feel strong instead of vulnerable. Even though I'm naked, I feel confident, powerful. Like I'm the one who decides what happens every step of the way. I never had any of that with Nox. He was too unpredictable for me.

Trying to banish his smirking image from my head, I decide to focus instead on the situation at hand. Raphael is snapping photos in my house this time, in my natural habitat. I'm surrounded by my plants and I feel safe. It's a nice feeling, to finally have that sense of belonging I've been looking for my whole life.

"You look perfect."

I let out a laugh, "Doubtful."

"You do, Dove." He clicks the camera again and gently touches his fingers to my chin, directing me so I'm facing the light. "So beautiful."

I feel a blush creeping into my cheeks. But instead of stopping Raphael, it seems to inspire him, and he fires off more photos, one after the other, *click, click, click.*

"Are you getting tired?"

"A little," I admit nervously.

"It's okay. The sun's about to set so we can stop now."

He puts away the camera and offers me the silk black robe I was wearing earlier. I accept it gratefully, allowing the fabric to swallow up my nakedness. Even though he's seen me naked a few times now, I still find it awkward. Not that Raphael is the one making it that way, not at all. He's always the perfect gentleman, never making a big deal, never mentioning it at all. But when he lets go of the camera, I always become acutely aware of my own body and my insecurities kick in.

"Do you want to stay the night?"

The question slipping from my lips shocks me, and I flush, avoiding Raphael's gaze. I hope he doesn't think I'm asking that because I want us to...

I flush even harder. I'm merely asking because I'll feel safer with him here. But he doesn't make it awkward, he just smiles and nods. And then there's the smallest, tiniest frisson of excitement. Like something could happen. This is the only time I've felt that since Nox came back – like I could actually see someone else in a romantic light. It's... refreshing. Different.

"I'm really proud of you, Dove," Raphael tells me and I smile with some uncertainty.

"Why?"

"You're eating better. You're not hurting yourself."

"I guess," I shrug.

"Aren't you proud of yourself?"

I think about his words for a moment, mulling them over in my head. I guess I should be proud. I am making big steps on the road to self-recovery. My trauma is being dealt with in proper ways and I've cut all the toxic people out of my life. And that includes Nox.

So why do I still feel empty deep down, where it matters most?

I shake my head to get the thought out.

"Yeah," I lie. "I'm very proud of myself."

CHAPTER THIRTY-SEVEN

NOX
1 YEAR LATER

My life is different now, but I'm still the same monster I've always been. Dove's absence has impacted me in strange ways. I'm quieter these days, more pensive. I'm not the man who left LA a year ago. I've outgrown him.

But today, my life has put me back in LA. After a full year of touring Europe and the States and doing shows, I'm finally returning to the city where I really want to be. It's as if Hodge knew how much this means to me and kept it away from me on purpose. Denying me the only people I actually give a shit about. Perhaps it's his own version of a fucked-up revenge plan for what I did to his daughter. Either way, I fucking deserved it.

The other difference from then to now is that I have money. I've done all those shows Hodge wanted me to, and I painted every single fucking day. I sold a lot, and now I have a substantial amount under my belt with more on the way. But Hodge's claws are in me, deeper than ever. The man fucking owns me, and he knows it.

I grit my teeth as I pace the luxurious suite. I don't know how long my stay will be, but the suite's paid for, for the next two weeks. That gives me enough time to check up on some things.

Surprisingly, I don't head to Dove's house first. I ignore every instinct. The siren call of my little bird is strong as ever, but I force myself to pay a visit to my other ward first.

Willa.

Over the past year, I've struggled with guilt like I'd never felt before. I made that little girl a promise and abandoned her the very next day. I can only hope I didn't fuck up her life too much. All will be revealed soon, and as worried as I am about the kid, I need to get answers, now.

I walk the path down to her house after taking an Uber to the neighborhood. I almost managed to forget what a shitty place Willa lives in. If she's still here.

When I round the corner and find the window of her bedroom, my heart fucking stops. There it is… the bear in the window.

I don't get overcome by emotion easily but seeing that fucks me up more than I'd care to admit. Swallowing my anger at the world, I approach the window. It's closer to night than evening now. I knock on the window gently. I can't see inside the room, because the shitty, threadbare curtains are drawn. But a moment later, they fly open, and there she is.

Willa looks… different. She's not much taller, but her face bears the brunt of the changes she's gone through this year. She looks older. Tired.

When she sees me, she crosses her arms and glares. It almost makes me chuckle, but I stop myself, motioning for her to open the window. She shakes her head no.

I put my hands in a prayer position and mouth pleases at her. Willa rolls her eyes, then finally opens the window. The look of hope in her eyes doesn't escape me, though. The kid is happy to see me, even if she won't admit it.

"How have you been?" I ask softly.

"Are you fucking kidding me?"

The sight of this little kid spewing curse words at me is kind of adorable, but I force myself to wince and shrug. "I'm sorry, Willa."

"You abandoned me."

"I didn't have a choice."

"That doesn't make it better," she hisses.

"I'm sorry."

"You better be," she mutters, rolling her eyes.

I know she's making light of the situation, but the pain behind that watchful gaze doesn't escape me. I've betrayed Willa. Left her here to deal with her family on her own, after promising to take care of her. I deserve to be on the receiving end of her anger. I did this to her.

"I'm back now," I get out.

"For how long? Are you going to tell me when you leave again?" She sighs, waving her hand. She looks oddly grown up. "Never mind. It's too late, anyway."

"I promise you, it's not," I say roughly, my voice hoarse and breaking over the words. It's fucking painful to see a kid this disillusioned with the world. "I'm going to take care of you from now on. Do you need anything?"

"Yeah," she mutters. "I need you here a year ago."

"I'm sorry, Willa." I really do mean it and my conscience has a vicious bite, reminding me once again of how much I fucked up the kid's life. Giving her false hope, then disappearing. What kind of monster am I? I never should've done what Hodge wanted. Willa was counting on me. "I won't disappear again. I'll tell you everything."

"So tell me." She crosses her arms, staring me down with the wisdom of someone ten times her age. "Where did you go?"

"I had to leave for work, I didn't have a choice," I grit out. "I... owed someone. And they were using something to blackmail me."

She nods, not offering any further commentary on my admission. "Then why are you back?"

I think about my answer. What am I supposed to tell her? That I took the first chance I got to get away from Hodge, come back here to be with my woman? Yes. I'll tell her the truth. Willa deserves it.

"There's a girl," I mutter. "Her name is Dove."

"That's a nice name. Is she beautiful?"

I look up into Willa's eyes, noticing for the first time how matted her once light blonde hair is. She looks... neglected, for lack of a better word.

"She's very beautiful," I smile weakly.

"Would she like me?"

In that one question the kid asks, there's a promise for so much fucking heartbreak it twists my stomach into knots. She wants Dove to like her. As if it will make a difference. Willa's doomed to this life, just like I'm doomed to mine.

"Yes, I think she would," I smile weakly. I'm tired. Tired from all the lies. "Maybe one day you can meet her."

Willa nods thoughtfully and I dig in my pocket, bringing out a phone and a charger and passing them to her. "Here, I got you this."

"A phone?"

"I assumed you didn't have one," I mutter, showing her how to charge it. "It's pretty easy. Keep it hidden. Call me if you need me. Whenever."

"You're not going to be walking by my house anymore?"

"I will if you call me," I grin darkly. "And this way, we can stay in touch even if I have to leave again. Is that ok?"

"Yeah," she mutters, quickly putting the phone and charger out of sight then scampering back to the window. "How long are you staying for?"

"A few weeks, probably," I mutter. "I'll come see you a few times, as much as I can."

"What about Dove?" she asks. My woman's name feels strange in this setting, but I kind of like being honest with this adorable kid. I see something in Willa, something that makes me want to take care of her.

"What about her?"

"Will she be happy you're back?"

I take a moment to ponder the kid's words. The answer is probably not. She was more than eager to get rid of me a year ago. But in that time, my obsession has only grown darker, deeper. I thought I'd start getting over Dove by now. That I'd be balls deep in another pussy. But the sad truth is, I haven't fucked a single other person. It's just me and my fucking fist, and the thought of Dove ever-present in my mind.

"Probably not," I smirk at Willa. "We got into an argument before I left."

She shrugs, her clever eyes on mine. "Then fix it."

I laugh out loud. "It's not that easy."

The kid grins. "It's always that easy, monster."

"Hey, who you calling a monster?"

"You," she smiles. "The scar looks scary."

"Do I scare you, Willa?"

She thinks about it for a moment, then shakes her head. "No. Monsters aren't scary. People are."

Her words hit me hard and I nod thoughtfully before pointing back into her room. "Get some sleep, kid. Call me tomorrow, if you want."

"Even if there's nothing wrong?"

"Yeah," I smile thoughtfully. "Even if there's nothing wrong."

She waves me off and I slink back into the shadows, my hands in my pockets as I walk away from her shitty place. Dove's next on the agenda. Of course, I have to be careful, so she doesn't see me. I don't want her to come through on her promise to call the cops if she sees me around her place again. I know it's been a year, but she seemed fucking determined to keep me away.

It's a long walk from Willa's to Dove's, and I take my time, dragging my feet and avoiding walking to Dove's neighborhood. As much as I want to see my little bird, I'm afraid of hurting her even more.

It takes me hours of walking around the city, dragging my feet along, to finally decide I can't stay away.

I tried to be good.

TYRANT STALKER

I tried to give Dove what she wanted.

But I fucking can't stay away.

It's early morning by the time I show up in front of her house. I don't recognize any of the cars parked on the street, which isn't much of a reprieve. Knowing that smug piece of shit Raphael, he probably upgraded his ride since the last time I was here. He seems like the smug type who always drives the newest model. Prick.

I find my spot in the shadows, remembering Sam. There's nothing left of him, not even the stack of newspapers and blankets Dove gave him. He's gone, erased. But he still left his mark on this world. I know, because I carry it in my rotten heart. And I think Dove does, too.

I wait in the shadows until the front door of Dove's house opens. My chest tightens as I watch him exit. Raphael. So, he was here. He was here all along, watching my woman, taking care of her when I fucking couldn't.

Instantly, jealousy and anger demand me to go over there and strangle the piece of shit on the spot. Is he fucking her? Has he been inside what's mine? The mere thought of it makes me enraged, threatening to unleash every single demon I've kept silent in my head. But I push it back, force it behind closed doors. He's not going to win in the end, anyway.

I watch Raphael walk up to a flashy car – just as I suspected, the newest Tesla. He gets behind the wheel and drives away while I grit my teeth and watch Dove's house for any sign of life. But there's nothing. She must be still asleep.

Jealousy's a dangerous fucking drug. Right now, it's making me lose my mind, imagining all the ways Dove betrayed me since I was last here. If this were a year ago, Raphael Santino would be dead fucking meat.

But in my year away, I've picked up some self-control.

Besides, it'll feel sweeter to rip her out of his arms. Make him fucking watch Dove pick me. Because the poor little photographer never stood a chance.

Dove Canterbury has always been my property. And I'm not letting anybody have a piece of what's mine.

With a satisfied smile, I pull away from the alley. It's not our time yet. But I know now for sure, I'm not giving up on the woman of my dreams. And I think I know exactly how to get my little bird back...

Whether she wants it or not.

CHAPTER THIRTY-EIGHT

DOVE

I examine my reflection in the mirror critically. I look good – even for my standards.

I'm wearing a skintight black dress which reaches the tops of my thighs, and a pair of black heeled boots. I slip on a coat over and take a deep, calming breath to steady myself. I can do this. I haven't promised Raphael anything. And he should know by now I'm not ready to do anything sexual. Aside from one very awkward kiss, we haven't even broached the subject... in a full *year*.

Sometimes I feel bad for him. Other times, I feel guilty for leading him on. But Raphael's all I have now. My best friend and my confidant, besides my therapist, of course. He's helped me heal so much and for that, I'll always be grateful. And to be fair, he hasn't pushed to sleep with me at all. So why should tonight be any different?

As much as I tell myself not to worry, there's no denying the special glint in Raphael's eyes when he asked me to come to his place. He's planning something and I'm not sure I'm going to like it. But it's too late to back out now. I can't be so scared all the time, anyway. I have to try to be open to new opportunities.

With that thought in mind, I grab my purse, lock up and get into the Uber that's waiting for me outside. The entire ride to Raphael's, I stare out the window, nervously chewing my bottom lip. By the time we arrive, my lipstick is gone.

I pay the driver and ring Raphael's doorbell. He answers in his calming, kind voice and lets me in. The elevator ride up is too short for my frayed nerves, but I do my best to keep it together. I tell myself it's nothing. Probably just a nice dinner he cooked for me. He's not going to hurt me. He's not... *Nox*.

The elevator dings and the doors slide open.

I take a deep breath and close my eyes. I've been holding back for nothing, because Nox is a thing of the past, and I'm going to make him stay there. On an exhale, I open my eyes and walk into Raphael's penthouse apartment.

"Hey," I call out, surprised he hasn't greeted me at the door.

"In the kitchen," he calls out. I hear the sound of clinking glasses and smile to myself, my fear dissipating. But then another voice joins Raphael's. A woman's.

Instantly, my smile fades. I walk into the kitchen to find Raphael pouring wine for himself and Elise, who's sitting on one of the barstools at his kitchen island.

"Hi, Dove!" She jumps up and comes closer, air-kissing my cheeks. Pepper is nowhere in sight and I'm relieved. But the fact that Elise is here concerns me. Did Raphael invite her? Why, after he was so dismissive of her that time we ran into her? "It's so good to see you again!"

I nod robotically. Even though I'm scared to admit it, it's nice to see Elise, too. She reminds me of a time I can never go back to. She reminds me of Robin.

"Would you like a glass of wine, Dove?" Raphael asks as I sit on one of the barstools.

"Sure." He passes me a glass and I wait for one of them to explain whatever the hell is happening here. "So..."

"So, Elise is going to help us with a little something today," he goes on. "Would you mind coming with us to the lounge?"

I grab my glass and follow them. My eyes dance between Elise and Raphael who seem to be in some sort of silent agreement over something I'm not privy to. I don't know what's happening, but I don't fucking like it.

Once I enter the lounge, the glass falls from my hand. The deep-pile carpet beneath my feet absorbs the spilled wine and the glass lies on its side, slowly leaking the last of its blood red liquid.

But none of us pay it any mind. I'm too focused on the set up in front of me. And before I have enough of a chance to react, Raphael grabs me by the waist. I struggle against him but he ignores my screaming, handcuffing my hands together. My resistance is of no use. He drags me to a chair in the middle of the room with added restraints and straps me in. My heart races. I stop screaming. Instead, I focus my eyes on the figure before me – Raphael. The only man I thought I could trust.

And he's just betrayed me.

"Don't scream," he tells me in a low, threatening voice. "You know nobody's going to hear you, right?"

I stare at him with pure contempt. "Why are you doing this?"

"Because, Dove," he says, his kind voice accented with toxicity. "I've waited long fucking enough."

Before I can answer, he pulls off his tie and ties it around me so I'm silenced, my mouth covered and my nose inhaling his scent coming off the fabric.

"Come here, Elise."

I remember the other woman then, just as she offers me a smug smile and saunters up to Raphael. She hooks her leg around his waist and he lifts her up in a movie-like kiss. I want to fucking scratch her eyes out, but I fight those urges and keep staring at the scene unfolding in front of me.

After their makeout session is over, Elise falls to her knees in front of Raphael. He looks right at me as he unzips his pants, but I refuse to give him the satisfaction of looking at his cock. Instead, I allow my gaze to penetrate him, wishing he'd turn to stone as he smirks at me.

"You left me waiting long enough, Dove," he tells me. "Any other man would've given up faster than me. So today, you get to watch what you can't have anymore. But

Elise can, isn't that right, Elise?"

The blonde looks at me over her shoulder, smiling sweetly as she nods. "Mm-hmm."

I can feel my cheeks igniting. Before I get a good chance to look, Raphael's cock disappears from sight as Elise starts to suck on it. Wetness fills my mouth, as if I'm the one pleasing him. I clear my throat, desperately shutting my eyes closed so I'm not forced to look at them go at it in front of me. But then the noises start.

Elise's desperate moans with her throat filled to the brim.

Raphael muttering curse words in Spanish, choking her as she sucks him off. My blood boils at the sight of them. I want to fucking slap her and scream at him to stop, but my pride won't let me. Instead, I furrow my brows and continue to glare as she slobbers all over her own chest. Raphael pulls his cock out of her and spins her around so she's facing me. Elise's blue eyes glitter as they meet mine.

"Look what you can't have, Dove," she purrs, making me want to explode with jealousy.

But am I really jealous? If this were Nox, I would've already ripped her eyeballs out, somehow. But not with Raphael. Yes, I'm upset, but it's more about losing my position of power and feeling uncomfortable because I'm being forced to watch them fuck. I don't want to watch, and yet I can't look away. It's like a train-wreck.

Raphael pushes her to the floor and the bitch lifts her ass for him. He lifts her dress clear and gets on his knees behind her. Elise's long pink claws dig into the carpet as he fucks her and she moans his name over and over again. I want to rip myself out of these restraints, but the more I struggle, the tighter they seem to get.

"Keep watching," Elise purrs in her annoying Barbie voice. "He's never fucked you like this, has he?"

"Let me go," I mumble through the gag. "Let me go right now. Or I'm calling the cops and telling them what you did to me."

"It's just a kinky game," Raphael smirks, thrusting into her.

"You're fucking with my head."

He pulls out of the blonde and pulls up his boxers. Then, he approaches me, eyes narrowed into dark, burning slits. "I thought that's what you like, *little bird*."

I want to fucking kick him but instead I struggle in the chair, doing everything I can to break free. Raphael finally rushes to my side as the chair topples over, with me still strapped to its legs.

"Stop fighting it," he mutters as he frees my hands. "I'm only trying to help you."

The moment I'm free again, I rip the gag from my mouth and spring away from him, avoiding the weight of his dark brown eyes. My heart speeds up with the betrayal that still feels so fresh.

"How could you do this to me?" I hiss at Raphael.

"I thought you didn't even care about me, little bird."

"Don't call me that!" My voice rings out, deafening in its intensity. I press my palms over my ears and groan as the sound drowns out everything else happening in my head. "Fuck, fuck, fuck."

Raphael makes a grab for me but I push him away and race to the elevator. He calls out after me but I ignore him, continuing to push my finger against the elevator button. When it finally arrives, I'm instantly inside, praying the doors will shut before Raphael can catch up with me. And they do.

Calming music begins to play over the elevator and I take a deep, healing breath as the descent begins. My heart is still faster than I thought possible, hammering in my chest and reminding me with each beat what I've just been through. It doesn't even compare to all the shit Nox has put me through, but I'm still angry with Raphael, feeling the fresh sting of his betrayal cut deep.

The elevator doors slide open and I stumble into the lobby. The lights are bright and the doorman is saying something to me, but I'm not paying any of it any mind. Instead, I stumble through the lobby until the fresh air hits me hard, like a punch to the gut. I take off running without a goal in sight. In my effort to get away, I left my purse at Raphael's. That's going to bite me in the ass later, I just know it.

I can't think clearly. I take deep breaths of the cool night air, trying to fill my lungs and my head with anything other than panic. But it seems to do the opposite. I gasp for air as I make my way to an alley by Raphael's building. I should keep running. Then again, why? Eventually, he's going to catch up with me and I'll be forced to come back with him, humiliated.

Fuck, I can't believe he did that. I can't believe he asked Elise of all people.

He's a fucking jerk. Not as big of a jerk as Nox, but close fucking enough. And I'm cutting him out of my life. I'm done with abusers treating me like shit.

Tears spring to my eyes and I wipe them off angrily. I don't want to cry right now, I want to be strong. But the memory of Nox, ever-present in my mind, hangs above me like it always does.

It only serves to remind me of everything I've lost already, and my guilty conscience whispers dirty, cruel things to me to make me feel worse.

You already lost Sam and Robin.

You could have at least kept Nox.

You could've been happy.

I shake my head to get the thoughts out.

Nox is a monster, and I need to stay away from him at all cost. All he wants is to destroy me, and I'm not going to let him.

I haven't changed my mind all this time, and I never will.

I take a shaky breath, convincing myself I believe those words even though I know it's all a lie.

CHAPTER THIRTY-NINE

NOX

I drop by Willa's place first, but she's nowhere to be seen, and when I question the neighbors, they don't give up much information. But her place is abandoned – emptied. And my stomach rolls with worry.

I shouldn't have followed Dove tonight. It's given me the perfect opening, and I'm not ready for that yet. But it seems like I'm not getting a choice.

As I watch her rush out of the building, my eyes narrow and I curse the prick who's done this to her. I should've gotten rid of Raphael Santino instead of Robin Canterbury. At least Dove wouldn't have any right to be pissed at me then.

Raphael follows her soon after, and I decide to trail him first. He searches for my little bird, and it takes everything in me not to fucking hurt him when he finally finds her, because the first thing she does is scream.

I don't know what the fuck the piece of shit has done to my woman, but I'm going to make him pay.

Dove resists Raphael and he holds out his hands to show her he's not going to hurt her. I can't see everything from my vantage point, but I can see enough to know

I may have to intervene. Even from this distance I can see the vein on Raphael's forehead, pulsating with anger. It reminds me of my father. I know if he strikes, he's going to hit fast and hard. Just like my dad used to.

I can tell they're arguing. Their voices are raised, still not loud enough for me to hear what they're saying, though. I can see his temper getting the best of him.

"Don't do it," I mutter to myself. "Don't you dare fucking try."

But I know he's going to. Some men just can't help themselves. And I know my little bird brings out this in them.

I start walking over there as he starts yelling and hits the wall. I hear him curse, holding his injured hand, but that's nothing compared to the broken nose I'm about to give him.

Dove doesn't see me because her back is turned to me, but her date does.

"Hey man, what the fuck are you –"

He doesn't get to finish his sentence because I've already slammed my fist into his face. The bastard curses out loud and stumbles, but all I'm focused on is Dove. She looks at me, and it takes a split second for the realization to sink in.

"Nox," she whispers. My name on her lips feels like a balm to my wounded soul. I want her to keep saying it, never stop. I'm somehow already turned on, just from standing so close to her, inhaling her rosy scent.

Raphael picks himself up, holding his nose that's spurting blood as he turns his bloodthirsty eyes to me. "Are you fucking insane, you piece of shit?"

"Probably," I mutter. "Now get the fuck away before I rearrange the rest of your face."

"You're a fucking madman." He looks like he's about to swing until Dove steps between us, stopping him from hurting me. "Dove, you can't be serious."

"You've done enough today," she tells him shakily. "I think it's time you went back home, Raphael."

"I'm not leaving you alone with him," her date hisses.

"That's none of your concern," Dove says, her tone softening. "Please, Raphael.

Go."

The guy looks at her with pure despair in his eyes. In that moment, I can see the Dove bug has bit him too. He's head over heels for her, he wants her. Maybe not as badly as I do, but he does. Too bad for him, because I'm not letting it happen. Ever.

"Fine," Raphael mutters, admitting his defeat. "You get yourself out of this one, Dove."

He leaves us there, and the silence that falls on the alley is deafening.

"What the fuck happened?" I ask Dove. "Why was he so upset?"

"It doesn't matter." She runs a trembling hand through her long dark locks. "It's okay now."

"I'm sorry I stepped in, but him hitting the wall... it looked dangerous for you."

"I can defend myself, Nox."

The moment she says my name, she exhales shakily. I can tell seeing me is fucking her up, and I hate that I'm doing this to her.

"I'm sorry, Dove," I say again. "I... I shouldn't have intervened."

"No." She shakes her head, still avoiding meeting my gaze. "It's good that you did. He was really angry, and I was scared."

I nod, not knowing what else to say. "I'll be on my way, then."

"Wait." The word means everything to me and I stop in my tracks. Our eyes finally connect and I see it all laid bare for me in her beautiful gaze. The pain, the expectations, the love. It's all there, and it all exists only for me. "What are you doing back in LA?"

"How did you know I wasn't here the whole time?" I ask, unable to resist my smirk.

"I... I didn't feel like I was being followed anymore."

"You told me not to," I remind her.

"I didn't think you'd actually listen."

I smile. She knows me so fucking well. "I... I left for work. I've done some shows around the globe. Life's been good."

I half-expect her to attack me. I know she thinks I don't deserve this. Robin is the one who should have had all these experiences, all this life ahead of him. But I ripped all that away from both him and Dove. But it's okay. I'm going to make it fucking right.

"I'm glad," she whispers.

"We should get out of this alley," I mutter. "Can I grab you a ride home?"

She nods, but I can tell she's hesitating. I don't mean to tangle her up in my business again, but I can't stop the question leaving my lips.

"Do you want to come back to my hotel? I promise it's not as shitty as last time."

"Why?" Dove stares me down.

"I have something to tell you," I go on. "And I have a favor to ask, too."

"A favor?" Her eyes darken.

"Yeah. Come with me. I want to tell you everything."

I can see the battle going on inside her pretty little head, but I don't want to pressure her any more. Regardless of her answer, I'm going to do what I came to LA to do.

"Okay," she finally whispers. "You still got your bike?"

I laugh out loud. "No, not anymore. I'll call us an Uber."

We wait in charged silence until the car pulls up. We get in the back and I tell the driver the address for my hotel. As the car pulls away, Dove's hand comes to rest between us on the seats. Slowly, I lay my fingers over hers, and she easily intertwines her hand with mine. I'm afraid to even breathe. I didn't expect this. I thought she'd be as angry as she was when we first went our separate ways. But Dove seems gentler, sweeter. It's surprising, but it doesn't change what I have to do to earn her forgiveness. Being with her tonight has only strengthened this belief. It was an idea first, but tonight, it has morphed into a plan.

We pull up in front of my glitzy hotel. If Dove's surprised, she doesn't show it. A doorman opens the car door for her and helps her out. We walk inside where I'm greeted by last name, which seems to surprise her.

"Going by Miller again?" she asks me softly.

"Why not," I grin. "I'm done running from my past."

We take the elevator directly into my suite. It's beautiful here, with gorgeous night views of the city. Dove carefully sits down on the white leather sofa while I pour us both drinks. Something strong, to get the nerves out of the way.

I hand her the glass and we both down our drinks in one go, sharing a nervous smile.

"So," she says. "Why are you really back here, Nox?"

"First, I want to tell you about somebody who's very important to me," I tell her with a smile.

"Oh?" Her eyebrows crease. Is that a hint of jealousy I'm seeing? It pleases me.

"Her name is Willa."

I watch Dove's face fall. She *is* jealous. It turns me the fuck on.

"Who is she?" she asks.

"She's a girl I met while I was... looking out for you. I think she's about seven, eight years old."

"Oh." Her face softens. "A little girl?"

I nod.

"She has a problematic situation at home. Here." I pass her a file in an envelope. "Everything you need is in there. Name, address, info on her parents. I'm hoping you can use this to help her."

"Why can't you help her? Do you have to leave again?"

"Yes," I nod. "Soon, I'll have to go. I only have tonight."

"Tonight?" Her eyes widen. "So tonight's the only night I'm going to see you?"

"For a while," I nod, feeling the pang of pain as I say the words. "Unfortunately, it can't be helped. But I think you'll like Willa. I think you need her as much as she needs you."

"What do you want me to do?"

"Find her," I mutter. "I've been by her house and it's been emptied. I don't know where she is, but her parents are gone, too. I need you to promise me you'll help her, Dove."

"Okay," she says. "I can do that. I'll find her."

"Good," I nod. "I've also arranged for money to be wired over to you."

"Money?"

"To take care of Willa while I'm gone."

"I have my own money, Nox," Dove tells me resolutely.

"Yes, but this is a favor I'm asking you for, and I want to help. Okay?"

"Fine," she sighs. "But why can't you take care of her? Why can't we do this together?"

The fact that she's even considering that fucking hurts. There's a part of me that wants to forgo my plan, tell her to forget it, I'm staying, all this was just a stupid fucking idea to please her. But it's more than that. It's a goodbye to my past self and I need to go through with it before I can start my new life.

"I'm going to explain everything," I promise Dove. "I will. It's just... I don't know how you're going to react."

Her eyes widen even more, burning me with their intensity. Dove doesn't say a word, just silently waits for me to go on.

"I'm going to the police tomorrow," I tell her resolutely. "And I'm going to turn myself in for Robin's murder."

"W-What?" Dove whispers.

"You wanted me to do that and I didn't understand why," I go on. "But now I do. I ripped something away from you, someone you cared deeply about, purely because I was a selfish fuck. I know and understand I can never make that right again. But I want to at least try and show you how remorseful I truly am. I want to pay for what I did. I want to show you I'm capable of redemption."

"But, Nox..." She swallows thickly and I can tell she's trying to find the right words. "What about the little girl? What about Willa?"

"That's why I need your help. I've been losing my mind trying to find her again, but I have a meeting with the chief of police tomorrow morning. I need you to find and take care of Willa."

"But I don't even know her," she whispers. "You can't... you can't leave."

"I have to." I cover her hand with mine. I can feel her fingers trembling. I anticipated a different kind of reaction from Dove, certainly not what I'm getting now. I thought this was what she wanted. But even if she doesn't anymore, I know it's something I have to do.

"Why?" Dove asks, her voice breaking over the single word. "Why do you have to do this now?"

I smile and squeeze her hand gently. "Because of Robin. Because he deserves this, Dove."

CHAPTER FOURTY

DOVE

My heart is pounding from everything Nox just told me. I'm trying to piece all the information together, but there's one thing that's sticking out, reminding me that my life is about to change for ever.

Nox wants to come forward as Robin's murderer. He's volunteered to tell the truth, without any pressure from me. And he seems determined to go through with it, too.

It hurts. It hurts because I know nothing he does now will bring my brother back. And yet there's a sick kind of satisfaction deep within me. Something inside me wants him to pay. I want justice to be served for Robin. I want Nox to realize how impactful his selfish decisions are. I want him to understand what he took away from me, ripped from me without giving me any choice in the matter. I want him to fucking pay.

"But..." My voice is weak, shaky. "How am I going to see you?"

"You won't," he says roughly. "I don't want you to visit me in jail."

"Why not?"

"Because that's not a place for a woman like you," he gets out through gritted teeth. "Besides, this is my punishment. Why should you have to pay for my mistakes?"

I can't say anything. I'm fucking dumbfounded, chewing my bottom lip nervously as I try to come up with an answer. Nox reaches for my other hand and we sit like that, with the weight of the world between us, so many things left unspoken.

"What if I don't want you to do this anymore?" I whisper.

"It doesn't matter," he says firmly. "I have to do it for myself, and for Robin. He deserves this. You still got that hoodie?"

I shut my eyes, nodding. I stashed it in the back of my closet, trying to force myself to forget it was there.

"Good. I'll need that for my confession."

"Nox." Panicked, I grab his hand when he tries to stand up. "Don't do it. Don't leave me. Don't."

"I have to." His words are final and they cut so incredibly deep it feels like somebody's ripping my heart out of my chest. This is the last thing I expected to happen. I never thought Nox would grow a conscience. But he seems determined, and something tells me I won't be able to change his mind now.

"But how am I going to..." I swallow thickly, embarrassed of the words that are about to leave my lips. "How am I supposed to survive without you?"

"You've been fine this whole time, Dove," he says, his gentleness surprising me. This is not the Nox I know. "What makes you think you can't handle more time away from me?"

"I haven't been fine," I whisper shakily. "I missed you... I need you..."

"Fuck." His hand slips from mine and he gets up, pacing his luxurious hotel suite. All of this is so different than what I anticipated. Nox is a different man now, one that wants to fix his past wrongdoings. And here I am, begging him to change his mind, because I'm so fucking weak. "I can't stay, Dove. And you need to find Willa."

"Let me have tonight." I drop to my knees. I crawl closer as he watches me with furrowed brows. "Please. You said you have to turn yourself in tomorrow. Just... let me have tonight to say goodbye to you."

"You want to stay here with me?" I nod, but he shakes his head, groaning. "We can't do that, Dove. It'll be too fucking difficult to leave you."

"Please, Nox." I know I'm begging but I'm not even embarrassed anymore. I need this, need him to make it right. "Don't make me leave. Let me spend the night. Let me be with you one last night."

"Dove..." My name on his lips sounds like a prayer. He wants me to stay, I can tell. He's just fighting his own conscience right now, battling his demons that are telling him to stay the fuck away from me before more bad shit happens. "What about Raphael?"

"What about him?" My face creases. "He ended his chances with me tonight. It's over."

"Did you ever..." He groans, running his hands through his dark hair. "No, I don't want to know."

I look up at him from the floor, softly saying, "No, we never did, Nox. How could I, after you?"

He growls my name and joins me on the floor. We're both on our knees, too afraid to touch, too lost in each other to comprehend this is all going to change in a matter of hours. I'm going to lose him. And this time, it might be for ever.

"Kiss me." I can't believe I've said it. That my innermost desires are coming out like this. But I'm so fucking desperate for his attention, for Nox to make me feel whole like only he can do. "Please, I want to feel your lips on mine, Nox, I can't say goodbye to you without that."

"No," he shakes his head vehemently. "That's a bad idea. The moment we cross that line, I'm going to want more and more."

"So?" I'm shocked by my own bravery. "Maybe I want it, too. Maybe I don't want to resist, either."

"Dove..." He grunts a curse word before scooting closer. He lifts a hand to my cheek, gently caressing the scar he gave me. "I don't want to hurt you anymore."

"Maybe that's what I want," I whisper, cupping his hand with mine. "Maybe I need the pain. Maybe that's what I've been missing all this time. Instead of fighting it all along, I should've been giving in..."

"I want to kiss you," he growls, and my lips part at the thought of his mouth on mine, making me submit to his wicked desires. I want to be his again. I want to be his good girl, opening myself to his abuse, giving us both everything we've ever dreamed of. "Is that okay, Dove?"

I nod wordlessly, already anticipating the touch before it comes. And then he leans in, capturing my mouth in a kiss that changes my world. Nox doesn't kiss like he used to. There's more pain in the way he steals from my lips now. Pain, sorrow, regret, all those things mixing into one as he swallows my cry and deepens our connection by pulling me into the dark abyss of our relationship.

"I can't resist you," he mutters darkly against my lips. "I can't stay away... I need you... I can't be without you. I'm nothing without you, Dove."

"That's not true," I manage to get out, allowing my fingertips to trace the scar I gave him. "You can live without me. You've been doing it for a year, haven't you?"

"Barely," he grunts, kissing me again. "This is so fucking tempting, Dove... How the hell am I supposed to say no to you when you're everything I've ever dreamed of?"

"Don't," I manage. "Don't say no."

He lays me on my back on the shaggy rug in front of the couch. His body cages mine and our kiss turns darker, needier. I'm stealing from him now, not giving a damn about his own needs and only seeing myself. I want him. I need him. I can't survive without Nox's cruel, punishing love. And the worst part is, I'm about to lose it all... All we have left is one night, with the minutes ticking by cruelly and relentlessly.

"When are you meeting the police chief tomorrow?" I whisper.

"Ten a.m."

"Stay with me until then," I beg desperately. "Please, stay with me... Love me..."

"Fuck, Dove." He tries to pull away but I grab the front of his shirt. The pain in his eyes cuts me deep as we look at each other. I'm hurting him. But I can't fucking stop. I need this. Need him.

"Yes," I mutter. "Fuck me. One last time, Nox... Please, show me how much I mean to you..."

"I know what you want me to say," he grunts. "You want me to tell you I love you."

"Don't you?" I ask softly, and he curses out loud. He picks himself up and I shift into a kneeling position. I can tell he's fighting something as his fists tighten and he grabs my long mane of hair. I yelp as he pulls me up.

"I don't love anybody," he says darkly. "But if you want me to fuck you, I can give you a night you'll never forget."

I whimper as he marches me into the impressive bedroom of his luxurious suite. The view from up here is amazing, not that I'm even getting a chance to properly admire it.

"Take your clothes off," Nox barks at me. "Slowly. I want to watch."

He sits on the bed and watches me critically. There's no music in the room but my hips begin to sway anyway to the melody only I can hear. Slowly, I slip the dress off my body until it pools at my feet. I stare right into Nox's eyes as I stand in front of him, raw, real and honest.

His eyes drink in the small curve of my tits and waist. He licks his lips. I know he wants me.

"Come here," he orders me. "Crawl."

I do as I'm told, the hardwood floor burning my knees as I crawl closer and lay my hand on his lap.

"Tell me what you want," Nox orders me. "Beg me for it."

"I want your cock," I manage breathlessly. "Please, I've been without you for so fucking long, Nox..."

"My cock?" he smirks, turning my head to the side so I'm forced to look at his handsome, carved-up face. "Is that all you missed, little bird?"

His old pet name for me feels like a salve on an open wound and I exhale, needy for more of his attention.

"Open your mouth."

I don't obey right away, so he slaps my cheek. My lips part as Nox unzips his pants. I gasp when I see his cock again, my mouth salivating at the sight. I want him. I need this. It's the least he can give me, if he'll really deprive me of seeing him after this.

He slowly pushes his cock in my mouth, then back out again. I let out a frustrated moan but he merely laughs at me.

"You better learn how to work for it, little bird, you don't have much time," he says darkly. "And I want you begging for every single fucking lick."

"P-Please," I manage. How fast the mighty have fallen. I'm so fucking desperate now, so eager for more of this. How was I okay without him only hours ago? I can't live without Nox. I don't *want* to live without Nox.

"No fucking way," Nox growls. "My cum is going somewhere else, Dove. Can you guess where?"

I look up at him, eyes wide. "My... ass?"

"No," he smirks. "Guess again, little bird."

My eyes dance over his features.

I'm not on protection. I don't know whether he knows that, but he doesn't seem to care much. He never did.

"My pussy," I finally whisper.

"That's right," he smirks. "All that hot seed is going right into your sweet little cunt. Tell me Dove, have you been saving yourself for me?"

I flush furiously. I want to lie to him. I want to hurt him by telling him how many men have been inside me since this, since him. But I can't, because it's not the truth. The truth being that I did save myself. That I kept walls up, walls nobody could break down, not even a man like Raphael Santino...

"You have, haven't you?" he laughs at me. "That's a good girl, Dove. I've been good too. So much pussy I could've had, and I turned it all down. For you. For my little bird."

"Thank you," I whisper in a daze-like state.

"Good girl," Nox repeats, pushing the tip of his cock closer to my lips. I open my mouth, eager for him to fill it, but he pulls back again. "I love toying with your mind, little bird. You look so fucking desperate. How much do you want this?"

"I –"

"No," he cuts me off, grinning darkly. "I want you to show me."

CHAPTER FOURTY-ONE

NOX

Dove seems to understand what I want right away. She pulls herself together with a deep breath, her hands coming to rest on my knees and her chin on top of them.

"You think you're the one holding all the strings, don't you?" she asks softly. "But I know the truth. I know how addicted you are to me. I know you can't help yourself, you have to keep coming back to me, taking more, stealing more from me. You're fucking obsessed, Nox."

"Keep going," I grunt, palming my swollen cock. "Fuck, don't stop, little bird."

"You're so fucking desperate for me to suck your cock," she purrs. "All that cum, building up all year, just so I can have it. How many times did you make yourself come thinking about me, Nox? I know there was nobody else, you don't have to tell me. I know what you're like. I know you burn for me."

"Suck it," I order her, presenting her with my cock, but the vixen merely smirks, barely touching the tip of her tongue to my wet cockhead, dripping with precum. "Fuck, Dove. Put me out of my misery. Suck my dick."

"Not yet," she says sweetly. "I like this role reversal."

"I don't," I growl.

"Sure," she laughs, swirling her tongue over the slit in my cock again and making me groan out loud. "You keep telling yourself that, Nox..."

Finally, I've had enough of her teasing and torturing. I grab her by the hair and pull her to her feet.

"You just had to provoke me, didn't you, Dove?" I smirk against her trembling cheek. "You thought you could get away with it, didn't you? Well, you're fucking not. And now I'm going to make you pay."

I push her onto the bed. She falls on her back and I rip my button-down shirt off, revealing my toned body. She gasps when she sees me again in my full glory, but I don't give her any time to process what's happening. My body cages hers and my cock sticks up between us, eager for the warm embrace of her sweet little cunt.

"You want it?" I tease her with the tip, pressing it against her panties. "Beg."

"Please," she manages to get out. "Please, fucking please Nox, put your cock in me, let me come on it..."

"Oh, already?" I laugh at her helpless struggling body. "I don't think so, little bird. Keep right there, on the edge, like a good little slut. Let me feel that tight cunt again..."

I shove her panties to the side roughly. The sight of her sweet cunt is almost too much for me and I groan, pushing my cock between her silky folds until I'm buried to the hilt in what's always been my home.

"Fuck yes," I growl as I start to fuck her. Dove's eyes are spinning across the room, gasp after gasp escaping her parted lips as I fuck myself closer and closer to an orgasm inside her sweet, forbidden pussy.

"Don't stop," she whispers brokenly.

"No fucking way," I grunt in return. "Not now, not ever, not even if you begged me to..."

"Come," she begs next. "Come in me."

"Not yet," I hiss, enjoying the way her tightness wraps around my cock and brings me back home. Fuck, this is what I've been trying to outrun? I never stood a fucking chance... Not with Dove Canterbury, my fucking woman, my fucking life.

"Please," she whispers, and then another thousand pleases escape her lips as I start fucking her. She's like a broken record now, but the sound is sweet to my ears as I continue my assault on her once innocent body.

I've corrupted her. Stolen from her. Ruined her for any other man. I don't know how Dove's going to survive me staying away from her. But I can't think about that now. I have to stay in the moment, right now, when nothing but us matters, when I own her pussy, her body and her mind. She's mine. And nothing's ever going to change that.

"I need your cum," she whispers. "Please. Let me keep it. Let me have it."

"Don't tempt me," I growl. The thought of protection hasn't even crossed my mind, but if she's cool with it, then so am I. Besides, I'm too fucking obsessed with her to stop now. I need to keep going. My cock demands it.

"Please, Nox!" Dove writhes beneath me, reminding me how much I missed her beautiful body, scars and bones and all. She's mine.

A ribbon of doubt unfurls in my chest. Am I doing the right thing by turning myself in for Robin's murder? Should I stay with Dove and help Willa instead?

No.

I can't.

I came back because I wanted to make things right, and I won't be able to rest until I've fixed the shitstorm I've caused in Dove's life. I can't let myself love her without paying the price for my sins. I have to go through with this.

I tune back into the sound of Dove's begging, her voice breaking over the millionth please leaving her lips. I smirk and slap her face, the cheek without the scar, hard. She's shocked into silence and her hurt eyes find mine.

"What?" I smirk. "Don't lie to me and say you didn't like that."

I can see the battle going on inside her head. Knowing she shouldn't like being slapped, because society has ingrained it in her mind that it's wrong. And then the submissive instinct that makes her my little bird. That wants her to give in.

"Beg for another slap," I tell her darkly. "Go on Dove, beg."

She's rendered speechless and I laugh out loud at her, punishing her with my cruelty.

"You don't want to? You want me to stop, little bird?"

"No," she cries out. "Please... I... slap me again."

I hit the other cheek this time and she gasps at the pain before her pretty eyes connect with mine and she breathes, "More."

"You want more?" I ask softly. "You want to get hurt, Dove? Is that what you want?"

She nods eagerly. "Hurt me. Please. Hurt me."

I smirk and attack her bra and panties, ripping them off. She shrieks as I do it, throwing the scraps of fabric on the floor as I lower my lips against her nipple, biting, hurting her. My palms wrap around her throat and I choke the next please out of her, making her succumb to me entirely.

"You asked for this," I remind her, my voice dripping with cruelty. "Begged for it. You love it, don't you? You love being my little abuse toy."

"Fuck." Dove's eyes roll back as I drive my cock deeper and deeper inside her. I can feel myself pulsing with the need to empty my balls into her tight little cunt. I want to give her what she craves so desperately, and yet I'm still holding back. As if I'm not going to give in to my needs... I never could help myself around Dove.

"Please fill me," she whispers. "Please. I waited so long. Give it to me, Nox."

"Say my name," I demand.

"Nox."

"No," I hiss. "Say my real name."

Dove's pretty eyes fly open, connecting with mine. Her voice is nothing but a whisper but the word that leaves her lips feels like a kiss, a caress. "Parker."

I unload my cum inside her then, filling her to the brim. Dove's eyes are alight with passion and something else I don't want to put a name to, because it will make leaving her that much harder. My cock erupts with seed and I hear myself groaning, muttering her name as I drive myself deeper inside, emptying my balls.

It takes me a moment to get it together again after I'm done. I slide off Dove and pull her against me, my fingers going between her legs. Some cum is already leaking out. I bury my nose in her sweet, rose-scented hair and push it back inside her. She has to keep it. It'll be the only memory she has left of me when I'm gone. She needs this.

She mutters my name as I hold her close to me, lost in a state of delirium. It's getting late – or rather, early – and we'll need to be up soon, but something tells me neither of us wants to sleep tonight.

"Why did you come back?" Dove whispers as I run my fingers through her dark locks.

"What do you mean?"

"I mean, you didn't have to. You could've lived your new life, moved on, never looked back."

"I didn't want to."

"Why not?" she asks.

"You really have to ask?" I kiss her forehead. "It's you, Dove. I can't be without you."

"But being with me means..." She bites her lower lip, avoiding saying it.

"I know what it means," I finish for her. "And I'm willing to do it. Because I..."

She pushes herself up on her elbows. Dove's eyes are beyond hopeful as they meet mine. I've only told her I loved her once, and it was a copout, un-fucking-fair on her. I'm not about to repeat the same mistake.

"You what?" she asks.

"Nothing."

She seems disappointed but doesn't argue with me.

"We should get some sleep," I mutter.

"As if that's going to happen."

Dove's devilish little smile makes me grin wide, too.

"You want to stay up all night?" I ask.

"Of course." She rolls onto her front and rests her head against me. "These could be our last moments together."

I don't answer. Dove taps her finger against my chest and I brush mine through her hair.

"Have you thought about that?" She already sounds choked up, and it makes me feel like shit.

"About what, Dove?" I ask with a sigh.

"About what you're doing to me," she whispers. "To us. You're leaving me. You're abandoning me again."

"As far as I remember, the last time you begged me to leave," I remind her, kissing her head.

"I never m-meant it." She's stuttering now, making me want her again because I love this shy, blushing side of her. "Please, don't leave me again."

"I have to," I reply firmly. "We won't talk about that anymore. You can stay with me right up until I walk into that station, if you want. There's a big chance we won't see each other after that, Dove. A long time might pass before we can be together again. Do you understand?"

I'm pouring salt into our wounds and my little bird does nothing to stop me. But I shouldn't have expected anything else. She knew I was going to do this, she asked me for it. Because Dove and I, we're always hurting one another. It's what we live for. And I'm not going to let her stop me now, when it's my fucking turn.

"You're such a little pain slut," I tell her in a low whisper.

"What's that got to do with anything?" she crinkles her forehead, offended.

"Nothing," I grin. "Just something I really need to remember."

"What else do you know about me?" she wonders.

"Everything." I wink at her. "Try me."

"What's my favorite dish?"

"Pad Thai," I laugh. "Too easy. Come on. Make me work for it."

"Hmm..." She looks up at me through those thick, dark lashes and smiles. I understand in moments like these why I've killed for her. And why I may never stop. "Okay, what about my mother's name?"

"Britta," I smirk.

"Are you kidding me?"

"What?" I shrug. "I know she goes by Brittany, but I figured you'd want her real name."

"Creep." She rolls over but I catch her, pulling her close to me.

"What did you call me?"

"A creep," she giggles as I bite her shoulder. "You're a fucking stalker."

"A stalker?" I whisper in her ear. "Fuck yeah I am. And you better keep looking over your shoulder for the rest of time, little bird. Because I'll always be fucking watching.

CHAPTER FOURTY-TWO

NOX

We spend the night together. Talking, touching, watching. I memorize the way Dove's fingertips feel as they glide over my skin. I commit her eyes to memory. I get hard and fuck her again. We lie together silently after that. The minutes are ticking by and we both know we'll have to say goodbye soon.

Her desperation kicks in as I get up from the bed, telling her I have to shower and get dressed so we can leave. She starts begging then, first softly, then louder, her words turning into sobs. It fucking breaks me to drag her in the shower and turn the cold water on above us. It showers us in a cool curtain that clears my mind and makes Dove crumble into a ball on the shower tile, sobbing my name and begging me to stay.

I expected this, so I'm prepared.

I wash her hair with her favorite shampoo that I bought when I first got to LA.

I whisper into her ear, telling her she'll be okay and that I'll always be watching. Who would have thought stalking her would be something I'd use to help her feel better.

After our shower, we dry our hair. I tug on Dove's waves while she fusses about her face devoid of any makeup. I tell her she looks beautiful, lying. I can't tell her how she really looks. Heartbreakingly gorgeous, so naturally stunning my heart breaks because I won't be there now, to watch her grow older, wiser, to have my children, to be my wife. I want to fucking cry, but my father showed me that's not a thing a man does, so I fucking don't. Instead, I wipe Dove's tears as she realizes she's better off with a bare face, since she'll be crying more and more as the minutes tick by.

She clings to me as I get dressed and dress her as well. I kiss her forehead.

"You don't have to come with me," I tell her.

"No, please!" She jumps up and throws her arms around my neck. "Please. Let me come with you."

"Only to the door, Dove," I mutter. "I'm going inside alone."

"Okay," she nods, eager. "Just let me come with you, please."

"Fine," I nod. "Come on. Car's waiting downstairs."

"Can't we walk?"

I glance at the clock. "We might be late."

"Please." She clings to me. "Please. Let's walk."

"Fine," I groan again, quickly cancelling the car on my phone. "Come on, we have to leave right now then."

I bag up Robin's hoodie. My heart and mind feel heavy as I take the bag with me.

She takes my hand and holds it firmly, not letting go even a little bit. We take the elevator downstairs, and I nod at the receptionist. Hodge will take care of everything here, and Dove has everything she needs to find Willa. This is my goodbye to the world. And it might be for ever.

I swallow thickly as we walk out of the hotel. I have to tug on Dove's arm to keep her walking. I shouldn't have agreed to let her come with me to the station. This is going to be hell.

She cries throughout the walk there. We talk. About the weather, about Sam. It's nice to revisit my memories of the old man, and Dove seems to be grateful for the opportunity to talk about her old friend.

Every once in a while she starts crying too hard to speak. I stop, knowing I shouldn't or I risk being late, and kiss her, and hold her. I whisper in her ear that it will be okay.

Finally, we arrive in front of the station. I check my watch, it's three minutes past.

"I'm late," I tell Dove softly.

"No," she shakes her head, shutting her eyes and biting her bottom lip. "Don't go in. Not yet. Please, stay with me."

"I can't." I kiss her nose. "Look at me, please."

She opens her eyes. Tears are already glistening on her lashes. They aren't black like I thought. Almost, but not quite there. They're a dark chocolate brown instead. Her natural color, probably – when she doesn't dye it jet black.

"I love you," I tell her.

"Don't." Her voice breaks and she holds in a sob.

"I do."

"No, Nox. Please, I..."

"Call me by my name, Dove."

"I can't," she whispers. "Please, I can't."

"Do it, I want to remember this moment." I hold her closer to me, leaning my forehead against hers. "You don't have to wait for me, Dove. I might not be out for a while."

"Stop," she whispers. "Red."

"No safe words," I remind her. "Not right now. I need you to listen. Find Willa. Help her. Promise?"

"Promise," she nods brokenly.

"And you'll take care of yourself for me."

"And I'll take care of myself for you," she repeats. I can tell she feels numb, lost, so I kiss her. Deep, unforgiving, reminding her of everything she can have with me. I'm not making her wait for me, and I don't think she should or will. But I'll carry this memory with me for a long fucking time. Until I see my little bird again.

TYRANT STALKER

"Miss me, little bird," I mutter in her ear, leaving the ghost of a kiss. "Miss me every day."

I pull myself away from her outstretched arms even though it's the hardest thing I've ever had to do.

I walk away without turning back once. I can't risk seeing her, because hearing her sobs is destroying me enough. Keeping my head down, I enter the precinct and prepare myself for the hell I'm about to be thrust into.

In the end, I needn't have worried about showing up on time at all.

The chief of police, a Mr. Brentwood, leaves me waiting for hours.

It gives me enough time to utterly destroy myself, thinking of Dove. Is she still waiting on the other side of that door? Is she still hoping I'll come out? Every time, I nearly get up to my feet and walk outside so we can talk. But I'm worried that's the moment Brentwood will pick to call me into his office, so I stay put.

I keep thinking of our last few moments together. How Dove looked at me, how she begged me not to go. It's not like I wanted to leave. But I owe this to her, and to Robin. Sam would be proud of me, too.

I close my eyes, thinking about how much shit I've been through since I realized I only wanted Dove. My mind goes back to all those days in the hospital when I was in a coma. I have the nurses there to thank for getting me back on my feet, but the truth is, there's more to it than that. I felt Dove beside me, holding my hand, nursing me back to health. She helped, too. I survived because of her. Because we're meant to be together.

Unfortunately, I'm not even realizing how much worse Dove's absence is going to hurt weeks, months, years from now.

I remember Robin then. How he was quiet and calm and so very protective of Dove. He always offered a shoulder for her to cry on and expected nothing in return. He was there for Dove even when I couldn't be. He took care of her. He made sure she survived. And I took that away from them.

Sometimes, I find it hard to believe I've fucked up so royally. That I actually did it – killed someone out of purely selfish reasons. It's Hawaii all over again. I'm letting my darkness seep through, even though I know I shouldn't. I've been trained and taught to keep it hidden. But with Dove, it all spills out. I can't imagine being this protective over anybody else.

For a long time, I was convinced I could outrun the darkness inside me, but I now know that wasn't what I needed to do.

The feeling of lightness... forgiveness... relief... it's all part of redemption. And I need to pay for my sins. Only then will I be able to spend the rest of my life – if that's granted – with Dove by my side.

But I've never forgotten one fact – that there's a death penalty here.

With those thoughts swimming through my head, I wait for my name to be called. Soon after, I realize Brentwood isn't even in yet, since his office is dark and his secretary seems fidgety. I paint myself a picture of the man but stop midway through. Who the fuck am I to judge him? In everybody's eyes, he's the saint, and I'm the sinner.

While I wait, I picture better days. Dove, next to me. The soft caress of her palm against my cheek. The whisper of her kiss against my lips. The scent of her, sugar and roses, multiplied by her closeness and the searing touch of her skin against mine. My fists tighten, needing to be wrapped around my cock. Fuck, I'm getting hard. This is beyond inappropriate.

But it's just what Dove does to me, has always done to me. She grips my heart with an iron grip, and she has a hold of my cock, too.

I'm already looking for an excuse to disappear to the bathroom as I picture last night. Her tight little body wrapped around mine. My name a dying whisper on her lips. My load running down her thighs. Fuck, she makes me need her so much. How the fuck am I going to survive without her? What if I never get to see her again?

Now, I'm desperate for another look, another touch. I push myself to my feet and watch the door, glancing between the secretary who's pretending not to see me, and the precinct's front door. Fuck. Should I leave? Should I find out whether Dove's still waiting?

I'm about to leave when a man rushes through the very door I'm watching, offering me a handshake and an apologetic smile.

"I'm Chief Brentwood," he says. "I'm sorry I'm late. Come through to my office, please."

I follow him past the relieved-looking secretary. I watch him take his coat off and place his cup of takeaway coffee on his desk.

"Okay, so what have we got here?" The captain sits down in front of his desk. "I must say, Mr. Miller, we're quite thrilled to have you – you have more than a few fans in the pen outside."

"Thanks," I reply stiffly, struggling to find the words to go on.

"That girl outside, she came with you?"

My heart leaps at his words – she's still out there.

"Yes?" My smile tightens painfully. "What about her?"

"Err, nothing," he replies, sensing the change written all over my face. He picks up his coffee cup and his hands shake. I get predatory when it comes to Dove. She's fucking mine. "She's your wife?"

"Maybe," I mutter. "Soon."

"Some of us know her," Brentwood nods with a sorrowful smile. "She was here a lot when her brother went missing. Never did find that young man. Some of the boys still think he ran off with another woman."

I feel my head getting cloudier. Fuck. Out of all the people working here, they had to give me the guy who knows about the fucking case?

Maybe that's my punishment. Facing the wrath and judgement of this man, who worked his ass off to find out the reason Robin went missing. Maybe he'll take a certain kind of satisfaction to learn I killed him. Or maybe, probably, it will only make him despise me more.

"I'm a killer," I say clearly. "Two years ago, I killed Robin Canterbury, that woman's brother."

"Wh-What?" Brentwood chokes on his coffee, setting the cup down. "You..."

"That's right," I nod. "I killed him and I'm here to confess."

"Mr. Miller, this is..." His face changes. The moment I foresaw happening is here. He hates me now. "You killed that young man?"

"Yes," I nod, signing my death sentence. "I killed him. I did it."

CHAPTER FOURTY-THREE

DOVE

The pain of leaving Nox is haunting me.

I'm walking home after waiting three hours in front of the precinct. But Nox never came back out, and I eventually got too tired to keep waiting. He told me he'd call me once he got the chance, but for now, that's all I know.

But now I have a new mission – something else to keep me going, because I can't bring myself to think about Nox yet. I can't let myself go there. I can't start picturing what could happen if this all goes horribly wrong. Nox told me it was in his favor that he was turning himself in, but he didn't want me to find legal representation. He seemed determined to pay... no matter the cost.

I keep thinking of the death penalty. When I was younger, I used to have arguments with my mother about it. I thought it was inhumane. I still do. And yet I think about the bright shining star that was my brother, and the black hole he left in my life when he was murdered. Nobody should get away with that. Not even Nox.

Conflicted with my own emotions, I realize there's no way for me to sleep just yet. Instead, I head to a café downtown and pull out the manila envelope containing the information about Willa.

I order myself an oat milk latte and slowly make my way through a blueberry and yogurt muffin as I peruse the file. There's not much there. A phone number – I try it, but the phone is turned off. An address, one I'll check later, even though Nox told me the house was abandoned.

A baby is babbling in a carrier next to me, and I smile at her absentmindedly as I peruse the file. Thoughtfully, my hand comes to rest on my own belly.

"Are you expecting, too?"

I turn my attention to the baby's mother, a younger-than-me redhead with bright blue eyes.

"Oh, no," I mutter with an awkward smile. "Just wishful thinking."

"I hope it happens for you soon," she smiles encouragingly. "It took my husband and me a few years, but we finally have our baby."

She points to the chubby-cheeked replica of her in the buggy who waves her little arms at me.

"She's adorable," I say.

"Thanks. Sophie-Ann is turning one this month, aren't you darling?" She tickles her daughter's chin, making me long for things I may never have. "We adopted her."

"Oh, that's wonderful!" I'm surprised in a good way. "She looks so much like you."

"Yeah," the young mom smiles blissfully. "She's our little miracle. Anyway, we have to get going. Nice meeting you!"

I wave her off and return to my latte, doing my best not to burst into tears again. But I force myself to stop thinking about Nox and focus on Willa instead.

I grab a sandwich for later and head to the address of Willa's house. When I arrive, I realize pretty quickly most of the building's been abandoned. There's one older man who still lives there, but he yells at me to leave, so I do. I keep walking through the neighborhood, soon realizing this must be a school route, since there are kids walking home in their uniforms. I follow them in the opposite direction until I finally reach a brick school. The sign reads Green Valleys Public Elementary.

Deciding this is as good as any guess to Willa's whereabouts, I head inside and ask to see someone on the school board, mentioning Willa's name. I don't have her last name, but I'm given proper attention from the start. The principal herself sees me, wearing a worried expression as she points for me to sit down in front of her desk.

"Is Willa okay?" she asks.

"Well, I was hoping you'd know more than I do about that," I say nervously. "When was the last time you saw Willa?"

"You're not her mother, are you?"

"N-No," I clear my throat.

"Then I'm afraid I'm not at liberty to discuss Willa Baudelaire. I'm sorry."

She gets up and offers me a hand to shake, and reluctantly, I do the same. At least I got the little girl's last name out of this.

As I'm heading for the door, the principal clears her throat. "Miss Canterbury."

"Yes?" I look at her over my shoulder.

"You should ask Mercy Waterstone about Willa," she nods. "The two are best friends. She'll be in the playground about now."

"Thank you," I smile gratefully. "I'm not going to hurt her."

"I know," she nods gravely. "But I worry her mother and stepfather might."

I swallow the bitter pill of what she's told me and head back into the playground resolutely. I pull out a picture of Willa holding a teddy bear. She's freaking adorable, with her pale blonde hair and forget-me-not blue eyes. Her skin is pale and covered in a layer of freckles. Her hair is matted and lacks shine, but nobody can deny what a pretty little girl she is.

I start showing some kids the photos, but most of them shake their heads before their mothers pull them away. I'm becoming a nuisance here, I have to work fast or I risk getting kicked off the playground.

I see the girl before she sees me. She seems feisty, with bright blue eyes and dark, chestnut brown hair. She approaches me and nods to the photo in my hands.

"Looking for Willa?"

"Yes," I nod. "Do you know where she is?"

"Who sent you?" The little girl cocks her head to the side and gives me a doubtful look.

"I..." I furrow my brows. "Nobody, well, I suppose... Nox."

I swallow his name. Fuck. That hurt more than I'd anticipated. Is this what it's going to be like now that he's away?

Unable to bear the weight of that question, I turn back to the brunette. "Are you Mercy?"

"That's me," she beams. "I'm Willa's best friend."

"Mercy, you have to help me," I beg her. "Willa is in trouble, isn't she?"

"Yes," she nods gravely.

"Where is she staying? Can you take me to see her?"

She shrugs. "I have to ask first."

"Please. Is she okay?"

She just stares in return.

"Look." I kneel down next to her. "Did Willa mention her friend Nox?"

She nods slowly.

"He's my friend, too. But Nox had to leave again, so he asked me to take care of Willa. Understand?" Mercy nods again, then glances over my shoulder, nervously biting her lips.

"My mommy's coming to take me home."

"Okay, Mercy," I nod. "Tell me where Willa is."

"I don't know," she shakes her head. "But she will come by my house tonight. I live on the same street she used to."

I think of the fancy new development that I saw earlier. They're tearing down those community apartments to build more expensive properties. I guess Willa's family was just one casualty of that.

"Her mommy died," Mercy suddenly says.

346

"What?"

"Willa's mommy. She never came back from the hospital."

"What happened?" I ask.

"I have to go now," Mercy goes on nervously. "Find my house, the white building with a cactus in front. Willa will be there tonight."

"Thank you," I nod carefully just as someone calls her name. She disappears and I do my best to blend into the crowd on the playground as Mercy's mother takes her home.

At least I'm a step closer to finding Willa.

That night, I'm waiting on Willa's former street at six p.m.

I didn't know what her friend meant, but I'm hoping she was right about Willa, and that she'll trust me enough to let me take care of her. I'm also trying to get my mind off the fact that Nox hasn't called once. I suppose they'll have to film the confession and get it on tape, but I'm still nervous as hell something terrible has happened. Thinking and looking for Willa has helped distract me.

I get lucky a couple minutes after eight when I see a nanny arriving at a white house and a couple driving off in an Aston Martin. A moment later, Mercy appears on the doorstep, nervously glancing around. And then, lightning fast, a small figure runs up to the door. Mercy hands her something and closes the door. The whole thing doesn't take longer than a minute. You could miss it in the blink of an eye, but I don't.

"Hey!" I call out after the girl and she slows down, risking a look over her shoulder. Her eyes and hair are wild, but her face is that of a child. "I'm Nox's friend. Are you Willa?"

She stops in her tracks. I see it. How much she wants to believe me. Then the pull of every lie she's been told by people she was supposed to trust, flashing in her eyes. She wants it to be true, but she knows it's probably not.

"Please, he told me about your teddy, and the phone he gave you."

Willa cocks her head to the side. "Did they tell you about my mom?"

She sounds so much older than her age.

"I'm not sure," I admit. "What happened?"

"My stepdad beat her," she mutters. "She died in the hospital. I ran away after he called home."

"Has he been looking for you?" I ask.

The girl shrugs. "He hasn't found me so far."

"Where have you been staying, Willa?" She shrugs again, her eyes heavy with pain. "Are you hungry?"

"Mercy gives me some food every day," she points to the bag in her hand.

"Would you like to take a shower? We can go to my place. Or, I can take you to someone else who'll take care of you," I rush to say. I want to help her so badly, but I can tell the little girl doesn't trust me.

"Where do you live?"

"In a small house," I smile shakily. "We'd have to take a taxi there. I can bring you back here tomorrow night, if you don't want to stay with me."

She stares at me critically. Her eyes settle on my scar and I feel my old demons coming out to play. I want to cover up, hide the scar.

"You have the same scar as Nox," she finally says. "Did you have it first?"

I nod slowly, not wanting to tell her more. But she doesn't ask. Instead, she comes closer and offers me her hand.

"Hello," she says, holding her little dirty palm up. "My name is Willa. I'm very sad sometimes."

She reverts to a younger role like this. I cock my head to the side and shake her hand. "Hi, Willa. I'm Dove. I'm here to tell you what happened to Nox and that I want to help you while he's away."

She nods thoughtfully. "Why did he have to go away again?"

"Nox did something bad," I admit. "He wanted to make amends."

"Okay," she nods. "Will he be back?"

I swallow the pain in my throat. "I hope so. But neither of us knows when."

"Can we go to your house now?" Willa licks her lips. "I really need to pee."

I call an Uber and we get in without talking, but with Willa's little hand still in mine.

She stares out of the window at her old neighborhood and I don't ask any questions until we arrive home. There, I take her hand again and I walk her to my house.

"I have lots of plants," I smile nervously. "It's kind of my thing."

"I like plants," Willa says as she enters the house.

In front of us, I see a semi-messy home of an eternally single plant mom. I wonder what it looks like through Willa's eyes.

"Do you like it?" I ask nervously. "I have a guest room... you can sleep there, if you'd like. And you can help me plant and water and take care of the plants."

"Stay here with you?" She looks at me with pained eyes. "Why?"

"Because Nox wanted that," I whisper. "And I think I might need you... more than you need me."

"I'll stay," she nods. "I'll help."

I smile at the idea of a seven-year-old helping, but there are tears in my eyes and somehow, I believe her.

Willa's going to help me get through this.

CHAPTER FOURTY-FOUR

NOX

Ironically, the first time I get my ass kicked in prison is because of Dove.

There's a man who used to know a man who used to know a man named Sam, and the rest is history. They know all about the prick who ruined Dove's life, and now they've worked it out I killed her brother, too. They don't know the good sides of our story. All they know is the bullshit I've put my woman through.

So I tell myself I deserve this. When one of the inmates spears me with a shiv, I grit my teeth and suffer through it. I don't fight back, but I still get in trouble. That's my first lesson about prison, and I learn it hard and fast.

I don't call Dove. I promised I would, but I know it would cause more trouble than it's worth. She needs to move on. I made her swear to me she'd find Willa, and I hope she's doing that and making sure the little girl is okay.

But it's all just a way to keep Dove on my mind. Dove, with her pale skin that bruises so easily. Dove, with her blue veins, pink nipples, dark heart. She's mine. Will she wait for me? She shouldn't.

Those thoughts get harder and harder to banish as the days slowly trickle by.

I've been locked up a week, with no way out for the foreseeable future. When I was in Brentwood's office, the death penalty came up. I found myself rendered speechless. My worst fears were coming to life. But I haven't spoken to Brentwood in a while. I've been assigned a state-appointed attorney who's spent more time looking for his glasses than he has questioning me about my case.

Because I brought the hoodie with me to the precinct and I gave them a confession, I'm going down for manslaughter.

Those first few weeks in prison are the worst because I'm not used to my new reality. Tossing and turning on a metal bunk bed. Taking a piss in front of my cellmate. Getting beaten, threatened, and constantly terrorized by the guards are just a few of the things I have to suffer.

But this is who I am now. A common criminal.

I set up my finances with Hodge before I got in here. All the money I make while I'm in prison is going into a trust fund for Dove, and one for Willa, too. At least I'll know they're taken care of if something happens to me in here. There are no guarantees in here, no way of knowing whether I'll get out alive or not. This is my life now.

I make friends, too. Men who are like me and gave in to the darkness at one point or another, like I did, soon realizing it wasn't for the best. This is a place where you repent. I'm alone with my thoughts for most of the day. My mind has always frightened me, but now there's no way to escape it. So, I think about them all, the people who shaped my life.

First, my father, June's mom. My brother, Kade. Then Dove. Dove's brother, Robin. Sam. Willa.

They all shaped and molded my life. And I let most of them down.

I make a solemn promise to myself to fix shit once – *if* – I get the fuck out of here. I'm not going to be the bad guy in all their stories. I want to make up for all my wrongdoings. One day, if I get the chance, I'll even make things right between myself, my brother, and his wife.

ISABELLA STARLING

June hasn't crossed my mind in a long time. It's strange to think that she used to be ever-present on my mind, the object of my affection and obsession. I was blind back then. Fucking blind. Dove was right in front of me and it still took me years to realize she was the woman for me. Back then, I was obsessed with having what others said was off-limits. My father planted a deadly seed when he tried to keep me away from June Wildfox. He only made my obsession worse.

But now I don't even think about Kade or June. All my attention is focused on Dove Canterbury. Just as it should have been from the start. She occupies my mind, owns my heart and soul. In here, I have too much time to think, too many opportunities for my mind to wander back to Dove, wondering what she's doing, whether she's missing me as much as I miss her.

Days turn into weeks turn into months. A letter arrives and it takes my breath away. A single Polaroid photo slips from the envelope and I stare at it in wonder. It's Dove. Shadowed and artfully positioned, with a hand on her growing belly.

Fuck.

It takes me a moment to realize what this means. My woman is having my baby while I'm imprisoned for the murder of her brother. The way life has worked out chokes me up, makes me feel dizzy. A life taken, a new life given – a baby, a son. Because I already know she's going to give me a son.

But there's no way for me to see him, meet him. I don't want him exposed to my current environment, so as much as it fucking hurts, I don't reply to Dove, don't acknowledge what she sent me. But every fucking second I'm rotting in that jail, I'm thinking about them out there.

My family.

Hopefully, they'll still want me back if I ever get the fuck out of here.

Hearings come and go, and then, almost six months later, my trial begins.

It all passes in a bit of a blur, my mind doing its best to protect me from the viciousness of the case and trial. I shouldn't feel sorry for myself, because I deserve this.

TYRANT STALKER

Every night, I torture myself by thinking about Robin and what I took away from him.

I plead guilty. I don't hesitate about it for a single second. I did it. I took an innocent's life, and now it's my time to fucking pay for a crime that never should have been committed.

Robin could've had a family too. Perhaps he would've settled down with that Elise woman, or maybe somebody else. He could've had children, little nieces and nephews for Dove. I took that all away from him.

I worry myself sick during the trial. I tell myself if they sentence me to die, I fucking deserve it. I took something I shouldn't have. Ripped a life away from someone who deserved life more than I did. For that alone, I deserve the worst punishment our legal system has to offer.

The verdict is delivered by the jury. Dove isn't in the room – it's closed to the public. The case hasn't garnered much attention and Hodge has done his job, keeping my name out of the papers. If I ever get out of here, my life could go back to normal.

They find me guilty of all charges. I await the sentence with bated breath. When it comes, I'm almost disappointed.

They haven't sentenced me to die. The head of the jury tells the judge they see a desire in me to better myself. They're going to be merciful.

The judge rules – fifteen years in prison, with the possibility of parole at five.

It's a long fucking time, but anything is better than the death sentence. I'm led away in handcuffs, my shoulders slumped. I'm going to pay for all my crimes in here. Even though the police only know about Robin, I need to repent for what I did to Hodge's daughter, and to my twin and stepsister, too.

I'm led back to my cell. My cellmates have been changing, but I'm informed I'm being moved soon, to a calmer, less dangerous block. That's a small relief. Ever since I've been attacked, I've been worried how the fuck I was going to survive years of being locked up in this hellhole.

They tell you a lot of things about prison, but nobody tells you anything about the lack of silence.

There are sounds all around me. Screaming, the sound of piss hitting the metal toilets. The guards clank their batons against the bars of our cells, scream, shout at us. There is no peace in here. This is where minds go to die.

But I force myself to nurture my thoughts. I find moments of peace by thinking of my favorite memories starring Dove. Her smile, her taste, her scent, all fill my mind until I'm convinced I'll never forget them. I commit them to memory, every move she makes, every word she said to me when we were together. I fool myself into thinking it helps, and for a while, it does. Except some nights, when I'm lying on my back on the springy mattress, staring at the ceiling. Those nights are the hardest because she feels the furthest away she's ever been.

I no longer believe I deserve to die.

And that belief gets stronger and stronger the more time I spend in jail. I start learning, reading books, taking classes. The prison accepts me as one of their own, the rotten, twisted criminals who are being punished for their crimes in here. I am one of them. I fucking got what I had coming.

But I grit my teeth and take it all. I don't question it, or fight it. I just take the cards life has dealt me and tell myself one day it will all get better. One day, I'll be free again. One day, I'll hold my son in my arms and tell him I love him.

For now, I don't even know his name...

I know it's a dream, but it doesn't stop me from enjoying it.

I'm imagining Dove here, with me. A place she should never be – or anyone else for that matter. But it's a dream, so I forgive myself.

My fist is wrapped in her long mane of hair and she's sucking my dick through the bars of my cell. Thick drops of spit fill her mouth and she groans my name with her throat full of cock.

"You like that, little bird?" I ask her. "I'm going to make you pay, too."

She gags and I take the chance to push deeper. Her eyes bulge and I laugh cruelly, enjoying her pathetic struggles. She looks so hot like this, on her knees, out of control. I want to stroke my cock to the sight, so I pull out of Dove's mouth, wiping it on her scarred cheek. She gasps.

"Filthy fucking girl, drooling all over my cock," I hiss, jerking off over her face. Dove sticks her tongue out, eyes begging. "You want to earn my cum, little bird? Offer me your fucking ass."

She pales, shakes her head. It's been a long time since I've been inside her tightest hole. Too long.

"I fucking miss it," I tell Dove. "So, turn around and let me see it."

Reluctantly, she crawls around, lifts her skirt and her ass is exposed to my hungry eyes. And fingers. Without warning, I spit on her ass to lube it, and slip my thumb inside her. She cries out in pain. Fucking adorable. I spit on her hole some more, making sure she's wet enough for me. I put another finger in, stretching her so the next time I spit, it drips right inside.

"Fuck, Nox!" she moans beneath me.

""Shut up," I growl, smacking her ass. "Unless it's begging for my load, I don't want to hear it."

Stubbornly, Dove presses her lips together. She doesn't say another word, her gasps silenced as she puts her palm over her mouth. I don't let that stop me. I pull my fingers out of her and replace them with the head of my cock. Dove isn't silent anymore.

"Please, Nox, please!" She looks up at me from behind. "I want you to fill me, I want you to give me everything..."

"Did you earn it?" I hiss. "Did you fucking earn it, little bird?"

And with that, I wake up to real life.

To handcuffs on my wrists, sometimes even when I sleep. To the cold room, where they put those of us who misbehave. We're treated worse than dogs. But I endure it.

ISABELLA STARLING

And I fall back asleep with a smile on my face, thinking of Dove.

Thinking of Willa.

Thinking of my son.

I'm doing this for them.

CHAPTER FOURTY-FIVE

DOVE
3 YEARS LATER

I worry my bottom lip between my teeth. My eyes remain firmly shut, my fingers fraying the edges of my black dress. I wait until they call out Nox's last name, Miller, then pick myself up and walk robotically up to the reception area.

Before he went in, before I found out they weren't going to kill him, I told myself I'd come see Nox every weekend. But then everything changed.

I got pregnant. I had a beautiful baby boy. Now it's just us and Willa. A family, one I'd never realized I needed, desperately so. But I'm not here to tell Nox that he has a son. I'm here because I need his dirty, depraved touch, and I'm fucking done making excuses about it.

I pin the visitors' badge to my dress, careful not to prick my skin with the needle. Then, I walk inside the room where Nox and I will have complete privacy for an hour.

He's already sitting down. I expected him to have cuffs on, but he doesn't. Nox lifts his head and looks at me. I want to cry at the sight of him. He's bruised, battered, but not broken. If I thought a death sentence would've been bad, seeing him this way knocks the breath right out of me. He's being punished for his crime. He's doing this for me. Yet, as I look into his handsome face, I don't know whether I can forgive myself for putting him in here.

I want to tell him so many things, but I stand frozen to the spot. There's a rickety bed in the corner of the room – a reminder this is a conjugal visit. That's what I requested.

"Little bird," Nox mutters and I smile on instinct, because his voice is still the same, and the butterflies in my stomach are still fluttering. "Come here."

I approach him, my heart threatening to beat straight through my chest.

"I can't believe you're here," he mutters, pulling on my hand to bring me closer. I notice the anklet around his foot then, controlling his every move. "I waited so long."

"Nox, I need you." All those words I'd been getting ready to say disappear. All that matters is me and him, and the fact that we're finally touching again. I become helpless in Nox's presence. He pulls me into his arms and we kiss for the first time in three years.

His lips are just as searing, just as passionate as I remember them. I touch the scar on his cheek to ground myself, unable to believe this is really happening, we're really being reunited.

Nox's hands begin to roam my body, and soon, they're impatiently tugging on my dress.

"Rip it off," I manage weakly.

"How will you get out of here without it?"

"I don't care," I whisper.

With a grunt, he rips my dress down the middle, exposing my lingerie. I wore this especially for him, purple and dark, accentuating my pale complexion.

There are so many things we should talk about, but they're all forgotten in the face of our reunion. I'm getting drunk on Nox's scent. He's nipping at my neck now, stumbling toward the bed with me in his arms.

"Wait," I beg him. "Please, we have to –"

"No," he mutters, too distracted by my body to listen. "Need you first."

"We only have an hour."

"I'll make it count." He nuzzles my neck. "Fuck, I can't get enough of it. To smell you again. To fucking feel you again. Fuck, Dove. Let me fuck you."

"No, please," I manage. "Not yet."

"Now."

His voice is so commanding, dark, twisted. It's everything I remember Nox to be, and I can't say no to him. He's the only man I can't pretend with. I'm so used to playing a role, being someone other people expect me to be. But not with him. Not here. Not now.

I lie on the bed. It's lumpy and I close my eyes, trying to pretend we're somewhere else. But Nox grabs me by the throat, making me gasp.

"You don't want to be here, do you?" he asks calmly.

"I'm here, aren't I?" I hiss in response, my defenses picking up. "I stayed away, Nox. I thought that's what you wanted."

"To find out I had a son through a Polaroid photo?"

"You don't even know if he's a boy." I scratch his arms until he lets go, smirking.

"Of fucking course I do. What's his name, Dove?"

I sigh, shaking my head, then whisper the answer. "Kellan."

He kneels in front of me then. He's different. So much different than the last time I saw him, and broken in too many ways for me to count. But he still loves me, I know it. Just like I love him.

"We don't have much time," I whisper. "Please."

He nods, takes a deep breath and picks himself up. When he's standing again, his eyes are so incredibly dark they look black. He pulls the belt from his waist, an orange one to go with the jumpsuit, and expertly ties it around my neck, connecting it into a knot around my tits and then wrists.

"You're learning some tricks in here?" I tease him, my heart skipping a beat as I realize I may have gone too far.

But Nox's dark humor is still there. He slaps my tits, the right one, then the left one. "Watch that tongue, little bird. Don't make me hurt you. Although, you'd probably love that, wouldn't you?"

"No," I lie through gritted teeth, smirking right back.

"Well, let's see just how big of a liar you are, Dove." He ties my hands with the belt to the head rail. I struggle uselessly. There's no way for me to break free now – I am his prisoner, at his mercy, and it feels so good. So right.

"Where should I begin..." Nox takes a step back, admiring his handiwork. He looks so alive. I hope I'm the one making him feel this renewed vigor for life. "Yes, I think I want to hurt those pretty pink nipples first."

I stare defiantly ahead as he pinches my right nipple between two fingers, then begins slapping it.

"You love it when I hurt you," my stalker whispers in my ear. "Don't you, little bird?"

"N-No." My voice breaks. "Please, don't stop."

"That's right." Nox's eyes darken with something I'm afraid of, but deep down I know he's never going to hurt me like he did when I was young. And he doesn't.

Instead, he kneels between my legs and slaps my knees apart. He slides my panties down and I help him, wiggling out of them until I'm exposed. He stares at me, devouring me with his eyes until I blush under the burn of his gaze.

"So fucking beautiful," Nox mutters, more to himself than me. "I'm going to remember this moment for ever. That you loved my cock so much you came to beg for it in prison."

"Asshole," I hiss.

"Shut up, little bird, you fucking love it."

He dives between my thighs then, filling his mouth with my taste and groaning as I moan myself closer and closer to an orgasm.

"God-fucking-damnit, Dove," he mutters. "You taste better than ever."

Suddenly he pulls away, as if he's done playing games with me now. He strips off the jumpsuit and his cock bounces free, erect, the veins on it throbbing with desire. My mouth fills and I do my best to keep my breaths steady.

It's not like I can outrun him, anyway.

"I'm going to fuck you so hard you'll have to crawl out of here," he growls. I whimper in response, but Nox is already pushing between my legs, his cockhead urgently pressing against my entrance and demanding my submission. "Goddamn, little bird. Look how you're making my dick drip... I'm so fucking ready to be inside you again."

He leans against my head, whispering in my ear, "To knock you up again."

My breath catches but it's too late, Nox is already fucking me. His cock pushes deeper and deeper, filling me up so much my eyes roll back in pure ecstasy. My toys or any other man could never live up to him. He's a fucking God, and I was born to worship him. Nox is my religion.

He fucks me like it's the first and last time combined, and I submit to him fully, allowing him in deeper than I've ever let anyone before.

"Time's running out," I manage to whimper at some point.

"Don't worry," he grunts. "I just want to keep fucking you until the clock strikes. Come on my cock, little bird. Fucking soak me."

I can't hold back once he says that and he laughs out loud at me as I moan his name, coming for him, letting him into my heart again.

"My fucking turn," he growls after, driving himself into me harder and harder until he builds up to another orgasm for both of us. We come together this time, our bodies writhing with pure pleasure as we come down from the unbearable high of being together again. "Fuck yes, Dove. Milk my cock. It's all for you, little bird."

Afterward, I'm numb.

Nox gently unties me. He takes off his orange shirt, stripping down to a white tank underneath and puts the shirt on me, covering up how indecent I am.

He carries me to the metal table and sits me in the chair. He sits opposite and holds my hands over the tabletop.

The alarm blares that our time is over. I sit there, frozen to the spot with my makeup smudged all over my face. I'm wearing the top of Nox's orange uniform, and he's smirking at me from across the table. I'm sure it doesn't take much guessing to realize what we just did here.

The double doors leading into the room are unlocked and opened. I stare stubbornly at the silver metal of the table while Nox stands up, still keeping his hands in mine.

"Sit down, Miller," the guard barks at him.

"Hey, he didn't do anything." I keep our fingers intertwined as I glare at the guard.

"Miss, I'd advise you to shut up," his friend tells me, reaching for his holster where there's a gun. I risk a look at Nox and the pain and anger in his eyes make me think he's going to kill both of them.

But he doesn't.

Instead, he swallows his pride and never takes his eyes off mine as they rip our hands apart. I know what his silent glare means. He's doing this for me, for us, because he wants us to be together as soon as we can.

As he's led out of the small room, my heart breaks all over again as he's dragged away. One of the guards kicks him repeatedly.

I close my eyes and give myself a moment to regain my strength. At least I got to see him. At least I got to kiss him. At least I got to be with him...

"Miss, are you coming?"

"Yes," I call out, fighting the fact that I'm on the verge of tears. I pick myself up and dust off the orange shirt I'm wearing, ignoring the gawking looks of the guards and leaving my ripped dress in the room behind me.

I walk past men who whistle and ogle me openly, out into the hot LA sun. I find my car – a Mustang Convertible in cherry red named appropriately as Cherry, because why not – and sit behind the wheel for a long time, collecting my thoughts.

Everything that's happened today in a single hour messes with my head, but I do my best to make sense of it all.

ISABELLA STARLING

All I know is, I can't stop waiting for Nox. Not now, not ever. Nobody else could ever make me feel the electricity he does, sparking between our fingertips like fireflies. We belong together – I've never been more sure of that. And whether it takes three years or thirty, I'm going to wait for him to come back to me, and spend the rest of my life showing him how much I love him.

CHAPTER FOURTY-SIX

NOX

If I thought it would be easier to move on after Dove now that I've seen her again, gotten my fill, I'd be wrong as fuck.

Her memory is fresh in my mind now, breaking me with every second that passes without her by my side.

But now I have a new mission and a new calling – to get the fuck out of here.

As opposed to the beginning, when I didn't care about ever getting out, I'm now more than eager to work on my case and prove I'm ready to return to society outside of the prison walls.

I meet with all the counselors, do volunteer work and make sure I'm on my best behavior. And by the time my parole comes up, two things shock me like a cold, hard slap to the face.

One – I've been in this hellhole for five years now.

Two – I have a real chance of getting out on parole and reuniting with Dove.

Time passes slowly in prison, but when you're waiting for the results of the jury deciding whether you get to be a free man or not, it's even more excruciating.

TYRANT STALKER

But then, five years and six months into my sentence, I get the word – I'm going to be a free man. I'll be on parole, I'll have to return to my job and report to my parole board officer, and I'll be wearing an anklet to ensure I don't leave the state. But nevertheless... I'll be free to be with Dove again. That is, if she's still waiting.

I anticipate the date of my release, but in the end, it ends up shocking me by creeping up on me. I wanted to contact Dove, to tell her, but I never got through when I called. So, I left a voicemail message to an automated machine, not even sure whether I still had the right number. I told her I was being released, and hoped the news wouldn't destroy her.

As I stand in front of my cell that morning, I finally allow the smallest ray of hope to shine through all the shit I put Dove through.

I paid for my crime, but I'm not done. I'm going to make sure Dove is treated like a queen every second of her life. I'm going to fucking worship the ground she walks on. If she's with someone else – even if it's Raphael – I'll keep my distance. I'll go back to the beast in the shadows, the stalker who's watching out for her. But I already know I won't be able to walk away. Not from her. I never could.

"Good luck, Miller," a guard smirks as he opens the cell door. "Welcome to the rest of your life."

His words ring true and hard with me as I walk out of there, a free man, with the ankle bracelet snug around my leg.

There's a long walk to the end of the driveway leading up to the prison, and the sun is beating down hard. I can't see up ahead, so I cover my forehead with my hand and walk into the distance. I have fifty bucks to my name and nowhere to go. But I've been worse off, and I know I'll make it through this.

I reach the end of the road and glance up and down, trying to find another driver who could lend me a phone or give me a ride downtown.

That's when I see the approaching car. It's a cherry red Mustang, a convertible, and there's a woman driving it with chestnut hair. In the back seat, a young girl sits with two little children. One's still in a baby carrier.

The sight almost fucking kills me.

Dove pulls up in front of me, kicking up dust. I can't erase the smile off my face as Willa kisses her baby brothers' foreheads and runs up to me embracing me.

"Hi, Nox!" she says, giddy.

I hug her back, staring at the back seat where the older boy is staring at me curiously. I see something in the boy, like my own darkness. But I think he's smart enough to keep it under control.

The younger boy is a toddler, but he's smiling wide, stretching out his arms toward me.

"Hello." I turn my attention to Dove now, my vision in black, except she let her hair go back to its natural color since I last saw her. She looks so fucking stunning. It takes me a moment to realize she has a scar. But then I remember my own, self-consciously touching my fingertips to my cheek.

"Dove," I breathe. My voice is ragged and pained, but her name still feels good on my lips. "You came."

"We all did!" Willa exclaims and I laugh as Dove embraces me, too.

Fuck. This is emotional beyond anything I could've ever imagined. I thought I couldn't feel anything, not after what my father did to me. But Dove and my new family have shown me my full range of emotions, and for the first time in my fucking life, I'm happy.

And I deserve it.

I sit in the front with Dove while Willa watches out for her brothers behind us. Dove slowly drives down a road I know, leading back to the house where she used to live all those years ago. I have to force myself not to keep glancing at the back seat, but I also can't tear my eyes off Dove. She looks fucking stunning. Irresistible. Sexy. Like everything I've ever dreamed of sent here to haunt me. But now I can finally have her. Now she can finally be mine.

I'm still staring when we pull up in front of her house. It looks just like it used to, except there are more plants, and toys scattered around the yard. I get out of the car and help Dove out too before turning my attention to the kids. The older one, Kellan, takes my hand trustingly and smirks at me. I'm gonna have to be careful around him, because so far, he seems exactly like me.

"What's your brother's name?" I ask Kellan as he helps me unstrap his brother.

"Zane," he says, and I grin. Dove picked cute names. I'm trying not to get too emotional but I already know it's no use fighting these emotions.

I help the younger kids to the house while Willa and Dove follow. Inside, it's chaos, but the kind of chaos I've been dreaming of while I was locked up. The boys run to their toys, and Willa, Dove and I sit down at the dining room table.

"How hard was it to find Willa after I left?" I ask Dove, still not quite able to believe I finally get to ask all the questions I've carried in my heart the past five years.

"I had help from her friend," Dove smiles, squeezing Willa's hand. The two look nothing alike, with Dove's darker hair and Dove's light locks and freckles. But I can tell their relationship is like mother and daughter. Dove adores my friend – my daughter – and Willa is looking up at my woman with pure adoration in her eyes. "After that, since her stepfather disappeared, it was easy to get custody. Too easy, almost."

"And what about Zane?"

"I realized I was going to have a baby a few weeks into getting custody of Willa," Dove smiles affectionately.

"Yeah, we went through it all together," Willa nods. I'm still marveling at the sight of her and how much she has changed since the last time I saw her. She's a young girl now, no longer a little kid. And I can tell her heart hasn't changed in the slightest. "Zane was a healthy baby and we were really happy."

"Even though he screamed all night for the first year." Dove winces, making me laugh. This feels like home. "But it was a learning curve. We get along better now."

"What about Zane?" I ask.

"He's two," Dove nods. "We just celebrated his birthday. He fell face-forward into his cake..."

She and Willa convulse into giggles and I smile along though deep down, I feel like I've missed out massively. But I put on a brave face, because I owe it to my family, and regardless of the past, I'm blessed to be here with them.

"Don't worry." Dove squeezes my hand. "There will be plenty more birthdays, especially with four of us."

"And I already know what I want for my next one!" Willa says in a sing-song voice.

"You're so not getting a phone." Dove narrows her eyes at me.

"Mercy has one!"

"So?" Dove sticks her tongue out at her and then Willa flips her off.

Before I can react, Dove flips her off right back. I'm about to scold them both when I realize it's an inside joke for them, and they giggle along. I've walked in on something here, something special and magical. This is what a family is supposed to feel like. This easy, breezy confidence that makes me feel comfortable, like I can share anything in the world with the people in this house.

Kellan and Zane come through to the dining room, each of them wailing for Mommy. It's so strange seeing Dove in this new role, but I shouldn't be surprised by how at home she feels in it. She wipes Kellan's scrape and bandages it up while simultaneously grabbing an ice lolly for our younger son. Satisfied, the kids retreat to the living room to watch TV, and this time, Willa goes with them, offering us some privacy.

All I want is to get my hands on Dove, but there's a quiet patience about it. I'll have her later, when the kids are asleep. For now, I'm happy watching light and shadow bouncing through the windows and off her beautiful face.

"Did Hodge send you money?" I ask her.

"Every month," she nods. "But we saved most of it. I spent some on the kids, and I paid off the debt on this property, so it's ours now."

"This is our home?"

She grins. "Yes, as long as you're happy staying here. The house is big enough."

"We might have to move if the family keeps expanding."

"Oh?" She raises her brows at me. "Planning something there, are you?"

"Not at all," I smirk. "First, I want you to myself for a few years. I'm not letting you leave my side."

"You sound so..." Dove leans against the counter, avoiding my gaze.

"What?"

"I don't know." She shrugs. "Different. Yet the same."

"I am different," I mutter. "Because I paid my debt to you, Dove. Not in full, never in full. But I want you to know how deeply sorry I am for everything I've put you through with Robin. Neither of you deserved what I did to you and I will be sorry for the rest of my life."

"Nox..."

"Wait." I hold a hand up. "There's something else. I started another trust fund for the kids and you. I'm hoping we can run a foundation with it, one that will benefit homeless youths."

"That's wonderful, Nox." She reaches for my hand, intertwining my fingers. "Because of Sam?"

"Of course, but I want to remember him in different ways, too," I grin. "I heard his granddaughter goes to the school Willa used to go to."

"Really?" Dove's eyes widen. "Wow. It would be so strange meeting her."

"Or her mother," I nod. "But we should try and find her."

"Yes," Dove nods. "That's a good plan."

We sit in silence for a while, the sun setting outside and coloring the dining room in its warm, golden rays of light.

"Dove..."

"Yes?" She looks at me right away, eager for me to speak.

"Can I..." I swallow my pride and force myself to get the words out. "Can I stay here?"

She stares at me before bursting out in a laugh. She pulls me up and embraces me, her lips an inch away from mine as she whispers, "You're never leaving me again. And this time, you don't have to stay in the shadows..."

EPILOGUE

DOVE
3 YEARS LATER

It's the day of Willa's sixteenth birthday and her brothers are driving me crazy.

Kellan and Zane have been bouncing off the walls since early morning when Willa opened some of her gifts. We haven't given her the main one yet, though. That'll be a surprise for tonight.

"Kellan!" My son stops with a smile frozen on his face. He's such a mischievous little boy, but it makes my heart sing to see him so happy. He's truly come into his own since Nox came back to live with us. And he certainly takes after his daddy. "Can you ask your brother to stop stomping, you're going to break the ceiling! The buyers will kill us."

He nods and disappears back into the living room, making airplane noises.

Tonight is another special night, because it's the last one in our old house. We've finally outgrown the home I bought for myself such a long time ago, and we're moving into a gorgeous villa in a safer, more family-friendly neighborhood. Willa says it's ritzy, and I almost want to agree with her. God knows the prices were outrageous, but I'm glad we made the investment.

Nervously, I wrap my fingers around the aluminum foil wrapped around a front strand of my hair.

"Willa!" I yell up the stairs. "You promised you'd help!"

"Coming!" she drawls out the world and I can picture her rolling her eyes. She rushes down the stairs. Every day I see her now, I'm amazed at how beautiful she's grown up to be. She was a striking but painfully thin child, and now she's a beauty that's as unmissable as she is unforgettable. "Oh God. How long did you leave it in for?"

"It's been about ten minutes," I admit sheepishly.

"Don't panic."

"Don't lead with that!" I yelp as she drags me into the downstairs bathroom, just as Nox opens the front door, balancing a huge cardboard box. "Nox! Don't let Willa see that, you know it's part of the surprise."

"Of course," he laughs, walking past us into the dining room. "Ten minutes are up by the way!"

"Bit late with that!" Willa calls back before closing the bathroom door. She sits me down on the closed lid of the toilet and unwraps my strand of hair out of the foil. "Oh my God."

"What?" I gasp. "Is it falling out? Did we leave it in for too long?"

"No," Willa grins. "It's white. It looks perfect!"

I turn around to look at myself in the mirror. My hair is chocolate brown, but now I have a white streak in the front. Willa thought it would look silly at first, but she tells me now how badass it is and that I look really cool.

"Do you like it?" she asks nervously.

"Yeah," I nod slowly. "I just hope Nox does too."

"Like what?" He squeezes into the bathroom making Willa groan as he kisses me deeply.

"Would you two get a room?" she begs.

"Not when we can embarrass you instead," Nox teases her, making her roll her eyes. But she still grinning as she goes in search of her brothers.

We've never broached the subject of Willa calling me Mom, or Nox Dad. But there's no question about one thing – Zane and Kellan are her family, her little siblings, and she treats them that way as do they her.

Finally, Nox and I are alone, and I melt into his embrace as he holds me close, kissing me deeply and making me submit to him in seconds yet again. I never could resist him, my soulmate, the man who both doomed and saved me.

We disappear into the bedroom while the boys nap and Willa gets ready for her party at her best friend, Mercy's house. We recently found out that Mercy is Sam's granddaughter, and we always encourage having her around. Even though her mother is a kickass lady and takes great care of her, we want to be there for Mercy, too. We've told her all our best Sam stories, and sometimes, even his daughter, Mercy's mom, listens in with a faint smile on her face.

While Nox explores my body, I close my eyes. I'm so grateful for how my life has worked out, what my family has given me. A place where I belong... And even my relationship with my mother has gotten a little less frosty. She adores the kids and has even been here to visit twice. She doesn't know who Nox is, and I doubt she ever will. There are some lines even I won't cross.

Robin lives in my heart, and in the rich tapestry of memories I share with the kids and Nox. I make sure Robin's a part of conversations, bringing up little stories and anecdotes about him, with Nox joining in. I don't know whether I'll ever be able to tell them the truth... but I can only pray that they'll understand, should they ever find out.

When it's time for us to get up, the house is bursting with activity for the night. A nanny is taking the boys and there will be a party and big sleepover at our house for the kids. We're actually letting them stay the night while we sleep in the new house – we trust Willa enough for that.

The caterers get everything ready and we wait for the girls to get there so we can give Willa her last present. The festivities are in full force an hour later and Nox wants me to himself, so we tear away the birthday girl and lead her outside with a blindfold on.

"Ta-da!" I say, slipping it off her eyes.

"Oh. My. Freaking. God." Willa covers her mouth before squealing. "Are you serious?"

"Of course," I nod. "We trust you, darling."

"You won't regret this!" she squeaks as she jumps up and down in front of the cherry red Mustang. "Can I take it for a spin?"

"You can go around the block now, but don't drive without us tonight," I nod while Nox kisses Willa's cheek.

She's not even listening anymore, begging Nox to come with her. He gets in the car along with Mercy and they drive off around the neighborhood, shrieking with excitement. I'm already worried, but I force myself to stop doing that to myself and make sure the girls are set up for the night. One of the girls' older sisters, who seems a bit more bookish, will be with them, and we'll only be a call away.

I tell myself Willa deserves this trust we're putting on her shoulders. She's a good kid and she'd never dream of letting us down.

Getting everything ready, I have a car waiting for us by the time they come back.

Willa is beaming from ear to ear and gives me the biggest hug. I tell her she deserves it and not to let us down. She just passed her driver's exam, so we figured we'd give her my old car as a memento and a way to get around. We've upgraded to a larger car that can safely transport us all.

As we're standing in front of our old house, the girls all head inside while Willa says goodbye to us. Just as we're giving her the instructions in case she needs us, a butterfly floats around us, landing on Willa's jacket.

"That's beautiful!" I gush, quickly snapping a photo. "So beautiful, Willa."

"You know, we have a saying about butterflies," Nox joins in, putting a hand around my shoulders.

"One you're about to make up now?" I tease him.

"Maybe." His eyes glitter darkly. "But they say the person the butterfly lands on gets their happily ever after next."

"Oh God, you're so cheesy," Willa whines. "I'm sixteen, not sixty!"

"Yeah, you're too young," Nox laughs, but I can see the lines in his face grow just a little deeper.

As the butterfly floats on its way, we kiss Willa goodbye and get into our ride. I don't know whether Nox's heart is as heavy as my own, but I end up wiping away tears from my eyes.

"Why so emotional, little bird?" Nox whispers in my ear. "Something wrong?"

"She's just so grown up," I whisper.

"I know. And the boys, too." He tugs on my new white strand of hair. "I like this, by the way."

"Thanks," I grimace. "Thought I should start getting ahead of my age. You won't trade me in for a newer model, will you?"

"Don't be fucking ridiculous," he smirks. "Never in a million years."

"You excited to spend the first night in our house, all by ourselves?"

"Beyond." Nox nuzzles my neck. "What is this, one of our first nights alone in years?"

"Definitely." I grimace. It's been tough getting away from the family lately, not that I mind. But Nox and I aren't as carefree. I'm forever worried about the boys and Willa, and Nox sometimes still seems like he's carrying the weight of the world on his shoulders. "Do you think the kids will be okay?"

"Of course." Nox nudges me. "Stop freaking stressing, little bird."

"I just worry." I fiddle with my dress and Nox pulls my hands away, kissing my knuckles.

"Tonight, you're all mine. The only thing you need to worry about is saying I do."

"I do?" I raise my brows questioningly. "What on earth do you mean?"

He just winks and stares ahead.

"Nox!" I squeeze his hand.

"I already said too much. You'll have to trust me with the rest of it and be a good girl." He smirks at me, the puckered scar marring his cheek making him just like me.

"Are you asking me..."

"Officially, I asked you two years ago." He points to the rock on my finger. "But you kept putting it off and off, so now I've taken matters into my own hands."

"Oh my God, Nox." My eyes are watering again, my knees getting weak. "Are we really getting married tonight?"

"It's just a small ceremony, just us and the priest."

"But what about our family..."

"If you want something else later, we'll do that too. But tonight, I want you all to myself. And I want to make our first night as a married couple in our new house beyond special."

"You already have," I admit in a low whisper. "You make me so happy, Nox. You've given me everything I've ever wanted. This is... this is a lifetime of happiness."

"For me too," he says simply, pulling me in for a deep kiss. And while his lips are on mine, I remember all the reasons I love him and why he owns me.

What he's been through because of me, for me. All the things he does for me, big and small, just to bring the hint of a smile to my lips.

Parker was a monster, but Nox isn't.

Nox is my soulmate, my heart's partner and the man who makes me whole. And after tonight, I suppose he'll be my other half, too.

"Are you sure you want to do this?" I whisper in his ear as we come to a stop in front of the new house. The dying rays of sunlight illuminate the gorgeous property. I feel tears in my eyes again.

"Of course I'm sure," he answers, getting on one knee. I gasp, covering my mouth with my hands.

"You already p-proposed," I stutter, making him smirk.

"This is for something else." He kisses my hand and presents me with a long velvet box. When he opens it, an infinity metal collar is inside.

"You want it all, don't you, Nox?"

"I do," he nods solemnly. "And you'll give it to me all, won't you, little bird?"

"Yes," I whisper, slowly nodding my approval.

Nox gets up and clasps the collar around my throat. It feels heavy and right against the hollow in my neck.

Before I can react, Nox gathers me in his arms and I giggle as he carries me over the threshold of our new home.

"Put me down, I'm too heavy!" I insist, and he finally gives up, laughing. When I turn to face him, his eyes burn with a dark passion. One that scares me... in such a delicious, panty-melting way. "Nox..."

"Hide from me, Dove," he smirks.

"This again?" I flush. It's his favorite game.

"I want to find you. Follow you." He smirks against my skin, leaving the ghost of a kiss against my scarred cheek. "Stalk you."

I pull myself away from him, but my eyes linger as I look over my shoulder. I smile, and Nox smiles back.

And then I hide from my tyrant stalker, and keep my fingers crossed that he'll find me again... And that he'll never stop following, hidden in the shadows.

THE END

Thank you so much for reading Dove and Nox's book! I hope you loved this dark, forbidden story as much as I enjoyed writing it.

Are you ready for more? Guess who's coming next!

WHAT DID YOU THINK?

Dove and Nox are the second couple featured in the Tyrant Dynasty series, but there is so much more yet to come. Before I tell you about that, I was wondering if you could review this book on Amazon, Goodreads or maybe even your bookish blog?

I love reading reviews for my books and discovering what readers enjoyed about my couples. It makes me so happy to read your thoughts on the characters I spend so much time with!

If you would be willing to write an honest review, I would be so grateful. You can tap the links below to review now, and I would love to see your posts on Instagram (tag me @authorisabellastarling) or via my email authorisabellastarling@gmail.com.

Thank you so much for reading!

Review on Goodreads

Read on for your exclusive sneak peek of Nox and Dove's story!

TYRANT DADDY
COMING NEXT!

Want to receive the first chapter of Tyrant Daddy as soon as it's available? Sign up to my newsletter, and join my group for the couple announcement!

CONNECT WITH ISABELLA

You can connect with me on Goodreads or send your review directly to my email authorisabellastarling@gmail.com and I'll thank you with a personal note.

Follow me on Instagram @authorisabellastarling

Like my page on Facebook @AuthorIsabellaStarling

Join my Facebook reader group

I can't wait to hear what you thought!

Printed in Great Britain
by Amazon